THE OTHER TYPIST

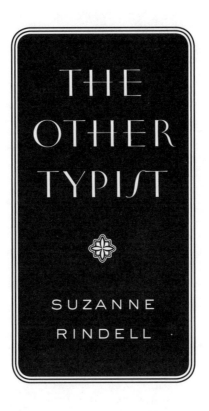

THE
OTHER
TYPIST

SUZANNE
RINDELL

AMY EINHORN BOOKS

Published by G. P. Putnam's Sons

a member of Penguin Group (USA) Inc.

New York

AMY EINHORN BOOKS
Published by G. P. Putnam's Sons
Publishers Since 1838
Published by the Penguin Group
Penguin Group (USA) Inc., 375 Hudson Street,
New York, New York 10014, USA

USA • Canada • UK • Ireland • Australia
New Zealand • India • South Africa • China

Penguin Books Ltd, Registered Offices: 80 Strand, London WC2R 0RL, England
For more information about the Penguin Group visit penguin.com

Library of Congress Cataloging-in-Publication Data

Rindell, Suzanne.
The other typist / Suzanne Rindell.
p.   cm
ISBN 978-0-399-16146-9
1. Typists—Fiction.   2. Nineteen twenties—Fiction.   3. Women—New York (State)—
New York—Fiction.   4. Police stations—New York (State)—New York—Fiction.   5. New
York (N.Y.)—History—1898–1951—Fiction.   I. Title.
PS3618.I538O84   2013   2013000995
813'.6—dc23

Printed in the United States of America
1   3   5   7   9   10   8   6   4   2

Book design by Gretchen Achilles

For my parents, Arthur and Sharon Rindell.

I owe you everything.

THE OTHER TYPIST

They said the typewriter would unsex us.

One look at the device itself and you might understand how they—the self-appointed keepers of female virtue and morality, that is—might have reached such a conclusion. Your average typewriter, be it Underwood, Royal, Remington, or Corona, is a stern thing, full of gravity, its boxy angles coming straight to the point, with no trace of curvaceous tomfoolery or feminine whimsy. Add to that the sheer violence of its iron arms, thwacking away at the page with unforgiving force. *Unforgiving.* Yes; forgiving is not the typewriter's duty.

I don't suppose I know much about the business of forgiveness, either, as my job has so much to do with the other end of it. Confessions, I mean. Not that I extract them—that is for the Sergeant to do. Or for the Lieutenant Detective to do. But it is not for me to do. Mine is a silent job. Silent, that is, unless you consider the gunshot clacking of the typewriter that sits before me as I transcribe from a roll of stenotype paper. But even then I am not the originator of this ruckus, as after all, I am only a woman—a phenomenon the Sergeant seems to observe only as we are exiting the interrogation room, when he touches my shoulder gently and says with great and solemn dignity, "I am sorry, Rose, that as a lady you must hear such things." He means the rape, the robbery, whatever it is we have just heard confessed. At our precinct, located in the borough of Manhattan in what is known as the Lower East Side, we are rarely left wanting for more crimes to hear.

I know that when the Sergeant uses the term *lady* he is being kind. It is 1924—soon to be 1925—and I am somewhere between what passes for a *lady* and a *woman* these days. The difference, of course, is partly a matter of education, which, in having matriculated at the Astoria Stenographers College for Ladies, I can—to a very modest extent—claim, but is also partly a matter of breeding and affluence, which, as an orphan with an income of fifteen dollars a week, I cannot claim. And of course there is the question of employment itself. Tradition holds that a lady may have *pursuits*, but never a *job*, and I, preferring a life with a roof over my head and regular meals to one without such things, am obliged to maintain the latter.

That is most likely what they meant when they said the typewriter would unsex us—it would deliver us out of our homes, not into the sewing factory or the steam laundry, but into law offices and accounting firms, where previously only male steps have fallen. That we would unlace our apron strings and instead button ourselves into the starched shirts and drab navy skirts that promise to neuter us. They feared the perpetual state of being surrounded by all those technological contraptions—the stenotypes, the mimeographs, the adding machines, the pneumatic mail tubes—would somehow harden us, and our soft, womanly hearts would grow rigid in an envious imitation of all that iron, brass, and steel.

I suppose it's true that knowing how to type has brought the fairer sex into some rather masculine work environments—like the police precinct, where we typists constitute a feminine minority. True enough, one has probably heard about or even glimpsed the occasional police matron in Manhattan—those stodgy old grandmothers employed to save the men from the false accusations of impropriety that all too often come along with having to herd prostitutes like so many sheep on a daily basis. But the Sergeant does not believe in police matrons and refuses to hire them. If it were not for the fact they need so much typing done and cannot do it themselves, there would be no women employed at our precinct at all. The typewriter is indeed my passport into a world otherwise barred to me and my kind.

Typing is not a brutish, masculinizing sort of work, mind you. In fact, one might even go so far as to argue that the work of a typist—the simple act of taking dictation, the crisp dance of fingertips with their dainty staccato over the shorthand keys—is perhaps one of the most civilized forms of work our modern world has to offer. And they needn't worry about the rest of it; a good typist knows her place. She is simply happy, as a woman, to be paid a reasonable income.

In any case, if typing were truly a masculine activity, you would see more men doing it, and of course you don't. It is always women one sees typing, so it only follows that it must be an activity more suited to them. I have, in all my time, only met one male typist, and that particular gentleman's delicate constitution was even lesser equipped than my own for working in a police precinct. I should've known from the first he would not stay long. He had the nervous carriage of a small bird, and his mustache looked as though it was trimmed daily by a barber. He wore a pair of very well-kept white spats over his shoes. On his second day a criminal expectorated a large stream of tobacco juice on them. The male typist, I'm sorry to report, turned very pale and excused himself to go to the lavatory. He only stayed one more week after that. *White spats*, the Sergeant had remarked, shaking his head. The Sergeant's clucking is often his manner of confiding in me. *White spats have no place here,* he said, and I knew he was probably glad to be rid of such a dandy.

Of course, I did not point out to the Sergeant that the Lieutenant Detective also wears white spats. The Lieutenant Detective and the Sergeant are two very different sorts of men, but they appear to have long ago struck an uneasy alliance. It has always been my distinct impression that I am not to outwardly tip my favor in the direction of either man, lest it upset the tenuous balance that allows for their cooperation. But if I am being honest, I will tell you I feel more at ease around the Sergeant. He is older and perhaps a little fonder of me than a married man ought to be, but I feel it is a fatherly sort of fondness and that he became a police sergeant in the first place because he is a righteous man and he honestly believes it is his mission to uphold the proper order of our great city.

Moreover, the Sergeant likes *all* things to keep proper order and takes great pride in following all rules to the letter. Just last month he suspended one of the officers, sentencing the man to a whole week without pay, because the officer had given a homeless waif who was waiting in the holding cell a ham sandwich. I could see why maybe the officer did it; the vagabond was such a sad spectacle—the outline of his ribs whispered indiscreetly against the thin cloth of his shirt, and his eyes rolled like haunted marbles caught in two deep, dark sockets. No one accused the Sergeant of being unchristian, but I believe he could tell some of the other men were thinking it. *Feeding such a man only sends the message that there is no profit in hard work and following the rules—and we can't afford to bankrupt these ideas,* the Sergeant reminded us.

The Lieutenant Detective outranks the Sergeant, but you would never know it. While he can certainly intimidate others at will, the Sergeant is not a tall man, although he is large in other ways. The great bulk of his weight sits around his waist, just over the rim of his uniform trousers, giving him a reassuringly paternal paunch. His handlebar mustache has taken on a sprinkling of salt and pepper in recent years. He wears it curled and also lets his sideburns grow long, which is no longer in keeping with the latest fashion, but the Sergeant cares little for changing fashions, and he does not go in at all for the newest shocking ones. Once while he was reading a newspaper, I heard him idly remark that today's modern fashions are proof of our nation's degeneration.

By way of contrast, the Lieutenant Detective has no mustache and keeps his face clean-shaven, which happens to be rather in fashion these days. Also in fashion is the haphazard style with which he combs his hair back using hair cream. Almost always, a lock or two comes loose and falls quavering over one eye, only to have him run a hand through his hair and push it back up. On his forehead is a sizable scar that runs from the center of his brow toward one eye and has the strange effect of enhancing his features. He is young, perhaps no more than one or two years my senior, and because he is a detective and not a patrolman he is not required to wear a uniform. His clothes are quite smart, but he wears them in a peculiar manner; he always looks as though he slid out of bed and just happened to fall into them. Everything about him has a jaunty slack to it, down to his spats, which have never once appeared nearly as white or as clean as the male typist's did. This is not to imply the Lieutenant Detective is unhygienic, but rather that he is simply not tidy.

In fact, although he appears perpetually rumpled, I am fairly confident the Lieutenant Detective's hygiene habits are regular. He used to lean over my desk frequently to talk to me, and I noticed he always smelled of Pears' soap. When I asked him once, wasn't that brand of soap generally preferred by ladies and not men, he colored up and seemed to take it very roughly, even though I hadn't meant anything by it. He left my question unanswered and avoided me for almost two weeks afterward. Since then he no longer smells of Pears' soap. The other day he leaned over my desk—not to talk to me, but rather to silently retrieve one of my transcripts—and I noticed now he smells of a different soap, one whose perfume is meant to imitate the aroma of expensive cigars and old leather.

One reason I dislike working with the Lieutenant Detective and prefer working with the Sergeant is that the Lieutenant Detective mainly investigates homicides, which means if I am asked to go into the interrogation room with him, it is most likely to take down the confession of a suspected murderer on the stenotype. There is no apology in the Lieutenant Detective's voice, as there would be in the Sergeant's, when he requests that I join him. In fact, sometimes I think I detect a hint of challenge in his voice. On the surface, of course, he is all very brisk and businesslike.

They think we are the weaker sex, but I doubt the men have considered the fact that we women must hear every confession twice. That is, once I've taken dictation on the stenotype, I must type it all over again in plain English on the typewriter, as the men cannot read shorthand. To them, the marks on the stenotype rolls appear like hieroglyphics. I don't mind typing and retyping these stories as much as I know I'm *supposed* to mind, but it *is* a bit off-putting to go over the details of a stabbing or bludgeoning just prior to, say, the lunch or dinner hour. You see, the trouble is once they've abandoned the notion of denying their crimes and they've decided to go ahead and come clean, the suspects are frequently very specific about the mess that results from such acts. As a moral person, I do not relish hearing these gruesome details, although I would be loath for the Lieutenant Detective to perceive my discomfort, as he would surely see it as evidence of my weak and womanly stomach. I assure you, my stomach is *not* weak on this score.

Of course, I'll admit there is something indirectly intimate about hearing these confessions along with another person, and I can't say I enjoy sharing such moments with the Lieutenant Detective. Quite often the suspect being questioned by the Lieutenant Detective has killed a woman, and more often than not in such cases the suspect has done some rather wicked things to his victim first. When taking the confession of a suspect who has attacked a young woman in the most brutal way, it feels as though all the air goes out of the room. Sometimes I am aware of the Lieutenant Detective glancing at my face when the confessor recalls the most violent parts, observing me impassively. During such moments I feel like a science experiment. Or perhaps like one of those psychological studies that have become all the rage these days. I sit and type and try my best to ignore him.

And yet—unlike the Sergeant, who worries out of consideration for me—the Lieutenant Detective doesn't seem particularly concerned that I'll hear something that will violate my supposedly pure feminine mind. To be honest, I'm not at all sure what he's searching for in my face. He is very likely wondering if I'll faint and crumple face-first over the stenotype. Who knows—he may even have a betting pool going with the other officers. But we live in a modern age now, one in which women have enough to do without having to trouble themselves with the obligation of fainting all the time, and I wish the Lieutenant Detective, for all his other modern manners, would stop glancing at my face like a curious puppy and simply let me do my job. Which, by the by, I'm quite good at. I can type 160 words per minute on the regular typewriter, and can get up to nearly 300 on the stenotype. And I am largely indifferent to the content of the confessions I must take down and transcribe. Like the typewriter itself, I am simply there to report with accuracy. I am there to make the official and unbiased record that will eventually be used in court. I am there to transcribe what will eventually come to be known as the truth.

Of course, I have to be careful not to let my pride over these facts get the better of me. On one occasion, as we emerged from the interrogation room, I called out to the Lieutenant Detective in a voice that was perhaps a bit louder than I'd intended and said, "I'm not a ninny, you know."

"Pardon me?" He stopped and spun around, his eyes traveling up and down the length of my person, that scientist-observing-an-experiment look on his face again. He took a step or two toward me, as though we were being confidential, and I breathed in another soapy hint of cigars and leather. I straightened my posture, gave a little cough, and tried to make my stand again, this time with more poise.

"I said I'm not a ninny. It doesn't frighten me. None of it. I'm not a hysteric. You can forget about having to fetch the smelling salts." I said that last part for effect; we don't really keep smelling salts at the precinct, and I doubt anyone travels with them in their pockets anymore these days. But I immediately regretted the exaggeration. It made me sound too dramatic, like the hysteric I had just claimed I wasn't.

"Miss Baker . . . ," the Lieutenant Detective began to address me. But the rest of the statement trailed off. He stared at my face for several seconds. Finally, as though someone had suddenly pinched him, he blurted out, "I have every reason to believe you could take the confessions of Jack the Ripper himself and not bat an eye." Before I could formulate an appropriate rejoinder, the Lieutenant Detective turned on his heel and strode away.

I am not sure he meant it as a compliment. Working in a precinct full of policemen, I am no stranger to sarcasm. For all I know, the Lieutenant Detective could have been having a laugh at my expense. I don't know much about Jack the Ripper. I do know that he was rumored to have been abnormally skilled with a knife.

I let the subject drop and did not bring it up to the Lieutenant Detective again. Life went on at the precinct in a more or less predictable harmony—the Sergeant kept to his uneasy pact of cooperation with the Lieutenant Detective, and in turn the Lieutenant Detective kept to his courteous-yet-always-curt interactions with me.

It all went on harmoniously, that is, until they hired the other typist.

I RECOGNIZED SOMETHING was happening the very second she walked in the door for her interview. On that particular day, she entered very calmly and quietly, but I knew: It was like the eye of a hurricane. She was the dark epicenter of something we didn't quite understand yet, the place where hot and cold mixed dangerously, and around her everything would change.

Perhaps it's a misnomer to refer to her as "the other typist," as there were other typists all along. I was one of three. There was a forty-year-old woman named Iris with a gaunt face, sharp jaw, and gray, birdlike eyes. Every day Iris wore a different colored ladies' necktie. Iris was always complaisant to do extra typing when it was needed, and this was much appreciated. (*Crime does not take weekends or observe bank holidays,* the Sergeant is fond of saying.) As far as social particulars went, Iris had never been married, and it was difficult to imagine marriage had ever been one of her aspirations.

Then there was Marie, who was in many ways an opposite composite of Iris. Marie was rotund and always merry and walked with a slightly hobbled step from where an omnibus had run over her left foot when she was just a child. Marie was barely thirty but had already married twice—the first of her husbands had run off with a chorus girl. Without being able to locate him to secure a proper divorce, Marie had simply shrugged away the legal contract and married her second husband, a man named Horace, who was kind to her but was sick all the time with gout. Marie worked at the precinct because she was under no illusion that Horace would be able to provide for her. She was a sentimental woman who had married for love, despite the fact the gout was bound to get worse and keep him off his feet more and more. The crude remark was often made behind Marie's back that between her mangled left foot and Horace's gout-swollen feet, they probably danced one "helluva" waltz together. People never said these things while she was in the room, but Marie was no fool and she was aware this joke was often bandied about. She had decided long ago to pretend ignorance. She was generally for anything that facilitated greater camaraderie, and in consequence everybody seemed to like working with her.

And then there was me, of course. I'd worked at the precinct for a little over two years and had already garnered a reputation for being the fastest and most accurate typist. Among the three of us we were able to keep up with all the precinct's needs, typing the paperwork for all the bookings, confessions, and correspondence. We were able to keep up, that is, until the Volstead Act triggered a serious boost in our business, so to speak.

In the beginning, the Volstead Act wasn't very popular among the officers at the precinct, and for a while enforcement of the act was distinctly halfhearted. The patrolmen grumbled and only offered minimal assistance as the Anti-Saloon League closed down one watering hole after another. Officers who happened upon flasks of bathtub gin often let the perpetrators off with a warning, taking care, of course, to confiscate the evidence. Despite the Woman's Christian Temperance Union's best efforts to make the nation think so, not everyone believed the devil was really in the drink. There were even judges who couldn't seem to muster the appropriate amount of outrage to earnestly punish the bootleggers who very fully and flagrantly flouted the law. *Seems only natural after a hard day's work a man should want a tall drink of something,* the Lieutenant Detective once said quite loudly for everyone to hear, shrugging his shoulders.

Things went on like this for a time. Periodically an assortment of men from the neighborhood—many of them husbands and fathers—were hauled in for selling moonshine and allowed to go with a simple rap on the knuckles. No one cared to do much more than this.

But they say it's the squeaky wheel that gets the grease, and in our case the squeaky wheel was Assistant Attorney General Mabel Willebrandt and the grease was us. I can't claim to be an expert on her legal career, but from what I've read in all the papers, Mrs. Willebrandt holds the dubious distinction of taking on issues of poorly enforced legislation her lazier and more prudent male counterparts won't touch, and then proceeding to tackle such issues with surprising gusto, often making headlines in the process. I suppose it is only natural Mrs. Willebrandt has made herself into a patron saint of lost legal causes; she is a woman, after all, and there is little risk in letting a woman have charge of the unpopular issues. When a woman fails at her profession it is considered something rather different from when a man fails at his. However, it was clear Mrs. Willebrandt had no intention of failing, and she proved herself to be both tenacious and resourceful. While she was unable to make much of an alliance with Mayor Hylan, she did succeed in talking some "good sense" into the mayor's wife, Miriam. Between the two of them, they succeeded in stirring up enough press to make the case that New York City should set more of an example for the rest of the nation and take more decisive action in trying to convert itself into a model "dry" city. I tell you all this because the result of all the political posturing was our precinct was selected to serve as a special apparatus of "the Noble Experiment." This is what I mean when I say we were to be the grease intended to quiet Mrs. Willebrandt's squeaky wheel.

The official decree was we were supposed to operate the city's first "crackdown unit." We were to set an example for other precincts to later follow. Extra men were added to our payroll, and we were commissioned with the task of ferreting out the neighborhood's major speakeasies and conducting raids. Of course, a police precinct is a funny thing; the chemistry by which it operates is something like a recipe, and when the ingredients are altered it can take a while until relations come into harmony again. The officers at our precinct were not keen on the introduction of new men, and even less wild about the idea of participating in the chaotic raids that were sure to make them more unwelcome in the neighborhood than they already were, but they had little choice other than to comply. While the men bemoaned these changes, the Sergeant appeared to take his new responsibility seriously. I got the distinct impression he saw it as both a professional opportunity as well as a moral honor, and the inevitable day came when he announced he wanted every individual who so much as transported a single bottle of whiskey over the New York–New Jersey state line to be prosecuted to the fullest extent of the law, a command that kept not only the officers but also the typists at our precinct very busy. It was not long before the unprocessed paperwork began to cause a bit of a clog in the whole system and the holding cell became nothing more than a place for bootleggers to meet their competition and suggest cooperative strategies to avoid future detection by the police.

That's when the Sergeant telephoned the employment agency and asked them to send over another typist.

ODALIE'S HAIR was not yet bobbed when she came in for an interview. If it had been, I doubt the Sergeant would have hired her, although I'm certain the Lieutenant Detective would not have minded. Even before Odalie bobbed her hair, I had my suspicions the Lieutenant Detective liked that variety of shocking hairstyle, and the kind of woman who dared to wear it.

I can recall the day Odalie came in and removed her cloche to reveal her jet-black hair swinging in a similar shape just beneath. It had been cut to her chin, the line of it very precise. I remember observing that the cut brought out something vaguely and fashionably Oriental in Odalie's face, especially around the eyes, and the sheen of her hair was very glossy, as though she wore a helmet made of finely polished enamel. I also remember catching the Lieutenant Detective regarding her from across the room. He complimented Odalie on her bravery and taste several times that day. As for the Sergeant, he did not officially comment except to mumble over his lunch, to no one in particular, that men were likely to get the wrong idea about a woman with short hair.

But all of that came later. As I said, on the day of her interview Odalie's hair was not yet bobbed. She arrived at the precinct that morning, her face demurely powdered, her hair slicked into a tidy chignon. I remember she wore white gloves and an expensive-looking ladies' suit that matched the robin's egg blue of her eyes, but it was really her voice that left the deepest impression on me, as it revealed the most about what I was later to understand was her true character. It was a husky voice with the kind of low rattling timbre that made you watch the childish curl of her lips very closely to ensure you'd caught the words that were issuing from her mouth accurately. Her voice was like this until something delighted her or made her laugh, and then it rose and fell musically, like someone practicing scales on a piano. It was a paradox of innocent surprise and devilish complicity that proved intoxicating to everyone who heard it, and I wonder sometimes—even now—whether that voice was something she had carefully crafted over the years or if she had simply been born with it.

The interview was brief. I don't imagine the Sergeant or the Lieutenant Detective needed to know much more about the woman to be hired as our new typist other than how fast she could type (they tested her with a stopwatch, and she laughed as though they had just come up with the most intelligent and delightful game), was she presentable, and did she have good manners. There generally just wasn't much more to vetting a new typist. And Odalie, with that voice, had them both instantly charmed. When they asked her would she mind having to hear about the often extremely unsavory acts of the criminals who were brought into the precinct, she laughed her musical, jingling laugh and then dropped into that husky timbre to joke that she was not the sort of girl you might call *squeamish,* and that it was only her meals at Mouquin's that she insisted on being particularly *savory* anyhow. I did not think the remark was really all that clever, but the Sergeant and the Lieutenant Detective both chuckled, already eager, I believe—even at that early stage—to be liked by her. I eavesdropped from across the room and heard them tell her she was hired, starting the next Monday. In that second, I swore Odalie's eyes flicked across the room and rested on my face for the briefest of instants, and that a tiny smile twisted itself into the corners of her mouth. But this impression was fleeting, and later it was difficult to be sure she had looked in my direction at all.

Damned nice girl, the Lieutenant Detective had said after Odalie departed. His summary was simple, but it actually described something I hadn't quite put my finger on at that point. The truth was I was probably younger—perhaps as much as five years Odalie's junior—yet the word *girl* applied to her in a much more powerful way than it did to me. Part of Odalie's allure was the way she carried with her a sort of grown-up girlishness. There was an excitement in the air around her, an excitement that might include you in some way, as though you were her secret collaborator. Her voice quivered with a sort of tomboy energy that suggested, despite her refined poise and sophistication, she was a robust individual—someone not above climbing a tree or beating you at a game of tennis. And in that observation was another thing I had begun to realize: The voluptuous glee in Odalie's demeanor hinted at privilege, at a childhood that had been filled with automobiles and tennis courts, things that had been absent from my own childhood, and—I would humbly venture to guess—absent from the Sergeant's and the Lieutenant Detective's childhoods as well. Yes, her mannerisms hinted at wealth, but perhaps wisely made no concrete claim. In this regard she was somewhat exotic to us, but in a way we probably only perceived unconsciously. And just as it is with all exotic creatures, we simply held our breath as she approached, for fear of scaring her off. No one at the precinct dared to question the reason this well-to-do young woman stood before us, laughing as though delighted to be considered for a lowly typist's job. I've always prided myself on my sharp instincts and critical eye, and yet even in my early state of disapproval the one thing I did not do was to question why Odalie should want employment. I can only say we are all susceptible to blind spots when exposed to the right dazzling flash.

That day, after she made her farewells and was told to return on Monday, she strode off in her childish, slightly tripping little walk through the precinct and out the front door. But as she did so, something fell from the lapel of her blue jacket and skittered noisily across the floor. My eyes instantly went to the tile where the object that had dropped lay glinting under the light of the bare electric bulbs. I knew I ought to call out to alert her, but I remained silent and Odalie continued on, seeming not to notice it. She disappeared through the door, and I simply sat frozen as several minutes passed. Curious, I finally shook myself into motion. I got up quietly from my seat and walked over to the spot where the object had been abandoned upon the floor.

It was a brooch—a very expensive-looking one, with opals, diamonds, and black onyx stones all set into a very modern starburst pattern. There was some quality about the brooch that seemed to mirror the very essence of Odalie herself, as though it were in some way a portrait of her in miniature. In a flash, I had stooped and quickly returned to my desk with the brooch concealed tightly in my palm, the sharp edges of its setting digging into my flesh. I sat and held the lovely object under my desktop near my lap—out of sight of the others—and simply gazed at it, mesmerized. It glittered softly, even in shadow. Eventually, I was called to do some typing and was forced to shake myself free from the brooch's spell. I opened a desk drawer and tucked it away, far into the back under some papers, telling myself I would return it to Odalie first thing when she came back to start her new job on Monday, and already knowing in the pit of my stomach that this was a lie.

During the rest of the day I carried an odd feeling around with me. I was plagued by a sensation of perpetual distraction; it was as if there were an object in my vision I could perceive but couldn't quite look at directly. Even then, I harbored the suspicion that Odalie had dropped the brooch on purpose, as a test to me. And in retrospect I realize such a tactic certainly bore her signature. With one simple act, Odalie had snared me in a trap that consisted of equal parts temptation and shame. I was bound to her from that moment on, always wondering yet eternally unable to ask if she was privy to my act of covetous theft. All this before we'd ever even shaken hands or been introduced.

2

It's misleading to insinuate I was aware at that early time of the *full* impact Odalie would have on my life, or on the precinct in general. I stated previously that I recognized *something* was happening the moment Odalie walked in the door, and indeed that much was true, but I would have been hard-pressed to tell you exactly *what* that something was, or the extent to which I would be affected in particular. Mostly, after that first encounter, the thought of Odalie inspired a mild disquieting feeling within the pit of my stomach, but nothing more complicated or concrete than this. A few times during the remainder of the week I opened my desk drawer and snuck a peek at the brooch and thought of Odalie—but my work obligations often cut my musings short. She probably owned a lot of brooches, I told myself once or twice. She may not have even taken note of the fact that this one was missing from her collection. She may not even care, I reasoned. I pictured myself casually returning it to her. I also pictured myself just as casually forgetting to return it. In both scenarios I refused to be impressed. The pretense was I didn't give a fig for the brooch; it meant nothing to me. It felt very liberating to imagine myself capable of such a blasé disposition, so indifferent to this new exotic creature and her rare treasures. And then the weekend came, and I didn't picture the brooch or Odalie at all.

At that time I lived in a boarding-house, as was the common custom for most unmarried ladies of my age and income. The woman who ran the house was a young widow named Dorothy— or Dotty, as she preferred to be called—with lank, dishwater-colored hair and four small children. The toils of childbirth and constant housework had aged her countenance somewhat, lending her complexion a reddish, splotchy, wind-stung appearance, loosening the skin below her eyes, and adding a pair of jowls to her jawline. But I would doubt she was more than thirty. In truth, I suspect she was closer to twenty-eight or twenty-nine. Of course, these days, it's not at all unusual to come upon a widow so young. Hers was a very familiar story: Dotty's husband disappeared into the now infamous war that swallowed so many young men of our generation whole without so much as spitting out the bones. If it weren't for the children needing her at home, she often said, she would make the journey to those pockmarked fields along the border of France and Germany to see his final resting place—the place, she says, where Danny no doubt succumbed to mustard gas.

Danny and Dotty; the sound of their names together suggested a cozy, complementary alliteration, a fact I'm sure only deepened Dotty's sense of loss and mourning. After too many nips of what she kept in the kitchen pantry and called cooking sherry (a supply of which mysteriously replenished itself without fail, despite the challenges presented by Prohibition), Dotty sometimes told the story of Danny's death as if she witnessed it firsthand. She felt very certain his body fell into a trench and now lies haphazardly buried there, lost in one of the hundreds of long, puckered mounds of earth that I've been told are still visible upon the French farm fields, like so many wormy scars. Dotty's youngest child was three and a half years old; I wasn't entirely certain the math worked out in her husband's favor on this score, but I never said as much to Dotty, as I was grateful for the reasonable boarding fee she offered and I had no desire to stir up unnecessary trouble. I had always been given to understand that loneliness during a time of war is a different and more potent kind of loneliness than any other in the world.

I know a little bit about loneliness myself, but not about being alone. In the boarding-house, I was never alone. The house was a rather tattered brownstone located in Brooklyn. I suppose it was in such a state because, as a widow, Dotty had no husband to do the routine maintenance required and limited disposable income to hire out for even the most necessary of repairs. It was quite a large brownstone when you imagined it housing one family, but not so much when you experienced it housing eight adults and four children, as it did during my tenure there. Needless to say, there was always quite a bit of noise and commotion.

Even my room within the boarding-house did not offer the regular amount of privacy one might expect. It was quite large, but it had been divided in two by means of several graying and badly stained sheets pinned to a clothesline strung up across the middle of the room. *Semi-private,* I believe the advertisement Dotty posted in the newspaper read. I do not think Dotty meant to be deceitful in this description, for after all it was somewhat accurate, and the price she charged was lower than I'd have likely gotten at any other boarding-house. But then, that amount doubled by two people was probably more than Dotty could've gotten renting the room to a single person. I suppose the relative quality of a deal is always a matter of perspective, really.

The other occupant of the room was an auburn-haired girl with chubby cheeks and dimpled knees who was close to me in age. She was called Helen—a name, I fear, that may have gone to her head, for she frequently acted as though she had confused herself with Helen of Troy. Perhaps that is cruel of me to say. It's just that I have encountered a number of cockatoos, but have met very few humans who preen quite as much as Helen did. She was constantly before the mirror, angling her face this way and that, feigning looks of surprise and rapture. With her fleshy face it was a bit like watching a soft lump of dough being molded into a series of baker's forms, and she was only moderately convincing in these expressions. She never admitted as much, but I suspected she was secretly harboring aspirations to one day take to the stage. At the time of our cohabitation she was a shopgirl, a profession she felt was infinitely superior to my own. She made no secret about what she thought of my job as a typist at the precinct. *Don't fret, Rose,* she often remarked to me, unsolicited. *You won't have to work in that ghastly place forever. I'm sure something better is bound to come along. And when it does, I'll help you replace those mannish clothes of yours and we'll find you some lovely, tasteful things.* Helen was fond of using the word *tasteful,* but I came to understand, during our time together, that it didn't mean quite the same thing to her as it did to me.

When I took up residence at the boarding-house, Helen had already occupied the room for some time, and had consequently selected its more advantageous half—which is to say, the side farthest from the hallway door. Having no reason to pass through Helen's side of the room, I generally left her to her privacy. But on her way in and out of the bedroom, teleology dictated she was obliged to pass through my side, and she had no qualms about making a ruckus or leaving her shoes and stockings on the floor in my half of the room. I also suspect she rearranged things before I moved in so that all the most prized pieces of furniture resided solely on her side of the room. But I suppose that's just human nature. Who's to say I wouldn't have done the same, had I been the first to move in myself?

In any case, during that particular week, Helen had been making a fuss about a gentleman caller she was to receive on Friday evening, so my apprehensions about work and Odalie were quickly consumed by Helen's theatrics the moment I got home that day. Of course, on the sojourn home I had no idea how thoroughly I would be made to play a role in Helen's social engagement. This latter discovery lay like a bear trap waiting to spring on me at the conclusion of my commute.

On my way home from the precinct, I ride the streetcar over the Brooklyn Bridge and finish the remainder of my journey on foot. Despite the passing automobiles and their intermittent low wail of Klaxon horns and nattering of engines, I have come to regard this process as a relaxing ritual, one that allows me to think over the events of the day. On that particular Friday, several abnormalities occurred at the precinct that had me especially preoccupied. In the morning we had taken the confessional statement of a man who seemed, at the first, quite sober, but who turned out to be extremely inebriated and perhaps not altogether sane.

I went into the interview room with the Lieutenant Detective and began taking dictation of the suspect's statement in the usual way. At first, things seemed quite normal—just your run-of-the-mill husband and wife kitchen knife stabbing. *An accidental crime of passion* is always how the lawyers describe crimes like that later on in the courts. Not that I always attend the trials, but I *do* like to sit in from time to time, and I have always found the pairing of the words *accidental* and *passion* to be an odd turn of phrase—as if the accident were loving someone, not killing them. In any case, the man's story was a very familiar one, and I took down everything he said with an automatic reflexivity.

But much to our surprise, ten minutes into the confession the suspect quite abruptly began describing a different crime altogether—something about drowning a man in the East River. Confused, I caught the Lieutenant Detective's eye, and we exchanged a hesitant look. The Lieutenant Detective shrugged, and his eyes seemed to say, *Well, if the chap wants to confess to two murders and not just one, let him hang himself.* Keeping all traces of urgency out of his voice, the Lieutenant Detective dropped his line of questioning about the man's wife and began to ask instead about this mystery drowning. He changed gears ever so gently, I noticed, and took a casual tack. The mood in the room significantly shifted, and it was suddenly as if the Lieutenant Detective was talking to a friend and discussing something as inconsequential as the weather. On instinct I felt my touch on the stenotype grow lighter and my presence recede into the wall, and it was as if they were alone. Finally, the man leaned over and dropped his voice to a whisper. The mayor had told him to do it, the man said; he was only following orders. I looked again at the Lieutenant Detective. I could tell by his external demeanor that he was struggling to maintain an unimpressed skepticism, but he had flinched at the mention of Mayor Hylan's name, and the corners of his mouth had gone taut with an involuntary tension.

"And why," the Lieutenant Detective asked in a condescending voice that clearly implied he was humoring our suspect, "would the mayor want you to attack this man?"

"Because," our suspect said, "he was part of the invisible government! The corrupt one!" It was then, as the man shouted, that I began to detect a premiere whiff of bathtub gin on the man's breath. He began to hiccup loudly. His mention of "the invisible government" was, I believe, a reference to a controversial speech Mayor Hylan had given, accusing men like Rockefeller of having too much control over politics. I realized we were hearing the mayor's speech repeated through a filter of booze and possible insanity. The Lieutenant Detective struggled to reclaim order over the situation and reorient his line of questioning, but before he could successfully accomplish this aim, the suspect began to hiccup more loudly and worked himself into a state of extreme agitation. He began shouting again. "The mayor told me to do it! I'm a soldier of righteousness, I tell you, a soldier!"

Just then, the Sergeant poked his head in the door to see what all the commotion was about. Our suspect took one look at the Sergeant and leapt out of his chair. He snapped his hand to his forehead in a salute.

"Reporting for duty, Mr. Mayor, sir!"

The Sergeant blinked at the man saluting him, utterly stupefied. The scar on the Lieutenant Detective's forehead rolled into a series of S's, configured by the deep furrows of his concerned brow. It took us all a few minutes to realize we were witnessing an absurd case of mistaken identity. Suddenly the suspect spun around in a frenzy, vomited with a startling ferocity, and finally ended his spasms by passing out cold on the floor, his cheek pressed against the tile and his tongue lolling thickly out of his mouth. The whole room filled with the wretched smell of rancid, partially digested alcohol. The Sergeant looked at us, unamused.

"Get him out of here" was all the Sergeant said, and disappeared. We sat there, stunned for a few seconds, until the Lieutenant Detective shook himself, sighed, and got up from his seat. He leaned out the doorway of the interrogation room and called to a couple of deputies to help remove the drunken man now snoring loudly on the floor. I set about tidying up the stenographer's desk and removing the used paper from the shorthand machine. What I'd been typing was likely useless. You couldn't take a drunk man's words down as testimony—at least not a man so drunk as to be incomprehensible. The suspect had become as inanimate as a sack of potatoes and barely opened his eyes as he was lifted and hauled away.

"I thought for certain that man was sober," the Lieutenant Detective murmured, more to himself, it seemed, than to me.

"I did as well," I said. "Couldn't smell a drop on him, and he was so lucid at the start. Guess he had us both fooled." The Lieutenant Detective looked up, surprised. This perhaps was the lengthiest exchange we'd shared in months. He regarded me for a few seconds. A strangely appreciative smile spread over his face, but it made me uncomfortable, and I was forced to look away. We went back to putting the room in order, both of us carefully tiptoeing around the puddle of vomit in the middle as we did so.

"He sort of does, you know," the Lieutenant Detective said.

"Who? Does what?"

"The Sarge. Look like Mayor Hylan."

I bristled. "How rude! Although I can't say I'm surprised by your disrespect, really." My voice came out sounding shrill, uncontrolled. I was vaguely horrified. I adopted a brisker pace in gathering together a stack of files and headed for the door.

"It's not an insult," the Lieutenant Detective said, his eyes widening in surprise. This proved to be too much for me. Almost to the door, I whirled about on him.

"Mayor Hylan has been called a communist, and as you very well know, the Sergeant is *not* some sort of dirty Bolshevik. He is a *good* man." I hesitated before adding, "You would no doubt be vastly improved if you were only *half* the man . . ."

I trailed off in this lecture, remembering my place and, more importantly, my desire to remain employed. Young and disrespectful though he might be, the Lieutenant Detective technically outranked both the Sergeant and myself. It wouldn't do to dress him down too severely, so I halted and waited to be reprimanded in return. But he only gazed at me for several seconds, a solemn, pitying expression creeping into his eyes. "I stand corrected," he said. This was unexpected, and I stood blinking and dumbstruck for the space of a full minute. Then, having no desire to stay and attempt to determine the sincerity of this comment, I simply turned on my heel and left the room.

It was all a lot to absorb. My job is often full of unruly men doing unruly things, but there was an air of absurdity—of dark absurdity—about the events of that Friday. And that exchange with the Lieutenant Detective! I felt humiliated, somehow, to have been brought down to such a level.

I got off the streetcar on the Brooklyn side of the bridge and began making my way home, absorbed in thought, still possessed by images of the crazy man who may or may not have drowned a man in the East River, of the Lieutenant Detective and his solemn expressions, of the new typist who had come in for an interview (the name of that latter individual playing musically in my head, tripping along to the pace of my own steps like a child's song: *Oh-dah-lee, Oh-dah-lee, Oh-dah-lee...*). I thought of the brooch and what the Sergeant would say if he knew it was tucked away in the back of my desk drawer. I mused on the fact that, secretly, I rather agreed with the Lieutenant Detective about the Sergeant's resemblance to Mayor Hylan. All of these thoughts and more skirted the edges of my reverie as I walked home automatically and with unseeing eyes.

Preoccupied thus, I wasn't at all prepared for the ambush that awaited me back at the boarding-house. When I walked in, the first thing I encountered was a blast of thick stew-scented air. This first part, at least, was typical. The house generally smelled of bones boiling in water on the stove—mostly all chicken, but sometimes also beef. It was such a pervasive odor throughout the boarding-house, I often wondered if this meant I carried the smell of beef stock and chicken stock around with me in my clothes and my hair, unwittingly trailing it about the precinct and among my coworkers, who were too polite to remark upon it. But today when I walked in the house I instantly noticed there were a few additional fragrances wafting in the atmosphere: the scent of coffee brewing and of cologne. And cigarettes—it smelled very strongly of cigarettes.

I peered into the parlor and was greeted by a dense fug of cigarette smoke. The chalky cloud appeared even more opaque where it drifted under the weak light of the overhead electric bulb—and this, too, I spotted as being unusual, as Dotty did not often allow us to turn on the electric lights during the day. I blinked, and as my eyes adjusted to the dim lighting and stinging smoke, I made out the figures of two men perched side by side on the sofa, each casually arranged so that his legs were crossed with one ankle resting on the opposite knee. I thought, at first, that the smoke had affected my vision, but presently I realized this was not the case. I was not seeing double, but rather a pair of identical twins, even dressed and groomed in a similar manner.

"You must be Rose," the one on the right said. Neither man got up from the sofa—a gesture that would have only been polite—and so I simply stood in silence, blinking at them. I noticed they were wearing similarly patterned but different-colored plaid jackets, complemented by identical boat shoes and straw boater hats. Somehow, though, I very much doubted the existence of an actual boat, as otherwise implied by their attire. There were ink stains on the thumb and forefinger of each man's right hand. Clerks or accountants, I guessed.

The silence was broken as Dotty and Helen burst into the sitting room, each carrying a tray full of coffee things, the cups chattering against the saucers like teeth in the cold.

"There you are," Helen exclaimed, as if my presence in the room was something they had long anticipated. Helen set her tray down next to Dotty's, and Dotty began pouring out slightly burnt-smelling coffee from a very tarnished silver carafe. "You're just in time to meet Bernard Crenshaw, my *beau*," she said, pronouncing his name *Burr-nerd*. "And Leonard Crenshaw, his brother," she finished, with a slight flourish of her hand. *Bernard and Leonard.* They had clearly fallen victim to the somewhat silly tradition of naming twins in a vaguely rhyming way, as if twins were not individual humans but rather two variations on the same theme. I knew there were lots of mothers who failed to resist this cozy habit.

"Actually, we mostly go by Benny and Lenny," the one on the right said. In an attempt to be amicable, I repressed the snort that rose reactively to the back of my throat. Even more ridiculous than the almost-rhyme of their given names was the rhyme of their preferred sobriquets, but it would be rude to laugh outright. I did not approve of rude behavior in others, and I couldn't very well permit myself a different standard. I regarded the twins again, trying to determine which one was Benny, Helen's "beau." Leave it to Helen to use a word like that. In addition to the faces she made in the mirror, there were times when her speech sounded inexplicably affected. *My people are from the South,* I once heard her drawl to an inquiring stranger. I knew that this was only true insofar as Sheepshead Bay could be considered the South, as her "people" were all Brooklynites, going back several generations.

Meanwhile, Dotty was flitting around with the distracted, burdened air of someone deeply inconvenienced by a surprise guest—and in this case, a guest who had inconsiderately duplicated himself. But I knew her too well; she was secretly delighting in the opportunity to entertain two young men, not to mention the pleasure she took in playing the martyred host. "Please forgive this old coffee service," she said, meaning the silver carafe. "I didn't know youse two would be staying for coffee or I woulda polished this ratty thing up." I think she meant to extract a compliment, but failed in this mission. She addressed mainly the twin on the right, whose plaid jacket was predominantly red.

I decided Benny must be the one on the right, the one who had spoken up to introduce their nicknames.

"We were just saying how, since Benny brought Lenny along, I should find a girl-friend to bring along, too," Helen remarked. There was a brittle, stretched quality to the cheerful tone of her voice, and suddenly her desperation was transparent—these were the strings that came along with Benny; wherever he went, his brother also needed to be entertained, a fact for which she had not been prepared. Suddenly Helen whirled in my direction. "Don't you look smart today," she said, the rhetorical comment echoing with emptiness. In an attempt to come up with a more specific compliment, she looked me over, her eyes traveling from my head to my toes. It did not appear they could wholly endorse what they found there. "You look . . . ," she began, still casting about wildly for something she might find pleasing about my person. "You look so . . . *healthy*!"

"Helen!" Dotty chastised.

"What? I'm paying her a compliment. Normally she looks so drawn and pale. But look, dear"—she turned back to me—"look how your complexion is just perfectly *rosy*! You'd be a fool not to come out with us.

"And of course you can borrow some of my things," she added quickly, making it clear that no matter how "healthy" I looked, she didn't want me stepping into public with her dressed in the suit I'd worn to work and still had on now.

"I would go if I could," Dotty interjected. "But of course, who would take care of the children?"

I suppose this was my cue to volunteer. Neither prospect seemed very appealing. At least with Helen and the twins I might get a nice meal. Dotty waited, and as the seconds ticked by, the look she gave me became increasingly laced with arsenic. In addition to Helen and myself, there were five other boarders, but they were all somewhat elderly, and none of them was reasonably equipped to babysit four small children. One of the oldest men who boarded at the house, a pensioner named Willoughby who had milky-blue eyes and who wore a copious amount of some sort of exotic, sickly-sweet cologne, would be all too happy to be left alone with the children, and I knew Dotty was guarding them from such an occurrence.

I looked from Dotty's genuinely miserable face to Helen's agitated, nervous expression and realized I had won this coveted invitation merely by default.

After a cup of coffee, my acquiescence was assumed, and I found myself whisked upstairs and forced to try on several rather frilly and ill-fitting dresses until one finally met with Helen's approval. Eventually we came back downstairs with Helen's dress fitted precariously to my admittedly scrawny frame by means of several black satin ribbons tied in strategic places. The quieter of the twins, the one in the blue plaid jacket—Lenny, I'd guessed by that time—made a halfhearted attempt to compliment me on the dress, a tactic I found somewhat offensive, as it had been made plain not more than fifteen minutes earlier that the dress was not something I could take credit for. A stickler for good manners, though, I mumbled a thank-you. Then we all said farewell to Dotty, who was tidying up the coffee dishes and doing absolutely nothing to conceal her disgruntled misery, and before I knew it we were out the door.

The agenda for the evening was dinner and dancing. At first I was inwardly curious about the dinner part—I envisioned the kind of restaurant I had never been to, one with creamy white tablecloths and napkins and exciting things on the menu I had never tasted, like oysters Rockefeller. But the meal turned out to be diner food at a greasy spoon owned by a friend's second cousin. The twins proudly informed us they received 20 percent off the total bill every time they dined.

The conversation, I'm afraid to report, was rather inane throughout most of the evening. The twins were both the quiet sort—so quiet, in fact, there was something a bit unnerving and unnatural about their silence. Always happy to assume center stage, Helen tried to fill most of the dead space with chatter, but despite the fact she had a number of memorized lines and embellishing accents at her disposal, I could tell she was running thin on material after only thirty minutes of the twins' stoniness. She was wearing an old-fashioned and rather fussy frock, and when she reached across the table her sleeve accidentally got caught in the puddle of murky gravy on her plate. The result was an extremely unbecoming brown stain running the length of her blousy forearm. She bemoaned this tragedy with great dramatic flare, and hinted—not too subtly, I might add—that as a gentleman Benny might think to assist her in the dress's replacement. Benny either did not catch on to her insinuations or else did an excellent job of appearing not to. After dinner, we piled into a taxi-cab and gave the driver the address of some sort of dance hall to which the twins claimed to have been specifically invited.

As had been the case with the restaurant, the dance hall was not as I'd (very optimistically, I now realize) pictured. The dance, they'd explained during the taxi-cab ride, was being put on by their club. Upon hearing this disclosure, Helen had turned to me, the delighted gleam of bragging in her eyes, and had hissed, *That's right, Rose; they belong to a social club!* The words *social club* loomed large in the air. Involuntarily, I pictured the lush oak-paneled rooms I had so often glimpsed through a high open window here and there while walking the city blocks near Grand Central. Behind those oak-paneled rooms I imagined marbled hallways and thickly carpeted sitting rooms and—with any luck—a swell ballroom with decadent refreshments and young couples dancing. And perhaps all these imaginings *are* what lies behind the oak-paneled rooms, but I cannot claim to be able to verify that, for the place we were destined to go was a cheaply lit café near Broadway as it crossed over Sixth Avenue and plunged deeper into the West Side. The "social club" in question turned out to be a volunteer sporting league, whose central organization was based in Hell's Kitchen.

Inside the café, there was a small elevated platform meant to serve as a grandstand for the orchestra. Four musicians were all that made up the entire "orchestra," but they played with tremendous enthusiasm, perhaps in part to make up for their lack of greater numbers. We found a table in a corner and sat down to take in the scene. A quick survey revealed a pathetic but sincere effort on behalf of the dance's organizers. Someone had draped black oilcloths over the café tables and set out mason jars that had been first scrubbed clean and then outfitted with little white candles that were now alight and burning brightly. The same someone had probably also hung the long strands of colored crepe paper that were draped in awkward abortive swags high up along the walls. There were only two couples dancing to the music in the middle of the room, and they were dancing a conservative and dowdy foxtrot. Even in my premature state of spinsterhood, I was aware this dance was beginning to go out of fashion. I peered over at Helen in an attempt to gauge her dismay, but her face showed a sort of haughty, imperial delight. I felt a strange inkling of pity for her. But like an evening chill, this sympathy passed through me and announced itself with the brevity of a shiver. After only a minute or two of sitting at the table, she insisted we take to the dance floor straightaway, and so we did.

It will come as no surprise when I say Leonard and I were a bit of an awkward abomination on the dance floor together. After three songs' worth of strained shuffling and tripping over each other's toes, I was dripping with perspiration from the effort and could no longer take Helen's mirthful shrieks and jibes whenever she and Bernard clipped close to us on the dance floor. I suggested to Leonard we sit it out for a bit. Ever silent, he nodded sternly and did not attempt to feign any great disappointment. We sat back down at the same table in the corner. There was a wilted carnation in the lapel of his plaid jacket I hadn't noticed previously. I commented on the "pretty" flower (it wasn't—I was merely trying to make conversation), and he very mechanically extracted it and handed it to me.

"Oh—no," I said. "I wasn't hinting."

"Take it. It'll have gotten crummy by morning anyway."

"All right."

I took the flower, but didn't know what to do with it. It didn't belong in my hair (carnations aren't really that sort of flower, are they?). After several minutes, I managed to get the thing tucked into one of the black satin ribbons tied about my torso.

"Thanks."

"S'all right."

The four-piece "orchestra" changed to a waltz, and we watched Helen and Bernard change their movements accordingly. A sweaty sheen was beginning to break out over Helen's fleshy brow, and her rouge had begun to run in ruddy rivulets down her cheeks, but her face bore a look of fierce determination that suggested all who witnessed her fatigue would do well not to comment on it. As we observed the couple's enthusiasm for dance tip slightly toward obstinacy and then back again, Leonard drummed his fingers on the table. I believe if Leonard and I shared anything that night, it was an acute awareness of being there solely to serve as chaperones for Helen and Bernard.

"What do you do, Leonard?"

"Benny and I are clerks over at McNab's."

"Do you like it?"

"S'all right."

"Been there long?"

"Going on four years."

"I see."

And so forth. I won't repeat the entire sum of idle chatter that Leonard and I occupied ourselves with that evening, as I'm afraid most of it was interchangeable and utterly unremarkable. It would seem this is the gift modernity has bestowed upon our generation: the practice of "dating," an awkward procedure where a man and a woman find themselves talking rot to each other in a darkened room. If it were up to me, I would say modernity can keep it, as I want no part.

When Helen and I crawled into our beds later that same night, we were both exhausted—she from the efforts of dancing and me from the efforts of making conversation with a man who if he were any duller might be declared catatonic by those in the medical profession. I could hear her sighing happily behind her side of the sheet that divided our room. I knew there was a sort of code to these sighs—Helen wasn't given the rush by boys very often. She was absolutely desperate to be given the sort of rush the female protagonists were always getting in the stories she pored over in the pages of *The Saturday Evening Post*.

"Thank you, Rose," she murmured in a very sleepy, pleasant voice. I have always known Helen to be an overly expressive person, but I realized this moment was the first time I had ever heard her express a sentiment of gratitude. For the second time that evening, I felt a tiny inkling of warmth toward her. She only wanted to be liked, after all—and this was something I could tolerate, even if Helen's primary desire was to be liked by boys as lowly and as dull as Bernard Crenshaw.

"Oh, but I meant to ask . . . you didn't go and blab about your job to Lenny, did you, Rose?"

"No," I replied cautiously. I knew where this tack was going. The friendly feeling I'd had just seconds before was already passing, as though a tiny sun had come out to warm my skin and was now tucking itself back away behind some clouds, leaving me colder than before.

"Good. You can't expect to charm a fella much by talking about typing in a police precinct! You might bend his ear a bit with the gruesome bits, but it's not exactly *feminine*, you know, all that business. Gotta always remember to guard your feminine mystique, or what have you." She paused as if deciding to hold her tongue, but the desire to restrain herself crumbled away quickly (as it so often did for Helen), and she pressed on with the terrible tirade of what she often liked to call *kind-spirited advice*. "And I wouldn't take it personally if Lenny didn't fancy you; his brother says he's very particular. Likes his girls to look like Mae Murray and all that." I heard her sigh again and roll over. "Don't worry, Rose. You're a sweet girl, and I'm sure there's plentya fellas that go for that sorta line, too." I knew she was succumbing to sleep as her true Brooklyn accent—an accent I rarely heard—was beginning to present itself. Her face went into the pillow and the next part was a bit muffled, but I think it was, "Next time we'll just have to gussy you up good an' right."

My only reply to Helen was an indignant silence that she utterly failed to register as she dropped almost instantly into a deep sleep and began snoring with surprising guttural force. The warm feeling I'd had toward Helen was definitely gone, along with any trace notion of sisterhood that still lingered stupidly in my head. Of course, it was easy to have thought as much at the time. By that very next Monday Odalie had arrived in my life, swathed in all her fashionable clothes and dark mystery. And unlike Helen, Odalie's influence turned out to be much more difficult to get out from under.

3

Our precinct is located in a very dank and humid old brick building. I am told that it is one of a small handful of buildings still standing in Manhattan that date from the time of the Dutch settlement and was originally intended to serve as some sort of storehouse for grain and cattle. I do not know whether this alleged architectural history of the building is accurate, but I do know that the brick walls are often wet with condensation and it is filled with the kind of humidity that does very little to keep a body warm. None of its windows receive the benefit of direct sunlight; instead they are filled with the kind of steady indirect light particular to dense urban spaces. As a result, the whole precinct is filled all day long with a somewhat eerie greenish glow, deepening the initial impression that you are either immersed in one great fish tank or else caught between several walls of them.

There is also a distinctly heady, air-thickening odor that pervades the place. In all my time working at the precinct and observing its characteristics, I have arrived at the conclusion that this odor is the scent of alcohol perspiring through the body's many pores. There is something very unique about the smell of whiskey or gin or whatnot souring on a person's breath, hair, and skin. You would think, perhaps, that this odor would come and go along with the varieties and quantities of men who import it, like a tide washing in and out. And indeed, the potency of the scent does wax and wane to some extent, but there is always a certain trace of it—however faint—that remains in our presence on a permanent basis.

Don't misunderstand me. I am actually quite fond of my job, and I have come to develop a sense of familiarity and loyalty for the precinct's environs. But usually when an outsider arrives, we are, all of us—the Sergeant, the Lieutenant Detective, the officers, the patrolmen, Iris, Marie, and myself—spurred by some native instinct to apologize for what we perceive to be its deficiencies, and this was certainly the case when Odalie arrived for her first day on the job.

On that particular morning, we were all crowded around Marie's desk having an impromptu meeting when Odalie walked in the door. The topic of discussion was our new status as a special crackdown unit, and how we all had an important part to play in the organization of each and every raid if we were to successfully shut down the neighborhood's speakeasies. The Sergeant seemed rather impassioned by the subject; he spoke to us in tones of measured emphasis and with a sense of great command, and I daresay the men seemed considerably motivated by his efforts. Earlier that month a rumor had made its way through the grapevine that if we successfully pulled off five or more raids in the coming weeks, we'd have our picture taken for the papers and the Commissioner would make a special visit to our precinct to shake everybody's hand. Naturally we were all very excited and nervous about this prospect; I looked around at all the eager faces and couldn't help but notice that the promise of our little precinct making the head-lines had even lured the Chief Inspector out of his office.

Usually the Lieutenant Detective is the highest-ranking offi-cer hanging about the office—although, to be honest, we all respected the Sergeant as the *true* overseer of the office, on account of the Sergeant's years of experience as compared to the Lieuten-ant Detective's youth and immature attitude. But that morning even the Lieutenant Detective's supervisor—our precinct's chief inspector—was there, hovering around Marie's desk with the rest of us. The Chief Inspector is an elderly, long-limbed man who has always preferred to deal with the paperwork generated by the Lieutenant Detective and the Sergeant from within the confines of his private office. His most notable features are his milky gaze and white beard, and in my opinion there is something faintly wraithlike about him. This impression possibly stems from the fact that most days, the only evidence of the Chief Inspector's exis-tence is the thin, sweetish aroma of his pipe tobacco emanating in slender wisps from the crack under his office door.

The meeting, as informal as it was, lurched to an awkward halt when Odalie entered the precinct. The door banged shut. We all turned to find Odalie standing in front of the threshold, peer-ing at us with her wide blue eyes and a faint smile on her lips. Her sudden apparition and elegant countenance were utterly incon-gruous with her surroundings. We were struck. Even the inter-mittent coughing and the rustling of papers that had thrummed along throughout our meeting as a backdrop of white noise sud-denly died down, deflating like a wind sock abruptly abandoned by the breeze. Odalie, to her credit, appeared absolutely unper-turbed. She calmly unpinned her hat (a tidy little velveteen toque hat, pinned over her as-yet-unbobbed chignon) and removed her gloves. The Lieutenant Detective hurried over and helped her off with her winter coat. She seemed to own, as I may have already mentioned, a lot of very nice things.

"Welcome, welcome. Glad you could make it," I heard the Lieutenant Detective say somewhat absurdly as he held her coat. It was as though Odalie had come for a dinner party rather than to take up her post as a typist. Odalie laughed in her free, easy, musical way.

"All right, boys, that's that," the Sergeant finally proclaimed, snapping our attention back to the matter at hand. "Let's all get to work now." He clapped his hands together twice, as though we were something dirty he was dusting off his palms. The meeting was over. The Sergeant knew a crumbling audience when he saw one. We scattered, each of us pantomiming immediate purpose in the hope that feigning rapt busyness would lead to actually being busy. Once again the Chief Inspector retreated back into his office, evaporating into his cloud of pipe tobacco and easing his nerves as well as our own. Slowly but surely, the pace of activity began to settle into its familiar clip—with one exception.

I unabashedly observed Odalie move through her first day at the precinct. After the Lieutenant Detective showed her to the coatrack and hung her coat for her (a billowing wrapover number, lilac in color; I believe it was cashmere, though I wasn't close enough to it to be sure), he escorted her in a promenade-like circle around the main office, introducing her by turns to each officer and staff member the two of them encountered along the way. Odalie, I noticed, was polite to all but modified her demeanor ever so slightly to accommodate each. With the Sergeant she was ladylike, formal. With Marie she was chummy; they laughed loudly together over a few familiar remarks. With Iris she turned a mirror to Iris's own aloofness—a professional distance, I know, Iris probably appreciated.

The Lieutenant Detective also introduced her to several of the patrolmen before they went out to walk their routes, or beats, as they liked to call them, short for *beaten paths*. I looked on as she extended a flirtatious hand to O'Neill, causing him to color slightly about the cheeks and lower his dark lashes shyly over his sleepy blue eyes. With Harley she allowed herself to chuckle indulgently at his suggestion they plot to play a prank on the Lieutenant Detective (the Lieutenant Detective looked less amused by this prospect). With Arp she nodded intently as he gestured nervously with his small hands and communicated to her in an instructive tone the importance of typing up a booking sheet with the utmost accuracy. With Grayben she shook hands firmly, looked him in the eye, and did not smile at his lewd jokes—instinctively knowing, somehow, that it was best to stake her ground with him straightaway.

And then, before I knew it, the Lieutenant Detective and Odalie were standing in front of my desk. I glanced up from the paperwork I had been proofreading and adjusted my expression to one of polite, detached interest.

"And last but not least, the lovely Miss Baker," the Lieutenant Detective said. I winced. I am no deluded fool, you see, and I have long since come to comprehend that *lovely* is not the adjective most people would use to describe me. To be blunt: I am plain. Hair the color of a common field mouse. Eyes the same. Regular features, average height. Clothes that attest rather frankly to my class and profession. I am so plain, in fact, that I am almost remarkably so. Having been in the police business for a couple of years now and knowing something about the nature of eyewitness reports, I am fairly confident that I could commit any number of crimes and get off scot-free, simply by virtue of being utterly unmemorable to a witness. My plainness was a fact, and a fact of which I'm certain the Lieutenant Detective was well aware. And so, wounded that the Lieutenant Detective was willing to mock me in front of an entirely new addition to our office staff just to settle an old score, I shot him an acid look. But Odalie took my hand in hers and instantly smoothed the air of discord.

"Of course; Miss Baker," she purred with that quaint rattling voice. "We weren't introduced, but I remember you from last week—I admired the blouse you had on. I remember thinking what nice taste you must have." I looked at her. She was hypnotic. I felt myself strangely compelled to believe her compliment in spite of my acute awareness that none of the blouses I owned were particularly admirable. But then I thought of the brooch and questioned whether this might be a veiled reference to its disappearance. I felt an icy apprehension creep into my veins. I hesitated.

"The other typists call me Rose," I said finally.

"Rose," Odalie repeated. She managed, somehow, by the tiniest trick of inflection, to make it sound more like the actual flower and less like the plain girl seated before her. "Well, Rose, it's lovely to meet y—"

Before she could finish her sentence, the door that led to the precinct's little holding jail burst open and an elderly wino ripe with body odor swayed wildly into our midst. The Lieutenant Detective, I noticed, stepped ever so slightly closer to Odalie, as if to shield her. But contrary to everyone's expectations, she did not require shielding. The buzz of activity around the precinct fell quiet and everyone looked on as Odalie composed herself and strode very calmly toward the escapee.

"Sir," she said in an unfazed, smooth purr while linking arms with the wino in a friendly manner, "you seem to have slipped away from your accommodations, and I'm afraid the establishment isn't quite ready to part with your company." The wino, a man who was perhaps in his sixties and was dressed in a badly tattered brown suit, looked at the arm that had so smoothly looped itself through his own and, with the combination of extreme confusion and intense concentration that is unique to the very, very drunk, followed the arm's length up to its owner's face. What he saw there shocked him into an awed, docile sort of submission. Odalie moved as though to imply great deliberate care of his person, and, unaccustomed to such treatment, he was caught off guard. He allowed her to lead him back to the holding cell as naturally and happily as if she were leading him to a dance floor or to a next hole of golf. Once there, she let go of his arm, patted his shoulder, and gave him a wink. Meanwhile, two deputies quickly stepped in and locked him back up safely behind bars. In spite of his reimprisonment, the old man grinned at Odalie euphorically as she walked away and did not appear to regret having allowed himself to be tricked.

When she reemerged from the hall that led to the holding cell and returned to the main floor, the officers and other typists collectively held their breaths for a moment, and then suddenly the whole room erupted with applause. Odalie smiled in a pleased way and nodded her head modestly, but—as I noted—did not blush.

"Well done, Miss Lazare," the Sergeant called in an approving bass from across the room.

The Lieutenant Detective walked over to her, extracting a handkerchief from his inside jacket pocket. He shook the hand-kerchief out, snapping it once through the air, then took Odalie's hands in his own and gently wiped away a few smudges of sooty dirt that had been transferred from the wino onto Odalie's own person during the course of her escort.

"Well, it certainly appears you are not above getting your hands a little dirty," he said to her, giving her a wink and allow-ing the corners of his mouth to curl up devilishly. I am not the sort of woman to whom men often utter double entendres, but I know one when I overhear one. To her credit, Odalie appeared uninter-ested. She smiled politely at the good-looking detective while he cleaned the soot off her hands, but then looked away absently, as though her attention had been caught by something more fasci-nating just over his shoulder.

As for our own aborted introduction, it appeared it had already been long forgotten. After the fuss over Odalie's smooth handling of the rowdy wino died down, the Lieutenant Detective handed Odalie off to Marie, whereupon she was shown to a desk and given her first police report to type up. For the remainder of the day, I watched her closely from my side of the precinct floor, but she seemed utterly impervious to my existence and did not look up or glance my way a single time. So much the better, I decided. I remember thinking at the time, aside from the simple fact of our gender, we did not appear to have much in common.

4

Of course, the mistakes seemed entirely genuine and unintended at first, and had very few irreversible repercussions. I suppose no one thought much of the little typos that began turning up here and there—if they even observed them in the first place. I noted them, but did not know yet the whole truth about Odalie's tactics, and so did not say anything. Like most people, I quickly arrived at the assumption that Odalie was simply careless at her job and told myself I would only bring it to the Sergeant's attention if she did not improve her accuracy over time. Out of a completely voluntary but enduring sense of conscientiousness, I took it upon myself to keep careful watch of her.

For the most part, we typists are expected to be incapable of mistakes. It is a curious phenomenon that whenever something is typed up it becomes, for better or for worse, the truth. I've sat in on a few trials myself and listened to words I'd typed with my own two hands read aloud by a prosecuting lawyer. The reading aloud of this transcript is always treated as though the information it contains is just as accurate and inviolable as the pair of tablets Moses brought down from Mount Sinai—even more so, for after all, Moses smashed those tablets on the first go-round and had to go back for a replacement set, and these transcripts seem more ironclad.

Even more interesting to me is how, as the confession is being read aloud by the prosecuting lawyer, the court reporter simultaneously types these same words in turn, creating a second, repeated record of the truth. Out of professional courtesy, I would never doubt the court reporter's accuracy (as I would not appreciate somebody doubting my own), but it is interesting to contemplate the number of hands—*feminine* hands, no less—and machines that must handle the content of the confession until it translates itself into a verdict and, finally, a sentence. This is, of course, a function of our modern times. Whether we've made the wisest choice or not remains to be seen, but either way we've gone and placed our faith in the fidelity of machines, in that we've chosen to believe what these devices reproduce will stay true to the original. Furthermore, we typists are considered an extension of the typewriter and the mechanical neutrality of all it produces. Once we've positioned ourselves in front of the machine itself, our legs crossed at the ankles and tidily tucked under our chairs, our fingers poised over the keys, we are expected to become inhuman. It is our duty to take dictation or transcribe everything exactly as it is. We are thought to be mere receptors, passive and wonderfully incapable of deviation.

I suppose this is also the paradox of justice. The disembodiment, I mean; that justice is supposed to be all-seeing and yet blind at the same time. We typists are expected to give up our opinions, but I suppose Lady Justice is expected to be even further deprived of her faculties, in that she is not even entitled to the prejudices of first impressions. Lady Justice may be obliged to be blind in order to properly do her job, but I'm not certain I could stand that particular handicap myself. I'll admit outright, I have always been something of a *voyeuse,* and I feel very little shame in this. I am quite skilled at watching people, and I believe this habit has given me something of a true education in the world—perhaps in more ways than one.

From the time of my early childhood years, the nuns at the orphanage often commented on my ability to successfully gather information by simply remaining silent and spying, unobserved. Of course, they did not put it this way. They only called it *spying* when I had been mischievous, and this was rare. Most times, they said things to me like, *My, but what an observant little thing you are, Rose! Always soaking up everything around you! See that your observant ways don't lead you into trouble, and you will go far in this life.* I heeded their advice. I was always good; I minded my manners and kept my hands and fingernails clean, and they never had to scold me about my chores or scrub at my face with the rough, wetted cloth of a washrag.

It was there at the orphanage that I learned that to be plain was a sign of superior virtue. Lucky for me I discovered I had a special talent for plainness. I had not been cursed at birth with any innately remarkable talents or features, so maintaining this lack was simply a matter of never cultivating them. I made a great study of plainness, and this was how I won many of the nuns over. As the years passed, I took care to absorb the criteria that informed their judgment. According to them, a plain girl would not grow up to be a vain girl, and thus would be forever safe from at least one of the seven deadly sins. A plain girl required very little fuss to be made over her, and was just as happy to make polite conversation as she was to extract a book from the pockets of her skirt and read quietly to herself. A plain girl was in little danger of getting romantic ideas in her head—or worse still, inadvertently stirring up romantic ideas in the heads of her male counterparts—and thereby causing a scandal. *If there's one thing we're sure of about you, Rose, it's that you'll never disgrace us by preening indiscreetly before the milkman,* they would say in approving voices.

The milkman who delivered our daily milk was a jolly bear of a man whose eyes twinkled with dark mischief as he heaped flattery on every girl at the orphanage who crossed his path, no matter her age or status. He heaped flattery on every girl, that is, except for me. Whenever it was my turn to receive the milk, his wide grin froze into a rather flat, stiff line as I threw open the door, and the curt exchange between us was polite enough, but unmistakably all business. I overheard one of the other girls ask him why it was he spared me so thoroughly from his many winks and compliments. *There's something not right about that one,* he diagnosed, shaking his head. *Can't put my finger on it exactly, but it's like the milk: Even when it's not yet spoiled, you just know when it's getting ready to go off.* To those of a more sensitive disposition, this would've caused great offense. But, of course, hearing this comment didn't upset me in the least, as only an utter ninny would align her personal conduct with the ideals of a milkman. At the tender age of ten I already had the wherewithal to intuit my own mental and moral superiority.

The nuns seemed to intuit it as well. For a couple of years they were thoughtful enough to send me to work as a maid during the afternoons for the elderly wife of a very wealthy Catholic businessman. The idea was I would learn manners and diligence, while also learning how a proper lady lived. My employer (I use this term rather loosely, as I was not actually paid an income—

although it must be said the orphanage did benefit from a few extra donations during those years) was a silver-haired, thin-lipped woman whose Arcadian ancestors had long ago followed the Saint Lawrence River out of the French colonies and into the British ones, until one day they woke up and found the world around them had changed and transformed itself into a new-fangled thing called America. All roads lead to Rome, or some version of it, and as far as I can tell this is how Mrs. Abigail Lebrun's forebears ended up adopting an eastward trajectory again, with the eventual result that the Lebruns took up residence in New York City.

As I knew them, Mrs. Lebrun spent her days overseeing a rather large four-story townhouse in an outer borough of New York, while Mr. Lebrun governed one of the city's largest furrier workshops. Mrs. Lebrun had quite a lot of other maids, but she managed to find work for me. Under her watchful schoolmarm eye, I learned how to polish silver, how to care for fur, how to clean diamonds without disturbing them from their pronged settings, and how to mend the most delicate of lace patterns. I also learned the great virtue of frugality from Mrs. Lebrun, who was something of a master at it. I believe she felt she was doing me a great service, and perhaps she was. According to her, my generation had gone and made the world disposable—we had filled the world up with cheap, ephemeral things and had neglected to learn the art of how to make anything last. In teaching me to extend the life of this or that feathered hat or silk ball-gown, Mrs. Lebrun had set herself the task of correcting my generation's flaws.

The nuns were quite pleased with the positive reviews I received in my stint as a maid, and considered perhaps even more could be done to help me. During the summer of my twelfth birthday they took up a collection, and it was decided when the school year resumed they would send me daily down the road to the Bedford Academy for Girls. This was so I might get a better education than the farcical one that was meted out in the single schoolroom at the orphanage by Sister Mildred, who was unfortunately eighty-nine years old and mostly deaf in both ears. I still remember how, at the time, the nuns were quite impressed by the education I was getting at the Bedford Academy and frequently expressed as much. *Oh, Rose, but how well you mind your p's and q's! They are making a perfect little lady out of you!* I don't know if it made me into a perfect little lady, but I suppose the Bedford Academy led to the Astoria Stenographers College for Ladies, and in this way I suppose the Bedford Academy had a hand in making a perfect little *typist* out of me (if I may be so bold as to use the word *perfect* to describe my impeccable typing skills). I may have mentioned already: I'm both extremely fast and extremely accurate in my typing. I believe this precision may simply be the result of my innate curiosity and my sharp eyes.

And so it was only natural that I trained these sharp eyes on the new typist. I watched Odalie carefully from the very first moment she began working at the precinct, but it was not until two weeks into her tenure that I started keeping a written record of her movements. It began very innocently; I jotted down simple notes about her comings and goings around the office and recorded the details of our limited conversations in the pages of a little notepad I kept tucked in the back of my desk drawer—right next to the brooch that still gave me a bit of a cold fright (and perhaps a simultaneous thrill) whenever I glimpsed it glinting at me from within the drawer, still nestled there. My notes on Odalie's activities were straightforward. Nothing terribly ambitious, just a road map, I suppose; a constellation of little landmarks I thought might lead me closer to figuring out the nature of Odalie's character. A sampling of extracts from these notes might read as follows:

Today when O came in she threw off the little capelet she was wearing like a magician and the satin interior flashed like silvery lightning. A clumsy kind of grace, but quite pretty. Entrances are always full of drama. Am beginning to look forward to her arrivals in the mornings, if only to see the show.

O inquired where I like to take my lunches. Could be she is simply after gastronomical advice, but I doubt it. Think she is trying to work up the nerve to ask me to join her for lunch someday. Responds to me differently than to Iris or Marie or any of the patrolmen. She is clearly intelligent and perhaps she has figured out we two are different from most of the others in the precinct. Not that I'm lonely, but it might be nice to have some clever conversations. I might welcome a lunch invitation after all.

Vaguely disappointed in O's typing skills—O botched two reports today. In six instances typed an "s" where an "a" should have appeared. When I pointed out her mistakes she blamed the typewriter and claimed the two keys have a habit of sticking together. Switched typewriters with her. Typewriter appears to be working fine.

The Lieutenant Detective came back from lunch today and deposited a small bundle of peanut brittle on O's desk. O acted very pleased, but as with all things to do with O, it was very difficult to tell if this was genuine. He said he just "happened" to be at the sweet shop this afternoon. Dubious, because the Lieutenant Detective takes his coffee black and has never been sighted eating a sweet.

O prefers tea to coffee. Earl Grey, with a little milk. Drinks it with her little finger curled. I admit I quite like this little habit about her. Perhaps a lady after all.

O crossed the room to return a report and lingered at my desk. Asked me what kind of music I prefer. I was perhaps a little too eager; said I like everything. The truth is I can't stand most of the modern noise one hears spilling out of the dance hall orchestras these days and really only like Bach and Mozart. But she put her hand on my shoulder and said we really must go to hear some music sometime. Wonder if we'll actually go to a concert together. Might even be able to tolerate some of that bizarre Stravinsky music if it meant keeping company with O. Have such a curiosity about her; my instincts tell me she is a very refined person.

Hinted to O today that I might go to the lunch-stand around the corner and that she might like to come along. She did not seem to pick up on my invitation, but I believe she is simply waiting until we can go someplace nicer together. She has very fine taste, and I'm quite certain she would want our first lunch together to be special. It was foolish of me to imply we should go somewhere as cheap and common as the lunch-stand.

O straightened her stockings while talking to the Lieutenant Detective today and didn't seem to care he was staring at her legs! Downright shocking. While sitting in chair, O reached right down to her left leg and began straightening the seam in the rayon. Stopped just short of reaching under her skirt and adjusting the very stays themselves, I'm sure. Very vulgar and inappropriate. Imagine the Lieutenant Detective was titillated, but the Sergeant would not have stood for it. Thank God for the Sergeant. There is such a thing as a moral and upright man.

Today O telephoned to a friend and stayed on the 'phone for several minutes discussing evening plans. Caught me looking at her when she was hanging up the receiver and began to ask me a question, but was interrupted by the Lieutenant Detective, who wanted me to go take dictation of a suspect's statement in the interrogation room. I think she was getting ready to ask me to go along with her and her friend that evening. Am almost sure of it.

Left her handbag behind when she went to lunch today. Saw a carton of cigarettes peeking out from inside. The carton had the name Gauloises *written on it. Never heard of the brand before, sounds foreign. But then, never smoked a cigarette before, either. Took advantage of a moment when no one was looking and slipped one cigarette out of the carton. Went outside to the alley to smoke it, but realized too late I had no match or Wonderlite to light it. Put cigarette in drawer next to O's brooch. Hope she won't notice one cigarette missing. She shouldn't be smoking anyway. Sends the wrong idea. Doing her a favor. If she only knew what a good friend I could be. Has all the makings of a true lady; just needs someone with a sharp eye to keep her from being too foolish.*

O took Iris to lunch today! Over me. Old, expressionless Iris, with her mannish little neckties. When they came back I was sweet as pie and asked all sorts of polite questions about their lunch, which

O answered as if the whole situation had nothing to do with me. Would be offended, but can't be bothered to care. Clearly I have overestimated O. She and Iris can have each other.

O came in a full twelve minutes late today. Did not apologize. The Sergeant said something to her about the time. Think she made a joke about it, but her voice was too low for me to hear from across the room. She laughed, and then to my horror the Sergeant chuckled a little, too. Am beginning to dread her arrivals in the mornings, for all the silly blustering that comes in the door along with her.

I ALWAYS ASSUMED my notes were patchy and sporadic at best, but reviewing them now, I see I was quite thorough. There are a great many more entries in my notebook—as I said, the ones I've included here only represent a sampling. But there is no great anomaly in my interest, only in my methods. From the very start Odalie was charming, and she could be very friendly and persuasive when she wanted. The false assumption that Odalie was what one might call a people person was an easy one to make. But in those early weeks, I uncovered a small truth: If one observed Odalie more closely, with a more careful eye (as I was wont to do), one might intuit that Odalie—for all her charm—did not care for most people. When people approached her desk, a very fine yet perceptible tension knit itself around the corners of her mouth, always preceding the wide smile she eventually spread superficially upon her face with the distracted, detached ease of someone spreading butter on toast.

And of course people always wanted to talk to her. If they couldn't talk *to* her, they settled for talking *about* her. The gossip began one lunchtime while a bunch of us were standing around the pushcarts that sold pierogi wrapped in newspaper and little paper cones of watered-down coffee on the street outside our precinct, and entered an immediate and vigorous repeated cycle that often went something like:

"I heard she went out to California with a fella, but he showed her all about how he had a right hook like Jack Delaney. So she stole his money and ran away."

"I heard she was in a moving picture once. She danced on top o' the table with Clara Bow."

"Oh yeah? How come we never seen the movie, then?"

"Will H. Hays got his meathooks on it and got it banned. Said it was too racy to be showed in public. Wasn't *decent*, if ya get my meaning."

"Well, that's convenient."

"What're ya tryin' to say?"

"I'm just saying I'll believe it when I see the picture."

"And I'm just saying I heard what I heard."

"Don't believe everything you hear. I think she's a nice girl."

"I agree. She's elegant!"

"Well, I don't know about that. I heard she was a gangster's girl. Yeah, see, that's how come she's got all that fancy loot—it's from *him*. They planted her here to get the lowdown on the bootlegging racket. You know how those gangsters are—always trying to plant someone on the inside."

"Careful, now," frequently interjected whichever good-hearted individual had conscientiously elected himself to serve as the Voice of Reason. "That's no laughing matter. You're potentially besmirching someone's reputation."

"I ain't sayin' it's true, I'm just sayin' I heard it. . . ."

It went on like that most of the time. Once started, it was like a steady chorus humming in the background that wouldn't—couldn't—stop. No one ever took credit for having started the rumors, but almost everyone was utterly unapologetic about passing them on. I suppose most of us at the precinct had gotten a little bored with the winos, the rapists, and the bootleggers. Odalie had become our sole source of entertainment, and the fabricators of these rumors (Grayben, Marie, and Harley, mostly) had let their romantic imaginations run off with them; they were trying to fit Odalie into the papers' latest headlines. Clara Bow, William H. Hays—it was all too recent. Just as with the paternity of my landlady's youngest child, the time-line surrounding these claims made their feasibility dubious at best.

If Odalie was aware of the rumors swirling around her, she did not show it. Her charm was like an electric switch she could flick on and off at will, and the rumors did not appear to have any effect on its flow. But despite having an abundance of charisma constantly at the ready, the surprising truth about Odalie was that she was not an open book and purposely seemed to avoid intimacies. Or so I intuited in the study I'd made of her behavior to that point.

When Marie deposited the week's reports to be typed on Odalie's desk, she always tried to strike up a conversation. Odalie was polite, but she rarely elaborated on her answers, and never asked Marie questions of her own—which kind of galled Marie, I think. I suppose on some level, being a bit reticent and choosy about company myself, I secretly approved of this. That is, I approved of it until she showed her utter lack of discretion and taste and invited Iris to be her very first lunch date. Perhaps it would've been more disappointing if it had been Marie, but oh—Iris! Harelipped, buttoned-up, flavorless Iris. I know I appear awfully plain on the outside, but Iris is one of those people who appears awfully plain on the *inside*. She said to me once, *Only children should have hobbies,* and she herself has none. No passions, not even any reading habits I know of—she reads only the newspaper, and she is even boring in her approach to this, for she reads it straight through from first page to last page, skipping nothing—not even the advertisements or obituaries or anything. And after she is done reading, she comments on one thing only: the weather. I might be the least authorized person to say so, but even *I* know Iris is a bit of a snore.

I don't go in for gossip much myself, and it's not as if I approve of Marie's nosy conduct and busybody chatter, but one thing I personally cannot tolerate is someone who makes you feel terrible for being interested in the business of others. After all, it is only human to be curious about others, and only a prude would deny it. But Iris is one such prude. Once, when I noted that the Sergeant had not brought in his lunch tin for more than a week and wondered aloud if there was trouble brewing between him and his wife, Iris was quick to quip, *Now, Rose, that's not called for. Best to mind your own business, else people might get the wrong idea about you and the Sergeant. Don't tell me they neglected to impart a proper sense of professionalism to you at the typing school . . .* I dislike gossips, but one thing I hate more than gossips are people who masquerade as though they are somehow above it all and have earned the right to condescend to the rest of us.

After Odalie and Iris came back from their lunch, I made some polite, perfunctory conversation and then returned my attention to the report I was typing. Of course I told myself my exclusion

from their lunch didn't bother me a bit, but something was nagging at me. I was agitated, irritable. Perhaps I had drunk too
much coffee that day, for my fingers jittered over the typewriter
keys in the worst way. I accidentally hit several of the wrong keys,
ripped the report page from the rollers and threw it away, inserted
a fresh sheet, and promptly made the same hurried mistake all
over again. Seething with annoyance, I decided to give it up. I put
on my gloves, took the cigarette from my desk drawer, and slipped
the contraband down the wrist of my left glove. It turned out the
gloves concealed the stolen cigarette quite neatly. No one so much
as looked up when I excused myself and walked outside.

I wandered several blocks to the alley I'd visited the first time
I'd tried to smoke the blasted thing. This time I did not forget to
bring along something to light it. The Lieutenant Detective had
been chewing on the end of a wooden matchstick all morning (a
habit he was prone to when he could not find a toothpick), and
when he left it unattended on his desk I took the liberty of adding
it to the small collection of bric-a-brac gathering in the back of my
desk drawer. (I'd like to take this moment to note: This makes it
sound as though I am by regular habit a thief, and I assure you I
am not. One can hardly own a matchstick—they are made to be
used by whoever might have need for them. And I have already
said my piece about the brooch being more of a *found item* insofar
as I only picked it up from the floor where it had dropped.)

When I got to the alley, I glanced around furtively. I was
acutely aware of how I must've looked. With a trembling hand, I
struck the sulfur tip of the match against a brick wall. It flared up
with a hiss. I'd never smoked, but I'd seen men do it plenty of times
in cafés. I held the flame to one end of the cigarette and sucked in

my cheeks slightly. Instantly my lungs felt a dry, hot, crackling sensation come over them. I coughed very ungracefully and shot a wild glance around the alley, still trying to make certain no one was watching me.

The cigarette seemed to be taking effect. My head began to spin and felt a little like it had turned into a balloon and had begun to lift away from my body. I wondered if this was what Odalie felt like when she smoked her cigarettes. Did she smoke them in cafés? At parties? Was she so bold? I thought of her and tried to hold the cigarette like she might do. My head got even lighter. I took several long, luxurious puffs on the cigarette, watching the butt smolder like a tiny red-hot coal as I drew in breath after breath. I felt quite relaxed until, very abruptly, someone thrust open a window in one of the apartments high above me. Startled, I threw the cigarette into a murky puddle and bolted down the alley as quickly as I was able. The sound of my heels hitting the pavement urged me on with a loud clapping that served to terrify me further. I didn't slow down until I neared the precinct. As I walked in the door and crossed the main floor, I tried to calm myself and put myself back together.

Luckily, my entrance was treated with just as much disinterest as my departure had initially generated—that is to say, no one even bothered to look up at me. I made an effort to catch my breath, squared off my shoulders, and calmly began to cross the room back to my desk. My thoughts raced with my new secret. *I've been smoking! I am a wild, smoking woman—just think of that!* The Lieutenant Detective would be so surprised to know, I thought with some satisfaction. The Sergeant . . . well . . . that was a less satisfying thought. I pushed it aside.

"Rose." I heard someone say my name softly. I flinched and turned to see Odalie looking at me, a faint smile of curiosity twisting her lips. "Is everything all right?"

"Oh! Fine," I said. "It's fine—all fine . . . I'm quite all right."

She cocked her head at me. "You looked startled just now," she said. She sniffed the air, and her smile twisted a little further as the curiosity died out of it and a hint of knowing trickled in. Then she shrugged as if to let me off the hook and let the matter go. "Only checking," she said. Her eyes lingered on mine for a second before she finally turned away and walked back to her desk. It was then that I turned my head and noticed the scent of cigarette smoke I was now carrying about in my hair. The scent was like the train of a gown, following me everywhere for the rest of the day, and I wondered how far it extended.

Later that afternoon my question was answered as I came back from the filing cabinets to find a packet of cigarettes sitting on my desk. The packet was new and unopened, and I knew instantly where they had come from. I crossed the room and held them out to Odalie, who was in the middle of typing something and looked up at me with a distracted expression.

"No, thank you," I said, shaking the packet in her face. "I don't smoke."

"Oh. Are you sure?"

"Yes," I said, still holding the packet out.

"Well then. I guess that's my mistake," she said, not sounding mistaken at all, and accepted the cigarettes with a smug, languid hand.

5

An incident occurred at some point during that period that had little direct connection to Odalie, but for some reason it always stands out in my memory when I recall her first weeks at the precinct. In fact, perhaps rather than saying the incident had "little direct connection," it would be more accurate of me to say it had no connection at all. The event in question didn't even happen at the precinct—it was just a small matter that happened back at the boarding-house once I'd already gone home for the day.

That afternoon, I was dismissed earlier than usual from my post. There had been a sort of lull after the lunch hour, during which a lazy mood settled over the office. At about half past three, the Lieutenant Detective ambled over with his loose, lanky shuffle and proceeded to half perch, half lean against my desk, sitting on the desktop as though it were a horse he was planning to ride sidesaddle. He pushed the papers lying on my desk around with an air of great interest, although judging from the unfocused gaze of his eyes I don't think he actually *saw* any of the words typed on the reports he was looking at. He cleared his throat several times and finally spoke.

"I believe you've already done the work of two typists today, Miss Baker. Perhaps we had better let you go home before you decide to demand twice the pay." His eyes flicked upward from the reports on my desk to meet my own, but, as though burned by something they found there, flicked away just as quickly.

"I don't believe the Sergeant has mentioned anything about my going home early today," I said.

"Well, as you know, I'm quite authorized to dismiss you on my own. And anyway, I'm sure the Sergeant would give his blessing," the Lieutenant Detective continued, his voice straining with affability. He balanced a paper clip flat on one fingertip and pretended to study it. "We wouldn't want to bring any trouble on ourselves from the union."

This last part was a joke. There were no unions for typists—or, for that matter, any profession where the fairer sex made up the majority of workers.

"Fine," I said brusquely, refusing to laugh at the joke. "So long as the Sergeant doesn't mind it, I'll take the afternoon off." I promptly set about packing my things up for the day. I reached for some papers under the Lieutenant Detective's seat and yanked at them unapologetically. With his eyebrows raised, he stumbled out of his sidesaddle perch and stood there blinking at me in a manner reminiscent of the winos who, upon their release from our custody, often staggered out from the darkness of the precinct only to stand on the pavement, dumbstruck and blinking in utter bewilderment at the much-too-bright sun.

When I had put on my gloves and slipped my handbag into the crook of my elbow, he was still standing there, blinking.

"But where will you go?" It was plain to see this exchange was not going as he'd planned.

I gave him a curious glance. "Why, home, of course. You said it yourself." He did not respond right away. I waited. I sighed and slipped the handbag back off my arm and let it land in the middle of my desk with a *plunk*. "Unless, of course," I said, "you're only having a laugh at me." I began tugging at the fingers of my gloves with irritation.

"No, no," the Lieutenant Detective said with haste. "Definitely not having a laugh at you." He had an odd, pinched look on his face as he watched me retrieve my handbag from the desktop and walk across the precinct floor to the front exit. He looked flustered, as though there were a sentence half formed in his mouth that was struggling in vain to the point of delivery. Perhaps he had expected a more effusive thank-you. But it was not my job to decode the motivations behind his enigmatic behaviors, and during my commute home, I made an oath to myself not to give it much thought or trouble myself over it.

Soon enough, I was nearing the boarding-house. The street that led up to it was lined with maples and elms, and as I rounded the block and reached the last leg of my commute, I found myself walking along the sidewalk ankle-deep in late autumn leaves. They had already lost their vivid colors, having transformed from their celebrated blazing reds and ambers to heaps of brittle, gray-brown papery scabs that rustled with the slightest stir of wind. There was an electric chill to the air, the scent of snow not far away; winter was almost upon us. When I finally arrived in front of the boarding-house, I remember peering up at the brownstone building where it squatted seamlessly amid the facades of its neighbors, and regarding its steep stoop and curlicue iron balustrade with a sense of comfort. *Home!* And it wasn't even dusk. I didn't care what the Lieutenant Detective's motivations were anymore; it *was* rather nice to arrive home in the middle of the afternoon. I felt a small twinge of lazy indulgence.

When I pushed the front door open, I was met with the usual blast of warm, stew-scented air. But that afternoon instead of insinuating a fuggy oppression, it was actually a welcome scent, stirring the first inklings of hunger in my stomach. I hung my coat up on a peg by the door and blew on my hands in an attempt to thaw my chilled fingers. Hearing voices in the kitchen, I moved toward them. I recognized the sounds of Dotty and Helen caught in the throes of lively chatter, their conversation rising and falling like two insects buzzing busily around each other. It might be nice, I thought, to join their cozy gossip sessions for once. I moved to enter the kitchen, but was brought up short just outside the double-hinged swinging door by something I heard: my own name. My heart gave a heavy pump, and I froze with my ear instinctively tilted toward the thin stripe of light that rimmed the door crack.

"Well, I don't know what you think I ought to've done. She's hopeless, I tell you. Hopeless!"

"You might try being a role model," I heard Dotty say in reply. "She could use one." I leaned a fraction to the right and could just see a peek of the room through the door crack. Helen was sitting in a chair holding a mug of tea. Hat pins stuck out at rakish angles from her reddish hair, but the hat itself—a rather large, outdated, and dramatic number—sat on the kitchen table by her elbow. Meanwhile, Dotty had her back to the room and was lifting something out of the oven, replying to Helen's conversation over her shoulder in a distracted manner as she went about her chores.

"Oh, I know—she's an orphan and means well and it's so sad and all that . . . But it's just that she's so painfully boring; talking to her is like watching paint dry! You can hardly blame Lenny for poking fun once her back was turned." Dotty turned around from the oven, and Helen peered up into her face with an innocent, doe-eyed expression. I recognized it immediately from the repertoire of faces Helen frequently made while looking in the mirror. When her voice came again, it was demure and sweet. "You think I'm very cruel to say so, don't you?"

"Well, you know what they say: Shouldn't judge till you walk a mile in someone's shoes 'n' all that."

"Ugh! But what *ugly* shoes they are."

"I've also heard 'em say a charitable heart looks smart on ev'ry woman," Dotty said in the familiar chastising voice I recognized as the one she normally reserved for speaking to her children. She slipped a soiled dish towel under the iron casserole dish she had just extracted from the oven and paused to wipe her brow. "Not that there's many who've shown me much charity ov'r the years, and you know, you think they would, too, what with Danny's death and the childr'n and all. . . . Wouldn't you know, Millicent Jasper, who used to be so chummy before Danny died, can't even be bothered to bring over a dish or two or offer to give me a hand with the childr'n ev'ry now and then. And, of course, then there's Helena Crumb, who's no better . . ."

Dotty began to list the people who had failed to demonstrate their ample charitable spirit with regard to her widowhood and the hardships of being left on her own to raise the children. It was a list I'd heard before, and one I knew she mentally updated on a daily basis. Helen, for her part, was clearly not as interested in Dotty's heroic strife as Dotty herself was. She tipped the saltshaker upside down, allowing a thin stream of bright grains to jet out, and proceeded to push the tiny snow-white pile around the kitchen table with her fingertip. She frowned as though deep in thought.

"Throw some ov'r your left shoulder," Dotty commanded upon taking notice of Helen's activity. Helen did so with a distracted air, the thoughts she'd been ruminating over rising to her lips.

"It's just impossible to be a role model to a girl like Rose," Helen said. "Her clothes and manners are just so *homely* . . . and she doesn't even *pretend* to be interested in feminine things."

"What do you expect, Helen? Lady Diana Manners? The girl was raised by nuns. They don't exactly emphasize puttin' on the frills, you must remember."

"I know . . . it's just that . . . well, she isn't entirely *unfortunate-looking*. It's a shame she can't be bothered to care a little more or do a little more with what she's got. Think what a clever girl could've done with those brooding Sarah Bernhardt eyes already."

"Not all girls are clever like you, m'dear. And even fewer are clever *and* charming," Dotty advised. "You should count your blessings and be kind to girls less favored by the boys. And in the first place, you can't expect all girls to have the same . . ." She paused in the middle of folding a dish towel and looked up to the ceiling, searching for the right word. "The same . . . well—*types*—of romantic goals . . . if you know what I mean."

"What *do* you mean?" Helen asked, looking up at Dotty with renewed curiosity. Dotty hesitated and looked around the kitchen briefly as though to ensure they were not being surveilled (little did she know, they were), then moved a little closer to where Helen sat at the kitchen table. She slipped into a chair just opposite Helen and lowered her voice.

"Well, the way I heard it, Rose was quite close to one of the nuns in particular. You know, kind of funny-close. A young novice named Adele, and things between them were quite . . . *entangled*."

Helen let out a small gasp. "No!"

Dotty nodded solemnly, trying to restrain the wicked delight that was threatening to break through the surface of her face as she delivered this piece of "regretful news." She leaned into Helen another half a degree and dropped her voice even further. "I even read the letter she sent here once."

"She? You mean the novice?"

"Yeah. She sent Rose a letter telling Rose to leave 'er alone and stay away. I steamed it open over the stove and then put it back inside and dabbed a little flour and water on the envelope to reseal it."

This was news to me. A fine mantle of sweat beads broke out over my forehead as my temperature turned wildly erratic. My cheeks burned hot; meanwhile, my blood shot icily through my veins. I knew exactly the letter that Dotty meant. But I did not know someone other than myself had ever read it.

"Did she say anything about Rose's behavior or what it is Rose might've done?"

"No, she just said—"

They halted upon hearing a loud clattering from just outside the kitchen door. Too late, I had tried to grab for the broomstick but narrowly missed it, cringing as it landed with a loud *smack* upon the wooden floorboards.

"What the devil?" I heard Dotty say as I quickly skirted up the stairs. In the brief flash just after the broom dropped, I had gotten my shoes off and was already carrying them in my hand, my stocking feet padding very softly on the tread of the staircase as I sprinted on tiptoe. By the time Helen and Dotty poked their heads out from the kitchen door, I imagine they found nothing but the broomstick lying on the floor, having been knocked over by an unexpected draft. It was not difficult to picture the scene in my absence—the two of them shrugging to themselves, righting the broom with an air of annoyed complaint, and resuming their conversation.

Up in my room I picked up a novel, but after my awkward exit downstairs I was agitated and couldn't quite focus on what it was that Mr. Darcy was saying—or *not* saying, I suppose, as was so often the case in Ms. Austen's books—to Elizabeth Bennet. I was flustered and frustrated. The luxurious feeling that had once surrounded the unexpected boon of free time had been stripped away in one fell swoop by the mean jibes of a girl I hardly even considered my friend. What did I care for the fact that Helen had nothing better to do than gossip about me? But there it was, eating away at me. And worse still was the fact that Dotty had read Adele's letter. I felt an instinctual wave of nausea wash over me as I recalled the words and details inscribed in that letter, and in my mind I read them over and imagined how they must've looked to Dotty's ignorant eyes.

I suppose I should explain about Adele. To be honest, I understand how people might *not* understand about Adele. But it was nothing underhanded or improper, I assure you. How horrified Adele would be to think her letter had ultimately resulted in Dotty's particular brand of mistaken impression! Perhaps if she had known an outsider would interpret it that way, she wouldn't have ever sent the letter in the first place. It really was an unnecessary letter in the end; there was nothing in it I did not already know.

Dotty had it a tiny bit right, you see, about how close Adele and I had grown over the years (nothing *unnatural*, mind you . . . we were just so like-minded and dear to each other, we were like sisters—or else bosom buddies, at the very least). I think it was guilt that made Adele write to me, saying the things she did. The guilt a person was bound to feel when one found oneself torn between one's ecclesiastical calling and one's . . . well, *secular* life. The latter being the sort of life I believe she wanted to lead with me. You see, I think deep down within her, Adele wanted nothing more than to shed the habit, run away from the convent altogether, and have a sort of second start at life. We talked about saving money and traveling to faraway places, about going to Florence and looking at all the lovely pictures in the museums there, or perhaps to exotic Stamboul, where we could spend all day at the Turkish baths and shopping in the bazaars for only a few pennies. Once I'd left the orphanage behind me, I wrote to Adele about these plans regularly—I didn't want her to think I'd given them up, and I was quite serious we should see them through. I admit I probably rhapsodized quite a bit in my letters, and perhaps my romantic vigor over the prospect of our future scared Adele somewhat, but I maintain these had once been our *shared* fantasies; it wasn't as if I were a madwoman pulling it all out of the air. In any case, I would venture to guess the mere suggestion to run away and give up the habit naturally made Adele feel very guilty, and there I was, tempting her with my impassioned accounts of the world that lay spread out before us, ripe for the taking.

This is not to imply I embodied some sort of corruptive force in my youth—I am hardly the type to play the seductress—and perhaps it would be wise to mention at this point that when Adele and I met, I was her junior. She was sixteen and I was fourteen. Unlike me, she was not an orphan, but rather a girl who had come to the convent after waking up one morning and telling her mother she'd had a calling to devote her life to the Good Lord. Her mother acted very quickly on Adele's proclamation and brought her straightaway to the nuns, who took Adele in on the condition she train for a few more years until she came of age and was of adult mind and body to take the vows she so longed to take. I overheard some of the nuns grousing one day about Adele's mother (you might not think so, but nuns grouse, too—although they almost always dutifully repent shortly thereafter), criticizing the woman's haste to dispense with her daughter's room and board. *Very convenient on the household budget,* I recall hearing them say. But I'm not sure this was an accurate assessment of her mother's motivations. I think the hastiness on the part of Adele's mother to take action had less to do with economic convenience and more to do with the fact that Adele's stepfather had begun "accidentally" popping into the washroom whenever Adele undressed to take her bath.

Adele told me about these unfortunate incidents one night when we were alone and it was very late. I remember being quite surprised by my own enraged desire to inflict bodily harm on a man I had never met. She never told me as much, but I think Adele made the mistake of also confiding her stepfather's history of misbehavior to old Sister Mildred, because one afternoon they met for many hours in Sister Mildred's tiny and often stale-smelling office that was adjacent to the schoolroom, and after that Adele was made to do a very long and exhausting penance of prayer and bathing and fasting "to cleanse her mind of impure thoughts." That would be just like Sister Mildred—to blame Adele herself for the offense that had been done to the poor girl.

Sister Mildred was from a long line of matriarchs very practiced in the art of insinuating that no woman ever received advances she did not herself invite. Her ideas about the world were antiquated, crusty things, a series of notions that had all been nibbled about the corners. To tell the truth, I think it was not that little room but Sister Mildred herself who smelled stale, as she was nicknamed Mildred the Patron Saint of Mildew by the other orphans.

Even if Sister Mildred's interpretation had been founded on something other than her own antediluvian assumptions about the world, I cannot think Adele ever intimated any desire for that loathsome man. I have heard Adele give her stepfather's description in great detail, and I assure you, there is nothing in his description I can believe a young girl could possibly want to invite closer to her person.

Adele's mother got her out of the house as quickly as she was able. Whether it was an act of feminine jealousy or maternal protection I cannot really say, as I have never met the woman. The fact remains that once she had delivered her daughter over into the capable hands of the Almighty, she never again visited the convent. I believe this left Adele feeling quite lonely. I don't have any memories of my own parents, so I can't say I understood exactly what Adele was going through, but I have a pretty good imagination, and I tried to demonstrate my sympathies by leaving little notes filled with words of encouragement and pressed flowers. In no time at all we were as thick as thieves.

Of course, there had been one incident in particular that caused me to realize for the first time how much I truly loved Adele. We were in the kitchen with Sister Hortense, kneading the dough that was to be eventually baked up and used for Communion, when Adele suddenly turned to me and said, *Rose, you have such a knack for this! The bread never comes out flat or mealy when you're on the job. It rises perfectly. Just absolutely perfectly!* Naturally, an unbidden rosiness appeared on my cheeks underneath the light dusting of flour that had settled there. But Adele just smiled and babbled on amicably, as though her thoughts were a liquid she might pour into the bread to give it some additional friendly flavor. *Maybe you inherited the gift from your mother,* she mused, *or maybe your father—yes, just think: Maybe your father was a master baker! Oh, but that would certainly explain it!*

Upon hearing this remark, Sister Hortense snorted loudly. Startled, Adele turned to look at her in surprise, but I was no fool. Long ago I had overheard the subject of my parentage being thoroughly parsed by the nuns. Time and time again, I'd heard them recall the evidence surrounding the circumstances that led to my entry into the orphanage. If the nuns' stories were to be believed, my parents were hardly the downtrodden *malfortunates* that so famously populate the novels of Charles Dickens—which is to say, my birth was not the inconvenient result of a lovelorn encounter in a slum, nor was my time at the orphanage the result of my guardians' having died tragically in a great house fire. They say fact is often stranger than fiction, but if you ask me, I believe truth has always been much more disappointing on this score. In the version of the truth I was told, my mother and father were a middle-class couple of relatively sound material prosperity. I suppose there was a decent enough chance my parents might have kept me and I might've been raised in the normal way, if my father had not contracted a certain venereal disease that one could only get by exposing oneself to a numerous variety of . . . well, I shall be frank and simply call them *ladies of the night.* As the nuns tell it, my mother "donated" me to the orphanage to spite him. She defied my father to try to retrieve me against her wishes. As far as I know, he never attempted to do so, leading me to conclude his fear of her wrath turned out to be extremely effective indeed. Her sense of justice was ruthless, but beautifully simple: If he wouldn't be faithful to her, she would refuse to keep and raise his children.

Of course, I would've much preferred a tragic house fire to this tale of petty jealousy and spite. I admit, as orphan stories go, mine is a rather lackluster one, which leads me to believe the nuns did not make it up. The bassinet in which I was found attests to my parents' middle-class standing, and my mother left a letter in the basket recounting the rather graphic details of my father's transgressions, while tidily neglecting to sign her name or reveal her identity.

When Adele began speculating about the identity of my parents, Sister Hortense promptly educated her on the subject and gave an abridged account of my father's misdeeds and my mother's attempt to even the score. Sister Hortense was not one for coddling girls, and I suppose I ought to be grateful the nuns did not infantilize me by ever lying to me about my origins. Nonetheless, my lips could not help curling into a faint, pleased little smile when Adele exclaimed, *Sister Hortense, shame on you! How could you suggest anyone would willingly give up such a delightful and clever girl as Rose?* Then she turned to me, took my hand in hers, and said, *Truly, Rose—you must know this horrid story can't be true; you're worth much more than that.* Sister Hortense only rolled her eyes, wrapped the dough she'd been kneading in a damp cheesecloth, and placed the lumpy mass in the ice-box. But still holding Adele's hand in my own, I could not have been more dizzy and affected than if I had just been knocked sideways by a wrecking ball. Something special was happening; a tiny door was opening inside my chest. I glimpsed a future wherein I would not always be alone, and I know Adele had glimpsed it, too.

I suppose after hearing Dotty's inaccurate and depraved assumptions whispered in the kitchen downstairs and feeling my stomach churn, I got to reminiscing and realized I still missed Adele very much. I sat and thought about her, about her very brown eyes and the little crinkle that was always present on her forehead, and the way she used to sing whenever the nuns gave her work to do in the kitchen, and how her hands were perpetually chapped from all the chores she did, and how she could never remember to put on a scarf, and how she sometimes declined to carry an umbrella because she worried that wanting to keep her hair dry counted as an act of vanity. There was so much to remember, and I sat there lost in my reverie, remembering all the details.

I snapped to attention when the door opened and Helen let herself into the room. I realized I had been waiting for this to happen all along, sitting in apprehension and turning the pages of my book without really reading what was written on them. She looked extremely startled to see me just then, perched upon my bed and reading a book, and I think this gave me a slight feeling of smug satisfaction.

"Oh! You're home!"

"Yes."

"I—we . . . we didn't hear you come in."

"Mm."

"Have you been home long?"

"I was allowed to take my leave for the afternoon," I said, "on account of my working so hard." I knew this was not an answer to her question, and I suppose I was hoping to needle her with my sidestepping of it. Let her worry about what vicious talk of hers I might've heard or not heard! Helen crossed the room to the vanity that straddled the curtained border of our two silently warring territories. I stared at her as she leaned down to catch sight of herself in the vanity mirror and nervously remove the hat pins still sticking out from her hatless hair.

"Home early—aren't you the clever one?" She gave a forced little laugh, and her eyes flicked warily at my reflection in the mirror, then back to her own countenance. "Oh goodness! Just look at me! I look like I've been in the salt mines all day." As she looked in the mirror, her body mechanically sank onto the stool that sat before the vanity, and she proceeded to fuss with her hair and pinch her complexion. I knew she was trying to ignore me, but I stared on mercilessly.

"I heard you and Dotty," I said in a low, quiet voice. For a fleeting second, Helen's eyelids fluttered and her mouth made a surprised little O shape. *Victory,* I thought. *Now she will have to grovel.* But just as quickly, an invisible automatic spring clicked into place and she regained her composure.

"Sorry? What was that, dear?" Her voice was breezy, saccharine. Perhaps she thought she was being politic, giving me a way to avoid the discomfort of direct confrontation. But I was not afraid. I pressed on.

"I said, I heard you and Dotty talking when I came in."

She drew a sharp breath and something caught in her throat, causing her to give a little choking cough, which she struggled to control. "Did you?" she said with curious innocence after she'd managed to clear her throat. "Then you must've heard me going on about that dreadful girl Grace at the shop." She tittered nervously. "So bad of me. You know I don't like to gossip . . . but, well, I suppose we're all guilty of it from time to time."

"I didn't hear you say anything about Grace. But I *did* hear you speaking of someone else."

"Oh, well, I'm sorry, but I'm sure I don't know what you're

talking about." She smiled—too widely. It was the craven smile of a nervous Dalmatian. Then she turned with a businesslike air and carried on grooming herself before the mirror. I couldn't believe it. She was going to insist on playing the innocent! But she'd already shown her cards, as far as I was concerned, and I could see her hands shaking.

"I don't suppose you've anything you think you ought to apologize for." I heard the words come out of my mouth and cringed. I sounded like a prissy old schoolmarm, my own voice going up several unflattering octaves as I reached the end of the sentence. I thought of Mrs. Lebrun from my childhood, scolding me when I'd once put the silver away in the wrong drawer. But I didn't care. Helen and I were in the open now, and I was ready for the relief of an all-out spat. I waited.

Helen turned to face me and blinked in feigned bewilderment. I recognized it again from the repertoire she often practiced in the mirror. "Oh!" she said, as though suddenly remembering something. "Why, yes, you're right; I almost forgot." She got up from the vanity, crossed to her armoire, and extracted something. "Here are your gloves back—I'm sorry I kept them so long." With an air of generosity, she moved to hand me back a pair of burgundy-brown leather gloves I had not seen since last year. I did not remember loaning them to her. I had thought them lost, and before winter had rolled around I had scrimped together some money to buy a much less attractive replacement pair in gray.

Now Helen was dangling my long-lost gloves before my face. With white-hot indignation still smoldering just beneath my skin, I took the gloves, the weight and sheen of them like the very slender, slack bodies of two small trout. So this was how she was going to play things. I told myself I couldn't be bothered any further to extract an apology from a girl who was too much of a weasel to admit when she was wrong. I turned and began to walk away. But then I changed my mind. It wasn't fair, I thought, to be left alone with the injustice of it all. I was quaking with anger, practically shivering all over my body. I retraced my steps back to Helen with a stiff, automatic gait, almost like a windup doll.

I drew up close and stood squarely in front of her, our noses almost touching. She looked into my face with a benign smile. Then, as if someone had pulled the plug on an invisible drain, I watched the color leave her face. It was in that moment, I think, she began to comprehend exactly what I was about to do, and what I was capable of doing if she angered me further. Still with a stiff, automatic quality to my movements, I lifted the hand that held the pair of gloves and brought them swiftly through the air, whereupon they landed with a satisfying *SLAP!* across Helen's cheek. Helen, for her part, began crying and carrying on immediately.

"You wretch!" she shouted bitterly at me. But I no longer heard anything. Calmly and deliberately, I pulled the gloves onto my hands. I fitted them neatly over each finger and exited the room with the notion of taking an evening walk.

I stayed out for several hours, dithering here and there, and didn't return until long after the dinner hour had come and gone. Once upstairs, it was obvious that Helen had retreated somewhat. I couldn't see her, as she was completely obscured by the sheet that divided the room, which I noted had been drawn so as to achieve maximum privacy. But I knew she was there; I could hear her sniffling a bit—leftovers, I presume, from the drama-filled "good cry" she'd likely had while I was out on my walk. I tucked the gloves away in a dresser drawer (certain only that they would disappear again very soon, as Helen was an incorrigible little thief) and crawled under the covers of my bed to resume the book I had been trying to read earlier.

I assumed it would be more relaxing now that I'd confronted Helen and a small measure of justice had been done, but it remained difficult to concentrate. Once more, I found myself turning pages without really seeing them. I could sense Helen on the other side of the sheet, probably thinking she'd been done a grave wrong. She would tell Dotty first thing in the morning—if she hadn't already, of course. She would probably even take the trouble to embroider the story here and there. They both would. I got up from bed and, with a vague tyrannical impulse, switched off the only electric lamp in the room. Helen did not protest. I crawled back under the covers and closed my eyes. I knew I was not likely to get much shut-eye for the night, but one thing was certain: This was no place for me anymore. Something had to be done.

Several weeks passed before Odalie and I grew to be close enough friends for me to confide my complaints about Helen to her in full. But once I did, everything changed.

6

"This Helen girl sounds like an absolute ninny. I don't see why you put up with it. You ought to just move into the hotel with me," Odalie decreed in her cheerful, bright manner when I recounted the story to her some weeks later. She gave me a girlish smile that was at violent odds with the thin stream of smoke she immediately blew from her lips. It hung for a moment, seductively coiling and recoiling itself much like that infamous original serpent, and finally rose to the airy vaulted ceiling of the restaurant. She detached her cigarette from an elegant bone ivory holder and crushed out the smoldering butt in the crystal cut ashtray, all the while completely ignoring the *tsk-tsk* sounds emanating from a pair of silver-haired biddies glaring at her from across the room. I knew, as it was, the cigarette holder represented as much of a concession as Odalie would ever make to such ladies, preferring as she did to smoke her cigarettes with no holder at all. With the cigarette snuffed out now, she looked up at me, fresh-faced, her eyes shining with such a gleam, I thought perhaps she was feeling rather moved by the idea of the two of us living together. My heart leapt.

Oh! But I am getting it out of order; I should explain how Odalie and I got to be friends in the first place. How she won me over finally and all that. The doctor I am seeing now tells me I should concentrate on telling things in the proper order— chronologically, he means, of course. He says that telling things in their accurate sequence is good for healing the mind.

And now these events should be easy to tell, as I can see them so clearly from the vantage of hindsight. The door to our friendship was initially cracked open in a very simple manner. She allowed me the luxury of rhapsodizing at great length about one of my favorite subjects: the Sergeant. I wonder, now that I know more about Odalie's character, whether she detected my weakness for the Sergeant and plotted to exploit it, or if she simply blundered onto the subject and was astute enough to see how much it pleased me.

I know I have already given a few of the Sergeant's particulars—his handlebar mustache, his sturdy stature, his intolerance for tomfoolery, his polite deference to general gentility. But even the sum of these qualities nevertheless fails to describe the essence of what I believed truly defined the Sergeant.

Of course, the Sergeant and I had a special understanding from the very first. When the typing school sent me to the precinct, it was the Sergeant who interviewed me. *I can read over the contents of this file,* he said, flipping open a cardboard folder the typing school had delivered to the precinct earlier that day via a messenger boy, *and allow these pages to tell me all about who you are. That you were raised in a convent, that you made decent marks in school, that despite being an orphan you lack the usual record of stealing or cheating . . . or*—he flipped the folder shut and tossed it on his desk, then leaned back in his chair and twisted one side of his mustache between his left thumb and forefinger—*I can simply sit across from you now and see quite plainly you are a lady of good conscience and honest disposition.* That was it. Our special understanding was established, and I was hired. As though to illustrate how certain he was of my vocational value, the Sergeant did not even check with the Lieutenant Detective or the Chief Inspector before pumping my hand and welcoming me aboard.

Minutes later, when he walked me to the exit, he put one hand on my shoulder and gave it a small squeeze. *I can't imagine it's been easy for you,* he remarked. I didn't know what to say, so I simply gave a slight nod. The Sergeant smiled, his paternal hand warming the curve of my shoulder through the artificial silk of my best blouse. *I can assure you, Rose, no one will give you trouble about your breeding here. I can see that even though you are just a woman, you know very well how to make yourself useful, and your industriousness will not go unappreciated in this office.* I was surprised by how well I liked the weight of the Sergeant's heavy, paw-like hand on my shoulder. I also recall feeling a sense of great reassurance. Not just reassurance in the fact that I had successfully obtained the job, but reassurance that good and fair-minded people—people who believed in administering a grounded, impartial justice—still existed and held sway in this world.

This is not to suggest the Sergeant is a timid, watered-down sort of man. Quite the contrary. He is a man of extremes. Even physically speaking, the fiery red hue of his perpetually ruddy complexion strikes a dire contrast with the icy blue of his eyes. But there was always—*is* always, I should say—an overall sense of equanimity about the Sergeant, an impression that all the contrasts in him are pulling in equal opposition.

At that time, Odalie's desk at the precinct was positioned directly opposite my own, and in this manner, one might think a natural rapport would arise between us. But at first there was only silence. As I said, I had a peculiar, uncanny feeling about the girl from the first moment I encountered her, but this did not equal an instant friendship. And when she took up with Iris (and then, to add insult to injury, dallied a bit with Marie's friendship), I took her for a fool and very pointedly turned a cold shoulder, which I was certain did not go undetected.

So I was surprised one day when Odalie emerged from the interrogation room and exclaimed, "He is just absolutely the law itself, isn't he?" As we were not in the habit of making conversation, I looked around to see who she could possibly be talking to. The days were getting noticeably shorter by then. We were headed into the long black nights of winter, and although it was only four o'clock, outside a cloudy sky was already turning from ash to soot. And yet inside the office there was still something vital, the peculiar sort of kindling that comes from human activity buzzing away in the falling dark of dusk. The electric lights still glowed, and the office thrummed with the sounds of telephones, voices, papers, footsteps, and the syncopated clacking of many typewriters all being operated at once. It could very well be day *or* night outside for all anyone cared; at that exact moment, everyone was quite busy, absorbed in what they were doing. And there was Odalie—still standing in front of her desk, facing me, her question (rhetorical though it was) still hanging in the air unanswered. I looked up at her and I remember—I remember this image quite clearly—the bare electric bulb that dangled above her cast a perfect shimmering halo around the crown of her head, a perfect corona of light caught in the sheen of her silky black bobbed hair.

"Yes," I stammered after a while. "The Sergeant is an excellent man."

Odalie cocked her head at me. Her eyes inspected me with a feline ferocity. "I'm curious," she said. "What can you tell me about the Sergeant?"

"Well, I suppose . . . he always gets his man, as they say," I said. I leaned my chin on my hand, pondering a longer answer, and ultimately happy to continue. "He's quite incorruptible, and his instincts are impeccable as a result. Whenever we have a stubborn criminal who is so very *obviously* guilty, we always leave it to the Sergeant; he has yet to fail."

"But I mean, what do you know about the Sergeant's personal life?" I stiffened, and Odalie, attuned to such things, noticed. "I hope you don't think me crude," she hurried to add. She lowered her very long black eyelashes. "It's just . . . you seem so . . . *perceptive* to the goings-on in this office."

"I wouldn't know about the Sergeant's personal life," I said curtly, and returned my attention to the report on my desk that wanted transcribing.

"Ah, it's just as well. I suppose it's exactly as one would imagine. A lovely wife and lovely children and all that."

"Well . . . ," some reflex within me prompted me to volunteer. "It's not *exactly* that way. . . . The Sergeant is very upright and morally correct, but if you ask me, I would venture to guess his wife is not exactly what one would call *appreciative* of such qualities. Can you believe, the Sergeant came in *twice* last week without his lunch tin? I suspect they were having some sort of row and she didn't pack it on purpose. Why, I can't imagine treating a virtuous man like the Sergeant with such utter disregard! If it were me, I would never—" I stopped short. Odalie's smile had changed from something charming and soothing into an amused, cynical little thing, and the shift made me feel quite self-conscious. "I only mean . . . It's just that . . . Well, you know how people can tend to undervalue a man like that . . . such a shame."

Luckily for my sake, we were interrupted by the Lieutenant Detective, who wanted me to trot over to the stationer and put in an order for all the paper, stenotype rolls, typewriter ribbons, and other sundries our office needed delivered for the month.

"And I suppose after the order's been put in you can go home for the day, Miss Baker," he said, looking at his wristwatch and observing the hour. He began to retreat to his own desk, then had a second thought and turned back. "And take Miss Lazare with you, so you can show her how it's done." Odalie smiled at me and tidied her desk, then went over to the coatrack and slipped into her coat, hat, and gloves.

Together we took the subway to Times Square, where the buildings suddenly rose into the sky, the tempo of the street skipped a beat, and reporters scurried about the sidewalks, hurrying back to their offices for the evening, where they would sit feverishly typing their stories before the midnight deadline, when all the newspapers went to press. The streets were still dry, but the dark sky was thick with rain clouds, and as we came up out of the subway a ripple of thunder echoed overhead.

At the stationer I put in the monthly order and listed aloud for Odalie all the details of how it was to be done. To my surprise, she did not take out the little notebook and golden pencil I knew she carried about in her purse, which I felt was a mistake—she was not the type who was likely to remember anything without taking notes—but rather stared at me the entire time with a pair of glassy, vacant eyes. After several minutes I gave up trying to give Odalie instructions and simply filled out the stationer's order form in silence and returned it to the clerk. He nodded, took the form, and thanked me distractedly.

Back out on the street we found ourselves caught in an unexpected downpour. Both of us were without an umbrella, and together we engaged in a game of trying to dodge about under the eaves and awnings of the buildings around us. But skyscrapers—those symbols of progress, with their sleek lines and soaring heights—nonetheless provide very little in the way of street-side shelter, as you might know. Soon enough we both found ourselves looking like a couple of drowned rats. We were forced to pause for a changing traffic light at a street corner, and a grocer's truck came along and mercilessly splashed me where I stood on the curb with a spray of filthy gutter water. Odalie began laughing hysterically. In a state of great annoyance, I turned to part with her. "Good night, Miss Lazare. I shall see you tomorrow at the precinct."

"Hang on," she said, catching my wrist. Her eyes quickly ran from my head to my feet. "What a shambles we are!" she exclaimed. Still laughing, still clutching my wrist in her hand, she stepped off the curb and raised her opposite arm to hail a taxi. "I think I may know a good remedy." Considering taxi-cabs a very lavish expense and rarely taking them myself, I briefly struggled to demur. But my instincts for economy were quickly overcome by my instincts for survival and comfort, and as the taxi slowed to a stop in front of us, I felt a wave of desperate gratitude wash over my cold, wet, tired body. Before I knew it, I had gotten in of automatic accord and listened as Odalie gave the driver the address of a hotel only slightly farther uptown.

I had heard of girls who lived in hotels before, but in my experience they had all either been very rich or else very improper. It made me nervous to realize Odalie might be either—or both—of these things. If I am being completely honest, I should admit it likely made me a little excited, too. When we pulled up to the curb, she paid the driver and allotted a generous tip. I followed her out of the cab door in a daze.

"Stay dry, misses," the driver said in a kind, grandfatherly tone as we exited from the cab. But he needn't have worried—we emerged under an electric-lit awning and walked the length of spongy red carpet that led up the stairs and into the gilded revolving door of the hotel. Inside the lobby, Odalie strode confidently over to the elevators, which looked to me like a pair of elaborately wrought birdcages. Stunned by the unexpected luxury of my surroundings, I followed her like a fawn staggering on new legs. Once the elevator had made its descent to the lobby, we got in and Odalie purred in a friendly voice, "The usual, Dennis." Evidently, "the usual" was the seventh floor, for it was at that floor that Dennis put the brake on and slid open the golden birdcage doors.

"Ma'am," he said cheerfully, and turned to smile at Odalie, who returned nothing but a grimace.

"Ugh," she said as though he were not still in earshot. "I hate it when they call me *ma'am*." She touched a hand to her hair, which was drooping and damp with rain. "Thank you, Dennis," she said to the now very distressed Dennis.

"Ma'am—I mean, miss?" he said, disconsolate. His dejection was short-lived, interrupted as it was by the demands of hotel business. Abruptly a tin bell sounded, and he retreated back into his gilded cage and cranked a lever. Odalie turned to me and smiled a rather rare, frank, thin-lipped smile. *"The young man carbuncular*," she said with a roll of her eyes, as though explaining something, and I suddenly had the impression that she was quoting something, although I didn't know exactly what.

She ushered me briskly down a long corridor. The carpet beneath my feet was plush, thick, red. My ankles wobbled ever so slightly as I walked on it, adding to the unsteady feeling that had already been building in my legs. I began to feel overwhelmed; it was all a bit too much, and the steam heat in the hotel was turned up rather high. But lured on by some entranced impulse, I followed Odalie as she drew up to a door, unlocked it, and threw it open. Inside was a large sitting room with fashionably modern green-and-white-striped furniture. Even the carpet was a deep, vibrant green and stretched wall to wall. I remember thinking there was something very clean and crisp-feeling about that particular shade of green. It was the color of a freshly mown lawn—and not just any lawn; the kind of lawn belonging to a golfing green or to the kind of wealthy estate I'd only ever read about in books. It was the color of money, in more ways than one.

I stood awkwardly in the middle of the room, idling like a forgotten croquet ball lost on too large an expanse of very green grass, still dripping from the downpour and not daring to touch the furniture. Then I heard Odalie latch the door behind me and felt her hands firmly on my back.

"C'mon," she said, laughing in her musical manner. "Let's get you out of these cold wet things." I was aware of being pushed in the direction of a bathroom. Once there, Odalie became a flurry of activity, opening the bath taps and unleashing a steaming torrent of water, extracting several little glass bottles and golden jars filled with all kinds of perfumed oils and unguents and adding them in different amounts as if by precise recipe to the bathwater.

When finally her witches' brew frothed over with a foot's worth of stiff, foamy bubbles, she shut the water off, pinned my hair up for me (I stood frozen, dumbstruck, watching in the mirror), and handed me a cream-colored silk robe. Less than an hour ago this woman had simply been another office girl, another typist, and now here I was, being given a glimpse into a life I could not have even imagined, being persuaded to slip into her bathtub and surrender my rain-soaked clothes. Seeing the consternation written on my brow, Odalie shrugged and giggled.

"Go on—hop in. I'll find you some dry things to wear when you get out," she said, and disappeared down the hall again. I looked around at the black-and-white tiled floor, at the marble sink and shiny brass piping, and then at the large enameled claw-foot tub, nearly heaping over now with bath bubbles. I hesitated for a few moments, glanced nervously at the tub, then unbuttoned my blouse and skirt, let them drop to the floor, rolled my stockings down, and finally slid out of my combinations. The silk robe in particular was an emblem of the kind of personal luxury I'd never known, and as I gazed at it the awe I'd experienced first in the lobby and then in Odalie's foyer reached an ultimate crescendo within me. While I do enjoy a good clean scrub, I admit my bathing rituals have always been of a very quick and functional variety. I was dimly aware I had somehow wandered far, far away from the world I'd always known and into some sort of wonderland. But a shiver brought me temporarily back into my body, and cold as I was, I had to forgo the robe altogether. The hot bathwater was calling urgently now, the soft crackle of popping soap bubbles like a siren's song. I stepped in carefully with one foot, then the other, and felt the sting of hot water on my very cold skin.

Odalie left me to my own devices for quite a while. It was

nearly forty-five minutes before she returned, and by then almost all the bubbles had dissolved and the whole tubful of water had turned a very foggy pale shade of aquamarine. I heard Odalie humming to herself as she came down the hall. I suddenly became aware of the fact there was no longer an adequate amount of bubbles to hide my rather scrawny nude body and stood up in the tub in an abrupt reflex. The water sloshed noisily, rushing into the vacuum of space I had left behind. I quickly grabbed at the brass rack for a towel to cover myself.

"How's this?" she asked, taking no note of my embarrassed posture and holding up a hanger to display a very lovely, peacock blue drop-waist dress.

"Oh," I murmured, blinking at the dress. "I couldn't wear that home. But just think . . . oh . . . Helen would turn absolutely green and die from envy."

"Who's Helen?" Odalie asked innocently.

And I began, for the first time since we'd met, to tell her.

THAT NIGHT MARKED the first night of our mutual confidence. Still warmed and relaxed from the bubble bath, I grew unusually loquacious. I described Helen to Odalie, along with all the petty thieving and snide insults I'd had to endure on a daily basis in my unfortunate role as Helen's room-mate. Odalie patted my arm and exclaimed over again and again, *What an obnoxious little wretch! I don't know how you put up with it.* Of course, in retrospect, I see how it was to Odalie's advantage to agree with me, to pet me and prop me up and ultimately fan the flames of my rage against Helen. But even so, I like to believe she would have thoroughly disapproved of Helen no matter what. As a manipulator, Helen did not possess one iota of the great store of panache Odalie had so carefully cultivated. But Odalie's charisma is another matter; I am getting ahead of myself again.

Odalie confided in me, too. Well . . . I thought she did, at the time. Once I was dry and dressed, we sat on great velvet cushions by the fire in the sitting room and drank from a couple of mugs of hot tea as I recounted the many details of Helen's habitual misconduct. I admit, I was in a daze and hardly knew where I was. It had taken me some time to get comfortable with the utter luxury of Odalie's apartment, but there's a funny thing about luxury I learned that night: Once you grow accustomed to it, you can't imagine being uncomfortable with it ever again. I was in no hurry to go home to the boarding-house in Brooklyn and back to horrible Helen, but good sense and proper decorum told me the time was drawing near. Never one to violate the rules of etiquette, I stood and prepared to make my departure when suddenly Odalie's cool hand was on my arm and she was peering into my face with a very bright and earnest gaze.

"Before you go, I suppose I should explain, shouldn't I? About the apartment, I mean."

Of course I'd wondered, but the restraint of good manners meant I never would've asked. I blinked at her and held my breath, worried if I said anything at all it might dissuade her from revealing the tricks behind the magic.

"My father pays the rent, you see."

I nodded.

"My family—we're a little rich, I guess. Not obscenely wealthy or anything in poor taste, mind. It's just that my father likes to know I'm well cared for, so here I am."

Still hoping for more, I remained silent and nodded again.

"The thing is," Odalie began in a coy voice, then hesitated. I got the sense I was about to be asked for something. "The thing is, I'm not sure the others down at the precinct would understand. But you, you're such a bright girl, Rose, with such an *enlightened* mind—you know that, don't you? Oh, well, you *should* know it; it's the honest truth! Speaking of how smart you are, I'm going to invite you to have coffee with my little group of bohemian artists. They're a wonderfully intellectual set; they keep me in the know about paintings and poems and such. You'll positively love them!" In a friendly gesture she took hold of my other arm and shook me gently by both shoulders as she said this, and I felt a familiar tingling warmth creep into my cheeks. I wasn't as sure as Odalie seemed to be about the prospect of my falling in love with what promised to be a group of derelicts posing as intellectuals, but I was becoming increasingly sure that I was about to allow myself to be charmed by Odalie herself. She gave a little laugh, cleared her throat, and looked at me again with serious interest. "But getting back to the matter at hand, I'd appreciate it immensely, Rose, if we didn't tell anybody about where I live. Or *how* I live. They might get some funny ideas about me."

I suppose more warning bells should've chimed inside my head than did at the time. Mostly, the whole incident had simply set off a sort of insatiable curious instinct within me. Perhaps, I remember considering at the time, Odalie was aware of the rumors that trailed her like a persistent cloud of gnats swirling over a fruit bowl. *She only wants to minimize all those silly tales of nonsense about her,* I said to myself. In any case, I nodded my complicity, and with great reluctance departed from the plush oasis that was Odalie's apartment and headed back out into the cold gray world.

And just like that, I had won the lottery for Odalie's friendship.

After that fatefully stormy night, she began regularly inviting me to lunch; Iris and Marie shot us sulky looks every noontime as we donned our coats and tripped laughingly together out the door and down the precinct steps. Or at least I imagined they did, for I was quickly learning anyone who fell just outside the ebullient rays of Odalie's attention was subject to the cold sensation of a dark cloud passing before the sun. I assume Odalie had finally discovered just how much of a frigid bore Iris could be, and had ruled Marie out on the principle Marie could not keep a secret and therefore couldn't amount to much as a bosom friend. Now, I had surmised, she was all mine.

Odalie also made good on her promise to introduce me to her "bohemian set." She brought me along one evening after work to a smoke-filled café not far from Washington Square. I am not certain what Odalie had hoped to accomplish with this introduction, unless it was to sound out my depths—which I'm certain she was surprised to discover are very shallow. I can't really stomach much of the newfangled nonsense that passes for art these days, and I find the people who chastise me to "broaden my mind" often have an offensively narrow view of how one should go about following this advice. My personal belief is that people who cannot work within the parameters of art's great time-honored traditions simply lack the talent and discipline to do so.

The night Odalie brought me along, her fellow *bohèmes* were rapturously reading and discussing a long poem that had been published over a year or two ago in a rather poor-looking magazine called *The Dial* and had evidently caused quite a stir in the process. If I recall correctly, the poet was called Eliot Something-Or-Another and the poem itself was all a bunch of jibberish, the ravings of an utter lunatic. But they ate it up with surprising zeal. At one point, the woman on my left turned to me and exclaimed, "Poetry will be forever changed after this, won't it be?"

I peered searchingly into her countenance for the tiniest signal of sarcasm, but found only earnestness. Her clear brown eyes and white cheeks were lit up brighter than one of the advertising billboards in Times Square. "Yes," I said, "I daresay it will be quite some time before the great institution of poetry recovers from the immense wrecking ball of a poem this gentleman has swung so brutally in its direction." I hadn't meant this as a compliment, but she gave a gleeful titter and smiled as brilliantly as if I had just proclaimed my deepest admiration. I watched the woman in puzzlement. She winked and held my gaze as she leaned over the table and allowed the man seated across from us to lift a match to her cigarette.

That was the first and only time Odalie invited me to join her "little group of bohemian artists." While I didn't exactly feel inspired by this outing, I can see now how it was nonetheless very smart of her to bring me, as the experience further inflected the impression of Odalie that was quickly taking shape in my mind. With that one little evening wherein I sat in a smoky café watching her argue passionately about expatriated poets and Spanish painters, she had, ever so subtly, managed to shift the light that would illuminate her actions. It changed the mind-set with which I would eventually perceive future events. Things I might have otherwise perceived as *illicit* would ultimately be reemphasized as *whimsical* and *avant-garde*. Whether she actually cared about the mad-minded experiments of Spanish painters I have little doubt; I know now she only cared about *looking* like she cared. In any case, once I'd had my single dose of *la vie de bohème,* Odalie did not bother to invite me back. She was an astute observer of human behavior;

I firmly believe by then she was already secure in the knowledge I had not tagged along because I craved artistic stimulation, but rather because I craved the privilege of her companionship. Already by that point, this assessment had become rather accurate.

The first two weeks of our friendship flew by, and it was suddenly as if I couldn't remember what life was like before Odalie had first smiled her brilliant pearlescent smile at me. Before I knew it, we were sitting in a restaurant staring at each other as our lunch dishes were cleared away, with the words *You ought to just move into the hotel with me* still hanging in the air.

"I've been meaning to look for a girl-friend who can take on a portion of the rent anyhow," she said in a brisk, careless voice.

"Doesn't your father pay for the apartment? He probably expects you to live there alone."

"Oh, sure, but he doesn't have to know about the room-mate, you see," she said, leaning in with a devilish smile and a sharp wink. I did see. There were no gleeful tears on the way. This was not an invitation for sisterly intimacy; this was a business proposition. My heart sank a tiny bit, but still not completely. We'd been fast friends for a few weeks by that point, spending all of our afternoons together. As I looked at her, the perfect cupid's bow of her mouth took on a slightly wicked, complicit expression. "The additional income would be quite beneficial," she said, and glanced at me sideways, "for both of us."

This was likely true. I'd come to the conclusion Odalie was something of an incorrigible spendthrift. Perhaps I could help her, teach her the art of frugality, I thought. I could impart the techniques Mrs. Lebrun had taught me. Over the duration of our friendship—a matter of mere weeks at that point—Odalie and I had dined in a total of nineteen rather intimidating and costly restaurants (and not just for dinner; for lunch, too! That there existed people who went to such extravagance over a meal as functional as a midday lunch absolutely fascinated me). We sat at tables draped in snowy white tablecloths and were attended by dapper waiters who wore tails and gloves. It seemed to me there was a man for everything, even a man whose sole job it was to stand at attention with a silver gravy boat and perpetually offer his ladle. These were exactly the sorts of restaurants I had previously dreamed of visiting, but had never had the proper occasion (or company). And so far, I had yet to catch a glimpse of a bill. When I asked Odalie how this was all possible, she always waved an imperial, dismissive hand in the air and said the same thing— that it was "no bother." Indeed, if there was one thing that was true about Odalie, it was that she never looked very bothered over anything.

Our meal that day was reaching its conclusion. With a silver tray in one hand and a white towelette folded tidily over the opposite arm, the headwaiter brought the coffee service to the table, along with a discreet slip of paper for Odalie to sign.

"Thank you, Gene," she said, and smiled again in her innocently bright, sunny manner. I had already observed that Odalie had at minimum one hundred smiles in her arsenal, but this one—the particular variety she was smiling now—was the one she called upon most often. Gene nodded and moved on. She dropped her voice: "I'll tell you a little secret: I can't recall if his name is actually Gene. But he's never said anything, and I've been calling him that for so long now, it may as well be!" She gave an amused giggle and, wanting to feel complicit, I couldn't help but join in with a laugh of my own.

I squinted at the slip of paper, but there were no numbers on it, just a place for her to sign her name. With a jaunty hand, she lifted the fountain pen that had been laid out next to it, scratched out something utterly illegible, and then looked up at me. She was still smiling and it was still a very bright smile, but now there was something also vacant about it, and I could tell she was already looking into the future and devising some sort of plan. I suspected she was doing sums in her head. Her lips held their pleasant pose, but something flickered behind her eyes.

"How much do you pay now?"

"Beg pardon?"

"For the room. At the boarding-house. How much do you pay? Say, nine or ten dollars a week?"

"Oh. About that, I suppose." It came out sounding guarded. The nuns had always taught me it was not polite to talk about money, and downright crass to name exact sums.

"Well, whatever it is, move in with me and just pay me the same."

"Are you in earnest?"

"Course," she said with a shrug of her small, narrow, boyish shoulders. "I'd be getting a leg up, and you'd be setting yourself up with a much better situation." I flinched, as any good American does when someone makes direct reference to a disparity of wealth. She shot me a frank, unapologetic glance. "Well, *you've* seen it." It was true; I recalled the night of my bubble bath. The grandeur of the memory had left a deep impression on me. "You'll have much more space, and it's not as if you have a private room right now," she continued. "And besides, I can promise you, I'm a whole lot more fun than that bitter little failed ingenue Helen and her ridiculous theatrical hysterics."

I hesitated, and then immediately worried Odalie had glimpsed my hesitation. Truth be told, I was desperate to jump at the idea. It wasn't just curiosity anymore; Odalie represented something new to me now. I'd already come to feel . . . well, not quite myself around her. The sensation of it was refreshing, as though unexplored possibilities were opening themselves up to me. I was not simply Rose—I was *Odalie's friend,* and every time this thought crossed my mind I felt a tickle of pride. Moreover, Odalie had also become something of a confidante to me. I'd told her so much about my childhood, about the horrible treatment I'd received at the gossiping hands of Dotty and Helen (although I tactfully left both the slap and the story of Adele out of the account). When she mentioned sharing her hotel room, I admit my imagination immediately conjured up an endless stream of late nights spent tucked under the covers and whispering secrets to each other as rosy dawn slowly crept in through the windowpanes. As these images entered my head, I felt a stirring of near-blind glee come over me. The idea was an exciting one, but at the same time a frightening one. I'd never lived anywhere other than the orphanage or the boarding-house, and in both cases the living arrangements had been contracted and secured for me. I glanced up at Odalie. If she saw my brief moment of hesitation, she chose to ignore it.

"What will I tell Dotty?" I asked, absently biting a fingernail.

"Tell her anything you like," Odalie said, lighting a new cigarette. I could see now we were going to be late returning to the precinct. I frowned. We had already been late coming back from lunch twice this week.

"What if she's very upset with me?" I pictured Dotty charging into the police precinct in pursuit of me with a hungry-looking, rangy-necked lawyer by her side. "Maybe she has rights," I murmured.

"Like fun she does," Odalie replied, and in that moment a sort of truth revealed itself—she already knew I was going to move to the hotel with her. When I glanced at her again, I realized I already knew it, too.

7

After Odalie extended her invitation, I moved in the very next week. As I had predicted, moving out of the boarding-house proved to be the trickiest part. Dotty stood at the bedroom door holding her three-year-old, Franny, on her hip and squinted possessively at every object that went into my suitcase, as though it were possible I might manage to defy physics and pack a lamp shade or an entire nightstand into my small suitcase the very second her back was turned. Franny, for her part, screamed and cried the entire time. Franny's cries were not for my departure, but rather for the penny candy Helen was eating downstairs in the parlor and not sharing. Dotty was well aware of this fact and could've quelled the tempest by simply feeding Franny a single spoonful of raspberry jam from the larder, but I think she liked the further sense of righteous indignation afforded her by holding a crying child in her arms. I had noticed in previous times—say, whenever bill collectors came to the house or neighbors knocked on the door to complain about the dog's howling in the backyard— Dotty had a tendency to lift whichever child was unhappiest onto her hip.

Despite the fact that the little girl was three, Franny still cried with the utter abandon of a much smaller infant, and her screams often ranged from inhuman, guttural, animal depths to shrill, ear-piercing heights, all in one breath. The scene was, to put it modestly, hardly a pleasant parting. But being that I did not own very many material objects to speak of in the first place, it did not take me very long to get everything into the suitcase, and before I knew it I had the crumbling leather straps cinched into place and was on my way down the stairs.

"Dotty always suspected you might do something like this" were Helen's only words to me as I passed through the front parlor, where she sat reading a magazine. I took one last look at her doughy face. She popped into her mouth a piece of the selfsame penny candy that had only minutes earlier driven Franny into a tantrum and smacked on it with her eyes slanted at me, and I knew by this gesture what she was really trying to say: *Tsk-tsk, leaving a war widow high and dry. . . .*

Oh, but it did little to move me. I very simply and sincerely couldn't be there anymore. Not with Dotty and not with Helen and not with the two of them whispering together in the kitchen about me and Adele, the latter whom they'd never even met but were happy to sit in judgment upon. By then Dotty had followed me down the stairs and into the parlor, and upon glimpsing Helen eating the penny candy Franny broke out into a fresh set of wails, exploring a whole new half-scale of notes that threatened to break the fragile membranes deep inside the human ear. The sound of it was all I needed to push me along those last steps out the door and down the front stoop. I walked quickly down the street and did not once turn back to look at the dilapidated brownstone that had served as my home for the last few years.

A couple of subway trains later, I reached Odalie's hotel. Under the awning on the sidewalk, I looked up at my new home, its golden doors lit up by bright floodlights. I felt myself grow intimidated. Everything about the move felt more frightening now that I was actually doing it. I ascended the carpeted stone stairs and heaved my weight against the revolving door with hesitation and the tiniest inkling of misgiving. Most residential hotels were quite . . . functional. Nothing drastically different from a boarding-house, really. Especially the residential hotels for women. But Odalie's hotel was a real, bona fide, tourist-class establishment. It had given me a thrill on that fateful rainy day of my first visit, but on that official moving day, the luxury of it only gave me a jumpy, nervous sensation. Dressed in a heavy coat and with my bulky suitcase in one hand, the revolving door presented a struggle. My grand entrance into the lobby turned out to be an awkward trip and stumble as the revolving door spat me out like a reaction to something bitter it had eaten.

The staff on duty did not recognize me. I could hardly blame them; my previous visit had been my only visit, and as I've mentioned I'd long ago perfected the art of plainness. They gave me some trouble when I made for the elevator in an attempt to go upstairs, and eventually they had to telephone up to Odalie's room to request she come down to collect me. Everyone seemed to know Odalie—or at least know of her—and it was understood that the proposition of her coming downstairs would take some time. The concierge showed me to a sofa and pointed out a booth that contained a courtesy telephone, saying, "If there's anyone you'd like to 'phone . . ." But he needn't have bothered. I wasn't acquainted with anyone who had a private telephone—just imagine!

Twenty-five minutes ticked by, and then at last the little golden birdcage of an elevator descended. Odalie stepped into the lobby. I couldn't help but notice the effect she had on her audience. As soon as the elevator's cheerful *ding!* sounded, all heads snapped toward the elevator and remained fastened there to Odalie's shape. She paused ever so slightly—a pause almost indistinguishable to the naked eye—then with a smirk took a snappy step forward, walking in her girlish sashay across the lobby. All heads pivoted with the kind of entranced synchronized unison usually reserved for tennis matches. As I rose to greet her, she slipped her arm through mine. I blushed, but couldn't keep the proud smile from forming on my lips.

"Memorize this lovely face, boys," Odalie said, meaning me. "Rose here has come to stay." She took me around to all the hotel employees and introduced me to each in turn, much the way the Lieutenant Detective had promenaded her around the precinct on her first day. She seemed to know all their names—or at least, as it had been with poor "Gene" at the restaurant, they did not protest her rechristenings—and I shook hands with each of them, allowing my bare hand to be held by white glove after white glove. It was difficult not to feel self-conscious. I was aware that adrift in the hotel's lavish setting my clothes and overall appearance suggested it was more likely I had come to wash the floors than to take up residence. Finally Odalie asked a baby-faced bellhop, who was either called Bobby or else renamed by Odalie as Bobby, to carry my suitcase upstairs. I thought of protesting, but my arm was sore from hauling the bag up and down the subway stairs, and the thought of someone else doing the lifting came to me as a relief. When we got to the apartment, Bobby brought the suitcase inside and Odalie gave him a dime for his trouble. To be fair, I think he would've much preferred a kiss from the way he watched her mouth as she smiled. He lingered for the slenderest of moments, then departed good-naturedly, as if he understood how much of a long shot his ambitions were, and why.

As soon as we were alone in what was to be my new bedroom, Odalie lifted the suitcase and plunked it down on a bed that had been nicely made up with a chenille bedspread and peacock-green satin pillows.

"Here's you," she said. "I hope it's all right."

It was more than all right. I surveyed the room. Upon my last visit, I had peeked into the doorway and glimpsed a study, replete with green-shaded bankers' lamps and a rather heavy-looking mahogany desk. But since then somehow the room had been transformed into a cozy sleeping space. A gold-leafed Oriental screen painted with the black silhouettes of long-legged cranes stood against one wall next to the bed. On the nightstand a large cut crystal vase sat overflowing with white lilies, the points of their petals curling with a sensual fullness. An old cylinder phonograph was positioned on the opposite nightstand, its amplifying horn shaped like a giant morning glory, equally shapely and eager to compete with the lilies. Odalie caught me looking at it.

"Oh! I hope you pardon that ancient thing. I move it around here and there, and I'm never really sure where it ought to go. Practically obsolete, you know, these days! I've got the latest model Victrola, and I keep that in my bedroom, but of course you're welcome to come in and listen to it any old time."

I was at a loss for what to say. Odalie's assumption of disdain had missed its mark entirely. I had never owned a phonograph—new *or* old—but had always wanted to. "I . . . I don't have any records," I stammered rather stupidly.

Odalie laughed—a musical trill in and of itself, no phonograph or records required.

"I've got stacks and stacks. I've practically got records coming out my ears," she said, gesturing to a tall pile of paper sleeves heaped on a nearby bookshelf. "You can play whatever you like, if you can stand that ancient thing!"

Suddenly her mood shifted, and she grew silent and cocked her head at me, deep in concentration. And then . . . a classic Odalie smile broke out over her face, like the sun breaking through dark clouds. She suddenly clapped her hands together, looking a little like a child who'd just been given a surprise birthday present. "You know what? This is an occasion! We really ought to celebrate properly!" She took my hand and pulled me toward her bedroom. My mind flashed to Odalie's bohemian friends and the lifestyle I assumed they espoused, and I suddenly felt my muscles grow tense at the prospect of what was about to happen.

"We're going out! Let's find you something to wear," she exclaimed, throwing open an armoire. My heart slowed back down to its regular rate. I was hardly in the mood to go out, but I didn't say so. She selected a very modern lilac shift with a black ribbon that was slung low around the hips and tied in a floppy bow. Odalie held it up to me, tucking the hanger up under my neck. I tried not to look critical. It was shorter than anything I'd ever worn. "Hmm. Yes. Yes. This might just do the trick," she said with a frown, more to herself than to me.

"I can't wear that," I said. When Odalie asked me why, I found myself unable to say what I really thought: *Because it's indecent.* But I don't like to feel indebted to people, and when I looked around at the lavish apartment that was my new home, I naturally felt a little guilty and a little awed. Before long, I had been overruled and the dress was on my person.

I was not at all sure where Odalie was taking me. Downstairs in the hotel lobby, she had ordered one of the bell-hops to hail a cab for the two of us in her imperial yet bewitching way, and once we were fussily ensconced inside with our scandalously knee-skimming skirts tucked neatly under our derrieres in defense against the sticky leather seats and our arms giving off the rich scent of powder, she gave an address not far from the police precinct. This struck me as rather odd; I didn't know of many entertainment venues on the Lower East Side. But then I must be frank here and admit I didn't know of many entertainment venues, full stop.

After the cab had been paid and we had successfully alighted curbside, I looked around but saw nothing. Or, at least, nothing that resembled the sort of merriment and revelry I had been anticipating. No mingled sound of music and laughter came drifting out from an open door, no glow of electric lights cascaded down from the windows above us. We appeared to be on a block filled with shops, all of which had long since been shut up for the day. Each abandoned shop front was dark and full of a bizarrely heavy yet inert sort of gravity, as though we were standing amid a row of sleeping giants. Our eventual destination seemed even more curious and shrouded in mystery than ever.

"Where in heavens—"

"*Shhhh!!*"

Odalie leaned into the empty street and cast a furtive glance in both directions, and suddenly I got the peculiar sensation there might be someone watching us. "All right. All clear," she reported in a charming, husky whisper. "But we might as well keep it down." She took my hand in hers, and we began wandering down what I was sure was an alley that dead-ended. My ankles wobbled a bit in the T-strap pumps Odalie had insisted I wear despite the fact they were half a size too big. I felt the coolness of the night close in around my bare skin, and as an idle breeze caught my skirt it fluttered against the backs of my thighs, reminding me that was precisely where it ended. Farther down the lane the shops dropped off, which came as no surprise. Alleys, of course, are not dreadfully good for business. But I spotted one shop, all the way at the very end of the alley. As we drew closer, I was astounded to see it was still open for business. It was a wig shop, dirty and poorly lit, with a sole clerk drowsing at the register. Odalie giggled, an excited giggle, and pushed her way in through the front door while a little bell tinkled over the tops of our heads. The second we walked in, the young man who had been slouching over the cash register perked up.

"Can I help you find sompin', ma'ams?" He was a strange-looking creature, with long greasy hair that fell down to his eye and oddly colored suspenders. I noticed he had a queer way of pronouncing *ma'ams*. He said it *mums,* as though he were British. Still young enough to be a *miss,* I wasn't accustomed to being addressed as a *ma'am,* and I'm certain Odalie wasn't, either. But I had never been one to insist on my youth and felt, for a fleeting second, a very slight inkling of authority.

"Why ye-es," Odalie answered with an air of distraction, her gaze surveying the contents of the store. She spun in a slow circle, evidently looking for something specific. Lined up on shelves along the walls were the bodiless heads of mannequins, each wearing a different fashion of wig and smiling the same pink painted smile. I was flabbergasted. Odalie possessed the lushest,

loveliest, darkest hair of any girl I'd ever known. I couldn't imagine what she could possibly want with a wig. Finally she reached
out with her tanned hand and slender wrist. With a deft motion,
she slid one wig off to reveal the bald head of its vacant-eyed,
still-smiling owner. The wig itself was a particularly wretched
thing: an elaborately Victorian bun that might have attracted the
likes of Helen, if only it hadn't been the most horribly drab shade
of iron gray. Odalie brought the atrocious wig to the clerk and
tossed it on the counter by the cash register.

"I hear this is lovely in chestnut," she said in a somewhat theatrical voice to the clerk. I looked on, incredulous, as her mouth
twisted into a flirtatious smirk. "But mahogany's twice as nice,"
she finished with a wink. I blinked. It was gibberish. The clerk,
evidently, did not think so. As though Odalie had just said something perfectly intelligible, he snapped to attention and, with a
very businesslike air, punched down a few keys on the cash register. As he struck the last key, a very loud metallic *CLUNK* sounded
and a panel in the wall behind him swung open to reveal a dark
hallway lined with red velvet curtains. Gay voices floated out, the
rising, falling murmurs of conversation punctuated every so often
with feminine laughter and the brittle clink of glasses. The sound
of Al Jolson singing valiantly along to the wry *wah-wah* of trum-
pets and jaunty *plinkety-plunk* of guitars was collectively droning
away on an unseen phonograph.

"You may enter, ma'ams."

It was a blind. I had heard of these but, having never seen one
for myself, was astonished. The whole wig shop business was a
bum steer. The proprietors of the store—whoever they might
be—had probably never sold a single wig in their lifetimes, or if
they had, it was purely unintentional. Odalie smiled at the young

man behind the counter and stepped into the hallway now exposed by the open wall panel. The clerk watched her slinky movements, and in turn I watched him watching her . . . until abruptly I realized she had disappeared into the dark and I was still standing in front of the shop counter, quite immobile. The young man returned his attention to me and looked at me with a skeptical eyebrow raised.

"Ma'am? Gotta be coming or going, now. Indiscretion's not good for business, ya know," meaning the open door, which I sensed he was already itching to shut. Something about his bossy yet sycophantic demeanor provoked my ire. I shot him a murderous look (triggering the skeptical eyebrow to rise even higher and turn ever so briefly into a question mark of fear, I noted with some satisfaction), then strode down the dark hallway in the direction of Odalie's disappearance. As soon as I stepped over the threshold, I felt the wall panel swing shut behind me. It was some minutes before my eyes adjusted, and I dared not move until I could dimly make out the floor again, afraid I would otherwise trip.

"Over here, Rose."

I walked in the direction of Odalie's summons, now sounding as though it had been enveloped in a din of other voices, and pushed through the velvet curtain at the end of the hallway.

I was unprepared for the scene that awaited me. I found myself stumbling abruptly smack-dab into the middle of a party in full swing. The room overwhelmed me. The walls were done in burgundy crushed velvet wallpaper. The lack of lighting caused the ceilings to recede in a dark, cavernous manner, and from the middle of an elaborate plaster medallion hung an unexpected crystal chandelier. The whole room was warm and humid with bodies, and the sharp tang of fermented juniper (from my time at the precinct I already knew very well this was the signature scent of bathtub gin) hung in the air.

The room was too packed to take in everyone at once, and I found myself focusing on the details of a few individuals who stood out. A couple of girls were shimmying a tight, frenetic Charleston in the middle of the room. Another young woman drank what appeared to be very frothy champagne out of a novelty glass shaped like a ladies' high-heeled shoe, her dress twinkling with glass beads that swung in pendulous strings from the very modern, straight-across line of her décolletage. A pair of short, stocky men were puffing on cigars and clapping each other on the back as they roared with hysterical laughter, their faces growing pink and clownish with exertion, each blow to each other's bodies more intimate and friendly than the last. Across the room a woman was sitting atop a piano, being urged by a small audience to remove her shoes and stockings. After making several halfhearted and insincere protests, she slipped off the requested garments and performed what sounded like an impromptu rendition of "Chopsticks" using only her toes.

"What'll you have?"

I realized I was being addressed. I looked in the direction of the voice, which was decidedly downward, and was startled to see a dwarf in red suspenders and a trilby hat staring up at me. Eggplant-colored dark shadows rimmed his eyes, and he was badly in need of a shave. I struggled to formulate a reply.

"No bathtub gin for this one," came Odalie's voice. She suddenly materialized by my side and slipped a very lithe, sinuous arm around my waist. "Let's start her on something a little more civilized. How about a nice champagne cocktail, Redmond?"

Redmond gave an almost imperceptible incline of his head,

then turned and toddled off with a stiff gait on his thick, truncated legs.

"Redmond's a sweetheart."

"Where have you taken me?"

Odalie only laughed. "Come on, I want you to meet someone." With her arm still entwined about my waist, she steered me to a far corner of the room, where a group of nicely dressed men stood clustered around a roulette table. Wordlessly I watched the shiny polished silver rudder of the roulette wheel turn in the air, the cross of its handle flashing as it slowly revolved. Odalie drew up short next to a tall, dark-haired man in an expensive-looking suit.

"Rose, I'd like you to meet Harry Gibson." On hearing his name, the man turned to us and, with no attempt to hide it, looked me over with a wolfish skepticism from head to toe.

"I go by Gib," he said, extending a courteous, indifferent hand. I shook it gingerly, and upon the completion of this gesture Gib immediately returned his attention to the roulette table. "C'mon . . . *c'mon*," Gib muttered under his breath. Curiously, he didn't appear to be rooting for any particular number, but rather *against* all of them in general. I watched his eyes flash as the roulette wheel slowed to the end of its spin and lurched precariously.

"Your drink, miss?"

I looked down to see Redmond had returned with whatever it was Odalie had ordered. He had returned with the drinks, but no bill, and I was soon to learn this was how things always worked with Odalie: drinks, meals, tickets to shows—Odalie received them all while handling the exchange of money for goods so discreetly as to render it nearly invisible. And now, by the simple virtue of being in her company, I was to receive all of these things for free. A dim realization of my new windfall crept over me as I examined the diminutive waiter who stood holding our drinks. His stocky arms were not quite able to clear the height of his head, but nonetheless he proudly held up a silver tray laden with two champagne glasses containing a cloudy, slightly greenish-tinted champagne. Odalie lifted one of the glasses from the tray directly to her lips and took a polite, appreciative sip. I knew a nice girl would never be caught drinking in a blind or otherwise, but I also sensed I was being tested; I could not refuse just now.

"What is it?" I asked as I hesitantly lifted the second glass from the tray.

"A little splash of heaven," Odalie replied. I gave her a look. She laughed. "One part absinthe, two parts champagne. Try it—it's positively lovely."

"I . . . I don't drink. What would the Sergeant say?" I blurted out.

Odalie laughed again, the music of her voice carrying throughout the noisy room. The white ball on the roulette wheel finally came tripping to a standstill, and a small uproar sounded all around the table. Gib turned distractedly back to us, frowning at my proclamation of temperance.

"Who is this friend of yours?" he said to Odalie, as if I weren't standing next to her.

"Another typist. From the precinct."

He started and looked at me with greater scrutiny. "Is she clean?"

Odalie scowled in annoyance—a rare look for her lovely face to display. "I'll vouch for her, if that's what you mean."

"You can't just bring anybody in here," Gib said in a low

warning voice. But it was a hollow warning; his attention had already been reclaimed by the roulette ball that had been thrown back into play, tripping along the fresh spin of the wheel.

"Have a drink of your cocktail, Rose, and show Gib here you mean no harm," Odalie suggested. I sensed it was imperative at that point to drink, and so I did, suppressing the urge to sputter back the fizzing licorice-flavored champagne as it burned the back of my throat. "Good girl," Odalie said approvingly, although I once again got the impression the conversation was not being addressed to me.

"Fine, have it your way," Gib said with an air of dismissal.

"Oh, Rose, let's get away from these dreadfully boring gambling bachelors!" Odalie suddenly exclaimed, winking at Gib and tugging me again by the waist. "I want to mingle." She pulled me so close, I had no choice but to move in tandem with her like a docile farm animal. The cocktail had already planted hot embers just under the surface of my cheeks, and I could feel it warming me.

Once safely across the room, I finally asked, "Who is he?" I meant Gib. Without missing a beat, Odalie understood.

"He runs this place. Well, for now he does. You mustn't be scared of him. He won't like you for it. Besides, there's nothing to be frightened of; once you get to know him, you'll realize he couldn't hurt a fly, really." She hesitated, smiling to herself and turning the words that came next over in her mind. "Also, he's my . . . my . . . well, I suppose you could say we are *enfianced.*"

I wasn't entirely sure I knew what she meant; I had never seen her wear a ring or speak of an engagement, and Gib's demeanor had struck me as so surly, I could hardly picture him proposing on bended knee. I glanced back at Gib. Upon observing more closely the brooding hue of his eyes and the dark shadow that ran the badly shaven length of his jaw, I realized I was offended by the idea of a man like that being engaged to the luminous creature standing next to me. It didn't make sense. Odalie didn't explain further, only gave me a wink, then immediately set about introducing me to what she called the notable individuals in the room. A number of the men were employed in the moving picture business, either as directors or producers, and a few of the girls had appeared as actresses in the background of several major films. One girl with extraordinarily yellow-colored hair had even appeared as an extra in a Charlie Chaplin film. Perhaps it was just my imagination, but I thought I recognized her, not from the film, as I'd never been to the movies, but from a photograph I'd once glimpsed in *The Tattler.* There were also artists and musicians, and still other people, too, whose occupations eluded me altogether. It was my impression that as the evening wore on, the people to whom Odalie introduced me grew increasingly vague about what it was they did for a living, but of course by that time Redmond had returned with his tray several times over and the whole room had begun to feel like a ship that had been pushed out upon a rocky sea.

My recollection of the night's events became significantly less reliable at some point. I believe, if I am not mistaken, I can recall taking to the dance floor with Odalie. I can't claim to know how to do the Charleston, yet I seem to have some memory of performing it. And I have a suspiciously vivid idea of what a cigar tastes like. I also remember sitting on a settee while speaking with a very large-featured man who, evidently feeling the need to educate me, pontificated at great length on the difference between stocks and bonds. A very wobbly and inebriated girl standing nearby kept cutting into the conversation only to remark, over and over again, *Sir, you have the most interesting nose I've ever seen. . . . That's quite a nose.*

I am not certain what hour it was when Odalie and I finally left the party. But I do remember my stomach had already begun to turn sour on me by the time we were in a cab and homeward bound.

"Mustn't. Go. To places like that. Again," I managed to mumble with a debatable level of lucidity. "Not. For. Nice. Girls."

"Oh, hush," Odalie said, and with a *shh* added for good measure, patted and rubbed my hand.

"The Sergeant would never approve," I mumbled. "Must tell him I'm sorry." I let my head loll to the side and closed my eyes. Suddenly I felt two very strong viselike hands gripping my shoulders, shaking a small inkling of sobriety into me. I struggled to open my eyes and found Odalie looking into my face intensely.

"Now you listen to me, Rose," she said in a cool, controlled voice. "There'll be no telling the Sergeant about any of this." My eyes began to droop and close, which must have offended her, because she shook me once again, this time harder. I was aware that the energy had shifted between us and something had killed the joviality of the moment; she was angry and she meant business. A bit frightened, I peered up innocently into her face and realized she suddenly looked like a stranger to me. She was trying to get me to understand something, and I understood on instinct she wanted me to make firm eye contact with her as a means of acknowledging her serious message. In my inebriated state, I willed my eyeballs to stop what felt like a repeated rolling motion. It took quite an effort, as my eyes felt like they were spinning in their sockets, left to right, left to right, left to right.

Perhaps this looked utterly pathetic to Odalie, for suddenly she laughed, gave a sigh, and released her grip on my shoulders. "What am I going to do with you?" came the rhetorical question, followed by another chuckle. "I suppose it's silly of me to worry." Now her tone was friendly, motherly—sisterly. She squeezed my hand. "You wouldn't tell anybody anything. And besides," she added, "you just got settled in. It would be a shame to have to look for a new place to live so soon." I dimly became aware of the threat that was tucked and folded so neatly into her words. "I certainly don't think Dotty would welcome you back with open arms, now would she?"

We both knew the answer to this question. I looked at Odalie, struck afresh by the state of dependency I'd gotten myself into in my new situation, but then my stomach did an impressive array of inner gymnastics, and I was forced to lean my head out the cab door and release some of the evening's champagne and absinthe.

8

I've always been the sort of individual to live her life by the rules. In the absence of flesh-and-blood equivalents, over the years I've taken a series of rules to serve as my mother, my father, my siblings, even my lovers—if an idea of love can indeed be derived from the sort of one-way devotion I cultivated in my regard for the rules. It's true no one may have tucked in the covers at my bedside, but there was a certain comfort in adhering to a strict rule of turning the lights out at nine o'clock. And perhaps it's true also there was no one there to tell me stories as I drifted off to sleep, but there was the list of prayers to be said, and the list of morning chores to go over in my head. Rules kept me safe. In keeping the rules dear to me, I could always be certain the nuns would clothe and feed me, the typing school would place me in a job, and the precinct would employ me. Until I met Odalie, the only god I knew was the God of the Ten Commandments.

So it's strange to me that with Odalie, I suddenly found myself breaking the rules I had once held in such precious regard. In many ways I suppose my love of the rules was supplanted by my love of Odalie, and I was surprised by the speed of the exchange.

The thing about rules is that when you break one, it is only a matter of time before you break more, and the severe architecture that once protected you is destined to come crashing down about your ears. I can only say I did it for the love of her, though the doctor I am seeing now hardly accepts that answer.

Of course, ever since the incident, the newspapers have painted Odalie as the victim. According to them, I am the one who has corrupted, who has lied, and who has committed the ultimate unspeakable act. Having forfeited my claim to having always followed the rules, I have unwittingly rendered myself plainly vulnerable to this attack. They may say whatever they want about me, and they do. They refuse to believe she might have bewitched me, but I can think of no more fitting word by which to describe the effect Odalie has had on me. Simply put, I have met no one more magnetic than Odalie, and I doubt I ever will.

During those early days of cohabitation, I was possessed by the idea of understanding and knowing Odalie, whose approach to dressing, drinking, and dancing enacted a sort of casual entitlement that was utterly alien to me. Many were the times I watched Odalie enter a room, the downy hair on her arms flashing golden against her tanned skin as she reached out a childish hand to steal the already-in-progress cigarette from between the lips of a man she'd never met. She was never once rebuffed, and the man—I say *man* here generically, because there were several—invariably introduced himself and reached into his pocket to fish out a lighter and a replacement cigarette, while Odalie puffed on her pilfered prize and regarded the gentleman with a sly, delighted expression, as if to suggest nothing he could pull out of his pocket could sufficiently replace the unique and spectacular treasure she had just stolen. During our time together, I was to spend countless hours observing Odalie, and I came to realize her little habitual interactions, such as her proprietary way with men's cigarettes, were never intended to be cruel or slighting gestures; they simply constituted her way.

There were also many behaviors deeply familiar to me that were completely beyond Odalie's repertoire. Blushing, for instance, is not something Odalie seemed able to do. Nor did she hesitate or demur. Her answer to every invitation, regardless of its relative legality, was to give the lanky, boneless shrug of a prepubescent teenager, a gesture often accompanied by the musical trill of her laugh.

And in no situation was this breezy, casual, devil-may-care attitude more shocking than as it concerned the physical act of love. I may never know for sure who Odalie did and did not take as her lovers, but I do know she was insufficiently scandalized by the reported conduct of the loose women who often attended Harry Gibson's speakeasies. She acted as though it were the most natural thing for a woman to do whatever she wanted, with whomever she pleased. This confused me.

You see, I didn't know then what I know now, which is this: Only the very rich and the very poor enjoy sex with a careless, indifferent abandon. Those of us who find ourselves somewhere in the middle—and here I must note I consider myself to occupy the middle, for although I was raised in an orphanage, the nuns did their best to equip me with the prudish values of a good bourgeoise (I have always quickened my step upon passing the ribaldry of the tenements)—only those of us in the middle class are obliged to maintain an attitude of modesty and discretion when it comes to sex. This is especially true of middle-class young ladies. We are the ones obliged to lower our eyes and blush during educational lectures on human anatomy; we are the ones who must *tsk* and shout *fresh!* with indignation whenever a young man tries to proposition us. We are given to believe we are the supreme keepers of sexual morality, and I, like any properly instructed schoolgirl of my day, earnestly felt there was something sacred in the keeping. Some keep it as a matter of burden, but I kept it as a matter of privilege.

I did not know anything about Odalie's childhood, and therefore could not know how she had been brought up. I suppose even if I'd had such facts at my disposal, they wouldn't have provided me any special insight, as the sexual habits of the very poor simply terrified me, and the sexual habits of the upper class were an obscure, opaque mystery to me. But the facts were Odalie seemed to feel neither the privilege nor the burden of upholding sexual mores, and as far as her own conduct—well, she did as she pleased with little sign of remorse. At parties she disappeared into darkened back rooms. She took automobile rides indiscriminately with anyone who amused her. When we went to dinner clubs, a special laugh of hers—a flirtatious one generally reserved for male company—could often be heard coming from within the walls of the coat check, muffled only slightly by a fur-and-cashmere buffer. I'm not certain why I took such a fascinated interest in Odalie's sexual conduct (or misconduct, as I saw it), but I did. When it came to Odalie's wild ways, I did not approve, but I was a silent judge, compelled as I was to follow and watch. Wanting to watch Odalie was a difficult impulse to resist, having as it does a kind of very potent and very dark draw.

A horrible disaster was looming on my horizon, so to speak, but from the very moment I met Odalie I was rendered utterly powerless to do anything other than watch it hurtle toward me. But, of course, if I am to tell it all in order, as I keep promising to do, there are other things I must tell first.

WE'D GONE TO the blind on a weeknight, and the next morning I still had yet to make a full recovery. That morning, as I walked into the precinct and encountered the usual heady odor of cheap whiskey and old wine that was carried in daily, I felt my stomach instantly recoil and prepare itself for an encore performance of its previous gymnastic routine. With a great effort of concentration, I managed to keep my breakfast in its proper place. In some ways I was actually grateful for the fact my workplace was regularly infused with such an unpleasant fermenting scent, as the odor of all those bootleggers and winos passing through the precinct went a long way to mask my own odor, which I was certain I was still carrying around on my person. Adding to my luck was the fact the Sergeant was unable to pay me much mind on that particular day. I would have been utterly mortified for the Sergeant to discover me in my state, but he was far too busy.

Unfortunately, however, the Lieutenant Detective was not. At some point during the morning he gamboled across the room to hand off a stack of reports to Odalie, and in passing he glanced at me and was forced to look twice.

"Looks like somebody could use a little hair of the dog," the Lieutenant Detective said, grinning in my direction.

"I'm sure I don't know what you're talking about," I said, mustering a sneer, then catching my throbbing head in both hands. Still grinning, the Lieutenant Detective approached my desk and sat on it in his old familiar manner.

"Somehow I'm sure you *do* know," he said. I lifted my head

long enough to give him a haughty look. Odalie pretended to observe the reports he'd just handed her with riveted fascination, but I was quite aware her ears remained sharply attuned to our conversation. "Look," he said, "I'm not the disapproving sort. I've found myself in the same condition on occasion." I felt my nostrils flare. What gall! To assume that I cared what he thought! To assume the two of us—the Lieutenant Detective and I—might have something in common! Blind to my indignation, he slipped something shiny and silvery out of his pocket, laid it flat on the desk, and slowly pushed it toward me in a sly gesture, all the while smiling crookedly. I became dimly aware he was offering me a flask. "A few sips of that," he said, "and you'll make it through the day."

Instinctually, I sniffed and recoiled. "I beg your pardon, Lieutenant Detective—"

"Frank," he interrupted, then leaned a little closer and added, "or Francis. But no one really calls me Francis." He paused and colored slightly. "Only my mother."

"I beg your pardon, *Lieutenant Detective*," I continued. He flinched as though I had just bitten him. "But I'm quite fine, and I'll thank you to remove your *property*, as it were, from my desk lest somebody fall under the mistaken impression that it is indeed mine."

He hesitated, then reached for the flask and slipped it back into his jacket pocket. As he did so, a small shiver of panic ran up my spine and I glanced about frantically, worried the Sergeant might be looking in our direction. I'd surely die of shame if the Sergeant were to glimpse the Lieutenant Detective trying to slip me a flask on the job. On the job or any other time, really. In the Sergeant I had always sensed my moral and ethical equal, and he'd always treated me as though the respect was mutual. As much as I felt compelled to impress Odalie and win her approval, I felt equally if not even more compelled to retain the Sergeant's approval and couldn't stand to have him think I'd transformed into one of those fast modern girls of whose lifestyle he thoroughly disapproved.

But at that moment it was only the Lieutenant Detective's disapproval I had to suffer. He stood before my desk in his rumpled suit and white spats, shoving the flask deeper into his pocket and pushing a long lock of hair out of his eyes. His lips moved in silence, as if attempting to draw words from the deep well of his throat. Finally sound came out.

"Here I was, thinking how nice it was that perhaps you'd turned out to be mortal after all," he said. "But I see you are as cold and mechanical as ever." He fixed me with a stern gaze and turned on his heel. I watched him walk away, then winced as a sharp splinter of pain raced between my eyes. I redeposited my aching head into the cool skin of my hands and dimly heard Odalie laughing beside me. There was a mocking lilt in her voice; it was not a terribly kind variety of laugh.

"You little fool," she said. "He was only trying to be a sport, and what he was offering would've helped you immensely." She meant, of course, the contents of the flask. But not having any familiarity with the practice, I didn't see how it could possibly make things better. I straightened my posture and stacked some papers brusquely. I rolled a blank document into the typewriter and began to punch out a report, feeling my brain cringe somewhere deep inside my skull with each loud *CLACK*. But I found there was a strange comfort in the excruciating pain. This was my penance, I was convinced.

At that moment, I began what I could not foresee would eventually become a long and repeated tradition of vowing to shun Odalie and failing. She was difficult to resist; she always seemed to possess one little thing you wanted, or one little thing that made you feel as though you owed it to her. The truth of the matter was the deal between us had been brokered the moment I'd agreed to move in with her. Well, sooner than that, perhaps. Perhaps it had been a signed and sealed matter from the very second I'd picked up the brooch Odalie had dropped on the day of her interview and neglected to return it.

With a shrug, Odalie dismissed the small scene between the Lieutenant Detective and myself and returned to her work without a second thought. But I was left to stew over the state of things for the rest of the morning and well into the afternoon. By quitting time I had come up with and refined several arguments I planned to present to Odalie, asserting why I could never again return to the speakeasy, not least of which was the fact it was illegal and a proper lady should never be caught in one, let alone a lady who works for the selfsame police force that was destined to someday burst in upon the scene. As every passing second brought us closer to five o'clock, I fortified my moral position and worked up my courage. But I never got a chance to enumerate such reasons to Odalie, and my eloquent pontification skills languished. As soon as we packed up to take our leave, she hijacked me in the most disarming manner, looping her arm through mine and whisking me off to a moving picture.

I had been resolved to say no to Odalie's next proposition, no matter what it was, but here I was at a severe disadvantage, as I had never been to a moving picture before. I see now why they refer to it as the silver screen. I sat beside Odalie in the velvety dark, mesmerized by the beautiful oval faces and thick, fluttering eyelashes of the starlets and the kohl-rimmed eyes of the villains as they were lit up by a shimmering shower of silvery light. On a platform to the left of the stage a tall, thin man with a narrow, angular nose played an upright piano, his spidery fingers moving with a jittery dexterity in perfect time to the film. Looking upward, I stared at the luminous moonbeam projected over our heads and was enchanted.

But even under the alluring spell of celluloid, I felt my attention drift away and my mind begin to wander back to the girl sitting next to me. Generally speaking, mysterious people made me nervous and I tried to avoid them. I could not understand why it should be the opposite with Odalie. Just like all the other fools around her, I had developed a taste for her brand of mystery.

It was a pleasant evening out, and when we left the movie house we decided to walk back to the hotel. Odalie was convinced a walk would do me some good. We strolled along the avenues, threading our way in and out among the cane chairs of the sidewalk cafés. It was perhaps one of the last days of the year still warm enough for outdoor dining, and there was a sort of buzz in the air created by eager patrons desperate to enjoy a last huzzah. Yellowy light spilled out from under each awning, turning the concrete beneath our feet golden and lighting up the faces of men and women who sat eating at the tables with a sort of jack-o'-lantern glow. We walked, unconsciously gathering fragments of conversations and the wafting odors of buttery garlic dishes, enjoying the street in a piecemeal way, like the pigeons who moved automatically along the same path gathering up crumbs. The fatted birds scattered as we stepped among them, then returned at some distance behind us, like a tide coming back in.

As we neared the park the sidewalks grew a bit wider, and I

was able to walk alongside Odalie easily. I had a mind to ask her directly, once and for all, to lay some of the rumors about her to rest. I have always admired good manners in people and have adhered to the notion that there are things in this world that are simply none of my business. For all of these reasons and more, I had—up to that point—never asked Odalie a single question about her past. Before it had always seemed intrusive, but now, of course, we were room-mates, and I felt myself more entitled to know about certain things. Moreover, we were sharing our present lives together, and I was growing increasingly conscious of the fact that her past may well indeed affect my future. I screwed up my courage.

"Your friend—Gib, was it?" I said. I was careful not to say *fiancé,* for the way Odalie had said *enfianced* that night had sounded very tongue-in-cheek, and I wasn't sure what to make of this. Odalie turned her head sharply at the mention of his name and arched an eyebrow. I gulped and pressed on. "He . . . ah, didn't say what he did for a living . . ."

"Oh, yes, well," Odalie said, waving a vague hand in the air. "I suppose you could call him an entrepreneur. Exports and small businesses, you know. The usual things." The answer didn't do much to put me at ease. She smiled, but there was a veneer about it. I had the impression I was getting the brush-off, and that this would be the permanent state of things when it came to my attempts to find out more information about Gib. I wondered: Had Odalie's speculators really gotten it right? I had to consider the very real possibility she was indeed "a bootlegger's girl," as gossips at the precinct had declared, and her job at the precinct was merely a means to keep him in the know, as it were. I knew the facts were not in Gib's favor. There had been so much alcohol at the speakeasy, and so many varieties. Someone had to be making it or at least importing it, or both, and it suddenly struck me that Gib had seemed like the party's overseer. All night long people had been seeking him out, like guests paying their respects to the host. I thought of asking Odalie in point-blank fashion whether Gib was a bootlegger, but she appeared to sense my struggle to formulate such a question.

"Look," she exclaimed, pointing as we neared the Plaza. "Let's take a victoria across the park! I haven't hired a horse-cab in ages." She hailed the driver, and before I knew it I was staring into the big chocolate eyes of a spotted gray draft horse who was craning his neck to see over his blinders, as though he hoped to inspect and approve of his prospective passengers before being made to lug them across the length of the park. We climbed in, and I felt the springing bounce of the carriage as it rocked against our weight.

The driver shook the reins and we were off at a slow roll. It was an open cab, and the night air was beginning to acquire a bit of a chill. I pulled my jacket tighter around me and watched the trees move steadily by, the last flames of autumn burning brightly in their branches.

"You really ought to give the Lieutenant Detective an easier time of it," Odalie said. I looked at her, shocked by this rather bold, unprompted statement. I opened my mouth, but no response offered itself up. Odalie was not looking at me; she was gazing thoughtfully at the passing trees. "He was nice to you, even after you shamed him."

I was confused. After I'd sent the Lieutenant Detective and his flask away from my desk, he hadn't spoken to me the rest of the day. "What do you mean?" I asked with a furrowed brow.

"Oh, nothing," Odalie said, turning from the trees to look at me.

"It's just that he kept deflecting Marie—giving her all those little tasks, keeping her busy and away from your desk." I shrugged. I did not see how that had anything to do with me. Odalie rolled her eyes as if I were a hopeless case. "If Marie discovers you've been drinking, how long do you think it'll be before *everyone* knows you've been drinking?" For a brief second, my blood ran cold in my veins. I had not considered this. Odalie read my expression and a little smirk appeared on her face. She gazed back at the passing trees. "And what Marie knows, the Sergeant certainly knows," she said, her voice flat and clear and full of warning.

On the other side of the park, we dismounted from the horse-cab, Odalie slipped the driver a few coins, and together we walked the few remaining blocks to the hotel in silence. Once home I realized, with little sense of victory, that I was finally entirely sober.

9

I have not explained yet about the little lapse in my professional discretion that has fallen under great scrutiny as of late. By this I mean the now-infamous report I filed at the precinct outlining the confessed crimes of a one Mr. Edgar Vitalli.

The advantage of hindsight, of course, is that one finally sees the sequence of things, the little turning points that add up to a final resultant direction. I've already mentioned my doctor's encouragement that I explain my actions with an emphasis on *chronology.* Life is a series of chain reactions, he says, and the relationship between cause and effect cannot be underestimated. And so, of course, I see *now* with utter clarity that the incident with the brooch was one such turning point, and moving in with Odalie was another, but typing up the confession of Edgar Vitalli was the most serious variety of turning point, as it marked the point of no return.

If you ask me do I feel sorry for Edgar Vitalli, I will tell you no. I am quite certain Mr. Vitalli falls into the category to which modern criminologists have given the name serial killers, and it is difficult to feel sympathy for a man like that. I understand now what I did was not right, but I cannot say in all honesty I fully regret the outcome produced by my actions. That I played some small part in Mr. Vitalli's being condemned gives me some satisfaction. Secretly I am only sorry his ultimate punishment has not yet been carried out. I say *secretly* because I know if I confessed my delight to my doctor I would be deemed an outright monster, so I keep my unrepentant feelings to myself. I am no bloodthirsty heathen, mind you. But like any truly moral person, I like to see justice prevail.

For the sake of consistency and of telling things accurately, I suppose I ought to recount a few of the details that led up to my transcribing Mr. Vitalli's confession. The difficulty is in knowing where to begin, but it's probably best to explain a little about Mr. Vitalli himself.

They say some men are simply not the marrying kind. This was not the case with Edgar Vitalli. Mr. Vitalli was perhaps *too much* the marrying kind—as the courthouse records had it, he married five times in four years. Despite the fact Mr. Vitalli was himself a youthful and handsome man, his wives were of a different ilk, all of them older and comfortably widowed. Moreover, this was not the sum total of what his wives held in common. They also shared the curious and uncanny fact they'd all suffered mortal accidents while taking a bath, and that they'd all been thoughtfully relieved of their wealth just prior to their deaths.

I suspect it was Mr. Vitalli's attitude that made the Sergeant's blood boil the most. You see, Mr. Vitalli was the worst kind of gutter rat (to use the Sergeant's vernacular)—the kind slicked down with snake oil. He was a confidence man; not terribly educated, but he had a way about him that suggested he thought himself rather smart. It might even be said Mr. Vitalli fancied himself a genius, for he implied as much on more than one occasion during his interviews with the Sergeant. Everyone who encountered him at the precinct felt instantly sure of his guilt, and all of us were eager to see justice served, and served swiftly. But twice he had gone to trial, twice he had elected to represent himself, and twice he had won over the jury's sympathies.

During his second trial I was curious to see how such a travesty of justice might occur. I sat in attendance for a day and watched Mr. Vitalli operate on the jury, removing their prejudices with the casual precision of a surgeon removing a patient's tonsils. With the men in the jury box he played the congenial drinking buddy, an average Joe, blameless for being glad to be free of the nagging, castrating constraints of marriage (*oh*, but he implied, *couldn't they relate?*). With the women who sat in the court audience, he simply licked the full, roguish pink lips that lurked under his black mustache and smiled with his long, wolfish white teeth as though to say to each of them, *My only crime against the world is I've been allotted more than my fair share of charm, and besides, I can't be blamed for being handsome.* The women appeared to agree and, perhaps as a testament to Mr. Vitalli's good looks, were even more sympathetic to Mr. Vitalli's cause than the men were. In the end he labored very little to prove he had not been involved in his wife's drowning. Instead, he devoted his efforts to proving even if he *had* been involved—*hypothetically speaking, of course (wink, wink)*—he was not to blame. Watching this, it was perhaps the first time I became conscious there existed a distinction between guilt and blame. Mr. Vitalli couldn't prove himself innocent, but he could prove he was blameless, at least as far as that weak-minded popularity club they called a courtroom was concerned.

Mr. Vitalli's high-valued stock was partly derived from his

attention to detail, as he never neglected the small civilities. He parted his inky hair down the middle with precision and oiled it carefully into place. He carried a silver-handled cane, gesturing with it like some sort of dapper circus ringmaster as he pled his case. When the court reporter unexpectedly halted in her typing and sneezed, Mr. Vitalli bolted with a genteel, catlike grace across the courtroom and waved a white silk handkerchief in her surprised face before the stammering judge was able to command him back to his seat. What's more, I believe the judge's reprimand only made the jury pity Mr. Vitalli further, as it seemed like sour grapes that the judge should punish him for only doing what every well-bred gentleman is taught to do.

In my humble estimation, justice was ultimately undermined by two principal tactics. One, Mr. Vitalli was always able to produce witnesses—sometimes multiple witnesses, always female, practically a gaggle of clucking geese—to attest they had seen him out and about at the time of his wife's death (I ought to say at the times of his *wives' deaths,* plural). And second, everyone was charmed by Mr. Vitalli, blinded by those white teeth and dapper manners, they simply could not picture him cruelly and savagely holding a woman underwater to the point of her death.

But the Sergeant and I, we knew better. We could picture him doing the deed with utter clarity, and had developed our own opinions of Mr. Vitalli's *capabilities.* There had, after all, been five wives! As wife after wife died in precisely the same curious way, we had interviewed Mr. Vitalli ad nauseam. And in that capacity, we had run through the repertoire of emotions he accidentally allowed himself to show; we had seen him cry crocodile tears, we had seen him sneer, we had seen him worry, we had seen him gloat in the aftermath of not one but two acquittals. We knew beyond a shadow of a doubt that Mr. Vitalli was, at his core, a true savage.

What's more: I believe either Mr. Vitalli could not help himself or else he got into a habit of taunting us with the crime scene. The freshly expired wives, you see, were all found in the bathtub in the exact same pose—a coincidence it was too difficult to over-look. With no air in their lungs, they sank to the bottom of the tub, where they lay staring upward in motionless silence, the sur-face of the water over them like a pane of glass separating the living from the dead. Their arms, which you might imagine flail-ing in those last seconds of life, were always crossed upon their chests in the manner of a perverse Lady of Shalott. Their ankles were also crossed, and photographs that were made of the five crime scenes conveyed a deeply unnerving, otherworldly ambi-ence. The crowning touch—a bottle of laudanum resting within an arm's reach of the tub itself—was so conspicuously placed as to seem utterly posed.

By the time of my report, it had gotten so Mr. Vitalli was visit-ing the precinct at regular intervals, being summoned as he was each time a wife of his turned up blue-faced and unblinking under a tubful of bathwater that had gone cold. I lost count of the times we saw him stroll in, but each time he arrived more dapper and dandified than the last. By the fifth death, Mr. Vitalli had decided to go out of his way to toy with us on purpose, although this devel-opment was not terribly obvious right away.

At our request, he came into the precinct voluntarily, or so it seemed. I remember observing him as he walked in the day after his fifth wife had been found. He shrugged out of his overcoat and hung it on the coatrack, a gesture that struck me as bizarrely familiar and at ease. He smiled around the room with a proprietary air. His body language suggested our precinct was in fact his home, and we were all visitors he had invited into the parlor with the glib idea we might amuse him. He was not bothered by bad nerves, or at least if he was, no molecule of his body betrayed as much. Neither did he seem to be grieving for the wife he had just lost. The Sergeant, thinking perhaps to rattle Mr. Vitalli, looked him in the eye and said firmly, "You must be devastated by this loss." But if intimidation was the Sergeant's aim, it missed its mark, for Mr. Vitalli merely smiled and put a theatrical hand over his heart.

"Such a fine specimen of a woman as she was," he replied, neglecting to refer to his late wife by name (I wondered, briefly, if he'd already forgotten it), "I don't know if I'll ever be able to bring myself to marry again." The words dripped with melodrama, and time stood horribly still as it fleetingly appeared he might even accompany the statement with a wink.

In that moment, it was clear to me the Sergeant would've liked nothing more than to ball up his fist and knock Mr. Vitalli's block off, but such a breach of professional conduct would've been extremely distasteful to the Sergeant, and he was professional to the very last. The muscles in his jaw visibly flexed as he ground his teeth in anger, but the Sergeant forced a polite smile to his lips and went through the formalities—shaking Mr. Vitalli's hand, escorting him to the interview room, offering Mr. Vitalli a glass of water as a matter of courtesy. As the Sergeant gave a quick crook of his finger in my direction (the same crook, I might mention, I'd watched Odalie give at least half a dozen waiters over the last week or so), I understood I was to follow the two men. I lifted a stack of typing paper from the supplies table and obediently fell into step behind them.

As we settled into the close quarters of the interview room, the Sergeant continued making polite conversation with Mr. Vitalli, who was voluble enough when it came to small talk. But then the mood shifted and the Sergeant segued into discussion of the crime itself. At that point Mr. Vitalli promptly transformed himself into a stone, simply sitting in silence and smiling as though he were the cat who'd caught the canary. He'd decided to clam up, as was his right. It was all a taunt: going out of his way to come in to the precinct only to stubbornly—not to mention smugly—refuse to answer anything directly related to his wife's death. The Sergeant, I could tell, was incensed. He wheedled, he threatened, he cajoled. As for me, I sat alert at the shorthand machine, tensed and ready to take the confession Edgar Vitalli refused to issue from his lips. This darkly comical state went on for the better part of a half an hour, until finally the Sergeant abruptly slapped his hand with tremendous violence against the wooden desk, causing both Mr. Vitalli and myself to flinch defensively. His eyes smoldering, the Sergeant leaned in until his forehead almost touched Mr. Vitalli's.

"Blast you! Get the hell out of here, man," the Sergeant growled through clenched teeth. Mr. Vitalli made no move to go, and I could see the Sergeant's mustache trembling. His chair scraped the ground with a bone-aching screech, and he stormed out, flinging the interview room door open with such force, I thought the glass pane would surely break as the door struck the wall.

For several seconds I remained frozen, mostly still shocked by the Sergeant's use of profanity (I had never heard him blaspheme before). Slowly I became aware of the fact I had been left alone in the room with Mr. Vitalli. Involuntarily my gaze flicked in his direction and a chill raced over my skin. Once you had glimpsed behind the curtain of Mr. Vitalli's charm, he was like that—there was something so profoundly absent from him that simply looking at him could make your skin crawl. I was instantly sorry I had glanced in his direction, for now he turned and caught my eye. A smile crept into his obscenely babylike, salmon-colored lips, and his black mustache twitched.

"Heavens. I had no intention of upsetting the good man," Mr. Vitalli lied in a falsely naive voice. I ignored this comment and gathered up my things from the stenographer's desk to go. "Do you think he'll ever forgive me?" Mr. Vitalli continued, the inflection of farcical glee in his voice growing bolder. "I'm so heartbroken over my wives, you see, and do so enjoy my social calls with the Sergeant." He reached out a hand, and suddenly I became aware he was about to take my wrist. For a split second, I was truly terrified—but only for a second, for almost as immediately another feeling came over me, a feeling I'm not sure I can adequately describe. Just before his hand reached me, my own hand sprang to life and clamped around *his* wrist with a viselike force. With a vicious aggression that seemed to come from elsewhere, I yanked him by the wrist and pulled him toward me so that we were staring eyeball to eyeball.

"I know you're used to playing the bully, and bullies often have trouble opening their ears and listening, but you'd better listen to me now like you've never listened to anyone in your life," I hissed. My voice sounded strange; I didn't recognize it as my own. And yet, I felt a twinge of inner pleasure as I realized I had now captured Mr. Vitalli's full attention.

"You may be an animal with no control of himself," I continued, "but believe me when I tell you, even animals get what's coming to them, and it's only a matter of time before the Sergeant puts you out of your misery."

The air between our locked eyes was thick with a tension that was palpable; it was as if we were staring at each other through an invisible brick. My hand—still moving by virtue of what seemed like an independent volition—squeezed even more tightly around Mr. Vitalli's wrist. His eyes widened, and suddenly I felt a trickle of something warm and wet. I glanced down and realized my fingernails had drawn blood. Four tiny red half-moons glimmered along the length of his wrist, and just as abruptly as I had snapped into my trance, I abruptly snapped out of it. I dropped his wrist and looked at the blood on my fingertips.

"Oh!" I stammered. "Oh!" I looked again at Mr. Vitalli and saw that his frightened expression was now developing into something else. It was genuine, it was familiar, and with a shock I realized it was the slow smile of a person recognizing an old friend he hasn't seen in a long while. I ran from the room, straight down the hall, and plunged through the hinged door of the ladies' room.

I did not see him leave. Even now, I do not know if Mr. Vitalli showed himself to the precinct exit, or whether he ever told the Sergeant about the little incident that transpired between us. Once in the ladies' room I remained there, trembling, for some time. I opened the faucet tap and let it run, plunging my hands under the bone-achingly icy water, driven by a half-mad hope that the pain of the cold water would wash away something more than those drops of Mr. Vitalli's blood. At some point I became cognizant that someone had entered the ladies' room and was standing behind me. Like a startled animal, my eyes flashed at the dark presence in the mirror, ready to do full battle with Mr. Vitalli if need be. But to my relief it was only Odalie. Her elegantly penciled brow was furrowed, and suddenly I felt a wave of shame. I shut off the tap and let my throbbing, frozen, blue-veined hands drip in the sink. My joints hurt, my skin stung. I reached for the dirty rag of a towel that hung on the towel bar and blotted them dry. When that was done, I stood there, fiddling, not sure what to do. I felt Odalie's eyes running over me.

Very slowly and meticulously—as if she were cautiously stepping around a murky puddle—Odalie approached and took the towel from my hands. I felt my grip loosen and the rough texture of the flour sack towel slip through my fingers as she pulled it away. She paused, and I summoned the courage to look up and meet her gaze. Then she took a corner of the towel and rubbed something from my cheek. I glanced in the mirror as she rubbed my face with the cloth and suddenly understood there had been a splotch of blood drying on the apple of my right cheekbone. I must've touched my face sometime after hurting Mr. Vitalli but before washing my hands in the sink, and had not been aware of doing so. Odalie wiped it clean and handed the towel back to me. She took a lingering look at me and smiled. Then she turned and exited the ladies' room without having ever uttered a word.

10

In looking over my notes, I see now where I got the idea that ultimately led to my undoing, and how Odalie herself planted the rather subtle and innocuous first seed. In many ways, the trouble truly began with those typos I've already mentioned. She was always making them, and now I see how it was a clever way for her to test me, to determine whether or not I was paying close attention and to find out if I would report her mistakes, correct them myself, or simply let them stand. And of course, the greater intimates we became, the more I became inclined to do the latter.

It escalated slowly at first. Over time, simple typos evolved into entire rewordings—the sort of thing that might still be chalked up to carelessness, yet not attributable to something as unconscious and mechanical as a broken typewriter with a couple of stuck keys. She was developing a very curious habit of, well . . . I suppose I might phrase it as *translating things*. And I could not know her motivations. When she transcribed reports, the Lieutenant Detective's handwriting focused on one set of details and Odalie's typing appeared to prefer another. Also, I supervised her a few times in the interrogation room and had observed the disparity between the suspect's words as they were spoken aloud and the words Odalie tapped out on the stenotype.

I did not know what to make of this new development at the time, but being that Odalie and I were getting along so well (not to mention that by moving in with her I had in some respects cast my lot in with hers), I was slow to make much of a fuss over the odd embellishments that increasingly appeared in her reports. Because they were usually about minor details and did not change the overall accuracy of the confessions, I often let them stand. Did it really matter, I asked myself, as long as the right people went to prison in the end? It didn't seem immediately apparent to me that anyone might be injured by this practice. My doctor here scoffs when I claim to have once been so naive, but it's true to say I was. (*Come now, you are hardly the naive type,* he says to me.) Of course, this was before I saw how bending the truth leads to breaking it, how Odalie would eventually twist the truth one way, and I another.

But all that came later.

In the meantime, the darkest day of winter came and went and yet somehow we barely took notice. Odalie and I spent our evenings insulated by the bright cheery interior of that white wedding cake of a hotel. We lay on the plush emerald lawn of the wall-to-wall carpet in the sitting room, sprawled out over the latest fashion magazines (Odalie even received all the Paris magazines; of course, between the two of us she was the only one who could read French, but I nonetheless enjoyed the illustrations). Sometimes when she was feeling particularly friendly, Odalie practiced a minor form of hypnotism on me, buffing my nails or brushing my long hair as we sat by the fireplace (she claimed to miss her own long hair, though her insistence on regular trims at the beauty parlor to keep her bob fashionably short and sleek would suggest otherwise). I can still hear how the smoldering logs in the fireplace popped and crackled arrhythmically, like bones cracking. Thinking about it now, I see I let myself get far too comfortable; we were spoiled, wasteful girls. We opened the valves on the radiator pipes to their fullest and walked around in nothing but our slips. We ate pretty little French pastries so pristinely decorated with ganache and gold leafing, the disarray inflicted by a single bite almost broke the heart. (At the time, I remember thinking of Helen and her sad penny candy, and for a moment I almost wished she could share in our bounty.) Above all else that winter, I came to learn that with enough money and modern steam heating, a balmy summer day could be created in just about any season. Together Odalie and I made summer year-round.

Two or three times a week, we visited a speakeasy or a private party of an equally lively nature. We tramped delicately over packed snow, wrapped in fur coats with the collars turned up, our hair wiry and untamable with the cold electric air of winter. Odalie clipped earrings to the fatty lobes of our ears—pendulous diamonds, as it was "our duty to out-sparkle the snow," she declared in her seductive, charming way—and these icy baubles swung jauntily just above our coat collars, grazing the fuzzy edge of the upturned fur. Once inside, it was always the same: Odalie pushed me around the room, introducing me to people with an air of gleeful whimsy—much like a young girl dancing with a broom—although I'm happy to report I never again consumed as much alcohol as I did on that first night.

And yet the feeling of astonishment I'd experienced upon my first speakeasy visit never completely left me. Each time Odalie led me into an otherwise lackluster shop front or a dubious-looking lunch counter and a cellar door or obscure passageway opened up to reveal yet another lush, boisterous party concealed within, I found myself just as overcome with surprise and curiosity as I had been on that first day. Absurd though it may sound, I could not determine whether it was always the same speakeasy or several different ones. What I did know was that the same set of people were frequently in attendance—more or less—despite the fact the location sometimes changed. And of course Gib was always somewhere to be found, standing square-jawed and stoic in the center of it all. In those days, I guessed he was the host of these parties. Or a front man of some sort. Slowly but surely, Gib and I began to develop a surly sort of rapport with each other. Or at least as much of a rapport as a person can have with someone who views you as a constant competitor.

I'm not sure what the right idea would've been, but it certainly seemed like Gib had gotten the wrong idea about me and Odalie—much the way Dotty had gotten the wrong idea about my feelings for my friend Adele. Which is to say Gib had the wrong idea about *me*. I will admit, a certain loneliness existed in my life and it's true enough to say these women helped alleviate that. Those trendy followers of Freud might say this neediness on my part has something to do with my mother, with how she abandoned me for no better reason than hateful spite. They might even imply there was something rather unnatural in my eagerness to be close to first Adele and later Odalie. But I don't give a fig for these dirty-minded diagnoses. I enjoyed watching Odalie from afar more than anything else. I suppose I didn't mind when she brushed my hair or traced light little circles on the palms of my hands. I didn't mind the way she wet her lips and leaned in toward me whenever I spoke (as if I were about to say something

absolutely riveting, only I didn't know it). And I'll admit I wanted
to be within eyeshot of Odalie at all times. But who didn't? It was
simply a side effect of her beauty. Or perhaps *beauty* is too crude a
word for it; rather, it was a side effect of the way Odalie's beauty
was uniquely animated, which was a phenomenon unto itself. It's
not as if I hadn't caught Gib watching her out of the corner of his
eye, keeping track of who she spoke to at the speakeasy, a voy-
euristic hawk in his own right. I'm sure you've heard it said a hundred times: The most objectionable people are often the ones with
whom you have the most in common.

Gib was all wrong for Odalie—I'm sure this much was plain to
everyone who saw them together. They made an absurd pairing:
Odalie was regal where Gib could only be described as sly-looking
at best. Other than the speakeasy—the inner workings of which
at the time I assumed were Gib's affair and Odalie only attended
for amusement—I could not see they had very much in common.
I could hardly imagine Gib attending one of Odalie's little bohemian gatherings, much less chatting at length about art or poetry.
Neither could I imagine where they must've met. They were an
odd couple to say the least, and I assumed it was only a matter of
time before I saw the last of Gib. But in the weeks after moving in
with Odalie, I began to see Gib had been a regular in her life for
quite some time already, and planned to go on as such.

In any case, Gib and I were building up a slow tolerance for
each other, the way some people slowly build a tolerance for a specific kind of poison. By the end of my first month at the apartment, we had learned to make the kind of civil conversation two
people might make while waiting at the same streetcar stop. By
the end of two months, I had learned to accept my somewhat sub-
ordinate position as a newer addition to Odalie's apartment as a

fact. After all, Gib did not need to be told which closet kept the spare linens for his shower and was no stranger to the bell-boys at our hotel, who greeted him by his first name (as opposed to the polite but generic *miss* they eternally lobbed in my direction). Accepting these things likewise meant accepting the fact there would be evenings when I'd listen for the sound of him letting himself out the front door but never hear it, and mornings when I'd wake up to see him grumpily slurping hot coffee from one of Odalie's little white china mugs at our breakfast table. As with all things that are unstomachable, I tried my best not to think about what objectionable things might have passed in the night and always maintained a civil front.

It was on one such morning Gib began to leak out information about Odalie's past. Or at least a certain *version* of Odalie's past. There was a pair of French doors that led from the dining room onto a fairly generous-size terrace that hugged the corner of the hotel apartment. That morning Gib stared out the window and sipped his coffee, observing the large, lumpy mounds of snow as they melted and made a soggy mess out of the terrace. He frowned. "We ought to glass that in," he said. "It's a waste in the wintertime, and with a little glass it'd make a damned fine solarium."

"Would Odalie's father approve of that?" I asked, holding a piece of toast over the sink and scraping away the blackened char. *Honeymoon toast*, the nuns used to call it whenever I burned the toast in the orphanage kitchen. An ironic choice of phrase, I had always thought, for a group of women utterly uninitiated in the ways of matrimonial life.

Gib's spine straightened. He looked up in surprise.

"Odalie's father?"

"Sure," I said, setting the plate of toast on the table and slipping into a chair. Despite my thorough scraping, the bread slices were still peppered with tiny black speckles. "Doesn't her father pay the rent for this place? I just assumed we would need his approval."

Gib cocked his head to the side, examining me closely with one eye as though he were a parrot taking in the sight of a new stranger. Suddenly an incredulous, somewhat sarcastic expression spread over his features.

"Oh. Is she calling him her father now?" Gib asked. "How interesting. I'd gotten so used to her referring to him as her *uncle*." He turned in a matter-of-fact way to the newspaper lying in his lap and snapped it open.

I blinked. "What do you mean?" I stammered into the thin newsprint wall hovering between us. "Do you mean to say Odalie's father is . . . is not . . ." I struggled to find the proper words, but there were none for this curious turn of events. ". . . not her father?"

Gib dropped the paper a few inches and studied my face. I cannot imagine what he found there, but after some minutes evidently he was able to plumb the depths of my ignorance enough to see greater explanation on his part was required. He gave a sigh and picked up a piece of toast, frowned at it as he turned it over for further inspection, then returned it to the serving plate. "If by *father* you mean the word in strictly the genealogical sense, then—no. The man who pays for this apartment is not Odalie's *father.*" Gib paused and gave me an assessing once-over, as though deciding something. "Of course," he finally proceeded, "a case could be made that you might refer to him as her *daddy.*" Upon pronouncing the word *daddy* he gave a disdainful, self-amused snort. A cool bar of early spring sunshine leaned in from the glass of the French doors and fell across his cheek, revealing the many pockmarks in his roughly shaven skin. Strangely, this defect rather enhanced Gib's features, much the way the scar over the Lieutenant Detective's eyebrow enhanced his. Gib looked at me again and rubbed his chin thoughtfully. "I didn't realize . . . ," he began, but trailed off. The newspaper floating before him sagged further, and finally with a sigh and a couple flicks of his wrist he folded it back up into a tidy rectangle.

"Hmm. I can see you're confused," he said. "I suppose it doesn't do to keep you completely in the dark." And then he cleared his throat and began, in his stiff-jawed way, to tell me the story of Odalie's "uncle." As soon as Gib began speaking, the image of Odalie I had diligently conjured in my mind up to that point melted away faster than the rain-pecked lumps of snow on the balcony, and yet another new one formed to take its place.

I shall paraphrase here, because I'm not at all sure I can tell it quite as Gib told it. In the months since I've been seeing my doctor, I've retold this story so many times it feels as though somehow the tale has always belonged to me, that I have always been the one who told it.

According to Gib, the French-speaking, fashionably coiffed woman I knew as Odalie Lazare was born Odalie Mae Buford to some people who owned a drugstore just outside of Chicago. The store was a small family-run affair, and from a young age Odalie proved herself useful behind the till, able as she was to make sums in her head while at the same time shooting the customers looks of sly curiosity from under those preternaturally long, dark lashes. But the family fell on hard times when Odalie's father suffered a sudden stroke and died, and Odalie's mother—a wiry, thin-lipped woman named Cora-Sue—consequently fell down the long neck of a bottomless bottle. Odalie, barely ten at the time, tried her valiant but youthful hand at keeping the books, but every trace of profit was drunk away very efficiently and speedily by Cora-Sue, who was sinking deeper and deeper into what my doctor here at the institution might call a state of melancholia. Odalie and her mother were eventually prompted to forfeit the drugstore to the bank. Deepening poverty forced them from the outskirts of Chicago and into the city proper, where Cora-Sue found she had limited professional skills at her disposal and promptly became a professional of a different kind.

The house where Cora-Sue found employ was of the usual requisite ill-repute, yet had a good reputation for being very "traditional." This meant it was a brothel in the old salon tradition, and most of the ladies who worked there, when not immediately engaged with a customer, spent their idle hours sitting in the parlor like proper ladies waiting to be called upon and courted. Well, perhaps ladies with coarser manners, for Gib informed me the "ladies" mostly occupied themselves with sitting around telling vulgar jokes and betting at cards. But despite the sailor's language and the gambling, a sort of drawing room atmosphere nevertheless prevailed. Oftentimes a man named Lionel, a student over at the music academy looking for extra practice, would even sit and play the piano, alternately pounding and trilling out everything from the latest popular band music to lovely little Beethoven sonatas, lending the overall ambience a jovial yet genteel, dignified air.

The proprietress of the establishment, a shrill redheaded woman who went by the name Annabel (it was rumored her given Christian name was really Jane but had been changed to avoid some previous legal difficulties), was not keen on the idea of hiring employees who came with children in tow, but when little Odalie introduced herself to Annabel by giving a flirtatious curtsy and a wink, Annabel immediately identified the miniature coquette's potential as a petite hostess who might amuse the customers by serving them drinks.

And so it was the two Buford women found employ and managed, for a time at least, to eke out a living Cora-Sue couldn't drink up the very same day. Cora-Sue took dollars for performing her services upstairs, while downstairs the men lifted their lemonades and whiskeys from a silver tray and placed pennies or the occasional nickel into Odalie's sticky palm, giving the tiny hand a small squeeze. Gib's description of what a hit the tiny Odalie was with the customers came as no surprise to me. A born performer, she stamped out tenacious little dances whenever she thought it might delight someone and even learned to patter out a few tunes on the piano at Lionel's instruction. The men delighted in her plucky nature, and it was not uncommon to find her seated at the card table, perched on some customer's knee and playing a hand of poker on his very amused behalf. As Gib recounted this chapter of Odalie's history, I formed the idea that this era must've marked a sort of early education for Odalie, as it was during her time at the brothel that she began to understand and hone her manipulative powers over people, and over men in particular.

There was one habitué (a term Gib said Odalie was fond of using—French, I'm told, for *regular*) who eventually took a more vigorous interest in Odalie. The man, one Mr. Istvan Czakó, was a dapper, middle-aged Hungarian of short stature but very deep pockets and an almost Baroque predilection for what one might call civilized perversions. Shortly after the Buford women began working and living at Annabel's place, Czakó rarely found the time anymore to make the journey upstairs to the second floor of the brothel, satisfied as he was to watch his new little muse dance and sing and to have her sit in his lap whenever she would agree to it. At first, Annabel did not mind, as Czakó stayed for hours and always managed to spend just as much money on the drinks he consumed while in Odalie's company as he would if he had engaged the private ministrations of one of the more *mature* ladies at the house. But when it was discovered Czakó was slipping money directly to Odalie on the side (and furthermore that it was a large enough sum to be paper money and not merely the kind that jingles), Annabel was outraged and demanded her proper commission. *The police would certainly want to know about his preference for the younger set,* Annabel suggested, with that telltale flinty gleam in her eye.

It cannot be said that Odalie was kidnapped exactly, for when Czakó elected to sail for France to avoid the persecution Annabel promised, Odalie packed her things and stole away quite willingly. There was perhaps a moment or two of remorse, of sorrow for the helpless alcohol-sodden mother she was leaving behind, but all such sentiments soon vaporized into a cloud of glamorous cigarette smoke once she and Czakó reached Paris. Czakó, who'd previously lived in Paris for many years, was only too happy to dazzle his young ingenue with the sights and sounds of the city. Together they took in museums, concerts, society salons, street cafés. It was during this time the myth of their familial relations first circulated. Required to explain the presence of a young girl in his company, Czakó was content to let strangers believe she was his daughter. For those old acquaintances who already knew him, he casually asserted she was his niece, born of a distant American relation and left in his charge for reasons that (I assume he very expertly and indirectly implied) were too sad to explain in any more than the vaguest detail.

They spent the better part of Odalie's formative years in France, living leisurely off Czakó's vast fortune. According to Gib, Odalie always maintained Czakó was a Hungarian aristocrat of some sort, which, from what I've read about aristocrats, might account in some part for his perversions. Eventually, Odalie was even enrolled in school and donned the ribboned cap, starched white sailor's collar, navy pleats, and dark kneesocks of a proper little *française* (a uniform, it must be noted, Czakó sometimes requested she wear during nonschool hours). By her late teens, she had grown into a polished young lady of many accomplishments. She was fluent in French and English (she had also acquired a smattering of Hungarian by then, though it was probably not useful in polite company). She furthered the studies in piano she had long ago begun with Lionel, and although she was not terribly gifted, she could always be counted upon to crank out a jaunty little tune.

In the days of her suburban Chicago childhood, Odalie had always been something of a tomboy, and even after her "finishing" years in France she was still at her core an athlete, having never lost that lanky, careless grace that was hers from birth. Czakó often took her south for the summers, where she excelled at tennis and golf and made the other hotel guests murmur in admiration of her fearlessness as she swam farther out than anybody else into the gold-flecked azure horizon of the Mediterranean. Meanwhile a proud and possessive Czakó looked on from a steamer chair, the wiry carpet of iron-gray hair on his denuded barrel chest shining dully in the Riviera sunshine.

Those were—Gib ventured to guess as he told the story—probably the happiest days of the Hungarian's life. Perhaps Czakó even allowed himself to believe Odalie would never grow up, and that the war—which by this time had begun in Europe—would never truly touch them. It wasn't until the sinking of the *Lusitania* that they finally felt compelled to gain a greater physical distance from the action, and together they made the journey back across the Atlantic on a stomach of nerves. They arrived in New York, which had grown boisterous with the politics of the Great War. Men stood on soapboxes and yelled about the divided interests of Theodore Roosevelt and Woodrow Wilson, but for a time Czakó and Odalie were able to skirt around all the commotion and go up the elevator to the newly insulated oasis of an apartment Czakó had secured for them on Park Avenue.

But their respite was short-lived. The trouble the Black Hand had stirred up at the start of the war meant there were fissures beginning to show in the great castles of Hungary. The aristocrats had already seen their finest hours, and were now losing some of their popularity. The commotion caused by the tussle between the anarchists and monarchists allowed for Czakó's private banker to reveal himself for what the fellow truly was: a capitalist. Czakó sent wire after wire, each one increasingly more desperate. But after three weeks it was evident the banker had no intention of ever being found. *Oh,* Czakó lamented regretfully for weeks after coming face-to-face with the realization that his banker would likely never be reached, *I should have seen it all coming and relocated my wealth into the hands of the Americans, or better still, the Swiss!*

It's not at all clear whether Odalie contemplated leaving Czakó at this point. Knowing her a little as I do now, it is likely she would have. But if she harbored seditious sentiments, she kept them to herself. Perhaps still feeling a little guilty for having left her mother at the nadir of their mutual misfortune, she remained with Czakó and convinced him they should live more frugally (he was inexperienced in such tactics and required instruction— though I found it difficult to believe Odalie was an expert in this practice), cutting back on their expenses and converting what was left of his fortune into Liberty Bonds.

With the end of the war and the rise of the Volstead Act, Odalie saw another opportunity for beneficial investment and suggested as much to Czakó. By this time, Odalie had long since left the greater traces of her childhood behind, and the dynamic that bound the two of them together had shifted. Czakó's trips to her bed had decreased over the years in proportion to the number of birthdays she had accumulated, yet his heed of her financial advice increased. For the first time in her life, Odalie was allowed to keep a separate apartment. This was perhaps a secret gesture on Czakó's part to protect himself. Czakó was aware their new business venture wasn't exactly legal, but he probably figured the less he knew about that, the better.

"You see, she's self-made in many ways," Gib commented approvingly upon the conclusion of his story. "I mean, just as much as John D. Rockefeller is, or any of those other slobs, for that matter."

I stared at Gib, my mouth agape, still trying to take in the deluge of information I had just been given. The notion that I'd been living with a woman who was quite possibly the nation's premier female bootlegger came as a bit of a shock. A queer magnetic field had dropped around me, and my moral compass was spinning. It was one thing to sneak into the occasional speakeasy; it was quite another to supply it and clear a tidy profit. For months I had hovered at Odalie's elbow sipping champagne, comforted by the assumption that if anyone's hands were dirty, so to speak, it was only Gib's hands and Gib's alone. This revised version of my evenings with Odalie was difficult to wrap my mind around.

"And—Czakó?" I stammered.

"Oh yes," Gib answered with an amused smile. "He's still in the picture. Checks in regularly and likes to take his piece of the pie, you know. And I suppose you have to admit it was his seed money. But it wouldn'ta come to nothin'—ya know—if it weren't for Odalie."

I looked at Gib's face. He had the very oily skin handsome, olive-toned men so often do. When he smiled, an event that was rare, his countenance positively gleamed. Now, as he posed as though contemplating Odalie's accomplishments with pride, his face shone brilliantly in the morning sunshine. I wanted so badly to disapprove—of Gib, of Odalie, of all of it—but I found myself in an even greater state of curiosity and awe.

Of course, I couldn't know then what Gib's smile secretly hinted at—that this story might very well be just that, a story, and that the truth of Odalie's childhood might never reveal itself to her admirers, obscured as it was by layer after layer of misdirection. It's funny; I have often imagined how different the world must look through Odalie's eyes, as hers are the only ones that have a complete view of the tricks behind the magic. I once read in a newspaper about Houdini and how he famously said his professional life was merely a constant record of disillusion, and I cannot help but wonder now if this is how Odalie, too, saw the world around her. Looking back now, I see it's quite possible.

11

There is something darkly thrilling about standing on the balcony of a very tall building and looking over the edge with the silent knowledge that it is in one's own power to jump. Jumping is, of course, very unwise—an act fated to resolve itself in total self-annihilation. Let there be no illusion in that. And yet one is nonetheless tempted to consider the dare. It was like that for me in the late spring of '25, when an opportunity presented itself for me to take a metaphorical plunge, a plunge from which I somehow sensed I'd never recover.

How to describe what transpired? I suppose I might put it this way: My work at the precinct came to something of a fork in the road, and I found myself unexpectedly torn—morbidly drawn to the dark moral abyss with the unabashed sentiment of a lover, like Mina self-destructively drawn to her Count Dracula.

Two months had passed since our—the Sergeant's and my— last interview with Edgar Vitalli. I remember winter dropped away in a hurry that year, like a guest who'd suddenly become cognizant he'd overstayed his welcome at the party. By April, the sun's rays beat down with a vital force, and the fresh breezes of spring were already laced with the thicker heralds of the hot, humid summer still to come. The bright light of the mornings struck a contrast with my dark afternoons at the precinct, which seemed filled to the brim with more gruesome details of grisly confessions than usual. This was possibly due to the fact the workload within our typing pool had been somewhat redistributed. Marie had gotten herself in the family way again, so the Sergeant had restricted her duties to the simplest of filing activities, as it was thought that hearing about rapes and murders might distress her and hurry the baby along before its time. The prospect of a woman succumbing to the labor pains of childbirth while at the precinct made the men more queasy than anything a suspected murderer could possibly recount.

"This is a perfect example," the Sergeant said once he had gathered us in a circle and reallocated our assignments, "of why women need to occupy themselves with different work than men." We all nodded somberly. I assume Odalie did, too, though she stood behind me and I could not see her. "I understand this is not an easy job for womenfolk. If it were up to me, I don't think I would have a single one of you ladies expose yourselves to what goes on in this precinct at all," the Sergeant continued. "But of course, we cannot function without someone to do the typing and filing, and the officers and patrolmen have proven themselves utterly helpless on that score." He turned a kind, paternalistic gaze on Marie. "And we mustn't forget, my dear, you have always brewed the best coffee," he said, the note of approbation not lost on Marie, whose doughy cheeks puffed with a smile. "I anticipate you can certainly go on doing that, and occupy yourself with the filing, and it will always be greatly appreciated." The Sergeant dismissed us with a wave of his hand, and the cluster of bodies around him broke up. Marie, Iris, Odalie, and I scattered our separate ways and resumed our previous work.

The Lieutenant Detective was not there that morning, but none of us thought there was anything very unusual about this. He was the representative from our precinct who was most often sent directly to the scene of the crime, and he often leveraged this fact so he might adhere to a schedule of his own making. It was no secret he had a distaste for keeping regular office hours, and we all assumed he would saunter into the precinct sometime in the afternoon, only pretending to have been somewhere on official police business earlier in the morning.

But later that week, I learned that the Lieutenant Detective had been called to a hotel in another district to give his opinion about a woman who had been found drowned in a bathtub in one of the hotel's rooms. Her body had been left in a familiar pose, and the contents of her hotel safe picked clean. Of course all of us at the precinct knew immediately who had done it, but it took the Sergeant and the Lieutenant Detective nearly a week to put together enough evidence to prove Mr. Vitalli was even acquainted with the victim, as this time he had not been married to the drowned woman. "He's not taking the time to marry them anymore," I overheard the Lieutenant Detective say in a low voice to the Sergeant. "Just goes straight to murder and theft. He's picking up the pace; we've let him get far too comfortable."

It took several days, but by virtue of sheer persistence they were able to compel Mr. Vitalli to come in for an interview, and at last he was successfully summoned. But our joy over this fact was short-lived; it was clear from the outset Mr. Vitalli—not even troubling himself to hide the amused sneer on his face—was anticipating a faithful reproduction of his previous interviews. As the Lieutenant Detective escorted Mr. Vitalli to the interrogation room (diplomatically calling it the *interview room,* which of course had a friendlier ring to it), the Chief Inspector put in an unexpected appearance, emerging from a cloud of pipe smoke that filled the doorway of his office as though he were a genie responding to a rub at the bottle.

"Irving," he said, using the Sergeant's given name and laying his spidery, long-fingered hand upon the Sergeant's shoulder, "I don't need to tell you how crucial having a confession has become to this case."

The Sergeant's mustache twitched. "No, Gerald, you don't."

"Good luck to you. Remember—he's a wily one. Best to be clever, try to lay the trap. . . ."

As the Chief Inspector's tepid, useless advice trailed off, the Sergeant walked away with a purposeful, determined stride. "Rose?" the Sergeant called over his shoulder, giving me the cue to follow him. My heart began to pound. After what happened last time, the prospect of going into the interrogation room with Vitalli again filled me with dread, but I could see no way out of it. With trembling knees, I fell into step behind the Sergeant. The regular whir of activity around us had lurched to a standstill in reverence for the task that lay before us. All heads turned in our direction. It was as if we were crossing a stage.

"*Psst,*" Iris whispered in my direction, and thoughtfully thrust an extra roll of stenotype paper into my hands as I passed her. "Let's hope the Sergeant gets something out of him this time," she said in a low voice, her necktie trembling at her throat and her tiny birdlike mouth not even seeming to move. I passed by Odalie, who arched an eyebrow—a skeptical gesture, but one I had come to understand was not altogether unfriendly and was, in fact, meant to convey a feeling of camaraderie. I walked past Marie, who was already looking quite shiny-faced and round-bellied in spite of the fact her pregnancy had only been announced a few days prior that week. She winked and gave me a stalwart nod, as though I were going off to bare-knuckle fight Mr. Vitalli myself.

Once inside the interrogation room, I swung the door shut behind me and scurried quickly across the space, sliding into the tiny stenographer's desk as innocuously as I could manage. Mr. Vitalli was already holding court, leaning back in his chair, giving a loud monologue that compared the virtues of married life to those of bachelorhood. Needless to say, it was not very polite fare, and I shall not repeat it here. I replaced the empty roll of stenotype paper with the one Iris had handed me (she must've known; leave it to her to keep a constant mental account of these things!) and waited. Mr. Vitalli flicked a glance in my direction and paused midsentence, his eyes narrowing as they locked with my own. I realized I had been afraid of this moment, that I had been nervous to come face-to-face with him again. It was clear Mr. Vitalli had not alerted anyone to the little incident that had transpired between us, but on instinct I understood this was not a gesture of complicity with me. He was simply waiting for the most advantageous opportunity, and he was not done sizing me up.

"You're a married man, Sergeant, are you not?" Mr. Vitalli asked in a patronizing voice, though we were all well aware he already knew the answer. Ordinarily, the Sergeant wouldn't have allowed a suspect to engage him in this way, but I knew the Sergeant was desperate to keep Mr. Vitalli talking by any means necessary. He cleared his throat.

"I am."

"Ah. Well," Mr. Vitalli said, throwing his hands in the air as though the Sergeant had just offered up perfect proof of his point. "Then you are privy to the fact that women are not always the angels they would have you believe they are."

"That so?" the Lieutenant Detective piped up in a relaxed, friendly voice, sensing an opportunity to steer the conversation. "Are you thinking of any of your wives in particular?"

"Oh, I wouldn't say *in particular* . . . more generally, I suppose." Mr. Vitalli turned, ran his eyes up and down the length of the Lieutenant Detective, and revealed his wolfish teeth in a knowing smile. "And you are of course a bachelor, I presume?" The Lieutenant Detective stiffened and flicked a wary glance in the direction of the Sergeant, who gave him a very slight, almost imperceptible nod.

"Yes."

"Then you can't know the ungainly secrets of the fairer sex as the Sergeant and I do," Mr. Vitalli continued. He lifted a hand to preen his mustache as he spoke. "You can't know that every angel of a woman likewise has within her the secret face of a demon. They all do. But you won't see this demon side unless you marry them." He paused. "Or become otherwise *familiar* with them." He gave a lecherous chuckle, as though musing over the different kinds of familiarity he had known, then coughed politely and continued. "They all keep this side hidden from public view, you see." As his eyes roved about the room, they landed on me again and stopped to linger. Suddenly his eyes narrowed. Now my heart was pounding so loudly, my ears began to thunder with my heartbeat. "Of course, from time to time a rare lady will slip up when she's not expecting to, and brazenly show her demonic face to a perfect stranger."

Now I knew for certain he was not going to let it go, that he was going to target me, and I felt the cold tingle of perspiration breaking out on my brow. Only Vitalli was looking at me; the Sergeant and the Lieutenant Detective remained riveted on his person, and for this I am grateful.

His tone was casual, but his gaze was white-hot with spite. "Take your young typist here. Rose, was it? I'll bet, as composed as she presents herself now, you'd probably imagine she is always quite the well-mannered *lady*, would you not?"

"All right!" the Lieutenant Detective said sternly. "That's enough out of you. It's time you spoke to the subject at hand and told us about your wives, not about our typists."

Mr. Vitalli's eyebrows shot up in the air, and he looked at the Lieutenant Detective, then turned to regard me, and finally turned back to the Lieutenant Detective. A look of amused recognition crept into his features, as if Mr. Vitalli was suddenly seeing the two of us for the first time.

"Goodness!" he said with a tone of innocence and a wicked smile. "Why, I had no idea you had already found romance, Lieutenant. And in the workplace, no less. How bold of you. I suppose I should shake your hand."

"I said that's enough!"

I glanced at the Lieutenant Detective, but he would not make eye contact with me. His eyes were fastened on the notebook lying on the table before him. A series of blotchy red roses had vined their way from his cheekbones to the roots of his hair, climbing in and around the pink rims of his ears. Even in my state of distress I felt a tiny prick of offense at this, as I can only assume he was mortified by the mere thought that someone might think we could be romantically involved.

"Settle down now, Vitalli," came the Sergeant's cool, calm

baritone. "We've let you have your bit of fun. I'm afraid it's time for you to start telling us the truth. If you come clean, perhaps we can help you reach a more amenable arrangement with regard to your sentence."

But it turned out Mr. Vitalli did not think he needed the Sergeant's help. In a repeat of the tactics that had worked only too well for him the last time, he simply sat there, smiling in silence, each time they asked him a question about the murders. For two hours, the Sergeant and the Lieutenant Detective put their questions to a man who might as well have been a mannequin. The silence that followed each question was so vacuous, it rang mockingly in our ears. The Sergeant and the Lieutenant Detective took turns pacing the room, while I sat with my fingers itching to press down the shorthand keys, my wrists poised in the air and my nerves all abristle, as though the stenotype sitting before me might go off like a gun. But as the minutes ticked by and the questions repeatedly bounced off Vitalli like rubber balls thrown against a brick wall, the spirit of determination in the room began to flag.

He'd only talk just so much as was necessary to keep us from giving up. It seemed as though his confession was nearby but always just out of sight. Finally, during a particularly long lull in the interrogation, Mr. Vitalli reached across the table, picked up a photograph taken of the scene, and inspected it with an air of professional interest.

"Did you take this?" he inquired of the Lieutenant Detective. The Lieutenant Detective raised an eyebrow and cautiously nodded.

"Our regular man was out sick." The Lieutenant Detective paused and cocked his head as though struck by a new stratagem.

He adopted an easy demeanor, his frown vanished, and the scar along his forehead smoothed itself flat. He grinned amicably. "But to tell the truth, I'm not very good at operating a camera. And as you can imagine, it's difficult getting a good photograph when you're obliged not to disturb anything. So I apologize if I didn't do justice in capturing your work."

Mr. Vitalli smiled politely at the baited compliment. Instead of affirming or denying the accusation, he cleared his throat as though a change of subject had just occurred to him. "Oh. Of course. But where are my manners? You want my statement, correct? How rude of me. Please, allow me to give my statement." He cleared his throat. The Sergeant and the Lieutenant Detective exchanged a sudden look, laced with the involuntary excitement of two hungry animals. They leaned in, struggling to maintain the skeptical expressions on their faces. Mr. Vitalli smiled and sat back contentedly in his chair.

"Well then. Here's my statement: Officially, I think you are in fact quite talented, Lieutenant Detective. I mean it. I'm quite genuine. There's a real hint of genius in these—a certain creative finesse, as it were. I envision a bright future in this for you. You ought to rent out a studio, do some artistic studies. Perhaps even acquire one of those charming little tripod stands and do some landscape work *alfresco*. You might even give that Stieglitz chap a run for his money. . . ." His mocking monologue went on for several more minutes. At one point the Lieutenant Detective slapped the table and abruptly stood up from his chair as though he might lunge at Vitalli in a fit of rage. But no sooner had he shot up than he caught himself and stopped short. He froze and slumped back into his chair as Vitalli looked on with a smile. The Sergeant's mustache quivered in frustration until, finally, he sighed.

"Frank, I'd like you to step outside with me for a moment."
The Lieutenant Detective nodded and rose again from his chair,
this time in a much more wilted manner. "Mr. Vitalli," the Sergeant continued. "I'll thank you not to go anywhere. And Rose—
you may have your coffee break."

"Oh, coffee, how civilized," Mr. Vitalli said. He turned to me.
"Why thank you, *Rose,* I would love some." He smiled, and I
checked the Sergeant's face to see if my orders were indeed to fetch
this vile creature some coffee. The Sergeant's mustache twitched
but his expression was inscrutable, so I employed my own judgment and took it upon myself to veto Mr. Vitalli's request. The
Sergeant exited without another word, but the Lieutenant Detective waited for me to get out from behind my post at the stenographer's desk and held the door for me. Once back on the main
precinct floor, he disappeared into the Sergeant's office, where I
assume the two of them hoped to scheme up a new interrogation
strategy, and I slunk back over to my desk.

"My, what dismal faces. I take it he's still not talking,"
Odalie remarked from the desk next to me.

"Not a single word, unless it's to mock us with some prattle
about the weather," I said. "I feel terrible for the Sergeant. He
works so hard, you know. And everyone knows this wretch is as
guilty as sin!"

"No way to con it out of him? He won't budge at all?"

I shook my head. "He's clammed up, says he knows his rights
and all that. He's stubborn. And boy! Nerves of steel, that one. No
one can shake his tongue loose."

Odalie put the eraser end of a pencil between her lips absently,
as though smoking a cigarette. She looked thoughtfully into the
distance. "But you're *certain* he's guilty."

"As I said, guilty as sin. He's gone to court twice already, but keeps finding ways to slither free like the snake that he is."

"And a confession would make all the difference?"

"Oh yes. A confession might scare away all those ninnies willing to lie for him and give him an alibi."

"Well then." Odalie's eyes finally snapped back from the tiny object she'd been contemplating far off on the horizon. Suddenly she was all business, as though she had solved our dilemma. "Then you'd better type up his confession."

I looked at her, suddenly annoyed. "I said he's not talking," I reminded her. "Not a syllable about his wives, or this woman in the hotel."

"Who says he needs to talk about them? Get him to blather about any old thing. What's more important is what *you type*."

What??? I blinked. My mouth fell open stupidly. "I . . . I can't just—"

Odalie interrupted me by rolling her eyes. "Yes you can. Whatever you type, that's what they'll look to in court, and you know it. He'll say, *'I never said any of that claptrap,'* but they'll just show him the transcript and say, *'Oh, but Mr. Vitalli, we have it all typed up right here—how can we have the report if you didn't say it to someone? These things don't just type themselves, you know. . . .'"* She stopped, then looked at me and leaned in very close, her eyes twinkling full of meaning.

"But . . . but the Sergeant, the Lieutenant Detective. They'll know it wasn't what he said. They'll know it's not . . . it's not . . . exactly *accurate*."

"The Sergeant won't chastise you for having the courage to do what you both know is just. He will probably even thank you for it in the end." I was speechless and stared at Odalie stupidly. As indifferent to my shock as ever, she shrugged and turned back to the pile of reports on her desk. "If it's the truth, it's the truth, no matter whether it comes out of your mouth or out of his."

"Do you really think he'll—"

"I do," Odalie said with absolute certainty, before I even had a chance to get my question out.

I stood up with a slight stagger. The door to the Sergeant's office was still shut, but I knew my coffee break would not go on forever. If Odalie was right, I was on the verge of losing an opportunity to stop Vitalli once and for all and set things right. My head was swimming with a newly minted, razor-sharp sense of uncertainty. I adjourned to the ladies' room, where I splashed some water on my face and held a long staring contest with the very plain yet perplexed girl who stood before me in the mirror.

What was justice, after all, but a particular outcome?

Then, for the briefest of flashes, I saw Odalie's face staring back at me from where mine should have been. Startled, I jerked away from the sink and knocked over a mop that had been leaning against it. As I recovered myself, the slow realization of what I was about to do came over me. I looked again at the mirror, but this time saw only myself. After a few minutes, when it became clear the staring match was destined for a stalemate, I shook myself free from my twin image standing on the other side of the glass. It was time to muster up some courage and do my job, the way I had always wanted to but had always been too afraid.

The Sergeant and the Lieutenant Detective were still inside the Sergeant's office when I crossed to the typist's desk. No one even so much as glanced in my direction, which meant my pale complexion and trembling hands went unnoticed, much to my relief. I took my seat and realized my mind had already made itself up. All I needed now was to transcribe the report. I hoped no one would notice there was no long strip of stenotype paper next to me. That's when I began to type, slowly at first as I coaxed the first few details forth with some hesitancy, then with increasing speed until I was typing in a frenzy as my imagination strung together a series of events with surprisingly vivid clarity.

The door to the Sergeant's office flew open, and the Lieutenant Detective stormed through the precinct alone. He strode across the main room and out the front door; likely they'd had a row over how to handle Vitalli and the Lieutenant Detective had decided the occasion called for some fresh air and a cigarette. I paused in my typing for only a fraction of a second to watch him go, then pressed on. My typing had reached an absolute fever pitch; I think if someone would've timed me with a stopwatch and counted the words I might've set a new record for speed. Once I had it—or enough of what would be needed—I reached to the typewriter's rollers and yanked the paper free with an exultant yelp, but then caught hold of myself before I attracted further attention. Odalie looked over at me and aimed the most luxurious, satisfied little curl of a smile in my direction, which I gladly returned. It was done. I had done it. So strong was my devotion to this vivid sense of justice, I could barely breathe with the ecstatic knowledge of it.

With the words typed into existence and now in my hand, I crossed the room to the Sergeant's office and knocked on the frame of the open door. The Sergeant's eyes were turned to the ground and his arms were behind his back as he paced back and forth. With a shaking hand I held out the report, but he took no notice at first.

"We've got to get this. We'll just keep at it," he muttered, as though giving instructions to himself. "We'll go at it from a different angle. Where is Frank?" He raised his head with sudden intensity. "Somebody go find the Lieutenant Detective. We can't let Vitalli just sit in there and gloat over his victory. We've got to really put the screws to him this time."

"Sergeant," I commanded. Without being in control of it, my voice spilled forth evenly in the same cool, controlled notes I had unintentionally used the time I had attacked Vitalli, and just as it had before, it chilled me with its unfamiliarity. My hand was still extended in the Sergeant's direction, and the typed pages wavered ever so slightly with the jittering of my grip. "I typed his statement," I said. The Sergeant glanced at the pages and his brow furrowed with an air of annoyance. An involuntary sneer crept into his face, and I could see his anger was now going to unleash itself on me.

"Have you now, Rose?" he said with ugly sarcasm. "Well done indeed. Some statement! We can't use any of the drivel he's been giving us. It's pure rot! The bastard knows he has us." He made to go, but suddenly something clicked in me, and my opposite hand shot out to grab his elbow. On a few occasions in the past, the Sergeant has tapped me on the shoulder in passing, but this marked the first time I had ever initiated such contact; as I reached out and touched the Sergeant, I realized this was not how I'd always pictured it. There was something bizarrely forceful in my grip. His eyes traveled from my face down to where I held on to his sleeve with astonishment. My brain played host to a fleeting recollection of the unfortunate interaction I'd had with Mr. Vitalli just weeks before, but I pushed the memory from my mind and managed to regain my composure. I dropped my hold on the Sergeant's elbow, but held out the report even more insistently.

"Sir, I typed Mr. Vitalli's statement. *I think you really ought to read what it says.*"

After a frown and a sigh, the report was finally lifted out of my hands, and I watched as the Sergeant's eyes moved over it. I could tell the contents baffled him—at least initially. He read it over several times, all the while looking from the report to my face and back down to the report again, as if he didn't quite understand how the two things he was seeing were connected. His brow knit itself, unknit, and then knit itself again. Finally, comprehension appeared to soak into him like water into a cloth. His shoulders unclenched, his posture straightened. There was a very still, very calm look in his eyes now—so still and calm as to be almost deadly. He cleared his throat.

"I see," he said in a low, quiet voice. We looked at each other for a long time, saying nothing. He understood now the totality of my offer, but had yet to accept. For a fleeting moment my throat thickened and I could not swallow, fearful I had violated his sense of propriety and that he was about to have me arrested. Truthfully, had that turn of events actually transpired, I might have drawn a strange comfort from it, as it would have confirmed my blind faith in the Sergeant's unwavering adherence to the rules. But his genuine consideration of my proposition quickly became apparent. "You understand this is highly unorthodox," he commented in a low voice. If there was a question in it, I did not respond. "What I mean to say is that this is not exactly in keeping with proper *protocol*. . . ." I nodded. "We must be absolutely certain we've got our man."

"I have no doubts," I said, and when I looked at the Sergeant I knew neither did he. I realized it was time to rally for my cause.

I gathered my poise and cleared my throat to speak. "I do not think I exaggerate," I said, "when I say the only thing more disgusting than this man's deeds—morally speaking—would be not answering to our consciences and allowing him to remain free." I did not say *as we have done so far,* but I could see the Sergeant was thinking it.

Further counsel on the matter was interrupted as the Lieutenant Detective came wandering back in our direction. "All right, all right," the Lieutenant Detective said, shaking out his shoulders and stretching his arms as if he had just completed a series of callisthenic exercises. "I'm sorry I let him get to me. Let's try it again."

"Frank," the Sergeant said, still speaking in that low, quiet voice. He gripped the Lieutenant Detective's shoulder in a confidential manner. "Frank, we got it right here." He handed the Lieutenant Detective the report, and the Lieutenant Detective read it over, the scar on his forehead creasing as he frowned at the typed confession.

"You got all this after I stepped out?"

The Sergeant looked at me and held my gaze for several seconds before answering. "Yes," he said in a steady tone. "We did."

At the mention of the word *we,* the Lieutenant Detective turned and took note of my presence anew, as if all morning long I had been nothing more than a piece of furniture, an extension of that very contraption by which I made my living. He raised an eyebrow. I suppose even then the accusation was already formulating, but the Lieutenant Detective only nodded and said nothing.

12

If I had it to do over, I would've put different things in the little journal I kept about Odalie's activities. In reading back some of the entries now, I see I've refrained from mentioning certain particulars about Odalie's business that might serve to exonerate me in my current position. Never in our time together did I completely cease to chronicle Odalie's activities in the little journal I kept, but I must admit that as the creeping heat of early summer reduced the perky spring tulips to nothing but the pronged, petalless stamens that drooped atop their rubbery stems, I had grown markedly less thorough in what I reported. Well, perhaps *thorough* is the wrong word. It might be more accurate to say I was still thorough in what I reported, yet was much more *selective*, thus allowing for strategic omissions. By then, I suppose it had dawned on me that there were some activities it was probably best not to inventory in my journal, as they might reflect poorly on Odalie's conduct, legally speaking, and I had grown rather protective of my friend.

As a result, my journal entries from that time (I am looking over them now) are perhaps a little fluffy and inconsequential, reading as they do a little like a ladies' magazine and focusing almost exclusively on the itemization of beauty and hygiene tips. Here are a few:

Today O purchased several pairs of stockings in that scandalous new "naked" shade Honey Beige. Bequeathed me a pair. Showed me how to fashionably apply powder to stockinged legs because shiny rayon is utterly obnoxious, she says. Legs should never be shinier than the chrome on a Model T, according to O.

Went to my first opera with O today. Have never seen such a fine theater before! Difficult to watch the opera itself and not simply gaze at all the well-groomed spectators dressed in their finest apparel, though must admit was a little disconcerted seeing that many diamonds on display. The show itself was a colorful yet somewhat ugly affair titled Pagliacci *about a clown who terrorizes his wife with jealousy. Afterward O and I talked about loyalty at great length; she seemed to understand completely my views on this, and it was a comfort to discover we might in fact see eye to eye. I knew I was not wrong in choosing her for my bosom friend!*

Today O and I stopped in at the beauty parlor. O got usual trim to keep her bob tidy. I got a wave. She suggested I might get my hair cut like hers someday so we could match, but I said I didn't know. Cannot see why girls these days are in such a hurry to chop off all their hair. I suppose they think it makes them appear brave. Shame they don't see it, but there's a rather large difference between brave and reckless. I did not say as much, but I rather like my long hair, and all the values that go along with it. Am beginning to realize

I'm more old-fashioned than perhaps I've admitted. And I believe, deep down where she doesn't show it, O is, too. Someday she will grow bored of the modern-girl life, and I intend to be there when she does. What a life we will have!

Tonight before O and I went out to the speakeasy O pinned my hair under to give me a taste of what it would be like to have hair as short as hers. Also applied rouge to my cheeks and lipstick to my lips. Despite myself, I was very excited to be dressed like O, as from the moment I met her I have wondered what it might be like to be her. A few times throughout the night different gentlemen approached, mistaking me for O—although this means it must've been very dark or else they were very inebriated, because I don't flatter myself to imagine I look much like O. Still, though, they approached, with a very friendly demeanor, whispering O's name. When I complained later about where they put their hands, she shrugged and laughed and simply said it was all a matter of wit, and if she could outsmart them then certainly so could I. Not so sure about that, because if I were her I would've known how to handle men like that, but instead of laughing them off and making them bring me drinks and stealing their cigarettes, I slapped their hands away like an uptight old maid and felt silly about it afterward anyway . . .

The temperature has been climbing steadily. O took me to the big fancy Lord & Taylor department store on 38th Street to go shopping for bathing costumes today, with the idea we might go to some garden parties and visit the beach out on the Sound. Together we picked out something I would never have previously considered in a hundred years. The nuns used to say the amount of flesh a girl is willing to expose is directly proportionate to the amount of black-ness in her heart and lack of character in her soul. But when I repeated this to Odalie, she looked horrified and amused all at the same time and suddenly I felt very small and stupid. She showed me how to roll the hems of the bathing costume down for the patrol-ling censors destined to be on the beach, and how to "peg" the hems so as to roll them up more fashionably when the censors aren't look-ing. In the end we bought matching bathing suits in a very athletic jersey-knit fabric, although it must be said she looks a fair sight better in hers than I do in mine. I could've looked at her in the fit-ting room glass all day, she looked so wonderful and vital and fresh—as though she were about to swan dive off the pedestal in the fitting room. At last—I can honestly say I feel I have a bosom friend, and I am so enamored of her! Oh, but I must stop talking about her this way. . . .

THERE ARE a great many more entries nearly indistinguishable from these; one gets the general picture. There are other entries, too, which I will refrain from repeating here. It suffices to say I see now I've spent quite a lot of time describing Odalie's person, down to the finest detail, and in so doing, I was quite effusive in my praise of her various features. It certainly wouldn't help matters to show these entries to the authorities. They've already got the wrong idea about my feelings for Odalie, and these entries would only serve to worsen this impression—I understand that now.

The lists of Odalie's paramours that I penned in my journal wouldn't lessen this impression much, either. As spring slid into summer, I became quite the little list-maker. I am looking at one such list right now. It reads:

April 16—*Harry Gibson*

April 20—*Neville Eagleston*

April 29—*Harry Gibson*

May 1—*Lonnie Eisenberg*

May 3—*Owen McKeill*

May 3 *(same night)*—*Harry Gibson*

May 10—*Jacob Isaacs*

May 15—*Gib again (after loud quarrel)*

May 23—*Bobby Allister*

June 4—*Gib again*

And so forth.

Perhaps you think me crude for keeping track of such activities. I suppose if I were a proper suffragette I would insist Odalie is "the mistress of her own body," as they say in all the birth control campaigns these days, and simply leave it at that. But never in my life have I passed myself off as a suffragette or pretended any great love for Margaret Sanger and those of her self-righteous ilk. I have no fascination with women who lobby for the political causes of the fairer sex—hunger strikes, marches in the street. All of that political nonsense holds no poignant allure for me, rankles no sense of outraged justice in my heart. I'm a far cry from a liberated woman. In fact, I'll go so far as to admit I can be a bit of a prude.

Of course, these lists aren't 100 percent accurate. There were many times when Odalie utterly vanished from whatever party or speakeasy we were attending, and there was no way of knowing where she went or what she did, and with whom. And there were times, too, when Odalie stayed out all night, returning to the apartment the next morning with just enough time to slip into fresh clothes and sip a cup of coffee at the breakfast table before having to be at the precinct.

Why did I like Odalie so much? I am still, even now, trying to formulate an answer to this question. When I found myself abandoned at a party, I never accused Odalie of being a bad girl-friend, though I might have been well within my rights to do so. Instead, I was quite the cool customer, if I do say so myself. By that time, I knew enough about Odalie's personality to understand it was imperative that I not be clingy, that I not make demands, or she would pull away from me permanently. And so I developed a routine. Whenever I realized Odalie had disappeared—one minute by my side, the next minute vanishing into a cloud of music, smoke, and shrieks of laughter—and it had become apparent she would not be reappearing anytime soon, I usually went home for the evening (alone, of course) and made a cup of tea. However, on one surprising evening as I was preparing to slip out and make my departure after finding myself once again sans Odalie, I became aware of a face watching me from a distance. The sight of it stopped me dead in my tracks. The familiar apparition crossed the room and came toward me.

"Fancy meeting you here."

"Lieutenant . . ." My voice trailed off. I was stunned.

"Given our surroundings, I really think it's best to consider abandoning your standing policy of austerity and call me Frank. At least for now," he said with a smile, throwing a cautious glance first over his left shoulder and then his right, making certain no one had heard.

But he needn't have bothered. No one was paying particular

attention to us. The crowd was engaged in its usual revelry. A bevy of girls appareled in dresses made entirely out of swinging strings of beads were shimmying atop a nearby table and attracting a great deal of attention. The beaded dresses were so reflective and bright, the girls' bodies shimmered with a watery mystique, like the opalescent scales of freshly caught trout. The room was dense with people, and I found myself at eye level with the Lieutenant Detective's chest as the crowd crushed us closer to each other. On instinct, I scanned the sea of faces for Gib, nervous as to how he might react to the Lieutenant Detective's presence. But he was otherwise occupied, frowning skeptically at a man doing amateur magic tricks for a small crowd that had gathered at one corner of the room. Near Gib's elbow I could make out the short, trilby-hatted shape of Redmond, waiting attentively for his boss's next batch of drink orders. For the moment, the Lieutenant Detective and I were adrift among the masses and utterly unobserved.

"Have you been following us?" I asked, recalling the strange sensation I'd felt while strolling around the city during the weeks previous. I'd noticed something had been amiss lately, some strange inkling causing me to cast a glance behind us as Odalie and I went about the town. It had felt like something was perpetually just out of sight—the flash of a familiar shape refracted in a shop window here and there, only to vaporize as soon as I tried to determine its location.

"Why would I do that?" It was a response, but hardly an answer, and I said so. He ignored my reproach, and after some minutes leaned in closer and touched my elbow in a confidential manner. "Listen," he said in a low voice. "I think it's best if you got out of here, and right away."

I didn't tell him I had been on the verge of making my

departure for the evening only some minutes before. His admoni-
tion had struck up something within me, something rough and
stubborn and flinty. Suddenly I had the urge to stay. I caught Redmond's eye and waved him over. The dwarf toddled in our direction, surprisingly deft at making his way through the milling
crowd. Soon enough he was at my side, his friendly, beady pupils
glinting up brightly from the dark purple shadows that perpetually ringed his eyes.

"'Lo, Miss Rose," Redmond said. "You look lovely tonight." I
appreciated the comment but did not let it go to my head; Redmond
was, rather like myself, always a creature of good manners.

"Why, thank you, Redmond," I said, borrowing Odalie's signature lilt with the inflection of my voice. "I think I could use another
champagne cocktail, seeing as how the night is still young."

"Course." Redmond threw a look in the Lieutenant Detective's
direction, but stopped just short of asking him if he also wanted a
drink. He waited a few moments for me to deliver an introduction
or friendly word, but when he read in my expression my utter lack
of welcome toward the Lieutenant Detective, Redmond shrugged
and turned to go. When it came to the mysteries of human behavior, Redmond was clever and had that particular blend of insight
and indifference that only those who are condescended to on a
regular basis possess.

"I'm not playing a game," the Lieutenant Detective said once
Redmond was out of earshot. "I really think you ought to get out
of here as soon as possible."

"Why? Because this is not a place for a *nice* girl to be?" I was
haughty now, indignant. "I bet . . . ," I began, but demurred, suddenly intimidated by what I had the urge to say. Then there was a
surge of spite and I decided to go ahead and finish the sentence. "I

bet you wouldn't mind bumping into *Odalie* here. You'll be sorry to hear, but she's already departed for the evening. And the gentleman who escorted her away for the evening appeared *very* entertaining." The Lieutenant Detective looked surprised, but not offended or displeased. He studied me briefly with a curious expression on his face.

"No, Rose, you don't understand." He put an arm around me, pulled me to his side, and pivoted my body so we were both looking in the direction of the entrance. "There's going to be a raid tonight, and I think it's best if you weren't here," he said in a low voice, as if to encourage me to concentrate on what was happening before me. My eyes began to focus on a handful of sour-faced men gathering there, the scattered group of them trying to appear nonchalant as they surveyed the room. All at once I took in the Lieutenant Detective's meaning. "We've dallied too much already; they're getting ready to close off the door and they're going to give the signal any minute. We've got to get you out of here."

We? Why was he helping me? I would've thought he'd have preferred to let them throw me in the clink and gloat at me behind the bars. But before I knew what was happening, the Lieutenant Detective had hold of my upper arm and was steering me through the room. My head jerked wildly about; I was trying to catch a glimpse of Gib or Redmond to see if they had detected the undercover policemen who were now positioning themselves in strategic corners of the speakeasy. As we drew near the entrance, I realized the Lieutenant Detective was going to have to explain about me.

"Wait," I said. I remembered something Odalie had shown me the last time we'd attended a speakeasy in this particular building. "There's a better way out." The Lieutenant Detective stopped and nodded. His grip on my arm loosened but did not relinquish altogether, and he allowed me to lead him in the direction of a tiny room in the back.

Once inside the back room, the Lieutenant Detective shot me a look of instant dismay. It was a small, claustrophobic room with shelves running along every wall, from floor to ceiling. The shelves were filled with unmarked bottles.

"Jesus, Rose, what is this? We don't have time for this."

"Hold on." I walked to one wall of bottles and looked for the empty one Odalie had shown me. I lifted one and looked behind it: nothing. I lifted another.

"Rose—"

"Ah!" Behind the last bottle I lifted was the handle I'd been searching for. I reached in and pulled it, but it was stubborn. A small shiver of panic ran through me. I gave it a stronger yank and suddenly felt its release. The bottle-laden shelf swung open on a pair of heavy-duty hinges as though it weighed nothing. I turned to the Lieutenant Detective. Through the dark I made out his eyes, wide and saucerlike as he took in the fact of the new exit that had materialized before him.

"I suppose I shouldn't be surprised." He shook himself and shifted back into command. "C'mon, let's go." Taking my elbow again he made to enter the passageway.

"I'm not entirely sure where it goes."

"Anywhere but here would do right now."

I was wearing a dress from Odalie that ended in a short pleated sailor's skirt with a gossamer overlay, and as the shelf of bottles swung shut behind us the gossamer floated up and got caught in the closing threshold. Too late, I tried to push back against the door. I heard the latch deploy with a heavy *thunk*.

"My skirt!" I said into the dark. The Lieutenant Detective produced a lighter from his jacket pocket, flicked it on over his head, and inspected the situation. Together we looked for a way to reopen the passageway door, but no opposing handle or latch could be perceived.

"All right. Hmm. Well." He took a breath and glanced up from my skirt to look me in the eye. "I'm awfully sorry about this," the Lieutenant Detective said, reaching into his back pocket.

"Sorry about what?"

Without answering, he produced a collapsible Opinel knife and flipped it open with one fluid snap of his wrist. At the sight of the blade, I involuntarily cringed and shrunk back.

"Take it easy." The Lieutenant Detective reached down to my skirt, gathered the cloth where it was now tethered to the doorway, and with one fast, hard slice, cut the fabric. I intuited the knife was very sharp, for the gossamer came away as though it were simply a piece of paper being torn in two. I was free. The remainder of my skirt drifted down, the freshly cut patch an awkward tuft that barely covered my derriere. "A shame," the Lieutenant Detective said, his mouth twisting into a strange variety of smile I had never before seen on his face. "It was a nice dress."

"I don't own it. It belongs to Odalie," I blurted awkwardly.

"Ah. Well, shall we?"

We walked the remainder of the tunnel in silence, the flame from the Lieutenant Detective's lighter guiding us along, casting the creepy elongated shapes of our own shadows on the tunnel walls as we progressed. At long last, we reached a wooden door. The Lieutenant Detective undid a series of bolts, locks that were only accessible from our side of the door, and suddenly we were met by a wet, humid blast of the hot summer night. We stepped out of the passageway and into a very nondescript alley. I realized I had no idea where I was.

"Clever," the Lieutenant Detective commented, still inspecting the door we had just exited. "All the doors lock from the inside. You can leave but never enter. Perfect for getaways."

"You sound admiring."

"I am."

"Did you organize the raid tonight?" I asked.

The Lieutenant Detective looked at me and held my gaze for several seconds. There was a full moon out and I could see the cold, clear blue of his eyes and the waxy-smooth skin of the scar on his forehead glistening in the silvery light.

"No," he said finally. He shrugged. "I don't disapprove of places like . . . like this." I didn't answer, and he continued, abruptly stumbling forward in a jittery voice. "Actually, I have a theory." His eyebrows shot up in a nervous gesture, as though he were about to commit high treason and was somewhat exhilarated at his own boldness. "See, my theory is society needs places like these. Places to let the steam off, you know? Prohibition isn't practical. It simply turns more citizens into criminals." A long silence followed, and the shoulders that had been hunched with excitement as he'd chattered now sagged. I believe he knew what my next question was going to be before I asked it.

"Then why—"

"Why did I agree to come along on the raid tonight?"

I nodded.

He shrugged and looked distantly toward the end of the alley. "I dunno." He returned his gaze to me and hesitated, as if weighing what he was about to say next. Then he gave a guilty grin and waved one hand in the direction of my snipped skirt. "I suppose you never know when you might come to the aid of a damsel in distress."

It was a line. But I had no idea why the Lieutenant Detective would try a line on me and found myself a little shocked. More shocking still was how, once he'd said it, the Lieutenant Detective looked down at the pavement and shuffled his feet awkwardly. I couldn't believe he might be in earnest. The ladylike reaction would be to feel sympathy for his awkward overtures, no matter how gauche they might be, but I didn't. Perhaps it is telling that my natural reaction to the Lieutenant Detective's confession was that of a cat reacting to the discovery of a wounded field mouse.

"Of course. I forgot to thank you for making a shambles of my dress." It came out of my mouth with even more of a sarcastic bite than I'd intended. But instead of apologizing, I found myself rubbing it in further with a bitter, mocking little curtsy.

"*Odalie's* dress," he corrected me with an equally belligerent air. I glared at him midcurtsy, and he glared back. Our eyes locked once again, but this time by a sudden feral flash of white-hot anger. We remained like that for several minutes, as though the silvery light of the moon had petrified us and transformed us into two stone statues caught midsnarl. But curiously, the clenched musculature of our two faces suddenly, and in simultaneous synchronicity, began to loosen and slide into a pair of mirrored grins. I was surprised to hear my own voice laughing along with the Lieutenant Detective's.

When our laughter had subsided, I was very aware that the Lieutenant Detective had inched a few steps closer. On instinct, I leaned away. "I ought to be getting back to our apartment. You know, to deliver the bad news to Odalie about her dress." I was suddenly very eager to make my farewells and get away, not only because the increasing proximity of the Lieutenant Detective made me uncomfortable, but because I was nervous he might attempt to see me home. By then everyone at the precinct was aware of the fact Odalie and I had become room-mates, but I had been careful to keep the location and luxury of the apartment a secret. I didn't want to slip up and botch things simply because the silly young detective before me fancied himself a gentleman.

"I thought you said she'd already found a suitable . . . ahem, *diversion* for the evening."

"She's likely at home already," I lied in a haughty voice. The Lieutenant Detective ceded two steps of the borderland between us. "She's probably wondering where I am."

"Then we ought to get you home." He began pacing in the direction of the alley entrance and gave a heavy sigh. I knew I couldn't let him see Odalie's apartment, but when he put down my protests with a surprisingly concise, forceful air, I realized he was going to escort me either way, and I elected to save my protests for another time. And when we heard the long, plaintive *WAHHHH* of police sirens moving in the direction of the speakeasy's innocuous entrance, I was secretly glad for the respectable company.

13

Upon turning the key in the lock, I was shocked to find Odalie actually home. I hadn't really expected her to be. She was swathed in a bathrobe made out of several layers of sheer, sapphire-blue material, and her lanky, catlike body was stretched out at length on the emerald-and-white striped upholstery of the divan. The heat of the day still lingered in the room and Odalie had thrown open the windows to let in the night air. The gauzy white curtains hanging in the window sashes somehow enhanced the overall feline impression of the scene by lifting on the breeze and giving an intermittent, syncopated flick—very much in the tempo of an annoyed housecat idling her tail. In contrast to the inky night sky that loomed in the windowpanes behind her, Odalie looked very vivid and bright where she reclined on the divan in a study of jewel tones.

She was reading a magazine and eating chocolate-covered cherry cordials from a silken confectioner's box. Odalie had a peculiar way of eating sweets. It differed vastly from Helen's method. Helen ate her penny candies with a guilty, surreptitious air that put you in mind of a paranoid squirrel desperate to secure

a nut before some bird or larger animal came along and forced it
to share. In an opposite manner, Odalie ate her chocolates languidly, haphazardly. Sometimes she ate with an indifferent, distracted demeanor, holding whatever treat was in her hand with a
slack wrist, a thing already forgotten as she squinted more closely
at the latest hats from Paris. Other times she put her whole body
into it. She was not afraid to *mmm* and *ohh* when she judged something particularly tasty. With Helen, the candy itself seemed like
the valuable thing, whereas on the other hand with Odalie, the
valuable thing seemed like her *reaction* to the candy. Perhaps
these differences are emblematic of yet another class difference to
which I was uninitiated. After all, Helen was stingy with her candies because they were in limited supply. Odalie, however, could
afford to be generous and perhaps even a little wasteful. Over the
months we lived together, I'd retrieved numerous half-eaten boxes
of chocolates from under Odalie's bed, only to cluck my tongue
and deposit them in the waste bin because they had grown a furry
whitish-green mantle of mold due to exposure and neglect.

"Oh!" she said when she looked up and saw us. I could tell she
was very surprised to discover a man standing in her foyer. She
was especially startled that it was the Lieutenant Detective, but I
think she would have been at least a little surprised by any man at
all. I had never brought a gentleman to the apartment before, and
I was still smarting from the sting of humiliation brought on by
the countless smirks and raised eyebrows of the hotel staff who
witnessed our entry as we'd made our way through the lobby and
into the elevator. Despite my repeated protests, the Lieutenant
Detective had insisted on seeing me all the way to the front door.
Now he stood loitering in the foyer, staring into the sitting room
with his mouth slightly agape. I believe he was a little stunned by

the trip upstairs and was still deciding what to make of the plush lobby, the golden elevators, and the fashionably decorated apartment in which he currently found himself. Odalie shot me a look of reproach; I understood by allowing the Lieutenant Detective to escort me home I had violated my oath to keep her living situation a secret. She was clearly not at all pleased with this development. But just as soon as her features stiffened with anger, she regained herself and they melted back into a repose of welcoming ease. She rose lithely to greet us.

"Goodness. Well, Lieutenant Detective, you'd better come in and make yourself at home."

"I was only seeing to it Rose got home safely."

"Nonsense. You're here now. Stay a bit." The Lieutenant Detective staggered forward in a daze as Odalie hooked her arm through his and sat him on the divan where she'd been lounging just seconds before. He seemed acutely aware of this latter fact and scooted politely so he was perched on the outermost edge of the upholstered seat. She gave him an assessing look, her mouth involuntarily wriggling in a way I understood meant she was deciding how to regain control of the situation. I knew she would be unsettled until she had extracted a tacit guarantee that the Lieutenant Detective wouldn't give away her secret, and to do so first she needed to size him up. "I could offer you something to drink," she said. He looked at her. "Something to calm your nerves," she said. It was clear she did not mean coffee or tea, and he seemed to understand his acceptance of a cocktail would in fact calm his hostess's nerves.

"Sure."

As Odalie got up to mix the drinks, the Lieutenant Detective's eyes followed her, and I took the opportunity to sneak down the hall and into her bedroom to change my clothes. If Odalie had taken note of the brutally shredded hemline of the dress I'd borrowed, either she did not care or did not care to comment. I knew it was not likely she would say anything to reproach me. Nonetheless I felt guilty, having ruined something I knew I could not afford to replace. From the other room the spurt of the seltzer bottle sounded in several staccato blasts. In the months after I'd moved in, Odalie and I had taken to sharing one big closet and I stood before it now, studying its contents. As I rooted about for something to wear I heard Odalie bring a tray of drinks to the coffee table, the ice tinkling as she crossed the room. The sharp fragrance of fresh lime drifted from the sitting room into the bedroom, and I guessed she'd elected to make gin rickeys. Odalie, never one to drink the concoctions of ethanol and juniper syrup sold in the speakeasies—commonly referred to as bathtub gin— had very likely used the last of the bottle of real English gin we kept in the kitchenette bar (it was destined to mysteriously replace itself the very next day). Curiously, my mouth watered in anticipation, a phenomenon I'd never experienced before, being something of an amateur drinker myself.

I stared at the wall of hanging clothes and tried to hurry up. If the Lieutenant Detective had diplomatically gone home like proper decorum dictated, the decision would have been simple and I would've put on my nightgown, ready to be comfortable for the evening. But I ruled this out immediately. My regular nightgown was not an improper garment, per se. In fact it possessed certain features reminiscent of the sexless nightshirts we were made to wear in the orphanage: bleached white linen of a coarse and scratchy variety, a high starched neck, and long sleeves with string-pulls that cinched at the wrists. But I knew I'd rather die than have the Lieutenant Detective see me in any nightgown, let alone that particular one. I searched about for something more suitable.

"That's a very nice pair of bracelets," I overheard the Lieutenant Detective remark to Odalie. Immediately I knew the ones he meant. She hadn't been wearing them earlier, but I had spotted them twinkling on her wrists when we walked in the door. The baubles in question were a pair of diamond bracelets, the like of which I'd never seen in my admittedly provincial life. They were far out of the range of anything I ever glimpsed in Mrs. Lebrun's jewelry box as she taught me how to properly clean precious stones and their settings. I will probably never see anything to rival Odalie's bracelets ever again. Most curious to me at the time was the fact I'd never seen Odalie wear them out. Instead, she had a queer habit of putting them on when she stayed in, wearing them around the apartment the way another sort of woman might wear a housecoat.

"Are they real?" he asked. I heard Odalie laugh, the musical peals of her voice striking a perfectly ambiguous note, implying *yes, of course* and *no, don't be silly* all at the same time. I had wondered about the answer to this question myself, but had never been so bold as to ask. Finally, I found something of my own buried deep in the closet. I threw on a very plain blue cotton dress and made my way back to the sitting room, but hovered in the doorway, just out of sight, peering in on them from a vantage point where they were not likely to notice me.

"Do you know," she leaned in excitedly, "they were a gift; I've never asked whether or not they're real." She laughed again. I noticed she had pronounced the word *gift* sharply, like it had a bitter bite to it. The Lieutenant Detective also did not fail to notice this.

"That so? A gift?"

"Yes. Well. An *engagement present*, to be more precise."

"Oh, forgive me. I was under the impression you were . . ." He reached around for the most inoffensive word and found none. ". . . a bachelorette," he finally concluded, feminizing the more familiar (and notably less offensive) masculine term. Odalie smiled, pleased and Sphinx-like.

"I am."

"Oh, I beg your pardon. Again."

Odalie did not reply to this last comment and instead stretched her wrists out in front of the Lieutenant Detective's eyes. "But they really are something, aren't they." It was not a question. She rolled her wrists slowly to the left and then to the right, allowing the diamonds to shoot off the full color spectrum of their tiny prismatic flares. He gazed at them with appreciation.

"I've never seen a woman wear bracelets on both wrists, matching like that."

The bitter bite came back into the shape of her mouth as she smiled at the Lieutenant Detective's impressed countenance and gave a brittle laugh. "Yes. They look a little like . . . like *handcuffs*, don't they?" She crossed her wrists together and posed. The Lieutenant Detective started at this grim comparison and glanced at Odalie in surprise. She leaned closer to him. "In fact, I'll let you in on a secret: That's what engagement presents always are, in one way or another." She cocked her head playfully, but there was something dark, too, in her demeanor. I felt the prickle of something proprietary awaken in me, but I wasn't entirely certain to which party this feeling was directed.

I held my breath as Odalie reduced the inches of empty space between them. "Doll a thing up all you want, but you still can't change what it is. *A rose by another other name...*" she said coquettishly. Hearing the homonym of my name stung my ears somewhat. "Do you think any of the suspects down at the precinct would be envious if they knew my handcuffs are fancier than theirs?" Odalie was grinning wolfishly now, her rouged lips stretched wide over the white of her teeth, her body almost touching the Lieutenant Detective. Suddenly the urge to enter the room overcame me. I coughed.

Their attention snapped in my direction, a couple of woodland creatures frozen instantly upon realizing they are not alone in the forest. The Lieutenant Detective's face colored up to his ears, and he rose reactively from the divan.

"Oh! Yes. Well. I should be going. I'm quite glad to have seen you home safely, Miss Baker."

"Thank you, Lieutenant Detective. For all your . . ." I searched for the right word, lamely shrugged, and finally murmured, ". . . *assistance.*" I hadn't meant it sarcastically, but I could tell that was how he took it. He straightened his spine in an aggrieved manner that simultaneously suggested he felt truly sorry for the events of the night—for having been caught making eyes at Odalie, for having ruined the dress, perhaps even for the raid itself. He reached for his hat.

"Oh, but *Frank*, stay awhile. You haven't finished your drink," Odalie complained, gesturing to the glass still half full with gin rickey. She reached a hand up to tug playfully at his jacket sleeve.

There was a familiar ease about the way Odalie pronounced the Lieutenant Detective's given name; it was as though she had said it that way many times over already. As I took in the image of the two of them there in the sitting room, it occurred to me the Lieutenant Detective did not look so overwhelmed and disconcerted by his surroundings as I had originally thought. For the first time a certain suspicion began to form itself in my head.

"No, no. It's late, and I've already had more than my fill tonight, no need to tank up before going home." Still standing where he had abruptly leapt to his feet from the divan, he made a halfhearted attempt to smooth his rumpled suit. Despite his best efforts, the suit still hung on him in its signature slouchy manner. I suppose I had always known there was something of the handsome rogue about the Lieutenant Detective, but just at that moment, as he looked up at me with the scar on his forehead furrowed in the lamplight and a crooked grin forming on his lips, I began to see why he was so often fussed over when he found himself in the company of ladies.

"Besides," he added, "it's been quite an eventful evening." At this, Odalie looked at him askance. "I'll let Rose—beg pardon, I mean Miss Baker—recount the particulars."

Odalie saw him to the door. "The other way . . . to your right," I heard her call softly as he went the wrong direction to find his way back to the elevator. The suspicion that had hatched itself in my brain only minutes earlier subsided a bit. I don't believe his disorientation was the product of too much drink. It was his first visit to the hotel, as far as I knew, and people often found themselves overwhelmed upon their premier visit to Odalie's apartment.

Odalie came back into the sitting room, and from the shift in her manner it was immediately clear she was expecting a thorough debriefing on the subject of my recent interaction with the Lieutenant Detective. "It was very *nice* of him to see you home like that," she said. She threw her body over the divan like a wet blanket. There was something perpetually fluid about her movements, even in spite of the fact she was mostly long lines and hard angles. For months now I'd been trying to understand this paradox, and I knew I was not the first to try to puzzle it out.

"And don't worry," she continued once I had failed to reply. "I won't get too cozy with him." I knew right away this was a lie. She leaned forward from the divan and reached to pat the back of my hand where it rested on my knee. "I can tell you wouldn't want me to." There was an excitement in her voice the way she said it, and I realized the Lieutenant Detective had very recently gained an element of true appeal in Odalie's eyes. But it didn't matter to me just then, as there was another matter of great importance at hand.

"Odalie," I tentatively began. "There was a raid at the club tonight."

She was in the midst of taking a sip from the Lieutenant Detective's leftover gin rickey. She spat it out in a fine mist, and the piney scent of gin and citrus lime hit the air. Within seconds she was on the telephone, barking out one 'phone number after another at a very flustered operator, who—I gathered from the sound of it—kept returning on the line with the unacceptable news that none of the parties requested could be reached.

14

The Sergeant had said *we*. When the Lieutenant Detective asked if the Sergeant had somehow managed, in a very expedited manner and against all odds, to obtain Mr. Vitalli's confession, the Sergeant had looked at me (with meaning!) and had said, *We did.* I felt those two simple words had never borne more weight.

You see, in the years I'd known the Sergeant, he was never a man given to frequent use of the word *we*. His habit of stinginess with that particular word only made my respect for him grow in weight and size. I suppose that's fairly common; we always value those individuals who make us feel it is really something to have their friendship, to belong in their club. The Sergeant had a very precise mental ruler by which he measured people. He never hid it from you if you did not measure up, and he did not give a fig for how it made you feel. In his mind, that was not his problem; it was yours.

I say this now because when he gave me that look and said *we*, I knew it meant something. I knew it was a moment of great significance! I believed with my whole heart the Sergeant was a man who always did things by the book, and here he was condescending to bend the rules with me. With *me*! I knew he had a very strong sense of moral justice and it was only in the most extreme of circumstances and only with very special, like-minded individuals that he would ever dare to force Lady Justice's hand. I don't particularly care for the word *vigilante,* for it has a particularly anarchical and rebellious sound to it and as such does not suit the Sergeant at all. I believe the Sergeant was something more finely wrought, something acutely attuned to a higher call. And you may call me a fool, but I believe—or rather, I *believed,* as the past tense is more accurate here—when he used the word *we* it was his way of saying, *Why yes, Rose, we are cut from the same cloth.*

I know I have said it before, but I will say it again: You mustn't think there was anything improper going on between the Sergeant and myself. There were absolutely no, shall we say, *exchanges* between us. Nor did I ever "give him the check to cash later," as Odalie was often wont to say of the promises she'd made to those suitors whose desires she did not wish to immediately gratify. No, the bond that united the Sergeant and myself was of a much more pure variety. In addition to being a role model in the professional sense, he was a husband and a father, and although I admit I was sometimes inordinately curious and disdainful about the creature who was his wife (a woman whom, by the by, I have never met), I did not necessarily want him to stop being these things. Nor did I want him to be anything less than a man of his word. I did not imagine myself his mistress. Why yes, on a few (very rare!) occasions, I had let myself imagine what it might be like to be married to the Sergeant, to have him come home and eat a meal I'd prepared especially for him, to have his handlebar mustache tickle my skin as he leaned in to kiss my cheek. To have his handlebar mustache tickle me, full stop. Oh! But I can assure you, I entertained these fantasies very sparingly, and only on special occasions.

Of course, I never let on that such images ran through my head. At work I was always the model of proper decorum and professional courtesy. Although it was plain to everyone that I'd lately fallen in with Odalie and her lot, I nonetheless believe the Sergeant knew I was not susceptible to becoming some sort of wanton flapper or else some despicable gangster's moll. There had never been an abundance of words between us, but we'd never needed them. I'd always felt he'd known me straightaway, from the moment of that first interview. And in typing up Mr. Vitalli's confession, I knew I had done something that went well beyond professional courtesy. Neither of us was particularly religious, but I think in some strange way we shared the abstract belief we were doing God's work. We were two morally upright souls, ridding the world of another foul injustice. I thought of the Sergeant and myself as being a bit cleaner than the other people around us, and somehow above the dirtier politics of life. Naturally, for all these reasons and more, I was very nervous about coming into the precinct after the raid on the speakeasy.

Odalie had been unable to do very much over the telephone on the night of the raid. The largest chunk of information she'd been able to procure had come from a fourteen-year-old street urchin named Charlie Whiting who sometimes delivered messages for Gib and Odalie. Charlie was paid to sit in a back room and answer the telephone like an office boy and write down cryptic orders like *Philadelphia, 110* (which Charlie usually spelled "Filladelfeea") or sometimes *Baltimore, 50* (which Charlie usually spelled "Bawlamore"). Charlie had emerged from the back room that night to deliver a message to Gib, and afterward had stuck around to see if he could get away with a few swallows of gin before somebody disapprovingly remarked upon his age. He was a smallish, almost elfin boy, petite even for a fourteen-year-old, and had always loudly lamented this fact. But in the confusion of the raid, Charlie had benefited from his smaller stature and had managed to slip out a basement window.

It was almost dawn when we received a very apologetic knock at our door—the 'phone line was tied up, the bell-boy explained, and we were needed downstairs to dispense with the rather youthful "guest" who had come to call upon us. Standing in the echoing cathedral of the lobby with his newsboy cap tipped far back on his head as he gazed in awe at his present surroundings, Charlie appeared smaller and younger than ever. But Odalie clearly cared nothing for the impressionable fragility of true youth. She marched right up to him and snapped her fingers in his upward-gazing face, in response to which he blinked as though coming out of a hypnotic trance. Almost immediately Odalie began reeling off a list of names, counting them down one by one on her fingers. To each name Charlie alternately said *yes, no,* or else *think so, ma'am* to indicate who had been "pinched" by the police, as he phrased it. By the time the sun had risen and we were dressed and headed to the precinct for a new day of work, Odalie had drafted together a sort of makeshift partial list.

When we arrived that morning at the precinct, Odalie fixed herself a cup of coffee and walked very slowly in the direction of the holding cell, tacitly gazing into the bars with a casual air. It was as though she were a visitor strolling down the salon of a large echoing museum, coolly contemplating the lesser-known works of a great master. Equally passive and reserved were Gib, Redmond, and the many other prominent faces I recognized from the speak-easy. Unflinching, they held Odalie's gaze but remained silent, not a single one of them giving the slightest indication they were already acquainted with the woman staring at them from the other side of the bars. I intuited a whole conversation was taking place, despite the fact not a word was spoken. I resolved I would watch Odalie closely that day, curious as to what her plan would be. It was a sure bet she had a plan.

Of course I was a little on edge about my own fate that morning; I was very aware of the fact I had been at the selfsame speak-easy that was now at the center of scrutiny. Although I had deduced from the tacit exchange of looks between Odalie and the men in the holding cell that her anonymity was assured, it was not entirely clear mine would likewise be maintained. Even the Lieutenant Detective was a source of worry for me, as he had neither made any of the arrests, nor explained to anybody at the precinct why he was suspiciously absent at the time the raid went into effect. I fretted over what he would say. Would my name be mentioned? I knew him to be a man who was quite content to stretch the truth when it aided his cause, but I doubted he would feel comfortable telling the Sergeant a handful of outright lies.

But as it turned out, all my fretting on this particular score was for nothing. A wave of relief swept over me when I was told the Lieutenant Detective had telephoned earlier that morning and would not be coming in. He reported that a sudden and very uncomfortable stomach illness had forced his early departure from the raid, and as it had not yet subsided he was going to have to absent himself from the precinct for the day. If I had to make a conjecture on the matter, I would guess lying is very likely less difficult when it is done over the telephone. It is interesting to me how technology has in many ways facilitated and refined the practice of deception.

Somehow Odalie got herself assigned to each and every case that bore any relation to the speakeasy. They started with Gib, as I predicted they would. It was one of the Sergeant's clever interview tactics. The formula of it was simple, and he always did the same thing: He started with "the big fish," as he called it, and had a dialogue about what the consequences might be if the big fish didn't come clean. Then the big fish was redeposited to the holding cell and left to grow increasingly nervous as one by one, smaller fry were extracted and escorted to the interrogation room. By the end of the day the big fish was usually talking, fearful the smaller fish had already given him up. I was sure Odalie would lose her cool when they hauled Gib from the holding cell, roughly shoving him as they did. But she never broke. Odalie never showed the slightest sign of elevated interest. Instead, she got up, coolly gathered together some files and rolls of stenotype paper, and *clack-clack-clack*ed in her high heels down the hall in calm pursuit of the Sergeant.

And then it happened.

I say *it* happened because still to this day I am not entirely sure what Odalie did, although now with the advantage of hindsight I have a handful of very strong theories. What I *do* know for certain is this: Fifteen minutes after Odalie followed Gib and the Sergeant into the interrogation room, we heard footsteps coming down the hall and, surprised that someone should emerge so soon, turned to look. We were further surprised when our eyes met with the sight of Gib, alone and moving in a casual stroll in the direction of the precinct entrance. Every head in the precinct turned to watch him. He was apparently free to go. I remember he was almost merry about it, which was in keeping with his character, for after all Gib always *did* enjoy having a good gloat. With an air of arrogant simplicity, he whistled a cheerful tune and slid his charcoal gray fedora back into place on his head, cocking the brim ever so slightly to one side in the style he customarily wore it. He pushed through the front door with a jaunty swing of his shoulder, and the last trace we saw of him was the silhouette of his hat bobbing in a series of disjointed flashes as his image broke up through the tessellated glass of the precinct's entrance door. With every passing second his shape grew further shattered as he ambled down the stairs of the stoop and away from the building.

I glanced around the room and made eye contact with Marie, who was filing reports on the other side of the room. Though she had always been a heavyset woman, it seemed like overnight Marie had grown very visibly pregnant, her belly already straining at the fabric of her dress with the queer, perfectly smooth roundness of a balloon. Her watery blue eyes were made more blue by the blotchy redness of her complexion. Even her posture had shifted all of a sudden; she stood with one hand or the other almost always balled into a fist and pushing into her lower back, wedged into her flesh deeply as if to leverage her spine. She caught my eye, rolled her bottom lip out, and shrugged, as if to say, *Who knows what these men are about? He looked guilty to me, too.* Then she returned to her filing.

In the wake of Gib's exit, the din of noise around me resumed itself. I couldn't help but wonder what Odalie had possibly said in order to secure Gib's release, for surely she must've said something to the Sergeant that made him agree to let Gib go in good conscience. At the time, it only made sense to me that Odalie must've had to cook up something rather elaborate in order to convince the

Sergeant, as after all the Sergeant was an upright man and would have little tolerance for anything that sounded remotely like tomfoolery. Sure, I thought, he had collaborated with me when it came to helping Vitalli's confession along, but that was something altogether different. As I've said, the Sergeant and I shared a bond, and together we answered to a higher calling. The affair with Vitalli was a matter of ensuring justice did not slip through the cracks, as it is all too often wont to do. I could not let myself believe for a second it would not be the same with the Sergeant and Odalie. No, I thought, Odalie must've had to trot out the best stuff her imagination had to offer, but Odalie was nothing if not creative.

Of course I felt a little funny about this, given my loyalty to the Sergeant. Odalie was tricking him, and after all, that is what she had come to the precinct to do. By that time, I had come to accept what I already knew to be the truth. The rumors had been right about Odalie—or at least half right. She had taken the typing position at our precinct in order to manipulate the system, but the bootlegger she was ultimately protecting was herself. Please don't misunderstand; I don't mean to imply I only just then comprehended that fact. I am not an utter dunce. From the very first night Odalie had taken me into the speakeasy, even when I thought perhaps she was a mere attendee and not its ringleader, I understood the simple truth that Odalie was in fact a woman who walked both sides of the law. What I didn't realize is that by putting my hand in hers and crossing into that very first blind, I *myself* had become a woman who walked both sides of the law. On the day after the raid, as Odalie pulled some sort of ruse on the Sergeant in order to free her cohorts, I could hardly raise an objection.

Whatever it was Odalie said to the Sergeant, it proved effective. For the remainder of the afternoon, the exoneration that had allowed Gib to gloat all the way to the front door and down the precinct stoop was reissued several times for a number of the other men in the holding cell. Their handling became routine: a brief questioning session followed immediately by a prompt and perfunctory release. Suspects that had been arrested at the speakeasy went into the interrogation room with Odalie and the Sergeant and reemerged after no more than ten or fifteen minutes, only to saunter through the main floor of the precinct and sail out the front door.

I suppose I should have been happy to see it, and it should have been cause for celebration. There was one moment, one moment I remember ever so clearly, when Redmond was released (no thanks to my own efforts), and he walked by my desk and looked me in the eye with a scowl on his face that said, *Thank you but no thank you, Miss Rose—oh, I see how far you'd go for your "friends,"* and I felt a small tremor of relief wash over me that Odalie had been successful in setting these men free. I felt truly bad about Redmond. The last exchange we'd had was my drink order, and then I'd gone and disappeared right before the raid, leaving him to his own devices. And I'd only very narrowly missed being pinched by the police myself, and if I'd been nabbed I'm certain desperation for my own freedom would've overcome any moral high ground I can possibly claim. When I saw Redmond released, I felt glad for a moment, and considered that perhaps what Odalie was doing wasn't so bad after all.

LATER THAT EVENING, with the events of the workday finally behind us, we took a taxi back to the apartment. Since moving in with Odalie, I hadn't so much as set foot in a subway car. We always took taxi-cabs to and from work. I thought of this now and realized the image of the many subway platforms I had previously haunted lingered only faintly in my memory, and it was as though I had dreamed them. I stared thoughtfully out the taxi window as we rolled along the Manhattan streets and worked up my nerve to ask Odalie what she had told the Sergeant to secure the men's releases.

"What do you mean?" she asked.

"You know. I mean, what was the line? It must've been something quite sturdy; the Sergeant is not an easy man to convince."

Odalie turned her head from the window and regarded me carefully. I had never directly questioned her about the stories she told; my pulse quickened as I worried I had perhaps just violated the pact of complicity between us. But Odalie's response surprised me. "Rose," she said, "you put altogether too much faith in the Sergeant. You really oughtn't." She returned her gaze to the skyscrapers rolling steadily by. "You'd do better to remember, my dear, he's only a man," she murmured somewhat distractedly.

I did not question her further on the subject, but Odalie's enigmatic statement plagued me for the rest of the evening. An uneasy feeling descended upon me every time I tried to puzzle out what Odalie had meant about the Sergeant. I became resolved not to think on it, but I was only somewhat successful in this resolution, as it remained niggling at the back of my brain. You see, doubt is a magnificently difficult pest of which to try and rid oneself, and is worse than any other kind of infestation. It can creep in quietly and through the tiniest of cracks, and once inside, it is almost impossible to ever completely remove.

After dinner, I spent the evening alone in my room attempting

to distract myself by reading books and listening to the phonograph. Five Mozart records and nine chapters of *The Scarlet Letter*
later, my mind was no closer to peace. With a sigh, I switched off
the electric lamp and crawled into bed. It was past midnight and I
was tired, but exhaustion had crept too far into my bones, and now
sleep was reluctant to come. I grew frustrated. I'd always had the
gift of falling asleep as soon as my head hit the pillow, and sleep
was one of the very sweet reliefs I'd come to count upon. In fact,
there were only two times I could recall having difficulty falling
asleep during all my years at the orphanage. Both times, Adele
had sensed my frustration and kept a vigil with me, keeping me
occupied with fairy stories in an attempt to induce drowsiness.
Once, she'd even snuck into the kitchen and warmed up a lovely
concoction of milk, cinnamon, and nutmeg for me to drink down.

Remembering this, I thought of the sizable and well-appointed
kitchen in our apartment and how generously stocked it always
was (Odalie had a standing order that fresh groceries be delivered
every third day). Very likely, I might find all the ingredients I
needed to re-create Adele's soothing cure—milk, cinnamon, nutmeg. I slid my feet into my slippers and padded toward the kitchen.
But as I crossed the apartment and turned into the kitchen, I discovered the light was already on, and somebody was already in
there.

"Oh!" said Odalie. "Well, fancy meeting you here." She was
dressed in a creamy off-white satin robe. The way she wore it, it
looked more like an evening gown than a robe. I observed the
manner in which it hugged her body in some places and strategi-
cally draped in others. She gave a girlish little laugh and took my
hand in hers as if we had just bumped into each other in a busy
uptown restaurant. As her tanned wrists emerged from her sleeves,

I noticed she was wearing the diamond bracelets again. It was curious to me; I wondered what mysterious urge had prompted her to slip them on. "Sandman hasn't come to fetch you for a date yet?"

I gave a skeptical grunt. "It appears I've been stood up," I said in a dry voice, volleying back the metaphor. "You, too?"

"Yes. But I have just the thing!" I sank into a kitchen chair and looked to where she stood at the stove. Something seemed incongruous, and as I blinked my weary eyes I realized I had never before seen Odalie standing in front of any kitchen appliance, let alone one in active operation. The aroma of cinnamon hit my nose and I started, surprised to smell a version of the very concoction I had come into the kitchen planning to make. "Trust me, this is divine," she said as she poured the contents of a saucepan into two mugs. She put one in front of me, where a snail's trail of stream curled upward to my nostrils.

"Careful, it's hot," she said unnecessarily as I lifted the mug. I blew across the lip of it to show her my willingness to be patient. She slipped into the kitchen chair across from me. My eyes took stock of her as we waited for our bedtime toddies to cool. She looked quite composed, even at such an ungodly hour. Her complexion was tanned and smooth, her inky black bob as shiny as if it had been freshly brushed. I had never noticed the fundamental disproportion of her features before: Her eyes were quite large, her mouth was quite small, and everything clustered toward the center of her face, as if all were bound eventually for the tidy rosebud shape of her lips. I felt a shiver of admiration, laced—as most admiration tends to be—with a tiny hint of envy. And then my eyes fell upon her wrists again.

"They're quite something, aren't they?" she said, catching me looking at the bracelets. They were indeed. I nodded. For a fleeting second I thought to ask her about the fiancé who had given them to her, the one she'd mentioned in passing to the Lieutenant Detective. But before the question made its way from my brain to my lips, Odalie spoke up of her own accord. "We were given them, my sister and I," she said, pushing the bracelet on her left wrist around with an idle finger. I stared at her incredulously. Slowly, my mind began to absorb the fact that my eavesdropping had gone undetected. Odalie did not think for a second I'd heard what she'd told the Lieutenant Detective, this much was clear. She had no plans to tell me the story of acquiring the bracelets as an engagement present. She sighed and continued.

"It was our legacy. My father gave one to me, and one to my sister," she explained. As she pronounced the word *sister,* a very theatrical and forlorn expression came over her face. I stifled an indignant snort. Surely she was joking, I thought. I had seen just such an expression on Helen's face many times, albeit with a much more amateurish execution. But she sighed again and I realized this was no practical joke. "He was something of a gambler, I suppose. Made a lot of money in steel, but then lost it all on the railroads." I felt for a fleeting second I was reading the latest headline in the *Times.* "He died when we were still very young," she said, her face solemn as the grave itself, "and left us only these—one for each of us. We wore them everywhere. It was as though they twinned us. We made all sorts of dramatic oaths to each other that we would never take them off." She laid a finger over the swath of diamonds twinkling around her wrist. "Of course, he also left us with his debt," she said, and smiled bitterly with that sort of tenacious, impecunious glee that suggests the bearer has known far more long nights and lean days than you have. "Her name was Violet," Odalie said. "And she was sweet and lovely, just like the very flower of her name." She pondered the meaning of this sentence, as though it was only just now washing over her anew. "Oh—like you!" she said, feigning sudden realization of the floral-themed similarity of my name. And then Odalie became quite serious. The corners of her mouth turned downward, something I'd never seen them do. It was a very unnatural pose for her features. "Violet took great care of me, made many sacrifices."

Her calculation was deliberate, and very precise. When she made statements like this, it left her listener to wonder what those sacrifices were, and to assume the worst. It was as though a shaft of heavenly light descended to illuminate the momentary apparition that was Odalie's imaginary saint of a sister. The long, plaintive notes of a string instrument would've completed the picture.

"You know, I have always felt the love of women was much truer than the love of men," she said, looking directly into my eyes. "Do you know what I mean?" I gave a polite nod. As she took a breath, her gaze flicked to my face, and she looked at me as though some sharp memory now pained her. "When she died, Violet handed over her bracelet and told me to wear one on each wrist and to think of us as paired for always and forever. Even when I had scraped lower than I'd ever thought I could go, I never gave more than a fleeting thought to selling these," she concluded, her chest heaving as though she had just swum in from some far-flung shore. Suddenly I wanted to laugh, to roll my eyes, to poke fun at this ridiculous creature sitting before me at that very minute. But I didn't ask the obvious question: Why, if her sister was dying and yet so precious to Odalie, didn't it make more sense to sell the bracelets and do what was necessary to ensure her sister's continued well-being? Instead, I bit my lip and proceeded to blow on the tiny rippling lake that was the surface of the liquid in my mug. Still debating whether or not to voice my disbelief, I took a sip. An abrupt jolt of pleasure overcame me.

"Oh," I exclaimed. "Why, that *is* good!"

"It should be. I used condensed milk to sweeten it," she reported, and smiled at me as though her tragic monologue had been abruptly forgotten. "You see, Rose, you and I, we're like sisters now," Odalie continued in a low purr. Before I had a chance to respond to this, she continued. "I know how right it was for you to do what you did about the Vitalli case; you only did what a righteous person is called to do. I think you're very brave for it. I really do. I admire you! And something else about sisters." She paused and smiled sweetly at me. "Sisters keep each other's secrets. I'm sure when the time comes, you'll keep mine."

There was something chilling in her voice as she pronounced this last statement. For a moment I had a flash of myself as the man who decides to paint the floor of his house and somehow manages to paint himself into a corner.

"Oh, but don't look so serious over it!" Odalie exclaimed. "All I mean to say is that I have come to think of you as my truest friend. My *dearest* and most *intimate* friend in all the world." She reached across the table and gave my shoulder a squeeze. "I'm so glad we found each other, Rose. It feels as though we've always belonged together." She reached to her right wrist and unclasped one bracelet. "Here," she said, taking my hand in hers. I had a moment of shyness, as I was aware of my palms being cold and sweaty while hers were warm and smooth. Before I could protest, she had slipped the bracelet around my wrist and was doing up the clasp. "Here—to prove to you how much I mean it."

I looked down at the treasure glittering on my wrist in disbelief. The diamonds caught the dim glow of the electric bulb overhead, releasing a million tiny prisms from even the smallest morsel of light. A hundred tiny stars winked up at me, as if the Milky Way itself had come to rest around my wrist.

In all my life, no one had ever given me a gift quite so nice. To be honest, I'd never even seen a piece of jewelry of that caliber close-up, let alone wrapped around my own wrist. The brooch that was tucked in my desk drawer at the precinct was also very lovely, but that didn't really count—Odalie had dropped it and I still meant to give it back to her eventually. Unlike the brooch, which I had merely found, or her clothes, which I only borrowed, here was something she was *giving* to me. I was dizzy with the thought of it. My lips fluttered silently as I tried to thank her. Seeing my condition, Odalie laughed, the sound of it rippling through the kitchen in a musical wave. We sat there, holding hands and comparing our matching wrists, all the while grinning stupidly at each other with maniacal glee. I looked into Odalie's smile and felt myself momentarily swallowed up by some sort of euphoric abyss.

It was moments like this, I would later learn, that would ultimately undo me.

15

All at once it got hot, and suddenly the only thing anyone in Manhattan could talk about was the weather. *Hot enough for you?* O'Neill and Harley said with a long whistle every time they came back into the office after walking a patrol beat. *Boy oh boy, could it get any hotter?* Upper lips glistened with sweat. Cheeks and noses glowed scarlet with permanent sun-burn. Outside, the sidewalks were empty, and the few remaining pedestrians (presumably either brave or daft) dashed from one tiny patch of shade to the next. Even the precinct, usually a dank, cool cave in the summertime, sweltered with the steamy heat. There was no escaping it. Which was not to say we didn't try to by any means possible. Feeling magnanimous and perhaps a little desperate himself, the Sergeant used some of his own money to buy a couple of electric fans, and the Lieutenant Detective spent the better part of an afternoon bolting them to the walls so they might cool our necks and faces.

"Are you able to catch a breeze with it like this?" the Lieutenant Detective asked, angling a fan in my direction and preparing to screw a hinge into place. The black wire cage faced toward me like some sort of dark mechanical flower, and suddenly the little hairs that had come loose from my chignon lifted to tickle my neck and shoulders. Papers fluttered on my desk, coming to life like a tree ferociously shaking its many leaves in the breeze. I rushed to anchor everything down and glanced over at Odalie, Marie, and Iris, all of whom were momentarily lost in their work. The papers on their desks remained at rest; it appeared my desk alone was receiving the benefit of this man-made vortex.

"I don't need any favors," I said.

"You don't ever need any anything." He winked and twisted the screw down on the hinge. Despite the breeze, suddenly the room grew even hotter—I felt a very sudden, heavy flush rise up to my ears. I rose without replying and went to the ladies' room to splash some water on my face.

Of course, the water from the taps was not cold or refreshing in the least, the pipes being too warm that day. But I cupped my hands and splashed some tepid water on my face anyway, letting it run down my neck and chin. It was difficult to discern where my skin left off and the droplets began. Everything was seething with a pulsing heat, my perspiration and the water felt so similar in temperature. As I stood dripping over the sink, Odalie came in. She crossed her arms and sighed.

"Do you know what we need?" she asked rhetorically. I silently prayed the diagnosis was going to be a movie in one of the famously air-cooled theaters in the East 50s. The line of her petite mouth curled at the corners in that signature way she had, and her eyes darted about the empty space just over my head. I could tell she was coming up with more elaborate calculations than a movie theater. "We need a little holiday . . . somewhere with an ocean breeze. I'll get us invited someplace nice. . . ."

I blinked. It was as if she had just spoken Chinese. I had never had a proper vacation. I took exactly three days off per year, and usually spent them at home with a stack of novels that would have never met with the approval of the nuns who'd monitored my reading habits throughout my childhood.

"But . . . what about work? How will we manage it with the Sergeant?"

"Oh, *pfft*," she said, throwing a dismissive hand back at the wrist. "Let me worry about him. I can manage that part. He's a pussycat, really." The way she pronounced the word *pussycat* proved rather unsettling to me. There was something almost obscene in the inflection. The doubt I had tried so hard to banish seeped back in, and my mind drifted to the day after the raid. But I could feel Odalie's eyes on my face, waiting for an answer now. I pushed my suspicions aside and forced a smile.

"A holiday would be nice . . . if we could manage it."

I had used the word *we*, but I didn't really mean it. I knew Odalie would be the one to manage everything, and she did. In record speed, too. By Friday we had been granted a week's vacation, and found ourselves riding across the Queensboro Bridge in a coupe driven by an accommodating Wall Street man who was so painfully short, he put me in mind of Redmond. It was a wonder his feet could reach the pedals of the automobile. As a matter of fact, perhaps he could only reach the accelerator; I don't think I can recall him using the brake at all, and we flew along at top velocity toward the broad white beaches of Long Island.

"So tell me more about what these squires do for you on the trading floor," Odalie was saying to the broker in an enraptured voice as he sped us along the highway.

"*Squads.*"

"Oh, yes, I mean what these *squads* do for you on the trading floor ... It's so fascinating, so *very* fascinating ... I don't know how you stand all the excitement of it!" With every question she asked the broker she sounded more and more like she was so utterly intrigued, she was on the verge of taking up the profession herself. Of course, by then, I had come to know her better.

Nonetheless ... just like that, we had escaped! With each mile we put behind us, I felt the air grow lighter in my lungs. It was as if the city had been one large pressure cooker, simmering in its own juices. With the top down on the coupe and a stalwart, man-made breeze blowing steadily in my face, I tallied the city's many summertime brutalities: the heat that radiated from the gray asphalt and made the air dance in wavy shimmers; the stagnant ponds in Central Park that turned a milky, putrid, almost phosphorescent green and incubated countless mosquitoes; the blasts of hot dirty air that breathed upward from every subway grate; oh, and how the loud noises pouring from construction sites even somehow seemed to further agitate and heat the air! Why on Earth we modern humans had signed a pact to live like that was beyond my comprehension.

After pulling off the main roadway and driving through a handful of seaside hamlets, the Wall Street broker finally proved the brake pedal was equally within his reach, applying it rather harshly as we turned into the long drive of a very large house. Oyster shells scattered and crunched as the coupe's tires rolled over the gravel. Parked automobiles were lined up, nose to tail, all along both sides of the drive. A few parked limousines still contained their hot, sweaty-faced drivers, and here and there from the interior of their front seats the flutter of an open newspaper could be discerned.

We rolled along toward a fountain at the top of the drive. The broker made one circle of it and, unable to locate anything more accommodating, found a very tight spot alongside some shrubbery that could have only deviated a hair's breadth from the exact measurement of his coupe. After much finagling that caused him to grunt and pant at the wheel, our impromptu chauffeur was able to wedge the coupe into position and cut the motor. The moment the engine fell silent, strains of music and laughter could be heard from somewhere out behind the house. There was, I surmised, some sort of garden party going on.

"Perfect timing! A minute more and all that driving would've driven me absolutely mad," Odalie announced. She reached an automatic hand to her hat to make some sort of invisible adjustment to the sporty cloche that had somehow managed to stay perfectly in place throughout the duration of our ride. I looked about to see where *here* was.

The house itself was a rather imposing two-story Dutch colonial, with deeply sloping gables. Perched on the highest level of the house was a small imitation of a lighthouse encircled by a widow's walk that together made up a sort of third story. The whole house was so brilliantly white and incredibly pristine, I had the brief hallucination I could smell the odor of drying paint. Even though no one came out to greet us, the front door was thrown open, and it was clear further guests were expected. Gazing into the dark cavernous space of the house, I could see all the way through it and out a back door, which had likewise been thrown open and acted as a frame for a bright patch of green lawn and a glittering smudge of blue sea. I turned to point it out, but Odalie was already walking a small way ahead of me. As soon as she alighted from the coupe, she had begun to move in the direction of the house's open door.

"Thanks so much for the lift, Edwin."

"Would you like to get your things out of the trunk?" Edwin inquired. He was still bubbling with self-important glee, having spent the duration of the car ride basking in Odalie's attention.

"Oh, not just now," she answered dismissively. A bit of puff went out of Edwin's proud pneumatic chest. "We'll have them send someone out to collect them later, once we've been . . . received."

A funny feeling came over me as Odalie made this last remark, and I began to wonder if we had been formally invited, or—a small trickle of dread came over me as the thought occurred to me—whether we were in fact that most gauche of all parasites: *gate-crashers.* Edwin stalked about, fussing with the car, realizing his passengers very clearly intended to go on ahead and leave him behind, and evidently deeply irritated by this development. "How'll I find you for later?" he asked in a gruff manner.

"Oh," Odalie murmured. "We'll find you. I'm clever at finding people at parties." This last statement was true enough, although I doubted she would prove her powers by using them to locate Edwin. He seemed equally dubious about his odds and shot her an overt scowl. Odalie tossed her head so that her shiny black bob swung in the sunlight and, with a giggle, made a halfhearted attempt at humor. "And if all else fails I'll hire a poodle and we'll have a hunting party and send up flares." She gave a nervous laugh and linked her arm through mine, whereupon I felt myself urgently propelled in the direction of the open door, and Edwin's grumbling gave way to the din of the party.

All morning the sun had been beating down on us as we rode along with the top down on the coupe. It took my eyes several moments to adjust to the dim light inside the house, and I shuffled in close step behind Odalie, instinctually following her as she navigated in and among the many dark shapes in the room. It was, I must say, a very elegant party in contrast to the rabble of the speakeasies to which I'd grown accustomed. We came near a grand piano, where instead of a drunk woman playing "Chopsticks" with her toes a hired pianist sat playing a very polished Debussy tune. Gilded mirrors hung on many of the walls, their opulence set off by the rich blue and gold of the brocade wallpaper. Oriental vases adorned with very clean-looking navy and white floral patterns lined the mantel. Trays of champagne glasses floated over waiters' heads like golden clouds drifting in and out of formation. Even the accents embedded in the partygoers' voices seemed to differ from those I'd encountered in the speakeasies; here the consonants of conversation were squared off with a stiff jaw while the vowels were inflected with a continental lilt.

I did not recognize a single face, certainly none from Odalie's usual scene in the city, to be sure. The women in the room had an air of polished athletic health about them, their tanned arms suggestive of days spent walking the golf course, their hair either clipped short or else very tidily swept up off their long, lean necks. The men were dapperly dressed in morning suits or more sportily dressed in polo shirts and smartly tailored knickers with their socks pulled up high. The collection of people that had been gathered together was so well-groomed, I suddenly felt a bit shabby and unkempt, even though I had on a very expensive dress Odalie had insisted upon loaning me.

"Don't start that," Odalie said, swatting my hands when she noticed my fidgeting.

"Who are we here to see again?"

"The Brinkleys, of course. Max and Vera." *Mr. and Mrs. Maximillian and Vera Brinkley.* The names rang a bell, but I was not comforted by this fact, as I quickly realized why. Maximillian and Vera Brinkley were socialites whose engagements and activities were regularly reported in the newspapers, along with their photographs. My earlier apprehension about being gate-crashers returned, and I had a sudden, panicky feeling about our mission there. I froze in my tracks and reached for Odalie's arm.

"Odalie . . . are you acquainted with the Brinkleys? Were we invited here?"

She shrugged, twisted open the clasps of her handbag, and proceeded to extract an envelope from its depths. She waved it absently in front of my face. "I have a letter of introduction. It's more or less like an invitation."

I was taken aback. My eyes goggled in the direction of the letter, but Odalie took little notice. She wasn't looking at me. Instead, her eyes searched the crowd, her head pivoting on her neck with the automatic, mechanical intensity of a submarine periscope. No doubt she was taking an inventory of partygoers recognizable for their appearances in the society pages. She seemed uncharacteristically jumpy, and I wondered if she had finally gotten us in over our heads. I pointed at the letter still clutched in her hand. I tried to think of who she might know with a great deal of adequately "old" money or else a sizable store of social influence.

"Is that . . . from the Hungarian?"

"The who?" she asked with an air of distraction, still scanning the room. She drifted through the main house and toward the backyard. I followed.

"The Hungarian. Or . . . should I call him your uncle?"

She suddenly stopped cold. Her eyebrows knit together, and she turned to fix me in her stare with something that resembled a flash of anger. I held my breath. But just as quickly as the flash of anger had sprung to her face, it melted away. Her shoulders relaxed with a shrug, and she tossed her head to let out a peal of haughty laughter.

"Oh, dear, dear, silly darling! You must have been chatting it up with Gib lately." She patted my hand and rolled her eyes. I felt supremely foolish as I began to comprehend the extent of my own gullibility. My mental picture of the barrel-chested Hungarian with his aristocratic background and monarchist sympathies began to evaporate as we proceeded to step out the back door and into the blinding, merciless light of the midday sun.

"I . . . I . . . Well, Gib said—"

"Oh, I know all about what Gib likely said." She rolled her eyes again to show her disdain. Then, catching the look of frustrated doubt creeping into my face, she suddenly softened her demeanor and took my hand in hers. She leaned in close, and I could smell her lily-of-the-valley perfume. "You haven't known him very long, so you can't know it, but Gib has *quite* the imagination."

The first part of what Odalie had said was true: I hadn't known Gib for very long. But the latter part . . . He had never struck me as a particularly creative type, and I very much doubted he was the secret possessor of a vast and potent imagination. It was unlikely he had conjured up the Hungarian all by himself. Odalie, on the other hand, I knew to have a very vital imagination. I was fairly certain that with the story of the Hungarian I had somehow managed to fall for one of Odalie's creative inventions despite the fact it had come to me secondhand. And then the story she had told the other night about having a dearly departed sister named Violet! While I had been extremely touched by the generous gift

Odalie had bestowed upon me when she had fastened the bracelet around my wrist, the gesture had not necessarily served to heighten the plausibility of the story that accompanied it.

What the ever-changing architecture of her stories was ultimately meant to conceal I still didn't know at that point. Curiously, despite all her subterfuge, Odalie retained a sympathetic allure in my eyes. When Helen told stories for manipulation or for dramatic effect, nothing bothered me more. I'm ashamed to admit I secretly, and sometimes not so secretly, relished the moments when Helen got caught in one of her lies and was unmasked, much to her own horrified chagrin. I felt a sense of downright glee whenever this happened.

But it was not this way with Odalie. I'm not certain I fully comprehended why I should feel so differently toward these two women—both of whom I realize are liars—and even to this day I often puzzle over it. Perhaps I liked Helen less because I found her to be a rather desperate and therefore unsuccessful liar, whereas the case could be made that Odalie was something of a virtuoso at it. Odalie lied for sport and never bothered to hide the fact that even she didn't believe a single word of her own lies. Helen lied out of a pathetic need to see herself through other people's eyes; I think she convinced herself that many of her own lies were true, and somehow this made her much more despicable than Odalie. My doctor says it is our animal nature to judge the weak more harshly, owing to how survival depends upon weeding these creatures out. He says I have *highly developed animalistic tendencies.* The way he says it, it does not sound like a compliment. He has formed other, equally unflattering opinions of me as well, although he does not always tell all of them to my face. He constantly writes notes on his little clipboard, and I try to pretend as if I don't notice, but the other day I leaned over and spied the words *acute cruel streak* written next to my name in blue fountain pen. I have complained before that he is not particularly keen on me, but when you are in the sort of institution where I currently find myself, they are hardly looking to take a survey—which is to say, the residents' assessment of the doctors is hardly taken under serious advisement.

Oh! But once again, I am getting away from my point. The truth of the matter is the two women in question were fundamentally different in how they treated the people to whom they lied. Helen's lies demanded that you affirm her, that you collaborate, that you play stupid. Her mendacity was an insulting nuisance if there ever was one. Odalie understood it was sometimes your will to want to be tricked; she did not need you to affirm her world. She would create it with or without you. Instead, she invited you in ever so casually, and somehow—even when her lies were shabbily wrought—you would find yourself *wanting* to go in, if only out of an insatiable curiosity. She knew, too, not to pressure you to proclaim your belief in her untruth. That would be asking too much; in asking for that, she would risk daring her listener to pull at the loose threads she carelessly left behind and unravel it all. Her comprehension of this simple fact made all the difference.

Just then I felt Odalie looking at me. The fringe of her bangs gave a fey little flutter along the line of her dark eyebrows as the ocean breeze lifted them with a gentle, lazy ease. "C'mon, let's not dwell on Gib's nonsense. We ought to be having fun," she declared. She led me toward a waiter shuttling a tray of champagne. "How about we have a refreshment like civilized people and find our hosts, eh?"

I nodded and we took off to roam the garden, Odalie still

holding my hand in hers. I had to admit I felt a twinge of irresist-ible pride, I realized, to have people look at us and see that we were such intimate bosom friends. I suppose this was because I liked for people to think I might have such a beautiful and charis-matic friend. Some girls don't like to stand next to a pretty girl, for fear they will look more drab by comparison. I know for a fact there were several shopgirls with whom Helen refused to become friendly for just such a reason. But I'd always felt as though my value increased when I stood next to Odalie. As if extraordinary people could only be drawn to other extraordinary people, I fanta-sized that some of my plainness melted away.

The unbearably hot day in the city had been translated into a very warm but pleasantly bright day in the seaside garden where we now found ourselves. I looked around, inventorying my sur-roundings like a settler happening upon a strange but fruitful land. Persian rugs covered a wide stone terrace where a series of tables were laid out with an array of picturesque delicacies befit-ting a sultan. White tablecloths flapped in the ocean breeze. Col-orful lanterns hung from every bare tree branch; they jigged about gently in the wind as though waiting impatiently for dusk so they might light the way for the festivities to continue late into the night. Among the stone statues of Apollo and Aphrodite, a string quartet played on a grassy knoll. The back lawn sloped a bit as it unfurled the distance downward from the house and finally gave way to the beach, its green tufted edge curling like a lip just over the beginning of a fine white sand. Far out on the navy sap-phire of the sea, two sailboats slid along the horizon, lazily exchanging positions. We laughed and careened around the gar-den, the points of our heeled shoes digging into the lawn as we strolled first in one direction and then another.

From across the lawn I saw a young man shading his eyes and squinting at us. He didn't wave, but as we staggered in sociable circles about the lawn, his eyes trailed us until eventually his body followed suit. At first, I thought nothing of it; Odalie often attracted attention wherever she went. But after thirty minutes or so it was clear this young man's interest was particularly piqued by our presence. He wore the simultaneously focused yet distracted expression of a person trying to place an old acquaintance, and I wondered if he already knew Odalie, perhaps from yet another version of her history I had not yet heard. Eventually, he approached.

As he drew up close, I saw how extremely young he was. There was a freshly minted collegiate air about him; he could not have been more than a year or two out of preparatory school. He was not exactly short, but he was small and lanky, with a very diminutive head and slender neck, all of which lent a costume air when combined with the heavy suit he wore, as though he were a boy playing in his father's clothes. I recall the word *doll-like* floated involuntarily into my mind. He had pale, baby-smooth skin, with the exception of two very angry-looking pink blemishes on his chin, the sores made all the more bright by the contrast they struck with his smooth white cheeks. His eyes were blue and clear, with very sparse eyelashes acting as a frame, and his hair was the lightest sort of brown that could've just as easily been called blond, given a slightly greater dose of sun.

"Why, hullo there. Don't I know you?" he called in a familiar tone as he approached. Surprisingly, his voice was a deep bass and struck me as oddly matched to its owner. His face bore a funny expression; it was a kind of shy half-smile. He seemed nervous about something as he tramped across the grass toward us. Odalie turned in the direction of the young man approaching us in order to better take him in and suddenly froze. For the slenderest of seconds she resembled a silent movie-star, in that both of her hands fluttered upward to stifle a scream that was never heard from the tiny hollow of her open mouth. But it was as though she had merely flinched, or experienced a sneeze or hiccup of some sort, for the reaction passed so quickly that it was difficult to be sure it had happened at all. Before I knew it, she was smiling at our assailant with her typical cool composure, her stony feline eyes revealing nothing.

"How do you do," Odalie said in a pleasant enough voice, yet with a decided lack of inquiring inflection. Mechanically, she put out a hand.

"Oh," he stammered in a baffled way, looking at the outstretched hand with the incredulous air of the uninitiated. It was as though he had never witnessed a handshake in his life and didn't understand why Odalie was offering her hand. "I'm Teddy," he said. Odalie sought out his hand with her own and finally, when she'd managed to acquire it, aggressively shook it.

"Of course. Nice to meet you, Teddy."

"Teddy *Tricott*," he said, touching his chest as though to ensure we understood who he meant and placing special emphasis on the last name.

"Odalie Lazare," Odalie said, imitating his gesture. She smiled smugly. At this, the young man's eyes went wide. He jerked his hand away.

"Oh!" he exclaimed. "Oh—I thought . . . oh . . . oh!"

"I'm Rose," I said, breaking into the rather awkward, inarticulate conversation with the hopes of hurrying it along. Having barely detected my presence up to that point, Teddy now turned to me, his eyes still wide, and appeared suddenly cognizant of my person.

"Oh, of course." He shook himself as though coming back into his right mind. "Sorry—yes. Of course, of course." He put out a hand, and I briefly gave him the tips of my fingers. As soon as he released my hand, Teddy resumed staring, goggle-eyed, in Odalie's direction.

"Forgive me," he said. "It's just that you look like—"

"I get that all the time." Odalie waved the apology away with a magnanimous toss of her wrist. I wondered which starlet Teddy had been about to name as Odalie's doppelgänger. There were several to whom Odalie bore an admittedly strong resemblance. At least now the boy's odd behavior was beginning to make a bit more sense. Odalie smiled again but could not hide the fact the smile had become hollow; I could tell she was quite done with the young man who stood before us and was ready to move on. "Say— Teddy, you wouldn't happen to know where our hosts might be hiding, would you?"

"The Brinkleys?"

"The very ones."

"Oh, uh, sure! Let me take you to them." Still a little shell-shocked from his mistaken movie-star sighting, he ambled in the direction of the stone terrace. Odalie hesitated, and I detected a faint reluctance to follow the young man. Then, pushing back her shoulders with an air of purpose and adopting a casual stroll, she trailed along in cool pursuit.

"How do you know the Brinkleys? Are you a relation?" There was a strange tone to Odalie's voice; something about it put me in mind of Helen rehearsing lines from one of the vaudeville plays she adored.

"Me? Oh, no. But I suppose I'm on pretty familiar terms. I like them well enough. They've always been very accommodating to me. Their son Felix would sometimes bring me home to their place in the city on weekends, back in the days when we were at Hotchkiss together."

"Well, that was very nice of him." Odalie had resumed her usual state of half listening.

"Indeed," Teddy nodded with a serious air. "Sometimes the trains to Newport were just too much of a nuisance, and it was nice to be able to get away from school and go *somewhere*, you know?" Teddy hesitated and looked at Odalie from the sides of his eyes. "Say—don't suppose you've spent much time in Newport, have you?"

Odalie stiffened. "Not particularly," came her vague reply.

"Ah," Teddy said. "That's really too bad." He continued stealing little suspicious glances at Odalie as we ascended the sloping lawn. When we reached the house, we followed Teddy through several drawing rooms and into a dark-paneled office where a group of people stood in a clustered circle, busily admiring an oil painting that presided over a stone fireplace. The diamond-patterned, leaded-glass windows in the room had been opened in an attempt to attract the ocean breeze beyond, but nevertheless the atmosphere was quite stuffy, and I had the instant sensation of claustrophobia.

"Yes, yes," a woman in a summery, lilac-colored gown was saying, waving a hand toward the painting. "Why, practically *everyone* says I resemble her, but even if that's so, it's entirely coincidental, because the relation is all on Max's side, you see."

I took a good look at the woman speaking, and my mind slowly clicked: This was Vera Brinkley. Her face was memorable. She was what people often referred to as a handsome woman. Her hair was carefully waved and swept back, revealing high cheekbones and delicate shadows of the hollows just below. She would've been beautiful if not for the length of her jaw, which ran a little too long and squared itself off a little too sharply, infusing her countenance with a vaguely horsey impression. Her body was thin and freckled and fashionably hipless, and she was of indeterminate age: Her face whispered rumors of her late thirties or very early forties, but her neck suggested another ten years could possibly be added to that score.

"Mrs. Brinkley?" Teddy tapped her discreetly on the shoulder. The woman turned.

"Oh, for heaven's sake, Teddy. You're not in school anymore. You're a college-man now. Call me Vera." Teddy nodded, but also blushed.

"I have some ladies here who've been hunting about for their hosts."

"Oh! Certainly, my boy. Max! Come over here, dear. Teddy has some people he'd like us to meet." A very prim man wearing a monocle and dressed in a morning suit looked up from the box of cigars he had presently unlocked for the benefit of a group of bankers. Just as it was with Vera Brinkley, Max Brinkley had an odd combination of youth and maturity about him. His body was quite thin, yet his fleshy face was as placid as a glacier lake and his cheeks ended in two rather slight but unfortunate jowls just under each side of his jaw. His snub nose gave him an air of youth that was instantly contradicted by the monocle perched on the apple of his left cheek. It was as though he were simultaneously twenty-nine and fifty-nine, but no age between the two. He crossed the room and peered questioningly from Odalie to me, and then back to Odalie.

"Mr. and Mrs. Brinkley," Teddy began, but, receiving a sharp look from Mrs. Brinkley, quickly modified his approach. "Ahem. Max and Vera, I give you . . ." He suddenly drew up short, realizing that despite our belabored introductions, he had already forgotten our names.

"Rose Baker and Odalie Lazare," Odalie quickly supplied.

"Yes—Rose Baker and Odalie Lazare," Teddy repeated, gesturing in turn to each of us. Apparently he had no trouble discerning which was which, as he made a gesture first to me and second to Odalie.

"Oh! I almost forgot," Odalie added, smiling one of her most endearing smiles. "I suppose I should give you this." She handed over the letter of introduction, which Max Brinkley took and lifted before his monocled eye. The corners of his mouth twitched while he read the words.

"Oh—yes, yes," he grumbled amicably once he had reached the bottom of the letter. "As I always tell my wife, any friend of Pembroke's is a friend of ours!" This statement seemed to tickle his funny bone, and he laughed aloud, a strangely low-timbred guffaw issuing from his thin frame. I detected we had just crossed over some invisible threshold. A mood of more relaxed welcome extended itself as though a train of dominoes were tumbling over. Vera laughed, Odalie laughed, Teddy laughed, and then I found myself joining suit, although still to this day I'm not certain I truly understood what was so funny. Mr. Brinkley folded up the letter roughly and stuffed it into an inside jacket pocket. "I hope you don't mind—there'll be others staying this weekend, too. A small party, in fact."

"We don't want to intrude, of course . . . ," Odalie said, but there was a veneer to her voice, and I knew immediately her protest was insincere.

"Nonsense. It's no intrusion at all. Besides, it's clear Pembroke wants you to be well cared for, and perhaps even"—he paused and winked at Odalie—"chaperoned." Odalie's lips tightened into a thin, polite smile. Mrs. Brinkley frowned, ever so briefly, at the floor. "I'll send Felton for your things," Mr. Brinkley continued. "He can carry them up and show you to your room. Felton!"

Only a matter of minutes later, we found ourselves happily ensconced in a plush, sunlight-filled bedroom upstairs. Odalie sat at the vanity and moved a brush through her glossy bob while I pushed open a window and gazed at the shimmer and twinkle of the sea beyond, slightly dulled now by the angle of the late afternoon sun. I can only assume somewhere out there in the vast populous world there really was a Pembroke, although I wouldn't go so far as to naively assume Odalie had ever made his acquaintance. As it was, I scarcely heard the name mentioned again, despite the fact it had served as the crucial turnkey to our seaside accommodations.

As I watched Odalie brush her hair and stare absently into the mirror, I realized she was not thinking of Pembroke, but rather someone else altogether. A distracted frown marred the lovely oval of her face. "Can you believe it! What ridiculous rubbish," she grumbled to herself. "Newport folk ought to know they're supposed to stay in Newport. Who ever heard of coming down here for the summer? It's absolute nonsense!"

I was taken aback by the vehemence of her tone and looked at her in puzzlement, but she took no notice.

"We've got to keep an eye on that boy," she murmured.

I wasn't sure if she was addressing me or had forgotten I was still in the room.

"What?"

"Teddy." She ran an absent finger over one smooth black eyebrow. "He's trouble." Her voice was full of the kind of deep thought and quiet calculation that forbids further prodding. There was a knock at the door, and Felton deposited our baggage in the room. I kept my questions to myself and set about unpacking our two suitcases.

16

One got the sense the Brinkleys' summer life kept a regular rhythm, and this rhythm consisted mostly of leisure sports in the mornings, garden parties in the afternoons, and tasteful feasts around the dinner hour, all followed by a waltz or two late into the more velvety hours of the night. If Mr. Brinkley had a profession, I'm not sure I could tell you what it was. One thing was certain: Whichever Brinkley had originally procured the family fortune had done his part at least two or three generations ago, as the Brinkleys currently in residence seemed to remain utterly unharassed by the so-called pressing matters of business. What's more, their estate accommodated all of their favored activities, and I daresay they rarely—if ever—left the grounds at any point throughout the entire duration of the summer. Instead, they became the center around which a small universe of New York socialites revolved, and Odalie and I were only too happy to fall into orbit.

Once we'd arrived and had been shown to our room, we dressed for dinner and reemerged just as the hot summer day finally stretched itself to the outermost end of its length. The final result was a bright, thin twilight. Coming downstairs, we made our way to the veranda and discovered four very long dining tables had been draped with pale blue tablecloths and set with white candles and white china. At the center of each table an enormous roasted pig rested on its belly, complete with a candied apple in its mouth. Place cards were laid out in front of each setting, and I thought I glimpsed the slight twitch of a frown on Odalie's face as she observed Teddy's name inscribed on the place card next to her own.

When Teddy came over to take his seat next to Odalie, he wore a vaguely embarrassed yet sly smile, and it occurred to me perhaps he had switched a few place cards from their original positions just prior to our arrival downstairs. There was nothing terribly shocking in this, and I hardly thought anything of it; men were always maneuvering to achieve a greater degree of proximity to Odalie. But what *was* surprising was that throughout the meal, Odalie kept her back to Teddy, refusing to make conversation with a polite but very stubborn twist of her posture. Even eye contact seemed a burden to her. I'd never witnessed anything like it. Odalie had always been one to hold court; she was kind to even the most lowly of her admirers (one never knew whose favors might come in handy). I couldn't help but wonder what sort of grudge she could possibly harbor against a boy who was not even old enough yet to have racked up any serious social offenses. All we knew of him was that he had mistaken Odalie for a movie-star (a far cry from an insult), he hailed from Newport, and at one time he had attended Hotchkiss—hardly grounds for the thorough snubbing Odalie was giving him that night as she sat with her whole body twisted away from him, more raptly engaged with my own conversation than she had ever been in the history of our friendship.

After dinner, he pursued her to the canvas platform where couples had already begun to pair off and float about in light-footed, airy circles. I believe he thought he might get a chance to dance with her. But if this was the case, he sorely underestimated Odalie's ability to fill up a dance card. She skillfully thwarted his advances at every turn, always remaining aloof but never being rude in any outright manner. So for the majority of the night, he stood off to one side of the platform and simply looked on, his hands stuffed awkwardly into the pockets of his high-waisted white suit jacket, the shifting tides of dancing couples swirling in eddies before him and the shifting tides of the actual sea ebbing and flowing at some distance in the darkness behind him. At one point, he crossed the veranda in my direction, and I may be mistaken but I believe he was coming to ask me to dance. Just prior to his arrival, though, Odalie was quite suddenly at my elbow. Her musical laugh filled the air as a string of gentlemen took turns bending at the waist and making a show of kissing her hand. I heard her making apologies about the hour being late. Seconds later I felt a light hand on my arm. Before I knew it we were upstairs in our room, turning down the bed and slipping into our nightgowns.

"Sorry to make us turn in early like a pair of sad old biddies," Odalie murmured while lying in bed with her eyes already closed. "I just couldn't have stood it a moment longer. If they'd have played a waltz I think I would've nodded off in some poor man's arms." She reached over to my side of the bed and squeezed my hand.

"I don't mind," I said, and realized it was the truth. Sometimes when she abandoned me at parties I came home early and went to bed—always alone—and I *did* mind that. But I never minded coming home early with Odalie at my side.

THE NEXT MORNING, I awoke to find the bed next to me empty. Whatever Odalie was up to, she had not left a note to say. I rose, washed up, and went downstairs to take breakfast on the veranda. Feeling too shy to introduce myself to any of the Brinkleys' other houseguests, I requested the butler bring me the morning edition and pretended to be extremely interested in the daily headlines. I pretended, that is, until one news item in particular very genuinely caught my eye.

At first it was Mr. Vitalli's photograph that stopped me cold, a teacup of coffee poised halfway between the table and my mouth. His pale, piercing gaze was as hollow and chilling as ever— although I noticed the egotistical curl of his lips drooped somewhat now, and his mustache looked badly groomed. VITALLI FOUND GUILTY, MAY FACE ELECTRIC CHAIR, the headline over his photograph read. *So*, I thought. *There is justice in the world after all.* And the electric chair! I suppose if there was ever a time I should have felt remorse for the helping hand I lent to Lady Justice, this would've been it. But instead I felt nothing save a deep sense of satisfaction that the jury had finally found their way to the truth. I tore out the article (*Representing himself, Mr. Vitalli failed to prove confession was falsified,* a line read) and tidily folded it up to take with me. I slipped it into my purse and hoped to show it to Odalie when she finally rematerialized.

I returned to my room to wait, but by eleven-thirty the day

had already grown quite sunny and hot, and I had become restless. Guests who stayed with the Brinkleys were invited to engage in a variety of outdoor activities. The accoutrements they provided were numerous: There were tennis rackets and tennis whites for those who wanted to venture onto the court; there were nine-irons and cleats for amateur golfers who wanted to improve their drives and putts; there were badminton sets and croquet mallets and colored balls, and also little leatherette cases of heavy leaden balls coated in shiny silver the butler assured me were required for a lawn game played by the French and called *pétanque*. Having grown up with a very thin introduction to most of these sports (and none at all in the cases of golf and *pétanque*), I decided instead of trying my hand at any of the games, I would take a simple swim at the beach. Taking a swim was something I could do alone, thus relieving the burden of having to awkwardly introduce myself to other guests (something I was loath to do without Odalie).

It was already balmy outside, but in the cool of my bedroom I shivered as I shimmied into the knit fabric of the bathing suit Odalie had picked out from Lord & Taylor earlier that month. After acquiring a towel from the butler (who raised an eyebrow at the length of leg peeking out from under the hemline of my suit), I set out in the general direction of the water.

There were two beaches to choose from. The Brinkleys' property spanned a swath of land that stretched from the Sound all the way to the open sea. I suppose a more romantic individual would've chosen the whiter sand and salty spray of the thundering Atlantic, but as I have already confessed a hundred times, I am a rather practical-minded person. I opted for the slightly murkier but much stiller waters of the Sound. When I got there I saw I had the beach to myself, save for the occasional motor-boat out for a pleasure cruise, whizzing by as voices of sun-burned hilarity carried in crisp ripples over the water. Some distance offshore a swimmers' raft bobbed softly, permanently anchored by some underwater means against the Sound's gentle currents.

By then the heat was rising from the sand in dusty, steamy drafts, and I was more than happy to ease myself waist-deep into the water. If I possess one unladylike quality of which I am shamelessly proud, it is how I'm actually quite a strapping swimmer. There has always been an inherent brute force to my strokes. Lots of girls can swim, especially all those fast, tomboyish girls who are popping up everywhere nowadays, but not so many years ago it used to be only the very rural or the very rich who knew how to swim. When the nuns arranged for me to attend the Bedford Academy, I gained some rather unexpected privileges, and having been properly taught my swimming strokes was one of them. They'd taken us on a handful of school excursions to a ladies-only beach, where we'd sloshed about in the waves, weighted down by the long, bloomer-style bathing costumes they made us wear, each of us waiting her turn to have her swimming stroke evaluated by the same gruff, broad-shouldered, freckle-faced female swimming instructor who was hired especially for the task once a year.

I gazed at the swimmers' raft bobbing. A small diving tower had been erected on the raft, and from the top a tiny orange flag fluttered in the breeze as though giving a wave of encouragement. I estimated it was only a couple hundred yards away and decided to swim to it. With a push and a gasp as the water enveloped my chest and neck, I was off, paddling happily along. I tipped my face into the water and attempted an earnest crawl stroke. I have always found swimming to be an exhilarating activity: the peculiar way one is obliged to move in the water, the reaching and stretching, the feeling of pulling air into one's lungs in great heaving gulps, the way the world simultaneously seems to fill up with both sound and its total absence. And there is almost always a moment of oddly invigorating panic, even if one is a very strong swimmer, during which one doubts the endurance of one's lungs and the strength of one's own muscles. It had been a long time since I'd been in the water, and I had one such moment just before I reached the raft. I felt fear awaken each inch of my body like a jolt of electricity, and when I finally pulled myself onto the wooden planks of the swimmers' raft, my limbs thoroughly turned to jelly and every nerve within me trembled with exhilaration— all of which quickly turned to exhaustion. I heaved myself atop the raft and lay there like a dead person staring emptily into the sky.

I have no idea how long I lay faceup like that on the raft. Enough time passed for the heaving of my chest to gradually subside, for my hair to begin to dry against my scalp in matted clumps, and for the world to become quite still and peaceful. The bobbing of the raft was hypnotic, like resting in a cradle. And then I slowly became cognizant of the fact the tempo of the bobbing was increasing. I turned my head to look toward the shore and realized another swimmer was approaching the raft. Glistening ripples spread in widening rings from his body as he paddled and kicked his way forward. He paused, briefly, in the middle of a crawl stroke and lifted his head from the water. There was a blur of a smile, and then a bright "Ahoy there!" sounded.

I sat up. I realized I was looking at Teddy, the very same young man who'd facilitated our introduction the previous afternoon and pursued Odalie all evening in vain. His face disappeared back into the water, and the windmill of his arms resumed. Finally Teddy reached the raft and found his way to the ladder. I had not anticipated running into him in this fashion. I must have frowned at him involuntarily as I watched him climb the ladder and grin with clumsy exhaustion, for he seemed to catch on to my displeasure.

"I would ask you if you mind the intrusion, but I'm afraid it can't be helped," he said in his prematurely deep bass of a voice, panting and trying to catch his breath. "I've got to have a break. It's a bit more of a swim than I'd realized. Guess it's no use changing your mind halfway out, eh?" He plopped down and laid his dripping body on the planks of the raft, eventually collapsing into the selfsame horizontal and heaving posture I'd been in only moments earlier. Once supine, he turned his head and squinted up into the sun to look at me. "Boy oh boy, you must be a swell swimmer." There was genuine admiration in his voice, and I felt myself involuntarily bristle with pride.

"Well, I enjoy it fine, I guess," I said very quietly, refusing to smile. I made a gesture to stand and go but balked, dithering between the ladder and the tower. I had originally hoped to dive from the tower, but now had reservations about doing it in front of an audience.

"Oh, wait—don't go," Teddy said, catching on to my intent. I looked at him and saw the earnest raised eyebrows and down-turned mouth of an innocent young boy. I don't know why I was in such a rush to get away from him. Odalie had yet to reveal the origins of her aversion to the young man. He had after all, I reasoned, eased our introduction to the Brinkleys and spared us from potentially appearing like gate-crashers. "Please stay," he said to me now. "I'd like the company." I hesitated, and he saw it. "And besides," he added, "swimming back is going to be rough. I may need a strong life-guard to rescue me and tow me back to shore." His panting had fully subsided by that time, and I could see this claim wasn't true, but I found myself lingering about on the raft anyway.

I leaned back on my hands and crossed my legs in front of me, then tugged at the hemline of my bathing suit in a futile attempt to cover myself up a little more. Several seconds of awkward silence ensued, punctuated only by the dripping of water that trickled off Teddy's hair into the small puddle that had pooled on the planks beneath him. I mentally ticked off the facts I knew about him, with the notion of selecting the one that might best facilitate some small talk.

"So—you're from Newport?"

Bizarrely, this question appeared to strike a nerve. Teddy shaded his eyes and gave me a very serious look, as though suddenly reevaluating me. "Yes. Do you know much about . . . the town?"

"Oh—no. I don't suppose I do."

He continued to search my face for several seconds, then—evidently not finding what he sought there—sighed. "It's pretty swell, I guess. Lots of good folks from old families." He tipped his chin sunward and closed his eyes. I dared myself to make a quick inspection. I had never seen a man in a bathing suit before, and although I knew on instinct Teddy was less of a man and more of a boy, I'll admit I was curious nonetheless. His shoulders were quite narrow under the tank straps of his bathing suit, and he was lanky all the way from his ribs down to his legs. His brow furrowed briefly, and he shifted as though uncomfortable, causing me to worry for a moment that he could feel me looking at him.

I looked away. Soon enough, the friendly drone of his voice resumed as he continued his summary of Newport. "Big houses. No crime to speak of." The putter and spat of a motor-boat engine moved nearer to us, and then just as quickly repelled into the distance. Teddy opened his eyes and sat up with a sudden air, as though an idea had just come to him. His whole body had gone rigid with tension. I discerned there was something very serious he wanted to tell me and he had struck upon his opportunity. I could also tell he wasn't going to come right out and say it.

"Well, as I said, no crime. But that's not to say there haven't been some rather serious . . . *incidents.*" He was looking at me with ferocious intensity now. I almost believed I could feel the pupils of his eyes beating down on my face, trumping the strength of the sun's rays. "In fact," he continued in a very slow and deliberate voice, "one of the most tragic incidents in the town's recent history involved my cousin and a very memorable debutante."

I was intrigued and somewhat baffled by this new line of chatter, but I said nothing. Although I wasn't exactly sure how or why, I felt as though I was being baited. But Teddy was not to be dissuaded. He took a breath and plunged forward.

"She was *something,* that debutante. People in town never saw anything like her before—and I'd be willing to bet haven't seen anything like her since. I only saw her once or twice myself, mostly in passing, too, but somehow you just don't forget a girl like that." He gave a low admiring whistle, but didn't smile. "Wide blue eyes with the brightest look of curiosity in them all the time. Long dark hair."

There was a pause, and it struck me there was an air of false casualness about it. When he spoke again, I knew why.

"Course she's probably bobbed it by now. Her hair, that is. She's the type who would."

A sudden comprehension tingled in my veins and I felt my pulse quicken. I sat up straighter. My body inclined itself toward Teddy by unconscious volition. For a brief moment he wore an expression of satisfied accomplishment; he knew the implied meaning of his statement had not gone unnoticed. It was clear there was more to his tale, more he wanted me to know, and he could take his time now recounting the details. *It didn't end so well for my cousin,* he warned me, just before starting at the beginning of the story.

I have since, of course, replayed the narrative Teddy told me that day several times in my head. It remains to be seen whether I've become its most accurate transmitter or its greatest distorter, but I will paraphrase here to the best of my ability.

Ginevra Morris was the ebony-haired, wide-eyed only child of a wealthy banker from Boston. Her father, some twenty-eight years her mother's senior, had retired when Ginevra was five and moved the whole family out to a very large and stately house on the shores of Newport so he might pursue his favorite pastime of building model boats while looking out the window at their life-size counterparts passing on the eastern horizon. By the time Ginevra was ten, she had discovered that with the slightest frown she could make her father return the velvety-eyed chestnut mare he'd bought for her birthday and exchange it for a dappled Appaloosa stallion. More amazing to her still was how with a second frown she could provoke him to turn around the next day and return the Appaloosa in order to repurchase the chestnut mare at twice the price. Ginevra was thoughtfully raised in the spirit of

Victorian traditions to excel in music, poetry, and art, and by the time she turned fifteen she made it clear she'd had quite enough of Victorian traditions. In an infamous standoff with her mother, just days before her sixteenth birthday and consequent debutante ball, Ginevra took a pair of scissors and, in one deft, coldhearted gesture, sheared the skirt of her ball-gown clean through in protest of something her mother was saying. Her mother, thinking it would humiliate and therefore teach Ginevra a lesson, made her wear the dress as it was: savaged, the hemline falling barely to the knee.

But her mother, a fairly young woman herself but already the high-collared relic of a bygone era, had severely miscalculated. The night Ginevra had her coming-out debut, her cowl-necked gown draped in an especially Hellenic manner, and she floated down the stairs in her scandalously scissored skirt with her head held aloft, causing a rippling murmur throughout the audience. That evening, she went from knock-kneed tomboy to Greek goddess in the space of twenty-two short, red-carpeted steps. One boy in particular, Warren Tricott Jr., the son of a mining magnate and a member of the wealthiest family in Newport at the time, took special note of her seemingly effortless transition. He pulled around her drive in his silver roadster the very next day, and every day after that for the next two summers.

Of course, Teddy said, he was quite a few years behind his older cousin. At eleven, Teddy's adolescence had not yet ripened fully enough to attune him to the subtleties of courtship, much less cause him to care very much, but even at that age he nonetheless understood how special and exciting everyone thought Warren and Ginevra were, and he noted how a hush crept into people's voices whenever they discussed what a wild, striking pair

Warren and Ginevra made. Teddy was away at boarding-school for the larger part of the year, yet whenever he came home to Newport the first gossip delivered to him was often about his cousin Warren and the mesmerizing young lady Warren took around on dates. Folks often spotted them motoring around town together, or taking the Tricott family yacht out for a sail. It was not uncommon to see the glossy black streak of Ginevra's long ebony hair fly down a town street or country back road, trailed by her musical, haunting laugh. Together they appeared to find a reason to delight in everything. Even the harshest winter to hit Newport in twenty years could not put a damper on their merriment. That Christmas, Warren gave Ginevra a little draft pony and a gold-painted sleigh, and together they sat upon the embroidered cushions with furs tucked over their laps and giggled uncontrollably as they searched out the highest hill to drive down.

The war was in full swing by then. Some defect, the specifics of which Teddy wasn't exactly sure—bad eyesight, flat feet—had kept Warren out of the Army. (There were those in town who suspected the defect in question was in fact Warren's overbearing mother.) However, whatever it was that prevented Warren from dying in an anonymous trench in a farmer's field in France also caused him to feel undermined. By the spring of 1918, Warren had watched all his classmates enlist and board a train bound for a southern state (Kentucky, Tennessee—Teddy could not recall exactly) to attend boot camp. All of them were given a hero's farewell despite the fact at that particular juncture in time they had done little more than visit the Army doctor in Boston, turn their heads, and cough. With each train that pulled out of the station, Warren felt a little more deflated.

Warren and Ginevra knew how to have a lot of fun together,

but their relationship was also often stormy, to say the least. When they quarreled, they did it with a variety of dynamite otherwise monopolized by rail barons for the purposes of blasting away bedrock. Ginevra in particular had a ruthless way with words. She knew precisely what to go for—the jugular, that is—and how to get at it most swiftly and efficiently. When Warren displeased her or made her cross, she wasted no time reminding him what people likely thought of men who sat on the sidelines of the war and let others do all the fighting. Folks who overheard these arguments guessed this was surely the reason Warren took up with other women on the side.

The other women never bothered Ginevra much. She knew about them in a vague way. Warren's dalliances were mostly confined to the other side of town, which is to say to women of a different class, who hadn't attended Ginevra's debut, let alone their own. And so, being the only proper lady with a claim on Warren's heart (not to mention on his trust), Ginevra didn't feel terribly threatened. Besides, it was a well-known fact Ginevra liked to have her fun, too—it was a constant effort to be the belle of the ball, and with Warren sometimes on the other side of town she felt free to maintain the affections of her numerous other admirers. As far as Ginevra was concerned, it was all wonderful and fun, and not even an inch of it was serious. When Warren asked her to marry him the next summer, she accepted his proposal without hesitation. After all, they were the ones who mattered. Warren set about picking out a ring.

What came next in Teddy's story changed everything. It marked yet another point of no return.

Details are such funny things. Having witnessed more than

my fair share of criminal confessions now, I can tell you it's true what they say: A lying criminal always trips himself up (or *herself*, I suppose, rare though that alternate scenario may be) by either giving too many details or else revealing the wrong ones. See, the thing about details is they're nearly impossible to fabricate with any plausible success. If you're telling the truth, you're telling the truth, and you'll get the details right, especially the queer ones. That afternoon Teddy recounted a rather unusual detail I don't think he could've made up. After all, we humans lack the graceful capacity the gods have for total chaos. We are unable to come up with a pattern so free of obvious categorization; instead we know the world by types, by only the most common chains of cause and effect, by the rote and the familiar. There is a reason they say God is in the details. It is the precious details that can prove your innocence, and it is the vicious details that can get you hanged.

Of course, I did not have all this ambitious philosophy in mind at the time. I simply sat and listened to Teddy as he told the rest of his story, which, with Warren headed off to a jeweler in Boston, I'd already guessed was ultimately heading toward the engagement of Ginevra and Warren. And it was. In a thoughtful gesture, Warren not only purchased a ring, but also had a special diamond bracelet made to give to Ginevra as an additional engagement present. Warren's thoughtfulness, not to mention his extravagance, had never been a handicap for him. In fact, he was so thoughtful, he even had an identical second bracelet made for a woman named Pearl who lived on the other side of town and who, if he'd been a married man instead of merely an engaged one, might otherwise be called his mistress.

Unfortunately for Pearl, Warren never got around to giving

her the second bracelet. Out of a somewhat ironic and misplaced sense of loyalty, Warren insisted on presenting Ginevra with hers first, and on the night he did so, a terrible accident occurred.

By all accounts, the evening in question had been one of those balmy, grass-scented summer nights. As was so often the case on such nights, Warren and Ginevra had spent the evening motoring around in his little roadster with the top down. The trouble happened when they took a road that ran through a switchyard a few miles outside of town and crossed over several sets of train tracks. The car stalled, and the tires somehow got stuck on one of the tracks that usually carried the nighttime freight train. By the time the engineer was able to make out the silvery flank of a roadster parked perpendicular on the track, it was already too late to stop. The freight trains that ran at night clipped along at a good pace and almost never had cause to slow up as they entered Newport.

The tragedy was not a complete holocaust. Ginevra had managed to get out in time and was saved. But Warren—poor, misguided Warren—had died attempting to throw the gear in reverse and save his treasured roadster by freeing the tires. There was a lot of talk around town that the two of them had been drinking, and that the whole thing had been a criminal act of recklessness. Some repeated the rumor of what the coroner had told his wife: that Warren's body—or what horrific gruesomeness was left of it— smelled suspiciously like whiskey. A few folks even suggested that Ginevra had gotten Warren drunk on purpose and that being on the train tracks was no accident. After all, it was no secret they'd argued at the restaurant where they'd dined earlier that evening. In a moment of dramatic flare, Ginevra had even thrown a drink in Warren's face. But when Ginevra gave her statement to the police officer who attended the scene she was as sober as a judge, and with very somber eyes, she swore Warren had been, too. Of course, it wasn't just her word. There was a witness—one of the switchmen who worked the night shift in the yard. The switchman (a tall, swarthy man with a rather pockmarked complexion) had seen it all and had given a statement to confirm Ginevra's story: There had been no negligence involved, and certainly nothing malicious. It had simply been a freakish and terrible accident. Case closed.

At this point in his telling, Teddy heaved a burdensome sigh. "It was sad for the whole town, but it was especially sad for my aunt and uncle." He squinted at the opposite shore of the Sound and frowned. "They don't speak of it, not ever. My own folks tried to keep it from me, too; I suppose to protect me. But I wish they hadn't, because it only left me with questions. Questions and a rather uneasy feeling about the whole business. You see, I'd grown up admiring my cousin so much—I was an only child, and he was like a brother to me—and then . . . then he was suddenly just gone. It took me quite a few years to finally lay hands on the newspaper clippings and to get people in town to tell me the details about it." He spoke in a frank tone and ran a hand through his hair, separating the clumps of strands where they had dried together. "I suppose it's a good thing she's so memorable— Ginevra, I mean. Because that's probably why people can recall the details. In fact, just the other day, I was talking to the police officer who attended the scene of the accident, and he remembered something. A detail I'd never heard before."

"What was that?" I asked. It came out in a more demanding tone than I'd intended. By that point, I suppose one could say I was invested in the story's outcome. Teddy flinched at the sound of my voice, as if he'd gotten so lost in the telling of his story, he'd forgotten I was there. He turned and looked at me, and when he spoke again I spotted something in his innocent face I'd never glimpsed before, something sharp and incisive.

"The officer remembered something funny about Ginevra that night," he said. "The accident had made quite a terrible picture, you see, and so he didn't really remember or focus on this fact until later. It might very well mean nothing. But . . ." Teddy paused as though to consider. He cleared his throat. "When she gave her statement, Ginevra was wearing both bracelets."

A chill raced down my spine. My mind had split itself into two halves—one half raced to list the coincidences, the other half raced along a parallel trajectory to refute them.

"Where is she now? Ginevra, I mean," I asked once Teddy had reached the conclusion of his story.

"Missing," he answered.

"How do you mean?"

"She left town shortly after the accident. Some people say it was because of the tragedy, some people say it was because of all the talk. Can't say I blame her, but it was quite a disappearing act she pulled. Left in the middle of the night; didn't even tell her parents where she was going."

"Have they made . . . an effort . . . to find her?" I asked. My voice sounded very small in the back of my throat.

"Nice families don't hire private investigators," Teddy said in a flat tone. "At least, not any they'd admit to, and the lousy ones they might hire on the side are never going to find anything anyway. But I'd really welcome the chance to talk to her. There are things that just never made sense about that night, and I'd like to get some of that business cleared up. I've been looking for her for . . .

quite a while. You understand how it is, of course." He turned to me and held me in a long, meaningful stare. My body was almost completely dry by that time, and I could already feel the beginnings of a sun-burn. It was not the least bit cold out, but nonetheless I felt a cold shiver run through me, and suddenly my arms and legs bristled with goose pimples.

I started violently when I heard my name being called. I stood up a little wobbly-kneed on the raft and shaded my eyes, only to see Odalie calling to me from the shore. "Oh!" I exclaimed. I don't know if she could see who I was with on the raft, but I recognized a certain urgency in her voice.

"If you'll excuse me," I said to Teddy. He nodded and smiled, tight-lipped but knowingly.

"Of course."

Forgetting completely about the tower, I made a shallow dive from the raft and began swimming diligently toward Odalie where she waited on the shore. I was a little overcooked by the sun at that point, and the water felt colder to me than I remembered it being during the swim out. As I swam I realized I had another sensation, too; I couldn't help but feel the tiniest bit of threat emanating from somewhere behind me, somewhere still floating idly on the raft.

17

We spent the afternoon avoiding Teddy. It was like a game of cat-and-mouse: We settled into one location, and when Teddy came along Odalie made up a creative excuse to move on to the next. Odalie never said as much, but it was plain to me that Teddy had her unsettled and distinctly on edge. Her open aversion to his presence did very little to soothe the suspicions Teddy had raised with his story about "Ginevra." I said nothing, but for the remainder of the afternoon I couldn't help observing how Odalie's jumpiness increased every time Teddy materialized and tried to join in one of our activities—and boy, did he: a round of golf (a game I had never played and found incredibly boring until he showed up), croquet on the lawn (Odalie taught me the rules of the game, and then promptly taught me how to cheat), even our after-noon tea. (*I'll let you in on a little secret,* she leaned in and said to Teddy, who gazed at her as though in shock that she should finally speak to him. *Afternoon tea is meant to be enjoyed by the fairer sex, not by your lot.*) He was persistent. But Odalie was even more per-sistent in her evasions and her fevered attempts to display her indifference. Her wonderfully enchanting smile was stretched a little thin by the end of the afternoon, but she was bent on having a good time and not letting him ruin it, or else she had decided she would knock herself out in the attempt to show as much.

I, by contrast, had finally relaxed into having a reasonably good time. The focus of Odalie's forced hilarity had landed on me, and suddenly she was absolutely breathless to know everything she didn't already know about me. That afternoon, we sat around a tea-table joined by a handful of the Brinkleys' other guests (mostly ladies and a few hen-pecked husbands). But despite the number of perfectly voluble and friendly guests at our tea-table, Odalie turned to me in an intimate way and started up a conversation in a confiding voice, as though we were alone. Even in my growing wariness, I couldn't help but feel more than a little flattered by this turn of events. I answered her readily as she peppered me with questions about my upbringing, and I was surprised at my own eagerness to talk about the childhood I usually kept private. I recounted for her the names of all the sisters at the orphanage, their relative holiness, and some of their more secular flaws. For her part, Odalie seemed curiously delighted by this information, memorizing the statistics of each nun as though I had just handed her a pack of holier-than-thou baseball cards.

I also recounted for her a random selection of memories from my time at the Bedford Academy—recalling how, for instance, all the buildings smelled like wet wool socks but that I'd secretly liked that about it, and how we all had to wear matching light blue dresses and I'd secretly liked those, too, despite the fact all the girls were socially required to act as though they detested them. I told all about the time I'd gotten an award for having the best penmanship in the entire school and how this meant I got to sit nearest the woodstove in our classroom, a position that was very coveted in the wintertime. I recounted how there had been a boys' school down the road and how there was one boy in particular when I was fourteen who used to walk by the school gate and slip letters inscribed with my name written in very elaborate calligraphy through the bars. I never opened those letters to find out what they said on the inside, and when Odalie asked me why, I told her it was because I knew nothing that was written inside could be as pretty and as perfect as the calligraphy on the outside. When I said that, she turned and looked at me with an oddly appraising gaze, and curiously, I got the impression she approved.

All the while I talked, Odalie listened to my mundane stories as though enraptured. That is, she did until Teddy joined our tea-table. Once Teddy sat down, her mood abruptly shifted. Unexpectedly, Odalie began to volunteer information about her own childhood, which, this time around, she remembered as taking place in California.

"What part of California?" Teddy politely asked. By then, everyone at the table had joined in our conversation and was listening intently, mesmerized, as people so often were, by Odalie's enthralling manner of telling a story.

"Santa Fe," she answered.

"I see," Teddy replied. Either no one wanted to confess they had not paid much attention to the geography teachers of their youth who had faithfully stood at the blackboard with pointer-stick in hand, or else no one wanted to contradict her, for all faces at the table remained pleasantly composed. "And how did you happen to visit all the way out there?" Teddy asked.

"Why, I was born there," Odalie replied with a sweet smile. I glimpsed a tremor of surprise jolt through Teddy's posture, but if Odalie detected it, she either did not care or else purposely ignored it. She continued on with her recollections.

Both the sun and the breeze were quite strong that day. As she talked, Odalie's sleek hair swung under her chin, the fine cut of her bob ruffling in the wind. Little bursts of bright sunshine flashed along the high cheekbones of her face as the yellow-and-white striped umbrella overhead fluttered. Everyone else at the tea-table seemed to put complete credence in Odalie's words, but this was not enough for her. She could not seem to ignore what she took to be a skeptical expression on Teddy's face, and I caught the lightning-fast flicker of her gaze as it flashed hotly in his direction several times. I knew this much from my time with her: She was not accustomed to being doubted. Her mouth twitched at the corners. When a woman named Louise cut in to contribute a story about the honeymoon trip she and her husband had taken to the little seaside village of Santa Barbara, Odalie excused herself and stood up abruptly to leave. I watched her storm away, wanting to follow her but feeling compelled to offer a polite excuse to the table.

"Was it something I said?" Louise asked, her face screwed up in earnest puzzlement as she looked around the tea-table for someone to affirm she'd done nothing wrong. "Heavens . . . isn't Santa Barbara near Los Angeles? I only brought it up because I thought she'd be tickled to hear a story about her old stomping grounds. . . ."

I took this as my cue for a tidy exit. "I believe she said earlier she has a headache," I explained to the group. "I'll go check on her." I scurried after Odalie, feeling Teddy's eyes burning into my back as I hurried away.

When I got upstairs to our room, I found Odalie angrily brushing out the tangles the wind had knotted into her usually silky-straight bob. I hesitated. I wanted to ask her about the things Teddy had told me—mostly, I admit, because I wanted her to tell me none of them were true. I was beginning to comprehend just how little I knew about the woman I was now beholden to. I remembered the fragment of gossip I'd heard at the precinct about Odalie and Clara Bow dancing on a table in a movie. The California story, I tried to convince myself, could very well be part of that. So many of her stories *could* be true, if only they didn't cancel one another out—that was the trouble. *If she looks me in the eye and promises me, if she says it like she really means it,* I told myself, *then I will decide to believe her, right here and now.* I would believe her, and all the rest of it wouldn't matter. Sometimes the truth of a situation was about more than simply uncovering the facts; it was about choosing allegiances. I screwed up my nerve and cleared my throat.

"Teddy said—"

But suddenly a hairbrush went flying through the air and smashed against the wall behind me. I followed its trajectory back to its original source and saw Odalie's face exploding in anger. "Teddy! What does he know! About anything! He's a pimply-faced undergraduate, for Chrissake! He's practically in *diapers!*"

I had never seen Odalie unsettled, much less losing her temper. The sight of it was both terrible and beautiful, like an angry comet hurtling down from the sky.

I didn't mention Teddy for the rest of the afternoon. I exited the room quietly, preferring an afternoon walk along the seashore to a pretended nap alongside a terrifyingly angry Odalie.

BY EVENING TIME, Odalie appeared to have returned to her customary cool state of being. Refreshed by her afternoon nap (evidently the sleep I would not have been able to achieve had been a total success for her), she was once again pink-cheeked and even hummed to herself as we dressed for dinner. She seemed to be in great spirits, and her energized mood was reflected in her selection of a bold red dress for the evening. I can still remember how the vibrant hue of the dress contrasted crisply with her dark hair, it made her bob appear as slick and shiny as a pool of spilled ink. She was a picture to behold, and a very striking one at that. Perhaps it's rather revealing to say so, but while I cannot for the life of me recall what I was wearing that evening, I nonetheless remember every little stitch of black embroidery on her red dress.

The stars were out in full force that evening; they appeared early—as though the Brinkleys had paid them to put in some overtime—showing up as bright points of light punched into the eerie bluish glow of the twilit sky. Dinner was served on the terrace just as it had been the night before (and this time consisted of rack of lamb with mint jelly), and the evening air was pleasantly tepid and salty. With some relief, I noted Teddy was not seated among our particular party. Once we'd come downstairs and Odalie had had a chance to survey the place cards that ringed our table, she became visibly more relaxed. Louise, the same woman who had been unintentionally snubbed earlier that afternoon when Odalie had bolted from the tea-table, was seated on Odalie's left, and this time Odalie made an effort to listen to Louise as she prattled on. In no time at all they were as thick as thieves, and I had to settle for staring at Odalie's back as she and Louise chattered and laughed. Of course I was annoyed, but I said nothing. Odalie was making up for her earlier trespass, I figured. So much the better.

Charity takes many forms, you see. And Odalie's particular form of charitable expertise was to make less attractive girls feel they could, by learning some secret trick, obtain at least a fraction of Odalie's inherent fluency in charm. But charity, when performed by such jolly unfeeling sharks as Odalie, is not without a sense of irony. Odalie could take a wallflower and flatter her into feeling like the belle of the ball. Just as chance plays no favorites, she sometimes did it for no reason at all, and with nothing to gain from it. Of course, I abhorred all these girls, never realizing I myself was one of them. But (lest we forget too quickly!) Odalie *did* stand to gain something from me. Quite a lot, actually, as it eventually turned out. But I'll get to telling about that soon enough.

The main course was served, and the air filled with the buttery musk of lamb. I had never tasted such tender meat before; my experience with lamb was limited to its much older relation, mutton, and as the soft morsels of lamb melted in my mouth, I temporarily forgot my irritation over Louise. But by the time dessert was cleared away, it had returned. I had become quite a snob during my months with Odalie, you see, and now I turned my newly haughty gaze on Louise. Despite being quite young, Louise was an annoying, prematurely ancient specimen, with her lackluster dark brown hair piled on top of her head with such a dismal air, it was as though some variety of backyard bird had begun construction on a nest and halfway through gave up on it. Each time she

laughed hysterically at something Odalie said, which was obnox-
iously frequent, she revealed a top row of slightly crooked teeth.
Even her clothing offended me—an offense I could've never afforded prior to Odalie's sponsorship of my own wardrobe. Louise
was wearing a dress that would've been hopelessly out-of-date if it
had not been for the beaded chiffon overlay, and even with the
overlay was only slightly fashionable. It was simply not possible
Odalie could be genuinely interested in anything Louise had to
say, I decided. Perhaps Teddy's presence set her on edge more than
I realized, and now Odalie was trying to fortify her position by
acquiring new friends.

"You know," Louise said, laying a hand on Odalie's upper arm
(as though I weren't sitting right there to note her bold advances!),
"I really ought to visit the city more often. All the best shops, all
the ones that carry the chicest merchandise, are there, like you say.
Do you know what? I'm going to ring you up, that's what I'm going
to do!"

"Oh yes, please do," Odalie exclaimed. I scowled an invisible
scowl to an audience who, evidently, was beyond perceiving me.
Louise extracted a tiny pencil and a little address-book from her
purse and took down our number at the hotel.

"Do you really think you could?"

"Could what?"

"Dress me to look like a movie-star?"

"Oh! Are you kidding me? Why, that'd be easy as pie!"

"Here's my card," Louise volunteered, extracting a white rectangle from her clutch. Quickly and upon instinct, I intercepted it.

"I'll take care of that," I said with a wide, generous smile. "For
the life of her, Odalie can't help but lose every single calling card
that comes into her possession!"

Odalie nodded kindly at Louise. "It's true," she said. "I'm afraid it's in better hands with Rose here."

"Oh," said Louise as her hand went limp, being more than a little reluctant to relinquish the card to my custody.

"There now," I said, taking the card and slipping it into my own satin-trimmed clutch. "Safe and sound." Odalie looked at me and raised an eyebrow. We both knew I would lose the card, but not by accident.

Without a second look at Louise, I snapped my clutch shut and surveyed the scene around us. Dinner and dessert had long since been served and cleared. Abandoned linen napkins littered the table like miniature deflated teepees, strewn amid empty champagne glasses and the stains and scraps of an evening's feast. From out one corner of my eye I perceived a male figure rapidly approaching our table, and from out the opposite corner I saw Odalie bristle.

"Pardon me," came Teddy's voice. He bowed deep at the waist in Odalie's direction, and it was understood he was requesting a dance.

"Oh!" The little involuntary exclamation escaped me. Suddenly all eyes—Odalie's, Louise's, and Teddy's—were trained on me. Unable to explain my shock away, I merely shrugged.

Aware that we were being rude, Odalie lifted her head in Teddy's direction and bared her teeth in what was a fierce and impenetrable second cousin to a smile. "Of course," she said through a set of stiff, glistening, perfectly white piano keys. Teddy took her hand, and she rose from her chair with her face tilted up defiantly, like a flower blooming in spite of harsh conditions.

Her body language plainly stated she did not want to be within half a mile of Teddy, much less cheek-to-cheek with him on the

dance floor. I'm sure she would've appreciated it if I had inter-
vened and deflected him somehow, but as a woman, there was little recourse available to me. I suppose I could have pressed myself
on Teddy in Odalie's place—insisting he dance with me instead
and perhaps even attempting to vamp him a bit—but such trans-
actions were utterly foreign to me, and in this capacity I was rather
hopeless. Instead I sat in silence, ignoring Louise as she prattled
stubbornly to me as though I were Odalie's proxy, and anxiously
watched as Teddy steered Odalie around the dance floor.

They cut a fine line, but the stiffness between them was obvious, even from a distance. Her head remained turned away from
him at all times, cocked to the right in a very serious manner as
though she were imitating one of those professional dancers who
perform flamboyant exhibitions in dance halls. I observed Teddy
was, in fact, very light on his toes; not surprising, given his thin
frame and slight stature. They danced a full waltz, and by the end
of it, to my relief, another man had cut in upon them. But Teddy, I
noticed, never strayed too far from Odalie, and cut in to dance
with her several more times as the evening wore on. Four orchestra songs later I dimly perceived someone hovering near my seat
at the table.

I was barely conscious of it when a thin, nasal male voice
inquired whether I'd care to dance with him. I looked up and in
astonishment saw Max Brinkley blinking down at me, the magni-
fied look of his monocled eye striking a comical incongruence
with his unmagnified other eye. Still a little intimidated by the
Brinkleys and apprehensive about the legitimacy of our stay, I rose
to my feet automatically as he reached for my hand.

"Please, Miss Baker, tell me why your friend seems to be having all the fun," he said as we set off gingerly in a foxtrot. "I'm

sure Pembroke, equitable old chap that he is, would want you to enjoy yourself, too."

"Well," I muttered with an awkward grimace, suddenly feeling like the imposter I was, "you know Pembroke . . ."

"Sometimes I wonder if you can *really* know Pembroke," Mr. Brinkley said. A tremor of panic ran through me before I realized Mr. Brinkley's comment was an epistemological observation, rather than a social accusation. "My goodness! Are you cold, my dear?" Mr. Brinkley inquired, noticing my involuntary shiver. He glanced up at the stars, as though some celestial thermometer might be hidden there. "I suppose it *is* a bit chillier than usual out tonight."

"Yes, Mr. Brinkley—"

"Max."

"Max. Actually I *am* cold, come to think of it. I think I'd better run and fetch my shawl, if that's all right."

"Of course, my dear." He stopped, mid-foxtrot, and took a gallant step back. "What kind of gentleman would I be if I forced you to freeze?" This was not an epistemological question; it was a rhetorical one. He bowed, his monocle staying miraculously perched on the apple of his cheek throughout, and I smiled. "Just don't forget, now, to come back downstairs and have a good time. That's an order," he said. I nodded obediently, recalling once having read in a society article that Max Brinkley had been a Navy man. I thanked him and scurried in the direction of the house, which was now lit up like a blazing Christmas tree.

I wasn't really cold, and didn't really want my shawl, but I did want to find Odalie. Both she and Teddy had completely vanished. I checked the interior of the house first (stopping by our room upstairs to pick up my shawl, just in case I should run into Max Brinkley again). The house was quite large, with many rooms, and there were so many people milling about that as soon as I had finished searching all of the rooms I worried that I'd perhaps missed Teddy and Odalie in passing and I searched the whole house all over again. By the second go-round, I was somewhat satisfied they were not to be found indoors. I'd grown sick of the house by that time, where the gay atmosphere had seemed to turn more septic than it had outdoors. The fug of cigarettes hung densely in the air of every room, making me cough, and in opening a broom closet I had accidentally blundered into a necking couple who were not in the least pleased to have me open the door and witness their activities.

Back outside, I surveyed the terrace. Teddy and Odalie were not at any of the tables. Squinting at the passing faces of each turning couple revealed they had not returned to the canvas platform for another dance. I strolled the gardens: first the wide lawn that led down to the beach, then the little topiary maze. Moonlight streamed down, turning the leaves of the hedges silvery and making the neatly trimmed foliage appear like walls of cut stone. I hesitated. I had never much liked topiary mazes or the impetus behind them; the notion that being lost could be fun had always struck me as the stuff from which nightmares are born. And then suddenly it came to me. I remembered seeing a greenhouse on a hill just beyond the topiary maze, a small distance off the west wing of the house. If Odalie had wanted to talk to Teddy privately and was fearful of what he might reveal, I could envision her choosing to do it there.

As I drew up to the greenhouse, the windows were dark. It was an elaborately white-gabled affair, a true relic of the Gilded Age. I walked along the inclined path that led to the greenhouse entrance with a feeling of foreboding so potent, it almost caused me to stop and go back. The sounds of music and laughter tinkled dimly from far across the lawn, as though it emanated from some ghostly echo of a party rather than the boisterous affair I'd just left. When I tried the door handle, I found myself half hoping it would be locked, but it turned easily enough. Once inside, a thick humidity instantly enveloped my skin, and I inhaled the rich aroma of moist peat moss and wet ferns. The echo of the door boomed loudly throughout the large space as I pulled it shut behind me, and I was very still for several minutes. As I stood there straining to listen, at first I could only hear the dripping of wet plants and the gurgling of an ornamental fountain or two. But then I heard it— the distant sound of two voices talking in hushed tones. I listened for another moment; the voices definitely belonged to Odalie and Teddy, and despite the commotion I'd made shutting the door it did not appear they had detected my entry. The sound was coming from the far end of the greenhouse. Very quietly, I made my way along the stone pavers that led in the direction of the sound's emanation.

I glimpsed the butt of a cigarette glow red as someone—it had to be Odalie—inhaled. Crouching down next to some sort of alien-looking, pointy-leafed bromeliad, I looked on and quietly tried to catch my breath. As my eyes adjusted to the dark of the green-house, the moonlight coming through the glass ceiling began to illuminate the two figures standing before me. Between them a cherub capered, a bow and arrow clutched in his chubby grasp and water gurgling at his stony toes. My ears eagerly worked to pick up the thread of conversation. Teddy was doing most of the talk-ing, and slowly but surely I realized I had walked halfway into some sort of long-winded explanation. For the second time that day, I listened to Teddy tell the story of his cousin's unfortunate

death. When he reached the end, Odalie exhaled a cloud of cigarette smoke and regarded him impassively.

"That's a very sad story," she finally said.

"Indeed."

"Oh, but I rather wish you'd never told it to me!" Odalie
exclaimed, suddenly looking up from her cigarette coquettishly.

"Why's that?"

"Oh, well, because I've always wanted to visit Newport. It
sounds so lovely! And now if I ever go"—she leaned toward him
with an expression of sweet sympathy—"I'll be sure to think of
your story and how terrible that gruesome accident was!" As she
spoke, a befuddled expression engraved itself with increasing
intensity on Teddy's face. Odalie glimpsed it, and in response her
own manner turned sprightly and cheerful now. "You see, I'd hate
to spoil it. I've never been."

"Never been!" Teddy spluttered uncontrollably. "Do you mean
to tell me you've never been to Newport?"

"I do," she replied. By now her tone had shifted. It still had all
the pretenses of friendliness, but there was also a deadly inflection
to it, as though you could almost hear the dry, papery rattle of a
venomous snake's tail. Teddy swallowed hard and stared at her
lips. She cocked her head innocently. "Yes. Never been to Newport. Can you imagine?"

"No . . . I can't," he stammered.

"Well, perhaps you should try," she said, the mocking innocence gone from her voice now and in its place a flat, dull tone.
And with that she strode away, swishing through the overgrowth
of the greenhouse and passing perilously close to where I remained
crouched and hiding. It was as though a bell had rung, and Odalie—

consummately triumphant boxer that she was—had been called back to her corner.

When I crawled into bed later that night, I knew two things for certain. I knew Odalie hoped to never see Teddy again. I also knew from the expression on Teddy's face as he watched her stride away that it would not be long before he came to find her.

18

And then, just as abruptly as it had begun, our beach holiday was over. If Odalie and I were ever to drop in on the Brinkleys again, I daresay they would not be very glad to have us back. For one thing, we finagled our way into a week's invitation but left after merely two nights. Moreover, we departed with the sort of abrupt haste that can only be interpreted as a total lack of common courtesy and respect for one's hosts.

As I remember it, after her exchange with Teddy in the greenhouse, Odalie retired to our room for the night. I followed her and feigned ignorance (she told me nothing of her interaction with him). We prepared for bed, but it was apparent there was very little rest to be had. Instead of crawling under the covers and joining me, Odalie turned out the lamp and proceeded to roam the room like an agitated jungle cat. I knew then it was unlikely we would be staying much longer at the Brinkleys' estate. As I slept (or pretended to sleep, rather), she paced at the foot of our bed in silence, gnawing indelicately from time to time at her fingernails. About an hour and a half before the sun came up, Odalie suddenly grew very still and very calm. She sat down in the middle of the rug on the floor and closed her eyes. I had never seen her do this before and found it very queer. It was almost as though she was praying, but even now, to this day, I doubt Odalie has ever prayed about anything.

When her eyes finally snapped open again, the morning sun was streaming in through the window. She telephoned for a taxi and packed our bags with a deliberate orderliness I was unaccustomed to seeing her exhibit. In general, Odalie's actions were dominated by a very haphazard air—the world around her conspired to collaborate with her rhythms, not the other way around. I remember finding it odd to see her move around in such a rigid manner. Somehow I knew better than to ask questions or strike up a conversation that afternoon; rather, I very simply and obediently followed suit with this change in our itinerary, grateful to be returning to the familiar city I'd always known. I was perceptive enough to intuit something dark was brewing, and I had it in my head I would be safer back home. One might be inclined to point out what a fool I was, but of course I couldn't know it at the time.

When the taxi pulled into the drive, the butler alerted the Brinkleys, consequently causing them to come down to see if anything was the matter. I still remember the look of reproach Max Brinkley shot me through his monocle, confused and thoroughly disapproving. Odalie conveyed a series of hasty and halfhearted regrets to our hosts, who shook our hands politely enough but who each arched an eyebrow and frowned over our shoulders the whole time at the driver as he loaded our luggage into the trunk. The final farewells were said, during which I felt Odalie's hand on my arm, the skin of her hand as soft as velvet, her grip as unyielding as iron. And then in record speed I found myself in the back of the taxi. The tires spun over the gravel, and the thin, frowning faces of Mr. and Mrs. Brinkley receded until they were no more than two expressionless blurs.

Of course, I assumed we were going to the train station, so when Odalie asked the driver how much he would charge to take us all the way into the city I was a bit surprised. I was even more surprised when he named an exorbitant sum and she agreed to it straightaway, not bothering to barter in spite of the fact we both knew she could very well have gotten him down to half the price he named. It took us three hours at top-notch speed, interrupted only by a solitary stop at a filling station, in order to arrive at our destination. Throughout our entire journey Odalie periodically twisted about to peer through the cramped, oval-shaped back window of the taxi. I looked back a few times myself and half expected to see Teddy running maniacally behind us, trying to catch hold of the automobile's bumper.

We arrived in front of our hotel without further incident some-time in the afternoon. During our ride back into the city, I had realized summer was lazily fading away. Already the days were beginning to grow shorter. For the remainder of that afternoon and on into the evening, Odalie appeared jittery. The lunch hour had come and gone while we were still in the back of the taxi, but Odalie did not appear to notice its absence, let alone the fact it was now time for dinner. There was a good amount of fresh food in the apartment ice-box, but she only took one bite of this or that simply to lay the dish down and walk away, forgetting all about it. She was the same with books and magazines. She picked one or the other up and turned a few pages merely to set it back down again, and all the while the blind, distracted stare never left her eyes. Several times she got up to open the curtains and peer out the window into the night and then, with a small, almost imperceptible shudder, drew them again as though recoiling from some unseen specter.

By the time the shrill ring of the telephone sounded, she nearly jumped out of her skin. It was Gib, of course. I could tell from her responses he was demanding to know why we'd disappeared and where we'd been. Or rather, where *Odalie* had been, as I suspect Gib was not in all honesty greatly concerned about my own whereabouts. From across the room, I could just about make out the tinny, canned sound of squawking that emanated from the telephone. Somewhere in the city, Gib was at the other end of the line, angry as spit. I listened to Odalie as she tried to soothe him with that mellifluous voice of hers.

"Oh, don't fuss so much. . . . Sometimes a girl just needs a little vacation. . . . Well, of course I'm always here if there's a problem. . . . What do you mean? What's happened?"

He'd sent little Charlie Whiting out on a delivery, and the dumb kid had gotten himself picked up by the police. Oddly, this piece of bad news seemed to wash over Odalie as something of a relief. Her rigid body melted back into its catlike slouch. She hung up the receiver and began plotting straightaway, happy to be presented with a new distraction. But before I tell all about how Odalie maneuvered to get Charlie off the hook the next day at the precinct, I'd like to take a moment here and explain a little bit about my state of mind at the time.

By now, the outside observer has probably intuited our interaction with Teddy had not yet fully run its course, and something serious was about to happen. It is important to me that I tell why I did not listen to my better judgment and distance myself from the impending catastrophe.

During my time with Odalie, I'd heard so many stories aimed

at explaining her origin, each new fable wonderfully fantastic and implausible in its own right. I suppose I'd gotten used to the idea Odalie's past was ultimately unknowable—and in some ways it made her rather mythical in my mind. But the story Teddy had told me out on the swimmers' raft somehow changed everything, and I'd be lying if I didn't say I suspected his story was the true one. Moreover, I sensed there was an element to Teddy's version Odalie wished to keep concealed from public view. It was the only way to explain her otherwise bizarrely potent aversion to the otherwise innocuous-seeming undergrad. And besides, the bracelets—those incontrovertible bits of mineral and metal—had somehow set Teddy's story apart from all the others. Unlike the Hungarian aristocrat, whose dapper suits and top hat turned to ash immediately upon contradiction and blew back into whimsical vapor from whence they came, the bracelets were very tangible objects I had witnessed on more than one occasion with my own eyes. Odalie's own explanation to me about the origin of their existence—a deliberately vague and shoddily wrought riches-to-rags story about a doting father and a tragically deceased sister named Violet—was never terribly convincing (when I brought up her sister's name less than a week after she'd told the tale she had absently responded, "Who?"—and uncomfortably, I had been forced to remind her). Not to mention the fact I'd overheard her the night she'd told the Lieutenant Detective the bracelets were an engagement present. Now it was looking like this latter bit of information may have very well been the truth. Or, at least, a half-truth.

I say all this because while one might judge me a fool, they would be mistaken to think me a total babe in the woods. I knew by then who and what Odalie was (although I readily admit I did not yet know in full—that would come later). Teddy's effect on her nerves did not bode well for her innocence. From my days spent sitting in front of the stenotype taking dictation in the interrogation room, I knew how to tell the difference between the agitated nerves of an innocent man and the agitated nerves of a guilty man, which with their raw, paranoid edges always jangled about more loudly in the end and gave him away. The long and short of it is I knew there was a good chance Odalie was in fact Ginevra. And I knew if that was indeed the truth of it, there was certainly a reason she had made the switch.

Why then, one might wonder, did I remain at Odalie's side, concealing her secret and following her around as she conducted further illicit business—the very brand of business, as I have already mentioned, of which I did not approve in the first place? I have said here I am no babe in the woods, and this much is true; I am no innocent. But only now, with the added advantage of hindsight, do I see how I may have appeared (to some) shrouded by the pall of malice from the very first moment I met Odalie. The word *obsession* has been bandied about rather recklessly by the newspapers. When I was not her condemner, I was her collaborator and, all too quickly following suit, her coolie. One might question why I was so drawn to Odalie, why I was so eager to ingratiate myself to her, if not for unnatural reasons. Yet I must insist again that there was nothing improper in my devotion to Odalie.

This is not to say I didn't want anything from Odalie. In the months we spent together, I watched countless others—men and women alike—as they swarmed around her, fawning over her, practically pawing at her, all of them wanting something from her. They had disgusted me. But I realize now how I, too, craved something from Odalie, and while in comparison to the desires of her other admirers my desire was much nobler in spirit, it was nonetheless like any other hunger in that it was driven by appetite and need.

It is difficult to put into words what I wanted from Odalie; language too easily corrupts, you see, and falls short. Once, while at the Bedford Academy, we were made to learn all about the carnivorous plants of the Americas. Most of the other schoolchildren were fascinated by the violent Venus flytrap, with its hinged leaves like a series of tiny bear traps. But I was more intrigued with the pitcher plant, with its much more alluring tubes shaped like upside-down bells, and the simple premise of its sweet nectar bait. Odalie was like that for me, and I suspect for other people, too. The promise of potentially being the recipient of her love and adoration was a sweet nectar one couldn't resist; like the insect drawn to his peril, you stepped toward it willingly.

Before you think me dreadfully Sapphic, perhaps it would do to remind you there's a great history of friendship between women—bonds that are pure and true and do not take on the more unfortunate shades of impropriety. Our mothers' generation certainly understood it. Why, isn't the cornerstone of Victorian girlhood founded on such wonderful intimacies? I believe, with all my heart, the generations before us knew a type of loyalty in love that our modern society does not understand at all. *An acute cruel streak*, the doctor here wrote next to my name. I suspect he thinks me an outright monster, but I am no monster. He misunderstands my motivations. I only wanted the giggles, the held hands, the whispered confidences, all the cool kisses upon my cheek that had evaded me throughout my own childhood. And in answering for the rest of my actions . . . well, it is natural for us to feel some measure of possessive zeal for the things we love. We cannot help the fact we humans are territorial creatures, after all.

I am rambling, perhaps, but there is a point to all of this. My point is *motive*. From the moment I heard Teddy's story, I became abstractly aware that an invisible clock had been set to ticking. I also understood this clock was ticking down to something, but why and to what event of course I could not know just then.

THE MONDAY AFTER we returned from the Brinkleys, we awoke to find a brilliant red dawn sky overhead. As the sun slogged upward and red gave way to blood orange, the colors vibrated with diminishing intensity. It was as if summer itself were burning off the last of its halcyon days. It was still warm out, but already the air was thinner and laced with the suggestion of cleaner, crisper days ahead.

Though we had arranged for a longer holiday, Odalie had determined we should return to work that day, in part, I assumed, to take care of the minor predicament into which Charlie had gotten himself. We rose, dressed, and made our way down to the precinct. Once through the entrance door, the Sergeant did not seem particularly surprised to see us. I think he had come to accept the fact Odalie would come and go as she pleased, and his choices were to either twist his mustache and grumble about it or not twist his mustache and not grumble about it. But Iris was flustered by our return. She was a woman who took comfort in routine. She had parceled out the work very precisely in our absence and now found herself obliged to spontaneously redistribute it. She huffed and huffed and hardly said hello, while Marie flew over to us and shook us with a friendly, brute force, her fingers now thickly swollen from her increasingly obvious state of pregnancy.

"Why on Earth would anyone cut short a holiday?! Oh, you little fools!" she exclaimed in an accusing voice, but her shining face betrayed her true delight.

"Just as I feared," the Lieutenant Detective chimed in. He sauntered in our direction, pushing a hand through his hair. "You cannot go more than two days without me." It might've been directed at Odalie, but for some reason he winked at me. I stiffened. I felt the back of my neck grow hot.

"Well, you could take a nice long holiday, Lieutenant Detective, and we could retest that theory," I replied on instinct. At this, Marie shook her hand at the wrist and whistled, as if to say *touché!* I watched as the Lieutenant Detective's grin slid into a frown, and felt that familiar sensation of satisfaction tinged with regret.

"No one's going anywhere," the Sergeant asserted. "We've got work to do." We stared at him, unmoving. "Marie"—he snapped his fingers—"coffee!" Whatever odd enchantment had temporarily rooted us in place suddenly lifted, and the office hummed again as we all went about our business.

"Let me help you with that, my dear," I overheard Odalie say to Iris, who had lumped all the case files back into one pile and was preparing to divvy them into a revised distribution. Odalie's voice was sugary and pleasant enough, but I saw the tendons above Iris's necktie flex defensively. Order and control were Iris's two best friends, and I knew by the end of the hour Odalie was bound to worm her way in between them, much to Iris's silent distress. If there was one thing I could consistently predict, it was that Odalie would always get her way.

Odalie had also not forgotten her promise to Gib. After a handful of casual, perfectly innocent-sounding inquiries, Odalie was told a representative was on his way over from the Lower East

Side Boys' Home to collect a young juvenile named Charles Whiting, who was being temporarily held in our precinct's holding cell. To any outside observer, Odalie did not appear dreadfully interested in the case. But nonetheless, the corresponding file somehow made its way from Iris's pile and into her own. It seemed a haphazard transaction, but I knew better. Before the lunch hour rolled around, a telephone call had been made to inform the representative he needn't bother making the trip, and a middle-aged couple had rung the bell at our front desk to sign the boy out. They were Charlie's parents, they claimed, despite the fact they twice referred to him as Carl (*It's a pet name*, the woman who introduced herself as Mrs. Whiting explained the mistake away).

Of course I was privy to the fact these weren't really Charlie's parents. Everyone at the speakeasy who regularly interacted with Charlie knew his father had died in the war and his mother had drunk herself to death the year after the armistice. But it wasn't until they had already departed, each holding one of Charlie's hands parentally tucked into one of their own, that I was finally able to place his "mother's" face as that of the woman who had once removed her shoes and drunkenly played "Chopsticks" on the piano with her toes.

19

I have as good as admitted the journal I kept about Odalie reads like one long love-letter; it details my initial intrigue with her and quickly evolves into an outpouring of the sisterly affection I spent so many hours cultivating for her. I understand only too well how it will appear to the eyes of an outsider, and I have endeavored to keep it among my private things for as long as that arrangement holds (the doctors here are not keen on privacy). We have access to very few books here—*Too much fiction may overstimulate the mind, and as you know, your imagination is already altogether too excitable,* they tell me. With little else to do and little ability to concentrate on the ridiculous "recreational" activities they offer here, I have now reread my journal several times over. It is striking how little is mentioned about Odalie's business affairs. At present, I can see only one entry that makes reference to the high level of Odalie's illicit entanglements. Of course, at the time, I failed to accurately interpret the meaning of this exchange, but I made note of it thus:

Today when I came home O and G were in the back bedroom and I heard them arguing about something. I would never eavesdrop, but they must not have heard me come in and they kept at it, and then of course it got so it was too late for me to interrupt or cough or make my presence known in some other way, and so I just held my breath and stood there, quiet as can be. Curiously, they weren't arguing over O having other suitors as they normally might have, but instead it was something about business, and O sounded a great deal more agitated than usual. At one point G shouted, Well, now that you've gotten your card from that almighty crook of a police commissioner, I suppose you think you don't even need me any-more. It was a curious thing to say—to my knowledge, O has never met the Commissioner. Finally, G came storming out and made for the front door, and when he caught sight of me he gave a rude snort and shouted back something horribly slanderous to O about my being a toady and a spy. Then he left without saying so much as hello to me and slammed the door. Thought G and I had achieved a peaceful treaty, but I see now I was a fool to think so. It is truly less of a treaty and more of a stalemate, I believe.

I KNOW MY PERSECUTORS would delight in much of my journal, but I believe this particular entry would disappoint them. Their explanation for entries like this one would be of a simple nature: They would say, of course, I am a madwoman, an unreliable raconteur. But I know the truth, and I'd be willing to bet if the Commissioner himself were to ever catch wind of this entry, the entire journal might even disappear altogether.

The fact of the matter is, my journal is rather devoid of further entries on the subject because I never knew that much about Odalie's business. I realize, of course, nobody here believes me when I say so, but I'm afraid it is simply the truth. The doctor I am seeing—Dr. Miles H. Benson; you may as well know his name, as it is no great secret—nods his head as though he believes me, but I know he is merely humoring me. He thinks if he nods his head in that sympathetic way of his I'll come to see him as an ally and confide in him. But in truth, I have not honestly been privy to the kind of secrets I'm sure he is salivating to hear. It's likely he has imagined a whole world for me, a world of racketeering and tommy guns and shoot-outs in curtained restaurants. Of course these imaginings are so false as to be laughable; the existence I led with Odalie was one of fine furnishings and delicate pastries and frequent trips to fancy department stores. At best, I possess a fragmented knowledge of the role Odalie played in the importation and production of alcohol, assembled mostly from bits and pieces of information acquired by indirect means (here Gib might snarkily point out that what I call "indirect means" he calls spying).

Of the facts I do know, here are some: I know the liquor at the speakeasies ranged from the very high to the very low, running the gamut from French champagne to grain alcohol. All in all, I realize now in retrospect a pretty decent-size operation must've been in place, and there was surely a certain amount of importation going on. During different intervals at the speakeasies there were numerous bottles of English gin, Irish whiskey, and Russian vodka all floating about. I had also gathered from the amount of bathtub gin and moonshine in circulation that a reasonable amount of production was likewise going on. I'd overheard Odalie on the telephone several times, and from her half of the conversation I made out that these homemade varieties of alcohol were being sold over the counter at several general stores and drugstores in a variety of locations from Philadelphia to Baltimore, and that the cryptic messages Charlie Whiting sat by the 'phone and took down had something to do with this business. Once I even answered the ring of the telephone in our apartment only to have a man with a rather uncouth Chicago accent rattle off a string of store names whose illicit supplies I can only assume needed restocking. The gentleman at the other end of the line was several minutes into his itemized list before I was able to stop him by blurting out, *I beg your pardon, but I'm afraid Miss Lazare is not at home presently.* Evidently the caller was greatly taken aback by this piece of news, for he rang off immediately.

In general, though, I remained rather ignorant on the subject of Odalie's business, and I must admit, my ignorance was of a rather self-imposed, willful variety. I am no dullard, so I suppose I should have seen the repercussions that would eventually come from my adopting this position. I did not know then—or rather, I did not want to know then—that there would come a day when I'd wish I'd taken more care to distance myself even further from Odalie's business matters.

BY THAT TIME, 1925 was already half over. As the sultry days of September stretched into an Indian summer, Odalie and Gib began to quarrel more regularly. While I realize it is very unbecoming of me to say so, I suppose I was inwardly delighted with this development. I never understood the draw Gib held for Odalie in the first place, and it seemed inevitable that Odalie should want to part ways with him. Whenever we spoke about it in private, I heartily encouraged her to take the steps necessary to effect this separation. While I never said so aloud, I even fancied that their increased proclivity to fight had something to do with my presence in Odalie's life, that I was perhaps unseating Gib in some significant way. Many of their quarrels during that time had to do with Odalie's whereabouts. When I first moved in, Odalie was very careful to keep Gib apprised of her actions at all times. But as my tenure wore on, she grew increasingly neglectful of this duty. Silly though it may sound now, I speculated that my presence in the apartment had emboldened Odalie in some way. She was breaking free of Gib, and I was helping her! Of course, this turned out to be true in the end—but not in the manner I imagined.

The result of Odalie's quarrels with Gib was that she needed someone to occasionally take up his role in business matters. She began to ask me for little favors. These were small tasks; typically they involved dropping off an envelope at this-or-that drugstore, or picking one up. I told myself I needed to go to the drugstore anyway, and the delivery of these envelopes was merely an innocuous little side-errand. But of course I knew better.

For her part, Odalie was extremely clever in the delivery of her requests. The first time she asked, we were on the terrace, lazing about in the late summer heat and sliding ice cubes along the backs of each other's necks in an attempt to cool down.

"Would you mind terribly?" she asked just after making her request. I hesitated, and she sensed it. "Why, Rose," she exclaimed, "the shape of your neck is just lovely. Has anyone ever told you that?" Indeed, they had not. "You really *could* carry off a bob in style, you know. Just think!" I felt myself blush up to the roots of my unbobbed hair.

Before I knew it, I had completed this same errand on her behalf no fewer than four times. I was unprepared, however, for her requests to escalate into something more than the occasional passing along of an envelope to a drugstore clerk. Odalie was careful to stack the odds in her favor at first, naturally. One night, we found ourselves curled up in Odalie's room on top of the bed-covers. She had been fighting with Gib, and ever the sympathetic listener, I had been playing the part of her attentive audience. We had been holding hands, as we often did, and just as Odalie dozed off, she pulled my hand to her lips and brushed it with a kiss. "A true sister," she murmured as she drifted off into a deep state of slumber.

The very next day she asked me a new kind of favor—one to which I found myself powerless to say no. It started off as a normal Tuesday, but eventually she compelled me to leave my post an hour prior to quitting time in order to run a "business errand."

"I would do it, but I'm behind. See this huge stack of reports that need transcribing here? All that's for the Sergeant, and I think he is growing quite intolerant of me these days. But you . . . you're always so on top of your reports, Rose! You can afford to step out for an hour. Oh, and it won't even be that! Much less, I'd say. Just slip out the door quietly, and I'll make sure no one notices you've gone," she said.

"Oh, I'm not sure—"

"It's really easy," she promised. "It's a little bit out of the way, but all you have to do is pick up a message."

As I began to demur, she stiffened and gave me a look.

"Oh, Rose, I can see you're put out. Please, never mind then. Don't bother yourself over it. I'll just telephone and ask Gib. . . ."

Of course I stopped her, and with a contradictory mixture of eagerness and reluctance I wrote down the address she gave. On my way out the door, she hurried after me and grabbed my wrist and said, "Oh! I almost forgot—for cab fare," while giving me an open-mouthed wink. As I hailed a taxi and climbed in, I glanced at the denomination of the bills clutched in my fist and realized she had just handed me enough money to pay a city taxi to chauffeur me all the way to St. Paul and back.

It had been muggy and overcast all day long, and though it was only September and not yet five o'clock, the sky had already turned a dark sickly green color. The driver, probably hoping for some semblance of a fresh breeze, had all the windows rolled down in the taxi, but it didn't seem to help much. When I handed him the slip of paper containing the address, he nodded and seemed to understand where we were going, so for most of the ride I simply sank into the back seat, leaning my head back and sweating rather indelicately on the leather upholstery. Eventually we pulled up in front of a brick building somewhere along the East River. The driver waited expectantly, but I was slow to make my move—the building didn't even look inhabited. Whatever the edifice was, it certainly wasn't a residential building; it appeared to be more of a disused factory of some sort. I noticed a few of the large glass windows on the upper floors had been smashed out, giving the building the air of a toothy jack-o'-lantern.

"Well?" the driver prodded, peering back over the seat and pushing the brim of his newsboy cap up so as to get a better look at me. I peeled a few bills from the wad Odalie had handed me just minutes earlier and paid him.

"You can keep the extra seeds." It was a slang expression I'd heard Odalie use at least a dozen times. Along with her clothes, I was evidently trying on Odalie's vocabulary and mannerisms.

"Thanks," he said gruffly. It sounded like skepticism, but I assumed he likely meant it in earnest, as I'd just handed him a rather large tip. I did not, at that time, consider the possibility his cynical tone had anything to do with the fact he'd picked me up in front of the police precinct and was now dropping me off along a rather dubious stretch of the East River.

Once out of the car, I approached the only door I could discern along the building's entire facade. I heard the cab pull away behind me. Somewhere out on the East River a garbage scow gave a great blast of its horn and the far-off shrieks of bickering seagulls echoed over the water. The door before me was heavy, wooden, and padlocked. By then I was certain I had written down the address incorrectly, but since the taxi was already long gone and there didn't appear to be a convenient way to telephone Odalie, I figured I might as well knock on the door. I reached up with a cautious hand and rapped on the wooden door timidly. It gave a mighty shake, and the padlock jingled on its chain. I looked around with an air of embarrassment, as I suddenly felt very foolish. I suppose I expected very little in the way of a response. But almost as soon as my feeble knocking died down, a rectangular peephole I had not initially detected slid open with violent force.

"What d'ya want?" a low voice boomed. I squinted into the dark of the peephole and, with a gasp, discerned a rather beady eye looking out at me. I stood there, blinking stupidly. "I said, now, what d'ya want?" the voice repeated.

"I'm here . . . on behalf of Odalie Lazare," I said. The peephole slid shut, its closure proving to be as violent as its opening. A heavy bolt sounded and keys jingled as a series of locks were undone. The door swung open, and I found myself staring at a thickly muscled, red-haired man wearing a fisherman's sweater and knit cap. He was quite large. The level of my eyes, I noticed, came to about the middle stripes upon the man's chest.

"Hurry up!" he barked, and without thinking I stepped over the threshold and plunged into the darkness inside. It was some kind of antechamber. The door was swiftly shut and bolted behind me. The padlock and chain were just for show apparently; the more I looked around, the more I realized everything that truly locked was bolted from within. Which meant, of course, the structure was regularly occupied by people—the last thing I'd expected.

"Odalie sent you?" the redhead asked. I nodded. He looked me over from head to toe, as though deciding whether the curious phenomenon in question was actually possible. He let out a huff that made me think the matter ultimately went undecided. "This way," he said, evidently no longer interested in the specifics of my person. He began walking rapidly down a hallway, and as he moved I realized his lantern was the only source of light around.

"Wait!" I said as I hurried after him. He ignored me. I stumbled forward in a scurry and caught up to him. When we got to the end of a seemingly endless labyrinth of hallways, he drew up short in front of a door.

"Dr. Spitzer'll be in there. That's him you'll wanna talk to."

With that, the redhead turned on his heel and the light from his lantern dimmed as he moved away. Confused and desperate not to be left alone in the dark in such a frighteningly unfamiliar place, I clawed for the doorknob. As soon as my hand found it, the door pushed open easily, and I was immediately blinded by a series of bright overhead lamps hanging from the ceiling in the room within. I blinked, my eyes adjusting to this new development, my brain on the verge of abandoning all expectations of normalcy.

"What in the world—?"

"Can I help you?" a man in a crisp white lab-coat asked as he approached.

"Oh! Why . . . no. No—I mean yes! Yes, please. I suppose I

should explain; you see I'm . . ." I suddenly felt reluctant to give my name. "Odalie sent me," I finished. I looked around. The room, as I have mentioned, was very brightly lit. There was a pair of very high, long tables running down the middle of the room, upon which a great number of beakers and flasks dripped and bubbled away. The air smelled strongly of rubbing alcohol and something else . . . something I couldn't quite place but that smelled a little like formaldehyde. "What is this place?"

The man in the lab-coat frowned. "Odalie sent you?" he repeated, just as the redhead had done. "Hmm." He looked me over. He had very dark, almost black hair, parted precisely down the middle, all of which was complemented by an equally dark, sharply trimmed mustache. As his predecessor had also been, the man in the lab-coat seemed skeptical of my connection to Odalie. Finally he shrugged. "Hmm, yes, well. Fine. I suppose that must be true enough. After all, who else would you be? We're expecting another chemist in soon, and surely you're not *him*. Hah! Unless . . . I don't suppose your name happens to be Madame Curie?" He rolled his eyes at me, gave me another assessing head-to-toe look, and before I could give an answer supplied one of his own in a snippy voice. "No . . . I don't suppose it is."

I remained silent, still staring goggle-eyed at the multiplicity of gurgling, steaming contraptions behind him. He followed my gaze over his shoulder. He turned back to me and grunted.

"You probably don't even know *who* she is," he said with a sneer, and I realized he meant Madame Curie. I felt my dander go up. A sudden rush of heat went to my cheeks, and the queer mechanical feeling I sometimes experienced came over me.

"Madame Curie is the winner of two Nobel Prizes," I said haughtily. It wasn't as if I'd never read the headlines growing up!

"Not to mention living proof that men often jump to the wrong conclusions, in more ways than one," I added for good measure. The man in the lab-coat raised his eyebrows at me and cocked his head. Almost imperceptibly, his posture straightened. "Listen," I said, hoping to take advantage of the footing I'd just gained in order to accomplish my task. "I'm sure you run a regular Nobel-quality operation around here. But I've only come to pick up a message." He gazed at me and remained speechless for several seconds. "Odalie said there would be a message," I prompted him.

At the renewed mention of Odalie's name, the trance was broken and he snapped out of his stasis. "Yes, of course. Well, there's no good news, I'm afraid." He turned away from me to attend the beakers with a brisk, businesslike air. He began making a series of minor adjustments to the contraptions located there. "You know how the gov'ment regulators are cracking down. They've really laid it on thick with the methanol lately. I can't promise any of this batch will be drinkable. Not if we don't want another chap dying, like last time."

"Oh! Why, you don't mean . . . You can't mean someone actually . . . !" I was utterly confounded.

Instantly, I could see my state of uninformed bewilderment had cost me my temporary superior footing with the man in the lab-coat. He rolled his eyes disdainfully at me, then sighed and cleared his throat. "Look Miss . . . Miss Whatever-Your-Name-Is, just tell Miss Lazare this: The batch is a bust, but I'll try it again. My friend is a chemist in a hair tonic factory; I can try starting from some of what they use." He thrust a bottle in my direction. "And here," he barked. "You can give 'er this."

I was slow to retrieve the bottle, and he shook it back and forth as if to nag me. "What is this?" I asked, and looked at the crude, unlabeled, green glass bottle.

"Proof," Dr. Spitzer replied, "that I'm not selling a good batch out from under her."

My fingers closed hesitantly around the bottle's neck. I peered into the glass and squinted at its contents. As far as I could tell, they were crystal clear. I swirled the liquid around, causing Dr. Spitzer to frown.

"Don't go drinking that now," Dr. Spitzer warned. "You have enough common sense to know that much, doncha?"

"Why . . . yes . . ."

"Figures. Course, you look more like the pampered type; probably more used to all that fancy imported stuff."

I blinked dumbly at him. I had never before in my life been taken for "the pampered type." The dim realization occurred to me that Dr. Spitzer's manners were turning increasingly rough by the second. As he looked me up and down rather uncouthly, any semblance of the imaginary university that had conferred upon him his title of "doctor" dropped away. The expression that took over his face was both wolfish and cruel at the same time.

"Yeah, I know all aboutcha: Leave it to all'a the blue-collar boys to drink the homemade stuff and let 'em try their odds, while you leave it alone." He gave an embittered sigh and shrugged dismissively. "Well anyway, just remember to relay my message."

I stood there, still absorbing the message to be relayed. Dr. Spitzer was irritable now, this much was plain. I felt as though I'd botched things; I'd managed to both offend him *and* prove myself a ninny. He pushed a button and somewhere an electric buzzer rang. Seconds later the redhead was standing in the doorway.

"Stan can show you the way out," Dr. Spitzer said in a flat, dismissive tone. He resumed his work as though my presence in the room was already a distant memory. I followed Stan with the same automatic step that had led me into the building, and before I knew it I was standing outside again, the heavy wooden door shuddering to a close behind me. A clammy breeze was blowing off the river, and looming above me at some distance I could make out the peaked trestles of the Queensboro Bridge. Self-consciously, I tucked the bottle clutched in my hand under my coat. It wouldn't do to be seen on a public street holding an unmarked bottle of alcohol.

But then I looked around and realized there was no one to see me. I had no mode of transportation; no bell-boy or doorman had telephoned for a cab to pick me up as I had nowadays all too quickly become accustomed. I began walking away from the graveled edge of the river in the direction of greater civilization. Though I had been ushered in and out of the building with great speed, the overall errand had taken longer than I'd expected. As I picked my way from the rubble-strewn industrial blocks and back into the major avenues, I gave a dismal glance at my watch and realized the ride back to the precinct would only get me there in time to turn around and go home for the day. I deliberated as I neared First Avenue, then hailed a taxi and gave the driver the apartment address instead. At least I could be fairly confident in Odalie's ability to conceal my absence.

Later that same evening, when I relayed the message to Odalie and handed her the bottle Dr. Spitzer had given me, she did not look especially surprised.

"Oh yes, he's a bit of a quack, Dr. Spitzer," she said, taking the bottle with unseeing eyes and setting it absently on a nearby side table. She shook her head. "Well, I won't hold my breath. Heaven knows why Gib hired him in the first place. Not much of a chemist in the end, I'm afraid." I thought of what Dr. Spitzer had said about the last batch—*Not if we don't want another chap dying, like last time.* . . . As if she could detect my thoughts, Odalie ignored the abandoned bottle now sitting on the side table, turned a page in the magazine she was reading, and with a faraway look added, "There are stories about him . . . believe me."

She didn't need to convince me; I believed her. The catch was, though I had gone to great pains to become her most trusted confidante, I was beginning to realize there were some things I'd rather not know.

Though Odalie's little "favors" forced me to step beyond the boundaries of my comfort, I continued to complete these occasional odd tasks, happy at least I'd finally secured the position I'd coveted for so long—that is, I had finally established myself as the most important person in Odalie's life, and she had clearly been appointed the most important person in mine.

It is impossible to explain to someone who has never made Odalie's acquaintance how glorious this is. It is not enough to say she had a way about her. If you were feeling heavy, she had some sort of trick to make you feel so light as to become giddy with it. If you were slighted at work, she made the person who slighted you the butt of an inside joke. When you were with Odalie, it was impossible to be an outsider. For me, this latter phenomenon was nothing short of a miracle. After all, I had been an outsider all my life.

And so, despite my growing unease with the little errands Odalie requested every now and again, I nonetheless think of those days as perhaps the happiest and most blissful time in all my life. I had reached a pinnacle. But of course, I didn't know it. Pinnacles are only defined as such by that which surrounds them, and in this case my high point was fated to be followed by a very low point.

Little did I know, my low point was looming just out of my line of vision. I would soon unwittingly turn a corner, and there it would be.

I REACHED THE CORNER in question when I caught a glimpse of a man in the holding cell whose face looked familiar. I couldn't be sure, but thought perhaps I'd seen him at the speakeasy once or twice before. When I alerted Odalie, she appeared to recognize him immediately, and I could tell she intended to take action about the situation. As she had in previous times, she managed to get herself assigned to the case. Once Odalie and the Sergeant had taken the man into the interrogation room, he was released only minutes later. I watched him amble through the precinct and out the front door. It was as though I was seeing an echo of Gib strolling leisurely out the door on that first day after the raid. I rose from my desk and walked toward the interrogation room. At the time, I told myself I was merely curious about Odalie's methods, but this was a lie. I see now I always knew what her methods were; I had quite simply and stubbornly blinded myself to the fact.

There was a long hallway along one side of the precinct that led to the interrogation room. Or, rather, the INTERVIEW ROOM, as was stenciled in brassy gold paint upon the window of the door. I turned into the hallway and immediately glimpsed Odalie and the Sergeant standing at the far end. I saw them plain enough from where I stood, but it was clear they took no notice of my presence in return. I was about to approach them when some instinct within told me not to. There's a certain sensation you get when you blunder into two people who are sharing an intimate moment, and as I turned the corner into the hallway I had that sensation. It stopped me dead in my tracks, and I stood there, dumbstruck, looking on. They seemed deep in conversation, but they were speaking in such low voices that I was at pains to make out what they were saying. And then a very simple thing occurred that stopped my heart in my chest.

As they were talking, Odalie reached a hand to the Sergeant's chest and idly fingered his lapel, leaning in and smiling flirtatiously as she did so. I was aghast. The Sergeant was such a painfully formal man, I expected him to immediately correct her errant behavior. But I awaited a reprimand that never came. Instead, he went on talking as though it were perfectly natural that Odalie should touch him so intimately. For a fleeting moment, I considered the possibility the Sergeant was being polite. Perhaps he meant to simply ignore Odalie's foolishness rather than point it out and cause her the pain of embarrassment. I knew he was capable of such gallantry. But as her hand slid from his lapel and came to rest on the upper shoulder of his sleeve, I was utterly disabused of this conclusion. When the Sergeant finally reacted, time slowed down and the warmth drained from my cheeks. As I continued to look on, the Sergeant lifted his own hand to cover hers, then traveled in a friendly way down and then up along the length of her lithe, short-sleeved arm.

I had seen enough. I was trembling with rage, and the sight

had instantly set the pains of nausea to twisting in my stomach. I quickly turned on my heel and scurried away in the direction of the ladies' room, where for several minutes I retched nothing but air into an empty sink. Then I stood staring at my reflection in the mirror and, for a while, everything went black.

Later, someone would point to a series of long, spidery fissures that now run the length of the bathroom mirror and claim that I had contributed to their creation. But I cannot see how this is possible, as it only stands to reason the mirror would've left some mutual evidence upon my person, and I don't recall having noticed any such scratches or cuts on my skin. In any case, when I finally reemerged from the bathroom I was still quite unsettled. My muscles quivered and quaked with an indignant sense of betrayal. Every inch of me was poised to take immediate action.

By virtue of pure disciplined effort I was able to go about my work as usual, but the scene I had witnessed haunted me for the rest of the day, flashing into my brain at inopportune times, each recollection of it more vivid than the last. Dr. Benson theorizes I have what he calls *an overactive imagination.* He says I am altogether too ready to jump to conclusions. During our sessions he lets his eyeglasses slip down until they barely have any purchase left at the tip of his nose, and peering at me from over the top of those empty flashing mirrors he often says, *Tell me, Rose, how can you be so certain there was something inappropriate going on between Odalie and the Sergeant?* Or else he will sometimes say, *How can you be sure your imagination wasn't playing tricks on you?* And I take offense to the latter question, because no one has ever accused me of having too much imagination, and even if what little imagination I *do* possess was to play tricks, they certainly wouldn't be tricks from the gutter. Once, Odalie described me as a "bluenose" to someone at a party, right in front of my face, and I wasn't a bit mad because, after all, I do think I have an exceptionally clean mind and would never think to be ashamed of this fact.

Odalie was too busy to talk to me for the rest of the day; otherwise I might've lost control of myself and chastised her in front of everyone—an event that, in the long run, would've ultimately humiliated me as much as her. In retrospect I have to say I'm still very glad I didn't do this, as it probably would've served as yet another piece of evidence to be used against me in my current situation. Instead, the minute hand moved twice around the clock during Odalie's absence, and as I watched it from the corner of my eye I devised another way to teach her a lesson . . . *I would withdraw my friendship!* Yes; ever so quietly I would pack my suitcase that very evening and let myself out the front door in the middle of the night, unobserved. The next morning Odalie would notice my absence, and upon checking the room where I regularly slept she would no doubt see all my things had gone missing during the night and she would intuit why I had left. As I typed up a stack of reports, I thought of the letter I would leave on my tidily made bed for her to discover, composing several rather dramatic drafts of it in my imagination and making several typing errors in the process. I debated which tone would shame and therefore hurt her more: an anguished one that expressed my heartsick disapproval of her, or a disconnected, indifferent one that would signal my superiority and disdainfully suggest that her transgressions were of a rather tawdry, cliché nature. Then I considered leaving no note at all, and decided perhaps that would hurt her most of all.

As for the Sergeant, I supposed there was no need to punish him. I cannot explain why, as I do not precisely know, but after witnessing their interlude in the hallway I did not have the same feelings toward both perpetrators. Waves of white-hot anger washed over me when I thought of Odalie; there was a sense of urgency in my feelings for her, a desperate need to punish her, to show her how incorrect her behavior was. Meanwhile, I felt nothing for the Sergeant but a cold, soggy sense of disappointment. In my mind, he had come down from Mount Olympus, and he had come down to stay. When I thought of him, I could only see his hand traveling up the length of Odalie's sleeve.

Of course now I see that while I had lost one god in the Sergeant, I had nonetheless gained another in Odalie, as I was more obsessed than ever with the uncharted depths of her manipulative powers, which I was beginning to believe had no bounds. She was not the clean, regimented sort of idol the Sergeant had been to me. Instead, she was something else entirely, something I could not yet name, for at that time I still lacked a panoramic comprehension of Odalie and of the effect she would ultimately have on me. I had no inkling then of how her most terrible power would show itself not in her own actions, but in what she was capable of driving others to do. Of what she was capable of driving *me* to do.

But all that would come soon enough. That evening, I went home with Odalie according to our regular routine. I made a point of being rather stiff and chilly with her, but I do not think she took much notice of my cool reserve. I decided it was simply best to bide my time until I could slip out unseen and protest Odalie's misdeeds with my absence. Gib slept at the apartment that night and was surlier than usual. Shortly after the dinner hour they disappeared together into Odalie's bedroom. I noted the date and his name in my little journal. I also wrote *Sergeant Irving Boggs*, then scribbled it out, and finally wrote it in again with a question mark next to it. Then I played a record on the phonograph on my nightstand. I opted for some tidy Bach concertos in an attempt to infuse the atmosphere with some manicured civility, and I began to pack my things. Through the wall, I could hear Odalie and Gib quarreling. And then I could hear them . . . not quarreling. Their passion turned to conversation, and the hum of their voices rose and fell like a tide until eventually, when it had grown quite late, they fell silent altogether. The last record I had put on finally ended, and the needle began to skip, threading into the final groove only to be pushed into the center of the disc over and over and over again. I lifted the phonograph's thick brass arm and switched the contraption off.

By that point my bags were packed—or rather my *bag*, I should say, as I had arrived with a sole suitcase and I intended to take exactly only what was mine. Of all the things I now had to part with, the clothes were the most difficult. It surprised me how attached I'd grown to the furs, the beaded dresses, the satin gowns. But if I was going to hold myself to a superior moral standard, I couldn't very well traipse around in Odalie's finery knowing it had all likely been gained via her improper behavior. I pulled open a dresser drawer and ran my hand over a pile of embroidered silk undershirts as though stroking a beloved pet one final goodbye. I lifted the diamond bracelet from where it lay cradled in the plush pile of a sable mink stole and shut the dresser drawer with an air of finality. I unclasped the bracelet and laid it lengthwise on my pillow, in the vacant place where my head would no longer rest. With a pang I thought of the brooch, still in my desk drawer at work—you see, I've always liked to be absolute in my measures. Oh, but that couldn't be helped now. I looked again to the suitcase where it sat on a chair in a corner by the painted Oriental screens. I had tidied the room with the utmost care, so as to make the space appear more noticeably denuded. I wanted my disappearance to have the maximum effect. As I surveyed the barren room with approval, I knew it was finally time to make my move. I stood to go and lifted my bag from the chair.

But then I hesitated. With my suitcase in my hand and dressed in my plainest calico blouse and long skirt, I stared at the door before me and swayed almost imperceptibly over my rooted feet. Some unnameable doubt was holding me back from following through with my intended departure. I considered the possibility Odalie might not even notice my absence for some days, or worse yet, not care. I pictured her poking her head into my empty room in that breezy perfunctory way she had, shrugging her shoulders, and going about her business as usual. I worried that while she mattered plenty to me, there was a chance I did not matter quite so much to her. I looked down at the suitcase where it dangled from my arm. Already it was heavy, already the trip wearied me, and I hadn't even taken my first step toward the door. I realized that in my eagerness to punish Odalie with my absence, I had not yet worked out where I was going—my mind had only gotten so far as to imagine the leaving.

I put my suitcase down and sat on the bed with a sigh. I was going about this all wrong. I wanted to send a message to Odalie, but I wanted something else from her, too. I wanted her to be sorry.

I decided to stay. At least for the time being. Slowly, meticulously, I dispatched the items in my suitcase and restored them to their proper locations in the room. Then, once dressed in a nightshirt, I crawled into bed. Now I was resolved to go to sleep and awake tomorrow to confront my new task—the task of loving Odalie and therefore forcing her to face the crucial fact she had wronged her most devoted friend, that her scheming and her risky behavior had to stop.

20

On Friday of that same week, an unexpected visitor came into the precinct looking for Odalie. As luck would have it, Odalie had gone to run some errands on her lunch hour. Exhausted and wary after my unexpected introduction to Dr. Spitzer, I didn't ask any questions about her errands this time. In any case, all this is to say she had a visitor that day, yet wasn't available when her visitor came to call upon her. I was seated at my work station, eating a sandwich and drinking coffee that had already gone cold, when I saw Teddy approach the receiving desk. Involuntarily, I gave a little yelp, which of course only alerted him to my presence. His youthful face lit up.

"Hullo, Rose!" he called in a cheerful voice across the room. He waved in my direction. I got up from my desk quickly, spilling the paper cone of coffee I'd been drinking down the front of my blouse as I did so. I didn't care; it was a blush-colored silk charmeuse number I had borrowed from Odalie and now it was probably ruined, but if I had learned nothing else by then I knew Odalie went through clothing the way other people went through talcum powder or toilet tissue. I hurried across the room toward

Teddy. All eyes in the precinct lifted to see what the commotion was about.

"Shh! Keep your voice down," I said to Teddy. "What are you doing here?"

"Well, I . . . I thought I might talk to Odalie."

I gripped him by the upper arm and steered him out the precinct entrance and down the stoop so we might talk on the street. "Honestly, Teddy," I mumbled as I tried to shepherd his lanky, adolescent body. As an obedient and loyal friend, I knew it would be ideal if I could get rid of him now, before Odalie ever caught wind of the fact he had come to find her. It's funny, but I swear I can recall thinking at the time, and rather prophetically, too, *That way nobody will get hurt.* Once safe on the street, I shook him and repeated my question.

"What are you doing here?" I released him and waited. He didn't respond straightaway. His eyes went wide, and when he looked down at his shoes, he shuffled his feet sheepishly. I took all this in and felt something soften in me. You see, I recognized my likeness in Teddy. There was an element of earnest urgency in his behavior toward Odalie I had to admit was not so different from my own.

The long and short of it is Teddy and I were both trying to make sense of Odalie's code of conduct. We were trying to get *the truth* from her, of all things! Teddy was trying to get the factual truth of her history, while I was trying to get the sentimental truth of her heart, but really we were not so very different creatures. We had both chased after Odalie and were now waiting for her to dictate the circumstances and outcome of the interaction.

As he looked at me with that pleading in his eyes, we had an unspoken exchange. I felt a tremor of sympathy ripple through my extremities. But then I collected myself. "Teddy," I said in a stern voice, "You can't be here."

His brow furrowed as though he were uncertain this was true. "I can tell she recognizes me, Rose," he said. "It's her. She's changed some things about herself, but it's *her.* I know it in my bones. What I have to ask her . . . it'll only take but a minute."

I surveyed him with a long and thorough stare, and it dawned on me that he might never give up. Convinced she was Ginevra, Teddy would not rest until Odalie had answered his questions to his satisfaction, a feat I wasn't sure she could accomplish, not ever. I thought through the long list of false stories Odalie had given me during our time together and about the number of times she'd purposely misled me. I thought, too, about Odalie and the Sergeant as I'd seen them standing in that hallway together. A tiny flare of indignant anger went up from somewhere deep inside my chest. As I looked at Teddy's face, still marked with that faint stippling of peach fuzz and acne so typical of adolescent young men, I realized I was approaching yet another fork in the road.

"I'll tell you what I'll do," I finally said, having made my decision. I produced a little pencil and note-card from my purse. "I've got to get back inside now," I said, writing down an address and a quick instructional paragraph with careful penmanship. "But here. Take this." I handed Teddy the note-card.

I left him standing there, perplexed and staring at the card, as I turned to trot back up the stairs of the stoop. "Thank you!" he called after me, once he'd gotten over his confusion. "Thank you, Rose." Halfway up the stoop, I froze.

"Don't mention it," I replied.

I suppose if there was any time I should have fretted about what I'd just set into motion—about what kind of potentially horrific collision I'd just initiated—it would've been then. But I didn't feel anything of the sort. Instead, I was peculiarly relaxed and calm.

As I remounted the last few stairs, I noticed the shape of Marie ducking away from the windows. So, we'd been observed. I knew that meant I'd have to endure Marie perpetually inquiring, *Who was that chap?* And *Wasn't he a little young to be my boyfriend?* I pushed through the precinct door and decided not to care. At the time I couldn't have anticipated how Marie's having glimpsed this scene might one day affect my future.

THAT NIGHT, we went to the speakeasy as was our routine. It began as one of those evenings wherein the moon loomed big and balloonlike, rising upward from one horizon before the sun had a chance to fully dip below the other. I remember standing on the apartment terrace and watching the moon make its slow, plodding ascent, a dusty pink half-crescent pocked with gray craters.

It had been another warm and sticky day, but now a cooling breeze was pushing the dirty haze of the city farther out to sea. The leaves would start turning soon, I realized, and I was surprised this meant that in a few months, I would've known Odalie for a full year. I mused on this revelation and must've gotten lost in my reverie, for I jumped when I heard her voice calling me to get dressed for our evening out. I rarely came out to the terrace, but when I did it was easy to be hypnotized by the way the electric lights of the city took on a supernatural glow as the sun ceded his territory to the sensuous moon and twilight turned to dusk.

When I came inside, I found Odalie had laid out a pair of outfits for us. To this day, I don't know if the resemblance of style between these outfits was a coincidence, or whether it was achieved on purpose. I can't imagine how she could have known the similarity would come in handy. Odalie is many things, and she has an impressive capacity to anticipate human behavior, but I do not believe she is an all-out clairvoyant. Nonetheless, presumably without knowing how it would help her cause, she dressed us that night in similar black evening gowns adorned with silver beading. Although one dress (mine) had a square-cut neckline and the other (hers) was strapless, the beading on both dresses was such that the silver beads gradually intensified as the pleated skirt flowed downward to skim the knee, giving the pair of us a crested-wave, mermaid-like appeal.

She also put hair cream in my mousy brown hair to darken it and make it shine, and pinned it under so it would swing at an angle along the line of my jaw—just as her bob did. I recall catching a glimpse in the mirror of us standing side-by-side just moments prior to leaving the apartment. We looked ever so slightly like twins. A beautiful, shining woman and her slightly duller, slightly dowdier counterpart. In an eerie final touch, Odalie had insisted we wear the two matching diamond bracelets—a peculiar twist indeed, as up until that point we had never worn them outside of the apartment. Once we slipped them on, our toilet was complete. Odalie promptly called downstairs and put in a request for one of the doormen to procure a taxi, and just like that, the evening had been set into motion.

Over the course of the last nine months I'd spent with Odalie, I had discovered the speakeasy—*her* speakeasy, that is—moved around sporadically, but mainly made use of about three or four regular locations. On that night (which was to reveal itself to be our last night) I suppose there was some sort of poetic circularity in the fact we found ourselves right back at the selfsame location as the first one I had ever attended. This time I felt like an old hand when the taxi drove to the Lower East Side and let us out upon a deserted street lined with darkened storefronts, and I barely batted an eyelash. As expected, one storefront still glowed with electric light. Upon pushing through the door of the wig shop, we found the same boy wearing the same pair of oddly colored suspenders sitting at the register. And he asked exactly the same question, a question I realized from the tone of his voice had long since become threadbare from overuse.

"Can I help you find sompin', ma'ams?" His voice delivered the rote line so the word *help* had been dissected of all trace elements of original meaning. He pushed a long greasy lock out of one eye and waited. Odalie ignored him altogether, taking out her compact and dusting her nose with talcum. I realized it was my turn to spring into action.

"Yes," I said, looking around for the iron-gray wig done up in an elaborate Victorian bun. They always relocated the wig to a different shelf in the store, so it was never in the same place twice. Perhaps this was part of the test to further separate the initiated from the uninitiated, or perhaps the boy simply did it out of boredom. Finally my eyes alighted upon the object in question. Truly it was a wretched-looking thing. I lifted it from the mannequin's unsuspecting head. "I hear this is lovely in chestnut, but mahogany's twice as nice." I knew when I said it that it did not come off sounding nearly as seductive as when Odalie had said it in times past, but nevertheless it proved effective enough. The boy plugged away at the cash register keys, and soon enough a loud *clunk* sounded and the wall panel behind the front counter sprang open.

"You may enter, ma'ams."

Odalie went in first, and I followed. Once again, as the wall panel clicked shut behind me, I felt my eyes suddenly peering into absolute darkness, working diligently to make out the shape and path of the hallway. The sounds of a lively party echoed all around us. I sensed Odalie moving in front of me, and I trailed blindly in her wake until together we pushed through a velvet curtain. We stood there for thirty seconds, but before we'd even had a chance to fully take in the scene, a woman rushed over and kissed Odalie on both cheeks.

"*There* you are!" the woman exclaimed.

"So good to see you again," Odalie replied with equal enthusiasm. I recognized the woman from my long-ago session with the bohemian group, but I could tell Odalie did not remember the woman.

"I was just saying to Marjorie—oh! See Marjorie over there? Wave, dear!—I was just saying to Marjorie, 'I wonder when she'll get here,' and right away you appeared, poof! Like magic—here you are!"

"Here I am," Odalie echoed. People were always coming up and talking to Odalie in this manner, and as a result she had developed a very graceful but vague manner of responding.

"You really *must* come over and say hello," the woman said, her breath washing over us in a hot whiskey-scented wave. Her arm was already linked through Odalie's in a manner that suggested she would not take no for an answer. She flinched with a silent hiccup and tenaciously pressed on. "There's a man by the name of Digby who's a downright wag of an impressionist. He's got some real funny stuff you really shouldn't miss! And of course the painter Lebaud is over there, too, telling all about how he plans to paint you in that new modern style where it's you but it doesn't look like you at all, where the features are all funny and out of order . . ."

The woman's dogged persistence was a success, and I suddenly found myself standing alone. I spotted Redmond from across the room, and he nodded in my direction. The misunderstanding that had occurred the night of the raid had never been discussed, but rather it melted between us a little bit at a time; a rigid ice cube slowly turning back to easy-flowing water that (I hoped) might soon run under the bridge. I watched as he toddled over to take my drink order. It was a terse exchange, but one I knew signified that we were progressing in a positive direction.

As I waited for Redmond to return with a champagne cocktail, I took a sweeping look around the room. A woman with a gardenia tucked over her ear was singing in a flirty voice that brimmed over with a sort of cheerful sarcastic glee, moving her hands at the wrists as she sang. It was one of those perky-sounding songs that turned out to be somewhat deceptive; it had a jaunty enough melody, but upon closer observation it was actually characterized by a spate of fashionably cynical lyrics. Couples that seemed impervious to pessimism danced in the center of the room, happy to ignore the lyrics and keep time instead with the upbeat tempo of the melody.

It's funny how that night things already felt changed. Perhaps I'm only imagining this now that I have the advantage of hindsight, but I swear that's the way it goes in my memory: Somehow I had the distinct impression a portion of the magic was already gone forever. Perhaps I am only remembering my sensitivity to the changing seasons. Who knows. After all, summer was over. It had abandoned us, leaving behind a feeling of dissatisfaction, and taking with it all those too oft unfulfilled beach-day aspirations of a brown-skinned, primitive freedom. The weather would turn cold before we knew it and drive us back into the cramped and stuffy steam-heated rooms we called civilization.

But I looked around me and felt there was something greater informing my feelings that night than simply summer's annual eulogy. In a flash it came to me, and I suddenly understood something about my own generation. It was the kind of comprehension only granted to a true outsider as she is looking in, and it was this: The couples dancing in the center of the room had seen many summers and many winters; they would reconfigure themselves many times, and had tacitly agreed to forget the waltz in favor of the foxtrot and then forget the foxtrot in favor of the Charleston. They would act as though each whirl around the dance floor marked the hilarious advent of something new; each kiss they gave out they would pretend was their first. In short, their youth was not an act, but their innocence most certainly was. Their youth was what kept them moving, a sort of brutal vitality lingering in their muscles and bones that was all too often mistaken for athleticism and grace. But their innocence was something they were obligated to go on faking in order to maintain the illusion something fresh and spontaneous and exciting was just around the next corner. I began, for the first time that night, to dimly perceive that the relative electricity in the air all hinged on this illusion. Somehow we had gone off to war and had come back world-weary . . . yet at the same time we'd managed to make a generational career out of pretending virginal adolescence. In short, I had come to the conclusion the whole pack of us were fakes.

I continued to look around. Without realizing it, I was searching the room for Gib. I had heard them arguing almost every day that week. Even in my state of displeasure with Odalie, I was nonetheless eager to see her cut him out of the picture at long last. I roamed the room. He was not in the cluster of men puffing away at their cigars. He was not hovering over the roulette table, watching for men purposely leaning against the rim of the wheel to slow it. He was not in the crowd of nervous bodies shimmying the Charleston (though to be honest, he rarely was). When I finally found him, it appeared Odalie had, too. They were seated upon a red velvet settee in a far corner by the bar, and together they were discussing something with great animation. Neither was smiling, and after several minutes it became clear their discussion was taking the form of yet another argument. Curiosity soon got the better of me. I set the cocktail that was already in my hand down on a nearby table and approached the bar, where I feigned thirst to the bartender and ordered a fresh drink. The entire speakeasy had grown impossibly boisterous by that hour, but I was nonetheless hoping to hear a fragment or two of Odalie and Gib's conversation.

But no sooner had I edged my way within earshot than a tipsy young girl tried to perch on the arm of their settee, and finding Gib's hand under her derriere, jumped up with a yelp. As she sprang from where she had accidentally sat upon his hand, she upset the contents of her martini glass over his head and proceeded now to flutter anxiously about the settee, squawking with apology. With an intermingling of bathtub gin and hair oil dripping into his eyes, Gib did not appear amused by this new development. Odalie, for her part, deftly extracted Gib's pocket square from the breast of his jacket and began blotting the offending gin from his face. In seconds she had sent the girl away and was soothingly urging Gib into a back room with her, where it seemed they intended to adjourn indefinitely.

With my reconnaissance mission thwarted and my curiosity unquenched, I let out a sigh and turned to regard the wild revelry transpiring in the center of the room. Someone had rolled a cart into the middle of the dance floor and stacked it high with a pyramid of champagne glasses. Meanwhile, a pretty little slip of a girl in a bright yellow dress stood atop a step-stool and poured a golden stream of champagne from a very cumbersome and heavy-looking magnum. The champagne frothed and bubbled over the glass at the very top until it cascaded down the small mountain of glasses, filling each along the way. People all around me, drunk and sober alike, applauded the girl's coordination.

For the briefest of seconds, I caught a flash of suspenders and spats and thought I'd glimpsed the Lieutenant Detective, standing just behind the makeshift champagne fountain. It wasn't him. Even so, the tremor of recognition had jolted me into a state of nervous alert, and I found myself suddenly restless. Perhaps even a greater shock to my system was the half-formed realization that I might indeed welcome his company. I was unsettled and couldn't remain leaning at the bar for long. Before I knew it, I had dumped down the glass of gin and vermouth in my hand and proceeded to do something I rarely did while still sober enough to remember the experience—that is, I ventured out to the dance floor and threw myself into the jittery crowd of Charleston dancers. I don't know how much time passed during my exertions on the dance floor, but it was likely a full thirty minutes later when I pulled off to the side to catch my breath. By then I had begun to sweat so much, my pinned bob had plastered itself to my cheeks and I tasted salt whenever I licked my upper lip. Red-faced, I stood to the side and watched as others carried on.

I had lost track of Odalie completely when all of a sudden her luminous oval of a face buoyed up at me, thrust forward into the candlelight from the dark. A bit startled, I staggered backward.

"Oh!"

"Rose, dear—there you are!" Her voice sounded funny; there was a brittle, accusatory quality to it. Something was wrong. Perhaps it was a trick played by the flicker of the candlelight, but it looked like Odalie's mouth was twitching. I slowly became aware of another shape standing nearby, just over her shoulder. It was the shape of a man. The shoulders were reasonably broad, but the hips were narrow and the head was disproportionately small. I blinked and looked more closely.

"Oh!" I said, startled all over again. Although to be fair, upon seeing his face I shouldn't have been startled at all. I had given him the address myself, not to mention a description of how to enter through the wig shop.

"You remember Teddy, don't you, Rose? From the Brinkleys'?" I believe she knew it was an unnecessary question. Of course I remembered. The overly polite tone of her voice was laced with a bitter anger. I had been planning all along on telling her I had been the one to invite Teddy, but now that the fateful moment of confrontation had arrived, I found myself swallowing nervously and extending a hand in Teddy's direction.

"Of course," I said. "Teddy. So good to see you again." He smiled and accepted my outstretched hand as if he had not just seen me mere hours earlier at the precinct. Once he'd released my hand, the three of us were left standing around awkwardly. No one made conversation for several minutes; meanwhile the party roared on all around us. I slowly became conscious of the fact we had come to constitute a static point amid a sea of vibration. Finally, Odalie spoke.

"As I'm sure you can imagine, Teddy and I need to have a little chat, Rose," she said. I nodded awkwardly, suddenly uncomfortable in my body. I knew my discomfort had to do with the guilt I now felt; I could see in Odalie's eyes she knew I'd brought them to this moment of final confrontation by giving Teddy the address of where we'd be that night.

"And we can't very well chat here," Odalie added. "Would you mind, Rose, taking him back to the apartment? I've got some things I need to finish up here, and then I'll be right over so we can all sit down good and proper."

I agreed to Odalie's request that I temporarily play host for her, but I didn't feel confident about any of it anymore. No sooner had my betrayal been revealed than I had immediately begun to regret it. I'm not sure what I thought would happen by giving Teddy the address to the speakeasy that night. But whatever it was, I still hadn't acquired the stomach for it.

Odalie flipped open a silver case and extracted a cigarette. Teddy fished around for a lighter and found one swimming in the depths of his jacket pocket.

"So, Rose'll show me to your apartment, and then we can talk more about . . . about Newport," Teddy said, holding up the flame. The tone of it rendered it half-question, half-statement.

"Oh, I'm sure we'll have plenty to talk about," Odalie said. "Go on, now. I'll be right behind you two." She patted his hand and winked, then disappeared back into the crowd of dancers, which greedily swallowed her up.

Content to wait for Odalie at the apartment as instructed,

Teddy held out a genteel arm to me. Together we headed for the back door.

Our journey over to the apartment was uneventful, despite the obvious tension. Silence prevailed between us throughout the trip. Twice—once in the taxi-cab and once as the elevator cage ticked off the floors, making its ascent—Teddy drew a sharp breath as if he was about to speak, but then seemed to think better of it. It wasn't until we were in the apartment and had been sitting there for some minutes that I broke the silence by asking him whether he'd like a drink. It was not something I historically had a habit of doing—offering people drinks, that is—but it was something Odalie would've done, and besides, I had begun to develop new habits during my tenure with her. I did not think Teddy, undoubtedly a charter member of the Boy Scouts during his youth, would accept the drink. But to my surprise, he did. Under ordinary circumstances I think he might've refused the drink; he seemed like the type to preach on about the virtues of "keeping a clear head." But I believe he found himself in extenuating circumstances that night; it was clear Odalie made him nervous. I found myself flipping through a little recipe book Odalie kept near the bar titled *Harry's ABCs of Mixing Cocktails,* attempting to build some sort of drink called a sidecar.

I felt Teddy watching me, looking on with sincere interest as I lifted a bottle of Cointreau from a shelf and measured out an amateurishly precise jigger. Whether the drink I built turned out to be a proper sidecar or not I don't know, but I shook the concoction over ice and poured it into two martini glasses. Less than twenty minutes later, I found myself repeating the process. The effort made my forehead bead up with perspiration, and stray hairs stuck to the sweaty skin, making it itch.

"It's a nice night. She may be a while. Why don't we take the air on the terrace while we wait?" I suggested. Teddy's eyes widened, and he shot me a sudden fearful look. It dawned on me this was an odd request—something usually recommended by a seducing lover—and I blushed. But Teddy coughed and shrugged, and after I'd mixed us a third drink, we adjourned to the terrace, where only hours earlier I'd stood watching the moon sail into the sky with its blood-tinged warning.

The muggy warmth of early autumn had left no trace of its oppressiveness behind on the night breeze. It had turned into the kind of evening I can only describe as delicious. The air was lukewarm and carried just the tiniest hint of a chill in it when the wind lifted. The crisp scent of wet leaves wafted over from the park, and the silvery light of the moon was so bright, our shadows stood behind us in sharp outlines, giving us the indirect impression we had invited a third and fourth guest to join us. We stood in silence for several minutes, resting our elbows on the terrace ledge and peering out over the city below. Somewhere several floors down and what seemed like a whole universe away there was a very low, faraway din of bustling traffic, of horns honking. I watched Teddy as he took a long pull at his drink.

"She's something of a sphinx, isn't she," he commented rhetorically when he finally came up for air and tipped his face away from his martini glass.

"What exactly do you hope to get out of her, Teddy?"

He looked around the terrace uncomfortably and shrugged. "The truth, I suppose."

"And what if the truth is bad?"

He regarded me for a very long minute. "How bad?"

I shrugged. "The worst you can imagine."

His eyes widened. "Do you know something?" he asked. There was a shade of eagerness in it, but there was a shade of terror, too. I shook my head quickly.

"No, no. I don't know anything," I said. "But don't you sometimes think . . . there are things you would rather not know?"

"No," he answered. "I don't." I searched the glowing white shapes of his face under the moonlight and realized he would not stop until he knew all of it—whether the girl he'd known as Ginevra was in fact Odalie, and whether she'd once upon a time been capable of retaliating in some tragic, irreversible way. I saw now his blue eyes were full of steel; he was going to know it all.

"What would you do," I began to ask, my heartbeat speeding up at the mere thought of his likely answer, "if Odalie admitted to . . . to doing something terrible, even if . . . even if it was only a fleeting impulse—and a bad one, true enough—but that she hadn't meant any of it?"

"I think you know, Rose, what I'd do."

I did. He would bring her to justice. Not the way I'd done with Edgar Vitalli. No, Teddy was not yet ready to strike that bargain and cross that threshold. In some ways he was an earlier version of me: one who desperately wanted to see justice done but who still (naively, I could argue) believed there were strict rules by which to achieve this. He would report her, and if one police district refused to entertain his claims he would go to another, and doggedly to another and another, until he finally found one bold enough to cinch a pair of handcuffs around Odalie's wrists. It would be the right thing to do. The very definition of justice, in fact. Nonetheless, my hands grew clammy as I realized I was having pangs of regret. I had betrayed the one bosom friend who had ever really stood by me.

Just then, a shape stepped onto the terrace with a sleek, feline grace. I wondered, for the briefest of seconds, how long Odalie had stood by the terrace door, and how much she might have heard.

"What a glorious night," she said. Her voice had that husky rattle in it, and she carried a small mirrored tray upon which three martini glasses balanced. As she distributed them into our hands, I wondered how she'd known to make sidecars. Then I remembered I'd left the open recipe book out on the bar. Suddenly Teddy's hand jerked, and he pointed at something. Following the arrow of his finger, I realized he was pointing at our wrists—first Odalie's and then mine. With a shock, I realized I had forgotten about the bracelets, which twinkled brilliantly now under the bright moonlight.

"Oh!" was all he could muster. "Oh . . . Oh!"

I felt my stomach turn, and I realized I was wild with a fresh terror. I understood what was at stake now, and I knew my fear was the dread of losing Odalie. Odalie, for her part, was unfazed. She ignored Teddy's distress and stretched languidly in the tepid evening air, finishing with a small, ladylike yawn.

"You know what I'd love? I'd love to stand out here and smoke a cigarette." Her teeth glowed eerie and phosphorescent in the silvery moonlight as she flashed a cool smile at us. She opened the clasp of her purse and pretended to look inside. "Oh! But I'm all out. Rose, darling. Would you mind terribly running to the newsstand and getting some?"

I nodded but was hesitant to go, unsure as to whether I should leave her alone. The instinct to protect her was surging strongly in me now. Whereas before I had wanted to see Odalie confronted, now I only wanted Teddy to go away, and as quickly as possible. I considered that perhaps if I dashed out for the cigarettes, it might give Odalie a chance to set him straight and send him on his way. As an afterthought I considered the walk might do me good anyhow; I was slightly fevered with drink by that time, and it felt as though hot embers were smoldering steadily under the apples of my cheeks. Odalie put some change in my hand, and I hardly remember riding the elevator—although I must have done so— for the next thing I knew I was walking in an awkward, aggressive stride along the city sidewalk.

The first two stands I tried were closed, so I tried a little corner-store I remembered on Lexington. I don't recall what the clerk at the store looked like, but I do recall making some sort of conversation with him about the weather (we both agreed it was cooling off and turning very fine—what a relief after that relentless summer!). As drunken citizens everywhere so often try to do, I tried my best not to appear as though I was concentrating too hard as I counted out the change. I could feel the warm glow in my face affecting my eyesight, and I was aware I was probably squinting closely at the coins to see which was which. But the clerk either didn't notice or else had long since ceased to notice the erratic behaviors of his late-night customers entirely. But it was clear I was not a prized customer, as he simply handed me the pack of cigarettes without putting them in a paper bag. On the way back to the hotel, I noticed a man out walking a rather sleek-looking greyhound. I made some pleasant remarks about the dog's winning countenance and stopped to pet it, then continued on my way. I wouldn't have been that familiar and easy with a stranger before my time with Odalie. I was really coming out of my shell, as they say. She had changed me, I reflected, and for the better. I would apologize to her for telling Teddy where to find her, and we would be sisters again. No more of these silly spiteful betrayals. Oh, the irony of my thoughts at that crucial moment in time . . .

It wasn't until I was a mere half-block from the hotel that I heard the sirens. By then a small crowd had gathered around, and already the policemen were working to keep the onlookers at bay. There was something everyone was pointing to in the middle of the crowd, something below their knees, lying on the ground. As I drew closer, my stomach balled itself into a tight fist. I could feel the warmth leaving my cheeks already, my eyes widening with the jarring clarity of sudden sobriety, my mind bracing itself for the harsh spectacle that inevitably awaited. By the time I got close enough to catch a glimpse of Teddy's body sprawled out in a broken posture upon the gray impassive concrete of the sidewalk, it was as if I had already seen it all before.

21

From time to time, I still puzzle over whether Odalie put the young elevator-boy up to it, or if it was an honest mistake and he was simply an overeager Good Samaritan trying to do the right thing. It doesn't matter, of course, but it would be nice to know. For some reason (now that I know Odalie for what she is) I've taken a measure of comfort imagining she went to great pains, resorting to all sorts of masterful plotting. But there are some things, I suppose, to which I'll never be privy, and I must resign myself to this fact. Either way, whatever motivated the elevator-boy's actions drew its power from a sure and steady source, for he did not falter as he stood across the circle of clustered onlookers and raised his arm to point a finger in my direction.

"There she is! *That's* the lady who rode up with him!" he cried. It was a simple statement—and a true one at that—but it struck me as an accusation, and I recoiled with a faint shiver of knee-jerk indignity.

"Excuse me? I beg your pardon, Clyde—"

"Name's not Clyde. It's *Clive*."

"Oh."

"Ask her—just ask 'er if she ain't the one that rode up with him!" Suddenly there was a police officer at my elbow.

"Do you know the name and identity of the deceased?" the officer asked. I admitted that I did. "And where are you coming from, miss?" he asked. I explained to him about the cigarettes, about going to the news-stands, the corner-store, and even about the sleek-looking greyhound. Already I could tell it was too much; he lifted an eyebrow. "And your friend, this *Teddy*, you say you left him alone up there?" He gestured toward the upper levels of the hotel.

I didn't answer at first, still under the spell of the impulse to protect Odalie. I glanced in the direction of where Teddy lay, but could not bring myself to look directly at the body. Surely he had not survived the fall. "Is he . . . ?"

"'Fraid so."

I let my eyes trail up the side of the hotel until I was looking in the direction of the terrace. From down here it seemed like a very alien, impersonal, faraway place. It slowly dawned on me the police were sure to go up there for further inspection. I swallowed. "I have a room-mate," I said, carefully trying to figure out how to volunteer this information. "She may know what happened. She might have seen the . . . the . . . accident." As soon as I said the word *accident* aloud it left a funny tang in my mouth. I was desperate to get upstairs, to see Odalie, to look into her wide-set eyes and read in them the truth of what had just occurred. The police officer (a patrolman; I was distraught, but still knew how to tell the difference between a beat cop and a real detective, of course) was silent as we rode up in an elevator cage helmed by the eagerly disapproving Clive.

After taking us to our floor, Clive proceeded to follow us as we left the elevator and walked down the hall. The officer did not say anything to stop him, and I could feel both men's eyes on me as I fumbled with the key to the front door. There was something loose and echoing in the air as I turned the doorknob to our apartment and swung the door open. A bottomless sense of vacancy permeated the sitting room, and I was overcome with a sick, panicky feeling. Right away, it was clear Odalie was gone. My mind attempted to piece together an innocent explanation as to where she was and why she had left, but already the threads of this were slippery and would not hold. The cop, to his credit, did not treat me like a crazy person straightaway, but rather conducted a polite-yet-perfunctory tour of all the apartment's rooms in an attempt to locate the room-mate I had promised was awaiting him. I trailed behind him as he moved through the apartment. We concluded our tour on the terrace. Less than an hour earlier the terrace had seemed balmy and pleasant; now it had taken on an atmosphere of oppressive foreboding. I watched the police officer take stock of things: the little mirrored cocktail tray left to idle on a low wicker table, the two empty martini glasses abandoned on the brick ledge (I never did find out what became of that third glass). He peered over the rail at the wreckage below, then glanced at the pair of martini glasses again.

"You say you were up here earlier this evening?"

"Yes," I said. Then, after a pause, I added, "I'm sorry I can't tell you more about how it happened." It was the truth; I was sorry, and getting sorrier by the minute. Perhaps it is laughable now, but at the time I was worried about Odalie. *Perhaps the shock of it was too much for her,* I thought, *but she shouldn't have left the hotel like she has.* If she'd ever been to Newport at any point in her past, if it looked like she and Teddy had been having a row before he fell, the whole ugly truth of it would come out and whatever had happened on the terrace tonight wouldn't look right.

"S'all right," the officer replied. "Somebody already 'phoned for a detective." I nodded. By then the Cognac I had consumed earlier had worked its way further into my system and my head was beginning to pound with a tight pressure. The daze I'd felt upon coming back from the corner-store was wearing off, and I looked down to see the carton of cigarettes still clutched in my hand. In an automatic gesture, I opened it and offered a cigarette to the officer. He gave me one of the queerest looks I have ever received in my life and shook his head, so I decided to smoke the rejected gift myself, thinking it might calm me. Odalie always said cigarettes had a wonderful calming effect on her. Still eyeing me cautiously, the officer reached over to light my cigarette. I noticed his hand was trembling. Mine, by contrast, was very steady as I smoked the cigarette. My nerves never showed themselves like that. I exhaled, tilting my head upward and allowing the smoke to curl from my mouth, imitating something I'd seen Odalie do a hundred times.

"What a terrible accident. Terrible, isn't it?" I said. It was an innocuous remark. Or so I thought, but the officer flinched. His head snapped in my direction, and his eyes widened with curiosity.

"Hmph . . . yes . . . *accident* . . . ," he murmured.

I finished my cigarette and stubbed it out, then deposited it neatly in the green bottle-glass ashtray that sat on the wicker table. In addition to the table, there was a little rug on the terrace, two wicker chairs, and a settee. Since it had become apparent we were waiting for something, I sat down on the settee and crossed my legs. A tiny twinkle caught my eye, and I looked down to see

Odalie's bracelet lying by my foot. Had Teddy torn it from her wrist? She wouldn't want it lying there, so I picked it up for safe-keeping. There was no better way to keep hold of it than to wear it, so I slipped it around my other wrist and did up the clasp. *Odalie was right*, I thought to myself. *They do look a bit like hand-cuffs.* I twisted my wrists slowly and admired the precious stones as they shimmered icy-cold in the moonlight.

Later more officers arrived, and they escorted me downstairs, where a car was waiting to take me to the local precinct. As I was helped into the car, I overheard the patrolman recounting our interlude to a group of fellow officers.

". . . and as I live and breathe, you shoulda seen 'er. She was just as cold as *ice*, I tell you! Stood there, smoking a cigarette, admiring her diamonds, calm as could be . . ."

SEEING AS HOW I was otherwise engaged, I can't say for sure when Odalie returned to the apartment, but I assume it was some hours later. Over and over, I've pictured it all now as it must've been: Odalie walking down the street toward the hotel and "discovering" the crowd of onlookers, the police cars, the newspapermen, and the blinding-bright flashes of bulbs popping on their cameras. There she is in my mind, drawing near the curb with her brow furrowed. Clapping a hand over her mouth upon glimpsing the coroner setting about his macabre work. Demanding to know what is going on while being bumped and jostled about by the crowd.

Oh, but I have a room-mate. Where's my room-mate? Where's Rose? I picture her saying to a nearby police officer. And then the officer—in my mind it is the same patrolman who stood with me on the terrace waiting for the detective to arrive—clamps a kindly hand on her shoulder to steady her and informs her of the bad news. Her eyes widen and the sunny tint of her skin pales, but she nods as she takes it all in, a small gesture to indicate horror, but not surprise. *Poor Teddy,* she says, her eyes glistening. *He didn't deserve such a thing.*

You ought to know, she implied you were up on that terrace tonight, he tells Odalie, relaying what has clearly now become my impossible accusation. He does not have to say *be careful of that one,* he does not have to call me a murderess and a slanderer; his tone says it all for him.

THERE WAS AN INQUEST, of course, and my trip to the local precinct turned out to be issued on a one-way ticket. That first night, I sat in an unfamiliar interview room being asked questions by an unfamiliar detective, while a typist sat quietly in the corner typing my answers with a dull receptivity. It was all I could do, when they first led me into the room, not to seat myself at her desk and poise my fingers over the keys of the stenotype merely out of habit.

The detective who interviewed me introduced himself as Detective Ferguson. He was quite a bit older than the Lieutenant Detective at our own precinct and was a full detective as opposed to a lieutenant. His dark hair was interrupted by two very white streaks at his temples that ran toward the back of his head with a comically sharp line of demarcation, giving him an abstractly skunklike air. Every time he asked me a question, he tapped out the beat of the words on the table between us with his forefinger, as if sending a wire over an invisible telegraph machine. Unlike

the Lieutenant Detective, this Detective Ferguson took a straightforward line with his questions. It was a bit unsettling, as I could
tell he was unsatisfied with my answers and that we were eventually headed for an all-out impasse.

Even more unsettling was the fact there was also a young
patrolman in the room I believe was training to be a detective,
and the kid bore a strong resemblance to Teddy. Perhaps I am
imagining it, but in my memory, he had sandy hair and an
earnest gaze and the same lanky, puppyish body, with narrow
shoulders and long limbs he had not quite grown into. To think:
Only hours ago I had been drinking cocktails and chatting with
Teddy. It had not sunk in yet that Teddy was really dead, and having his twin sit across from me at the interview table did very little to help me come to grips with things. I think I would've been
more at ease, too, if the kid had talked. If he had, he might've
demonstrated a funny accent or odd mannerism—something,
anything, to dispel the notion the two young men were in any way
related—and then the distraction caused by his presence would've
been alleviated. But as it was, he remained absolutely taciturn
throughout the duration of my interview, content to sit in silence
and scribble furiously into a notebook. He remained so, that is,
until I had my little "episode."

Of course, now that I've had some time to reflect upon the situation, I see the ways in which this interview marked yet one more
irreversible turning point for me. In my defense, I was not exactly
myself that night. Too much drink and the shock of seeing a body
had very likely warped my perception of things. And so I can
hardly be blamed for the scene that occurred during my interview.
But I suppose it's important that I tell this part, for I'm sure my
outburst helped speed me on my way to the particular institution

in which I now find myself. I will try to recount, to the best of my memory, the exchange as it took place.

The interview promised to be interminable, stretching on into the early hours of dawn. Several times the officers and the typist took little breaks, and I was left alone in the interview room, sitting very still as the air around me stagnated, listening to the ticking of the wall clock, my eyelids closing with weariness. I say all this because I believe I also was suffering from sleep deprivation, and this too may help explain my state of mind. In any case, each time the detective reentered the room, he did so with a renewed charge of energy and a fresh stack of file folders, not to mention a fresh cup of coffee. Knowing a little bit about how these things go, I understood they were taking statements from people. Most likely the entire hotel staff had been interviewed, and perhaps some onlookers on the street as well. The detective was biding his time with me while the eyewitness accusations accumulated and strengthened his case.

I believe my own interview went off the rails somewhere around the time the detective informed me that Odalie had already given a statement (*Odalie!*). I was very confused; this was both good and bad news to me. At first, I felt a flood of relief. I had been worried about her, but if she had indeed given a statement like the detective said she did, then at the very least it meant she was in a physically sound state. And yet when I thought about what had likely occurred on the terrace, my distress over her disappearance very quickly converted into distress over the contents of her statement. I wondered what the police might know about Odalie, feeling anxious over what I ought not reveal. Detective Ferguson pressed on, asking me questions aimed at diagnosing my relationship to Teddy and my living situation with Odalie. It began benignly enough, and I was not uncomfortable when he first took this tack, leaning back in his chair with an open posture and adopting a casual tone as he put some very direct questions to me.

"I take it, Miss Baker, you and Mr. Tricott were carrying on a relationship of a . . . *romantic variety?*" the detective asked me. My brow furrowed in confusion.

"Sorry—me and who?"

"Theodore Tricott."

"Oh! You mean Teddy. Romantic! Oh, heavens no. I hardly knew him."

"Witnesses saw him visiting you at the precinct earlier today. They said you seemed quite familiar, and that your conversation got quite *heated.*"

"Sounds like Marie has been gossiping! Fine—yes, I talked to him, but he hadn't even come to see me in the first place. He came to see someone else."

"Who?"

The hard flint of loyalty kept me silent.

"All right, well. You say he's a new acquaintance, then. Are you in the habit of inviting men you hardly know to join you for a cocktail in your place of residence?"

"Of course not; don't be absurd."

"Do you deny you invited Mr. Tricott over for a cocktail at your apartment?"

"Well, yes—and no, too."

"Which is it?"

I hesitated, and finally decided to be truthful about my part of things. "Yes, I admit I mixed a drink for Teddy and kept him entertained on the terrace while we waited for my room-mate to return. But no, I didn't exactly invite him, and it's not exactly my apartment."

"Do you mean to say you don't live there?"

"I live there, but it's Odalie's apartment."

"That's not what she informed us."

"Beg pardon?"

The first inklings of true betrayal began to enter my blood-stream, the alternating twinges of disbelief and dread tingling in my veins. Suddenly I was feeling a little light-headed. It was probably a case of dehydration, on account of all the alcohol, I thought.

"May I have a glass of water?" I asked. We took a brief break while Detective Ferguson sent the typist to go get one. I hadn't paid the typist much mind before, but when she walked back into the interview carrying a tall glass of water I took a closer look at her.

She was somewhere in her mid-twenties and painfully plain. Her hair was the same lackluster shade of light brown as my own, and her features were small and regular, with the exception of her teeth. Her teeth were small but very pointy in the front, and she had an underbite that made her lower jaw stick out ever so slightly. The unfortunate combination of her teeth and jaw gave her an air that was at once both timid and carnivorous, reminding me of an illustration I had once seen in an encyclopedia of a hungry pira-nha. I did not like the look of her one bit.

"So? Miss Baker?" Detective Ferguson prompted me.

"Beg pardon?" I had difficulty remembering where we had left off and was feeling distracted. I watched the typist slide back into her desk. Immediately her fingers commenced their fluttering over the stenotype keys. I narrowed my eyes at those fingers. They suddenly seemed like spidery, sinister things.

"Miss Lazare informed us you pay the rent on that apartment, and that it's rented in your name. What do you have to say about that?"

I blinked, but kept my eyes trained on the typist's hands as they continued to flutter over the stenotype. It seemed to me she was typing even when I wasn't saying anything. "I say it's simply not true," I replied with a frown, wondering where Detective Ferguson was getting his faulty information. Odalie could not have possibly said such a thing.

And then it happened. For the briefest of seconds, the typist allowed her eyes to flicker up at me, and the tiniest flash of a smug smile quivered on her lips. *The villainess!* I thought, my mind racing. *Of course she's in on it!* I mean, after all, I of all people knew how easy it was to tamper with a report, to plant ideas in a detective's head. Perhaps she had been angling for this, priming this detective for weeks! How could I have been so blind?

"The apartment is let in Odalie's—I mean, Miss Lazare's— name," I informed them. "I don't suppose it's any of your business, but that apartment is a bit out of my reach, I'm afraid." I paused and twisted in my seat to give the typist a meaningful look. "Being that we're in a similar line of business, I'm sure you can imagine the limits of my salary." I turned back to the detective. "Odalie has . . . well, *family money,* you see." Upon hearing this latter statement, the typist stopped typing, and Detective Ferguson's protégé suddenly looked up from his notebook.

"That's a horrible joke, Miss Baker."

"I'm not aware of making any joke."

"I don't see how you can make light of Miss Lazare's situation, seeing as how she was raised in an orphanage. That seems quite cruel, even for you."

"What?" I felt myself increasingly conscious of a great chasm opening up somewhere in the floor beneath me. "What? Who told you that?" There was a pause in which no one dared speak and I felt the constellation of conspiracy arranging itself around me from all sides. My heart began to beat faster. "Who told you that?" I demanded again. I sprang up from my chair and whirled about, and suddenly my gaze fell on the typist. "What have you been typing? I know what you've been about! You've been typing lies about me! Someone—quick! Check her reports! She's typing lies!" I realized I was now screaming, but I didn't care. The typist was staring at me, the whites of her eyes revealing her fear, which I took to be a sure sign of her guilt. Suddenly I understood it all. "You think you'll get rid of me with these lies! You want her for yourself! I know what you're about!" Before I knew what was happening, I had thrown myself at the typist and my hands were around her neck. Detective Ferguson and the young detective-in-training rushed to pull me off, but it wasn't until several more officers had charged into the room that they were sufficiently able to sever my hold on her.

Perhaps it will come as no surprise to you that less than an hour later I was ensconced at the institution where I find myself currently. I have resided here now for two and a half weeks, and am officially being held for "further observation purposes," under the supervision of Dr. Miles H. Benson, the doctor whose name I've already mentioned.

The appearance of one's innocence is a funny house of cards; you start by shifting the smallest thing, and before you know it the whole structure has come crashing down. In my case, it all began with the elevator-boy. I still wonder, sometimes, if it hadn't been for Clive pointing a finger at me, how the night might've played itself out differently. But there are other times when I understand: Elevator-boy or no elevator-boy, my fate was—and had always been—in Odalie's hands.

22

The slope that leads toward insanity has the paradoxical distinction of being both steep and yet undetectable to the person sliding down it. That is to say, crazy people rarely know they're crazy. So I can understand it when, while attempting to attest to my own sanity, it just so happens I am not readily believed. Despite all this, I must assure you I am not crazy. It's true, they caught me at a particularly inconvenient moment, and I can see how it must've looked, attacking that fellow typist as I did. But I have had ample time to review the situation now, and I have disavowed all of the nonsense I was spewing at the time of my little "episode." All of which is to say I see how unlikely it is that the poor woman was meddling with my statement. Even more unfounded is my fantasy that she hoped to unseat me in my role as Odalie's bosom friend. But that's the funny thing about treasure—we assume everyone wants what we hold most dear. And yet you really must take me at my word: It was a momentary lapse. In retrospect I understand how my convictions about the other typist merely constituted an extrapolation of my own fears.

My doctor (I believe I've already mentioned him—the re-

nowned Dr. Miles H. Benson, M.D., Ph.D.) says I am given to what
he calls *theories of conspiracy.* We humans are categorical think-
ers, he says, and we all try to fit our experiences of this world into
patterns. *Some of us*, he says (and by this he means me), *will completely overturn reality in an effort to uphold a particular pattern
that we prefer.* Then he leans back in the metal chair regularly
brought into my room for him to sit upon while we chat and later
taken away so I won't get any funny ideas about standing upon it
and devising some way to hang myself. He leans back in the chair
and lets his glasses slide down his nose, and once that happens I
know we are about to segue from the general to the personal. *Can
you think of how you might be fitting the facts to uphold any particular pet theory, my dear?* he asks in that didactic, singsong voice
of his.

During our first few chats, I used to challenge him. *Can you
think of how you might be fitting the facts to uphold any particular
theory of your own, Dr. Benson?* I simply cannot give credence to
his suggestion that the Saint Teresa of Avila Home for Girls has no
record of my time there. I do not believe Dr. Benson, or anyone
from this so-called hospital, has truly even checked. When I
inquired after the name of the nun who was contacted, Dr. Benson mumbled something and promised to "consult his files"—
which, of course, he never did. *You cannot rob a person of her whole
childhood history merely to uphold your belief in my insanity,* I
would say to him rather accusingly.

But that was during my first few days here, and my complaints
fell on deaf ears. Now I sit and let him build a case for his precious
"reality." He is very dedicated to the cause and can often have a
very convincing demeanor. Dr. Benson is the proprietor of a very
full and spectacular mustache, and I suppose I have a habit of

putting my faith in men with formidable mustaches. Dr. Benson's is nothing quite so grand as the Sergeant's flamboyantly twisted pair of handlebars, but it is nonetheless quite impressive and lends him an air of authority, and when he tells me his version of my own history, a version I can't quite seem to recall living, I have become complacent to sit and listen with rapt attention, as though he were spinning out a very mysterious and enchanting fairy-tale. He is so vehement about certain facts—like the fact the orphanage has no record of my growing up there—sometimes I nearly believe him. In fact, I thought perhaps there was a chance I had remembered the name of the wrong saint and sent Dr. Benson chasing my ghost in the wrong direction, that perhaps the place where I'd known Sister Hortense and Sister Mildred (not to mention my poor sweet Adele) was maybe named after Saint Catherine or Saint Ursula. But no, it was most certainly Saint Teresa. Saint Teresa the mystic, who despite all her prim and proper faith was known for her sensuousness as well as for her bouts of madness. Saint Teresa, the patron saint for removing maladies of the head. I know what you are thinking, and I am not so insane that I fail to see the irony in all this.

Of course the dim outlines of Dr. Benson's fairy-tale ring a bell. I have heard some of this before. According to him my name is Ginevra Morris. I was born in Boston, but shortly after my birth my family relocated to Newport, Rhode Island. If it were at all possible my parents might visit me here, Dr. Benson is sure it would prove helpful, as it would no doubt cause a rift in my fabricated history I would be at pains to reconcile. *In layman's terms, it would jog your memory, Ginevra,* he often says—and because the name is still so unfamiliar to me, I look over my shoulder at the nurse before realizing he means me. But alas, laments Dr. Benson, my parents are deceased; my father passed away two years ago from liver failure, and my mother died last spring in a rather unfortunate automobile accident. (Dr. Benson presented me with the newspaper clippings and took my intense interest in them as further proof of his theory. *Remember, Ginevra? How your mother always was a poor driver? The neighbors said it came as no surprise,* he urges.)

There is another story Dr. Benson also likes to tell, about an old fiancé of mine. Apparently we had a terrible row the night he died. The circumstances surrounding the young man's death— his car stalled at an inopportune time while upon some railroad tracks—never did sit quite right with the townspeople. *You have to own up to your actions,* Dr. Benson advises me. *You might've been able to vamp the whole town into looking the other way for a time, but that time must end here.*

This makes me snort and show all my teeth as I most heartily laugh aloud, a behavior I can tell rattles Dr. Benson. *I am hardly a seductress, Dr. Benson,* I say with a chuckle. *You can see as much with your plain eyes.* At this, Dr. Benson remains quiet and stares me down with a skeptical look, and I have to wonder if all the time I spent with Odalie has changed me more than I realize.

Oh, but there's more to this story! The first time Dr. Benson told it to me in its entirety I almost fainted with utter shock upon hearing the details. I say "almost fainted" because of course I have a very strong constitution and did not faint, though it might've been nice to slip into unconsciousness at that juncture in time, just to stop Dr. Benson's mouth from spewing the hateful narrative as it continued to spring forth. That first time telling it, the good doctor prattled along rather innocuously at first, urging me as he always did to remember my life as Ginevra. *You vamped the whole town into looking the other way,* he said that day, stroking his mustache as though recalling the story from his own memory, *and you nearly had everyone pledging their undying faith in you, too, Ginevra—until you ran off with the train yard switchman.* I sat up straight upon hearing this, my brain suddenly racing to fit together what I should've suspected all along—Gib! *Tell us when he began blackmailing you, Ginevra,* Dr. Benson said. *Did it begin right away, that first night, out on the train tracks, with the wreck of Warren's crumpled roadster still steaming and groaning in the background behind you?* I looked at Dr. Benson and realized I wished I knew the answer to his question. I felt a fleeting twinge of sympathy for Odalie. So Gib had had her under his thumb the whole time! That arrangement must've been excruciatingly painful for her, free-spirited creature that she was. But the fleeting twinge of sympathy I suffered was just that: fleeting, for Dr. Benson's next line of questions was to have an even greater effect on me, and they have consumed me ever since.

How long did you plot to kill Gib, Ginevra? Dr. Benson asked, leaning forward to better look me in the eye. *How long did it take you to formulate a plan?* Of course, the first time Dr. Benson asked me this I was quite befuddled, and it took me some minutes to piece together the fact that Gib was dead. Over the last two weeks of my confinement, I've managed to procure more of the specifics. Evidently Theodore Tricott hadn't been the only one to suffer a tragic accident that night. Harry Gibson had been helping to host an illegal wet party (otherwise known as a "speakeasy") when he drank a particularly lethal cocktail that was one part champagne, two parts non-potable methanol. The drink had a surprisingly quick effect. The nerve damage set in almost immediately, the coroner speculated, and soon after paralysis set in upon Gib's lungs. By the time Teddy plunged off the terrace, Gib was already dead, and "Ginevra's" misdeeds had brought the insular circle back around upon itself.

It was at that point I began to protest my innocence in earnest. Ever since they'd told me about the statement Odalie had given and I'd attacked the typist in the interview room, my faith in my dear bosom friend had been crumbling away like a sand dune in the wind. Now, Dr. Benson's question tormented me: *How long did you plot to kill Gib? How long, how long, how long?* plagued my brain every night as I lay on my cot in the institution, desperately seeking sleep. And it was with a stomach-churning sense of cold and absolute dread that I realized the answer was: at least about a year. I had not been watching Odalie; she had been watching me. She had thrown down her bait—that brooch—and from the very second I picked it up she knew she had her magpie: someone she could distract with her sparkle as she laid the foundation of her master plan.

Tragically, however, by the time I had a better vantage on the panorama of my situation it was too late. Everything I explained about Odalie, about her connections, about her manner of insinu-ating herself into people's lives, went unheard. There was a time when I considered perhaps Dr. Benson knew the truth of it and had been somehow bribed by Odalie as well, but I don't think so presently. The good yet pig-headed doctor seems so sincere when he speaks to me about *accepting the truth of reality* that I have come to believe he really does buy into all that. I've seen myself through his eyes, and I understand he thinks my reality, insofar as it diverges from his own, is a fiction.

Of course, there are places where my reality and Dr. Benson's reality have some overlap. For instance, I have been presented with a few anecdotes from my history I know to be very real. At one point, they brought "Dr." Spitzer in to identify me. I say "Dr." with mocking only because it turned out Odalie was right when she said he probably wasn't much of a chemist. Technically, he wasn't one at all. He'd been arrested for his own crimes, and in return for a shorter sentence he was only too happy to point me out as "Miss Ginevra" and, of course, as the woman to whom he'd given the bottle of improperly re-natured alcohol that brought about Gib's untimely death. According to him, he'd never heard of Odalie; I was the sole proprietor of my own enterprise, not to mention the chief purchaser of his services.

And, of course, I still remember the day Dr. Benson came in and asked me was I acquainted with a girl named Helen Bartleson. She'd claimed to know me from the time I'd tried to "lay low by living at a boarding-house," and had given some statements that were of particular interest to the police, Dr. Benson informed me, although I can't imagine what. I told him Helen was a nincompoop, and in any case knew nothing about my life before or after I left the boarding-house. But obviously I had to say yes, I did know her. *We were room-mates for a brief time,* I replied. Dr. Benson asked was this prior to my arrangements at the hotel apartment. *Yes,* I said. Did I recall slapping her across the face with a pair of leather gloves? Dr. Benson wanted to know. *Well, I didn't relish it and it was not my place, but someone had to discipline her and it was clear Dotty wasn't going to do it,* I answered. When I said this, Dr. Benson smiled.

We are finally making progress, he diagnosed, but I didn't see how.

The worst was when I thought it might help me to come clean about Edgar Vitalli. I was trying to make a point—that not everything recorded while in a precinct was always 100 percent accurate. Dr. Benson asked a lot of questions about this, and then a couple of chief inspectors from different districts asked many many more. And then they brought in the Police Commissioner himself. It's funny; all that time working at the police precinct, preparing for the Commissioner's visits, and this was how I finally made his acquaintance. The first thing I noticed about him was his temples bulged when he was telling a lie. Like how he claimed he'd never met Odalie and didn't know what I was talking about when I brought up the business of how he'd given Odalie a white card. He was sure to ask all the questions during that interview, of course, or else I would've pressed him further about the card Gib accused Odalie of purchasing from his offices.

It was a longer interview than I would've liked. I really shouldn't have told them anything, but the stress of constantly being convinced I did not know reality from fantasy made me want to tell the truth about absolutely everything, even about Edgar Vitalli, just to lay it out all straight in my head. But oh, what a fuss they made! It was in all the papers: how I'd doctored the confession, making it sound like Mr. Vitalli knew all sorts of incriminating details about the crime. How I'd charmed the Sergeant and seduced him into complying. I was a wicked, deceitful seductress, they claimed. One reporter even compared me to Salome, dancing for King Herod and asking for the head of John the Baptist! The result of all this was that the Sergeant withdrew into a swift and silent retirement. A retroactive mistrial was declared, and I am sorry to say Mr. Vitalli was thereby acquitted of all charges and released from prison. His ugly smirking face glared out at me from every front page. I felt very bad about this, and for a while I collected all the newspapers I could lay my hands on in the common room, clipped the photos, and pinned them to the wall in my room at the institution just to torture myself with that hideous taunting face. It was my way of doing penance (I suppose I had to be declared insane before finally getting some religion). Eventually Dr. Benson noticed the eyes were scratched out in most of the photos and forced me to take them down and hand them over to the nurses on the basis that my collection demonstrated what he called *an unhealthy preoccupation.*

There are times when Dr. Benson likes to tussle with me over moral conduct and justice, especially on the subject of Edgar Vitalli. I find this a bit more than vaguely insulting, as I was the only one who actually cared about seeing to it that justice got done. *A man's life was in your hands . . . how can you justify condemning him with no proof?* Dr. Benson asks me. I try to tell him Mr. Vitalli's guilt was plain to see, that it was *obvious*, yet no one was willing to go to the lengths I was, that I was the only one willing to do what was necessary to make sure justice was done. If I were a man and had spearheaded the official investigation, I would've been congratulated! But Dr. Benson only shakes his head at me. *You cannot appoint yourself judge, jury, and hangman, Ginevra*, he says, as though I am some sort of righteous loony who has gone on a tirade.

But perhaps the greatest injustice, the one that offends me the most, is the fact Odalie will never understand how much I loved her. Ironically, I think it was Gib who might have had a grasp of this, albeit an incremental one. A person simply cannot see what they are not looking to see, and I have finally come to grips with the simple truth that Odalie was never seeking my devotion. It's true she wanted my loyalty—for a time, at least—because it proved useful to her. But *devotion* is a word whose definition reaches a depth that threatens to swamp this current generation.

The modern world is a strange place indeed, and I fear it is one in which I do not belong. It's not as if I'm daft; I've seen the world, leaving me behind in fits and starts. And from the very first, I knew Odalie was a creature born of this new time, with her golden-hued skin and skinny boyish arms and sleek black bob. There is much to admire about these new modern girls, superficially speaking. That much I fully admit. I know when people think of romance they will think of Odalie, standing in the moonlight, the beads on her dress like a galaxy's worth of stars come temporarily to rest, the sheen of her hair refracting a halo. But of course this notion is something of a bum steer. All along, all those nights we spent searching out back doors and reciting lines of gibberish to enter those innumerable speakeasies, it was really Odalie who was the true blind. Her breathless charm and musical laugh are promises that true romance, the most exciting variety of life-changing romance, is just around the corner. But the truth of the matter is Odalie herself possesses not one romantic bone in her entire body, and she has little patience for sentiment of any kind. She is the mirage that moves constantly before you, always a fixed distance away as you step deeper and deeper into the desert.

No, between Odalie and myself, I am the romantic. A relic from an already forgotten era. The world has no patience these days for the formalities of ladylike conduct. Nor does it have any interest in nurturing the bonds of sisters, of mothers and daughters, of bosom friends. Something—perhaps it was the war; I cannot say—has torn these bonds away. I realize if I am to survive in this world, I must sooner or later evolve. Evolution. Another modern innovation to reverse the old thinking that the meek shall inherit the earth.

But enough. I know this is all simply a lament—surprisingly, not one for Odalie, but for myself.

EPILOGUE

They tell me I am to have a visitor today. They informed me of this fact when I first woke up this morning. I think the nurses fancied themselves thoughtful for telling me, believing it would give me something I might look forward to, but since they are not allowed to reveal the identity of my visitor I have spent the last few hours agonizing over who it could possibly be. I've always had difficulty eating the watery oatmeal the hospital serves as our breakfast each and every morning, and today my overexcited nerves made it even more difficult than usual.

Why, Ginevra, you're not even making an effort, one of the nurses scolds me as she takes away my still-full tray. Visiting hours are from one o'clock to four. By noon I am nearly crawling out of my skin. I am not sure whom I am hoping to see.

Actually, that's untrue.

I *am* sure whom I am hoping to see. Old habits die hard. But the cynic in me already knows the truth: She will not come here to see me. If nothing else, she is very clever. Coming here would be a mistake; there would be no benefit in it for her. And yet I find myself looking anxiously in the direction of the door, hoping to see the silhouette of a stylish cloche appear. The heart is a funny organ, with such stubborn biases. Yesterday I went to bed making a careful list of all Odalie's unforgivable faults and reminding myself of all the reasons I ought to hold myself in superior regard. And then, this morning—in the time it took for a silly gossiping nurse to let it slip that I was to have a visitor—my every grudge against Odalie immediately lifted. And now I sit here, wretched instinctual creature that I am, my eyes hungry once again for the sight of her.

But at precisely a quarter after one, all my soaring hopes come crashing to the ground when Dr. Benson comes to tell me my visitor has arrived, and as a special reward for my good behavior as of late I will be allowed to visit with "him" privately in my room as long as I heed the rules of proper conduct, of course. *The orderlies will be watching,* Dr. Benson reminds me. I nod. *So,* I think with considerable disappointment. *My visitor is a man.*

I suppose there was a time when I would've been cheered to see, say, the Sergeant stepping over my threshold. But sadly, now that time has passed, I admit: From the moment we met I'd placed the Sergeant on so high a pedestal, he could not help but eventually fall. In my adulation, I overestimated him. His was not an unbending constitution after all, for in the end Odalie bent him to her will as she did with so many things. If I were to see him now, I fear I should be preoccupied, speculating over exactly what the—ahem—*rate* of exchange was between them. It is best to remain ignorant of certain things.

I am markedly disappointed now, but still full of apprehension. I sit and fidget until I realize I am practically wringing my hands, so I stop and concentrate on sitting very, very still.

The last person I am expecting to see is the Lieutenant

Detective, but suddenly there he is, slouching in my doorway, his hands jammed into his jacket pockets like always. *May I come in, Rose,* he asks, and I realize it is a strange comfort to hear my given name, even though under normal circumstances I would prefer for him to call me *Miss Baker.* Never one for bad manners, I invite him in. He ambles in comfortably enough, but once in the center of the room he looks uncertain of what to do next. I gesture to the metal chair the orderlies have set out for expressly this purpose, and the Lieutenant Detective coughs and sits down.

Rose, he says.

Lieutenant Detective, I say.

He doesn't speak for several minutes. The nerves I felt just minutes earlier have mysteriously disappeared. I feel more calm than I have in weeks, though I can't exactly pinpoint why. The Lieutenant Detective, by contrast, looks more jittery than I have ever seen him. I watch as he extracts a cigarette from his inside jacket pocket. Absentmindedly, he pats a different pocket (for a match, I assume), but then, with a glance at the NO SMOKING sign posted in the hallway just outside my door, stops and holds the cigarette as if unsure what to do with it. He twirls it over his knuckles until it slips to the floor. Our eyes trail to where it falls, but he makes no move to pick it up.

Rose, he begins again. But this time I interrupt him.

They call me Ginevra these days, I say. His eyes widen. I can see them raking over the contours of my face, searching for something.

Yes, about that . . . , he says.

Why have you come here, I interrupt again.

I've come because . . . , he says, but stops when he senses a shadow over his shoulder. An orderly passes by my door and pops his head in, aggressively swiveling it once in each direction—making sure, I suppose, that no funny business is going on, that the Lieutenant Detective is not slipping me a spoon and a map with instructions on how to tunnel my way out. I picture this scenario playing out and suddenly laugh aloud. Startled, the Lieutenant Detective looks up at me, and I catch something familiar in his expression— something I realize has always been there but that I haven't ever put my finger on before. It is fear. The Lieutenant Detective is afraid of me. All this time, and I am only just now seeing it has always been so.

You would think they might trust a man of the law and just leave us be, I say about the orderly having just put in a none-too-subtle appearance. I mean this kindly, in the spirit of solidarity, but I can see my comment further disturbs the Lieutenant Detective.

Yes . . . well. You know, technically speaking, I was above the Sergeant . . . and so responsible for his conduct, as he was—of course— for yours, he tells me. *That Vitalli business got me into a bit of hot water as well.*

My apologies, I say, but he doesn't answer. Lost in thought, he looks to the floor where the cigarette still lays without really seeing it. Several minutes pass, and then he finally clears his throat.

You know I don't believe it, he suddenly blurts in a confessional tone.

Believe what, I say.

All this business, he says. *About you. I can't believe you were behind it.* Again I feel his eyes raking over my face; I wish he would stop trying to read whatever it is he believes must be written there in invisible ink (oh, so he thinks). *Especially when it's clear she's . . . she's so . . .*

Where is she, I suddenly demand. At this, he gets up from his chair and ambles over to the small window at the far end of my room, pretending to look at the view. I know he is pretending because I have seen the view and I know there is nothing much to look at. One tree. The corner of the opposing brick building, speckled in moss. An unsightly amount of barbed wire atop a fence. *Where is she,* I repeat.

Gone, he says, and although I know it is the answer I have been expecting all along to hear, I feel my heart sink. He turns around. The scar on his forehead crinkles into the folds of his brow. *It happened right after—right after . . .* He hesitates. *She said she didn't feel safe, that she needed to start over.*

Of course, I say. *Of course she did.* Inside I feel my soul curl up into a small, knotted thing. But then the Lieutenant Detective says something I am not expecting to hear.

She asked me to give you something. He reaches deep into his right jacket pocket and produces a box. My heart immediately sets to pounding again—the way it did this morning when the nurses told me I had a visitor and I had dared to hope it would be her. It is a small box, about the size of a jewelry box, and covered in paper printed with roses. No detail was too small for Odalie. This embellishment cannot be a mistake. I reach out for it and take it in my hand. Inside I discover a single object. It is a brooch—a very expensive-looking one, with opals, diamonds, and black onyx stones all set into a very modern starburst pattern. *She got it from your desk,* he needlessly informs me. She said you would want it.

I hold the brooch in the palm of my hand and gaze at it. It is a lovely, mesmerizing sight; the shapes of it are now sharp and jagged and bittersweet in my mind. I understand what she is saying, and her cruelty has knocked the wind out of me. My eyes well up, but I do not cry.

Are you all right, Rose, asks the Lieutenant Detective. When I do not answer, he crosses the room and stands directly in front of me. *Are you all right?* He puts his hands on my shoulders. We are face-to-face. So close our noses are almost touching. I look into his eyes and see a soft, vulnerable spot somewhere deep within the dark of his pupils. Something vaguely malicious comes over me. I hear him give a little gasp of exhilaration and I feel him draw in his breath sharply, and I understand finally he has been wanting me to do this all along. I have never kissed a man before, but I have observed Odalie on more than one occasion, and I find myself taking action with a natural ease, as though executing by rote memory the scenes I'd witnessed. It is slow and warm, until I feel a sense of urgency in the Lieutenant Detective's lips awakening an inkling of urgency in my own lips, and for a moment I almost believe in the truth of this gesture. But seconds tick by and before the kiss is over, I remember the knife he used on the night my dress got stuck in the door of the passageway exit at the speakeasy, and I feel my hand automatically reach for it. The Lieutenant Detective does not appear to feel a thing. When I pull away from him, he is gazing at me in a daze, a slow smile spreading over his face.

Then he looks down and sees the knife in my hand. I flip it open.

Rose, he says, his eyes going wide.

I put a finger to my lips and I shake my head. And then, in a flash, I have gathered all my hair into one hand. The knife slices through it in a single clean cut, and I feel my unevenly bobbed hair tickling my cheek. Suddenly, there is a great commotion all about me. Two orderlies have caught on and have rushed into the room. The Lieutenant Detective staggers backward. The orderlies pounce on me and take the knife from my hand. They start to wrestle me to the ground, but when they feel no resistance from me they stop and seat me in the metal chair, where I sit with my body gone slack like an abandoned marionette. They shout down the hall for Dr. Benson.

On the ground there is a pile of mousy brown hair, already netted together like some sort of absurd bird's nest, and somewhere underneath the pile lies a single cigarette. I bend down and, brushing the hair aside, pick up the cigarette. *Would you mind terribly giving me a light,* I say to the Lieutenant Detective. For a moment, I think he is going to turn and run out of the room. He is looking at me with a different expression now, one I have never before seen on his face, and I know this will be the last time he comes to visit me. Slowly, with a shaking hand, he reaches into his pocket and pulls out a matchbook. He strikes a match, and the flame dances with his quivering hand.

As I lean down to the match and inhale, I think of Odalie on the infamous day she strode into the office with her freshly cut bob of hair. I remember it was a Tuesday. In my mind, Tuesdays have always seemed like the most ordinary and mundane of all weekdays. But there she was, making Tuesday into a day none of us would ever—could ever—forget. I hardly knew her then; at that point she was still just the new girl in the typing pool with pretty clothes and a careless way with her jewelry. We had yet to share the secrets that were still to come, the late nights over hot toddies, the drowsy chat sessions spent reclining together on the same bed. She walked in that morning and the entire precinct held its breath. It was as if someone had stopped the very ticking of the clock. Then, someone—I can't for the life of me remember who— paid Odalie a compliment. She turned her head to acknowledge it, and as her voice rode those familiar musical scales in a mellifluous trill of laughter, the glossy black of her newly shorn hair swung in a jaunty embrace of her cheeks. With that short hair it was as though every angle of her was crying out, *I am free! Oh, how free! And how much freer than you!*

The match goes out, and the Lieutenant Detective slowly retracts his trembling hand. But no matter; my cigarette is lit. I take a nice long drag on it, tilt my head upward, and exhale. If I am still sorry for anyone, it is Teddy. But as I've already explained in great detail, there must always be sacrifices along the road to evolution. For the briefest of seconds, I see a flash of Teddy's face, his eyes wide with terror as he falls downward toward the concrete below.

How about that, Odalie, I think, and take another drag of the cigarette. *Two can play at this game.*

ACKNOWLEDGMENTS

I would like to thank my agent, Emily Forland, for so many things: her intelligent feedback, her perpetual calm demeanor, and her outstanding professional social grace. Thanks also to Emma Patterson and Ann Torrago of the Wendy Weil Agency, who, together with Emily, I am confident will keep the legacy of the amazing Wendy Weil going strong. Wendy will be missed. My deepest gratitude to Amy Einhorn for her expert editorial guidance, deft insights, and refreshingly straight-shooting approach. I am still extremely thrilled to be working with someone I so admire! Thanks also to Liz Stein, who is one smart cookie and a hardworking wonder. I am also very appreciative of the editorial contributions made by Juliet Annan; the sharp insights she added were invaluable as I honed the manuscript. Thanks, too, to Sophie Missing. I would like to thank Emma Sweeney for giving me my first job in publishing, and for paving the road that led to this manuscript finding a home. A tremendous thank-you to Jayme Yeo, my dearest friend for over a decade now, who patiently read and reread many early versions despite having a doctoral dissertation of her own to finish. I am deeply indebted to Eva Talmadge for many things: her carefully considered insights, her constant professional encouragement, and her friendship over the last two years. Thanks also to Julie Fogh, a one-woman support network extraordinaire! Thank you to Rice University and all my colleagues there. Thank you to Susan Wood: poet, mentor, and dear friend. Thanks to Colleen Lamos for directing my graduate school interests in modernism and to Joe Campana for setting an admirable example of how to accomplish good work as both an artist and an academic. I am grateful to my publishing girl-group for their fellowship and support: Hana Landes, Julia Masnik, and Laura Van der Veer ("Reading Rainbows," unite!). I would like to express my sincere appreciation for the following people who read early versions of the manuscript and gave helpful comments: Brendan Jones, Mark Lawley, Melissa Rindell, Susan Shin, Ning Zhou, and Olga Zilberbourg. I am grateful to the Weldon family, who rented me an affordable apartment in East Harlem during the time I wrote this book. Thanks also to my New York roommates, who were supportive of this endeavor: Clare Brower and Matt Bessette. A big fat thank-you to Brian Shin, who has provided unconditional love and support throughout the years; I don't know what I ever did to deserve a best friend like you, but whatever it was, I'm sure glad as hell I did it. On a similar note, I am extremely grateful for my family: Sharon, Arthur, Laurie, and Melissa.

Lastly, I should mention there are one or two moments in this book wherein I humbly aspired—in my own small way—to pay deliberate homage to the first true love of my teenage years: Fitzgerald's *The Great Gatsby*. My admiration abides.

ABOUT THE AUTHOR

SUZANNE RINDELL is a doctoral student in American modernist literature at Rice University. *The Other Typist* is her first novel. She lives in New York City and is currently working on a second novel.